Eg

Carey Harrison is a novelist and playwright whose work has been described as 'intricate webs of fantasy, erudition and comedy' and 'a superb mix of slapstick, surrealism and tragedy'. Born in London in 1944 to actor parents Sir Rex Harrison and Lilli Palmer, he was raised in the United States and Italy, and educated in Britain. As a dramatist his performed work includes some sixty television plays and episodes of series, among them the BBC-2 *Freud*, a six-part dramatized biography termed 'a superb analysis' by the *New York Times*. Two trilogies for Radio 3, *The Sea Voyage* and *A Suffolk Trilogy*, have been widely praised; the latter includes the Giles Cooper Award-winning *I Never Killed My German*.

Egon is the third novel in a quartet entitled *To Liskeard*, a modern-day *Canterbury Tales* in which, as the travellers recount their separate adventures, each story, and each book, brings them closer to a reunion in the small Cornish town of Liskeard. The first two volumes of the quartet, *Richard's Feet* and *Cley*, were published to great acclaim in 1990 and 1991.

Carey Harrison lives in Dublin with his wife, artist Claire Lambe, and their children.

Also by Carey Harrison

Freud, A Novel
Richard's Feet*
Cley*

*available from Minerva

CAREY HARRISON

Egon

Minerva

A Minerva Paperback
EGON

First published in Great Britain 1993
by William Heinemann Ltd
This Minerva edition published 1995
by Mandarin Paperbacks
an imprint of Reed Consumer Books Ltd
Michelin House, 81 Fulham Road, London SW3 6RB
and Auckland, Melbourne, Singapore and Toronto

Copyright © Carey Harrison 1993
The author has asserted his moral rights

A CIP catalogue record for this title
is available from the British Library
ISBN 0 7493 9844 2

Printed and bound in Great Britain
by Cox & Wyman Ltd, Reading, Berks

For Claire, my wife

For JVS; for Jeremy, for Jonathan, Aileen and Lawrence,
writers, for their skill and sustaining kindness;
and for Ian and Paul who, like Egon, landed in England...

My lark, my weaver of spells,
My bow, my arrow, my love...

—Lewis Glyn Cothi's elegy for his son, *Lament for Siôn y Glyn*, translated by Joseph P. Clancy

there, I hope?

'Of *course* I know my *name.*'

You can remember what you do, where you live?

Something the matter with my eyes. Wait—wait, it's coming. 'Say again?'

'You can remember what you do and where you live? Your address?' Now I can see him, watch him speak as the blur sharpens. A young sandy-haired fellow, jacket and tie, seated across the desk from me. Haloed in window-light.

'Yes of course I can.' In my testiness I don't even sound like me. It's only fear. I must not panic. 'I know perfectly well who I am.'

But I can't stop myself confirming it quickly in my head and as the name comes, *Alec Simmons*, it comes with a troubling sense that I'm devising it (for whom? for him, or for myself?), that I'm not an Alec at all.

I must have said the name aloud because he nods, and after all he has my name, my file, in front of him. I *am* an Alec. It already feels right.

Easing in the chair I shift Alec's thighs, Alec's back and buttocks. Studying the fellow opposite. Restless Alec can tell, I note, that the man doesn't have much time for this interview. A raw face, red-headed, a pimply hairless jaw, it doesn't look as if he has to shave much.

That's it: I'm in a cottage hospital. And instantly the thought

3

comes, how do I know that? And as soon as I realize that I'm asking myself that, I know there must be something wrong with me, still wrong with me whatever the man says, because *of course* I know where I am. If there wasn't something wrong, why would I be so surprised to discover that I know? Why would I even ask myself how it is that I know, unless preceding the instant of knowledge there had been a blank, a darkness?

That's normal, the doctor persists. I know he's been telling me this for some time, and I know he isn't going to let me stay here, occupying a bed, that's what the interview is all about. Pen between the first two fingers, the butt of the pen tapping his thumbnail. All you're doing, he explains once more, patiently now, is inspecting ordinary, perfectly healthy thought-processes, holding them up to the light, as it were, don't you think? Putting them under the microscope and finding that they're not really instantaneous at all, they're a matter of little stages. Of searches. That's absolutely normal.

'But *why* am I doing this?' Putting everything under the microscope. Yet I know the answer: because you're still in shock.

'Look,' he says at last, 'is there anything important that you don't remember?'

Crafty question—or else plain idiotic. Because how would I know? But he wants to be done with me and I mustn't delay him. I do know what he's getting at, of course. *Yes*, that's just it, I say, there are whole years missing. And people's names, they've gone too.

'People close to you?'

'No,' I admit, reflecting blindly. No names at all come to mind. 'No,' I say, I suppose not.

'Don't you think it might have been like that before this happened?' He smiles and indicates the cluttered desktop with a nod. 'I mean, I don't know where I'd be without my files.'

A faint sugaring of sleep clings to the corners of his eyes, like a child's, with a fly-speck on one sandy eyelash. Gets up, doesn't have to shave, comes straight into the office.

'We do forget people's names, don't we, from time to time? Increasingly often, in fact.'

How old *am* I? He must be trying to tell me that I'm getting on, mustn't expect too much from memory.

4

You see? he says. 'Look here, if you named a year and asked what I was doing then, I'd have to think. I doubt if anything would come to mind, for a moment or two. I'd have to ask my wife.'

I try to picture this beardless fellow's wife. 'I don't have one to ask.' Why doesn't she wipe the sleep from his eyes before he goes to work? A sweet plump lazy thing perhaps, sleeping in.

'But you do see what I mean?' he continues gently. 'Poor old brain's not up to every question you put to it.'

'I understand that. But that's... well, it's only part of it.'

He doesn't look at me.

'There's a kind of continuous hesitation,' I explain, 'up here.' Tapping my Alec-brainbox. What I can't bring myself to say: that I seem to take my cue from *outside*. From outside my head. And how long can I go on like this?

'It'll pass,' he says. Looking into my eyes now.

It's all I want to hear.

BACK IN MY room, packing, frantic, why is Alec hurrying?

I have discovered this: when I move (when I stir, even minutely, and almost before I know it) I am he, I am Alec. Alec moves, stirs. Acts. Inside my head I am I. But this is wrong. Is *I* not Alec? Does *he* not think?

Calm down: I am what I have always been, I am entire and everything *is* present, all of me, even if it isn't present as memory it's here as instinct, appetite, some cunning surely too, acquired along the way, the sum of everything I've lived no matter how little memory yields. And—*this* is the thing to understand—since I may never know how much or how little I could recall before this thing happened, I must make do. And let it come to me. I will *not* panic. Remember everyone's in the same boat, that's what the chap was trying to tell me.

Can this be normal, though? Without looking up (the world of light seems to have shrunk to a circle around my feet) I know the shape the ivy makes around the window, I know each leaf as though I'd counted them for days to fill the void, and now, making its way across the outer sill, raising its back inchworm-fashion, a green caterpillar with one red tufted pennant of a tail: words coming with it, 'You beautiful caterpillar,' absurdly, I want to stroke it, 'you beauty!'

But when Alec looks up there are no leaves at the window, no caterpillar, a winter fog is rolling in like giant's breath through conifers and across a sandy parking space with a handful of cars, a harsh midwinter by the look of it.

And now the caterpillar seems to me to belong to another window fringed with leaves, I'm lying sick in a child's bed, and I feel overwhelmingly grateful for this memory that's mine, unbidden. My Alec-body leads me to the bed, mouth open, basking in it, holding on his lap a brown suitcase I don't recognize at all. Perhaps somebody's lent it to me. It's what I contain that matters.

And then I have it, I know where the caterpillar came from. A brick house-front with red window-frames, a sallow Cornish landscape unfolding around it. I feel on the edge of a breakthrough.

But my ordeal isn't over. Alerted by movement at the edge of vision, I sense that my suitcase has come alive. An immense beetle, dark greenish-grey like a fat, rainsoaked goose-turd but with legs and great curved horns, is climbing slowly and precariously along one rim, as if choosing the most perilous path, or retaining the option to move onto one or other plane of the suitcase. I can feel my whole body flushing with Alec's fear, not mine—since to me the poor beetle seems sluggish, roused from hibernation or else on its last legs perhaps, a survivor past its season. Staring fascinated, I note that it sports long, corrugated antennae, shaped just like miniature heads of ryegrass, sprayed black. At last I let Alec look away, shuddering, willing it to be another creature out of memory and to be gone when he looks back again.

It is. Gone. Just the suitcase, as before. The horror of it still sings in his nerves, prickling at his fingertips, and to be sure it's disappeared and not just flown away or fallen off he searches the floor and the bed, in vain, shaking out his clothes, reluctant to believe a reverie could have fashioned anything so strange, so minutely specified, antediluvian in shape yet so alive.

I'm fond of caterpillars, but like the Alec in my veins I've had enough of this insect-haunting and pray silently for it to stop: sitting now on the visitor's chair, well away from the bed. Where could my mind have got it from? I've never studied bugs or beetles, that I can recall.

ALEC IS (I think, pending revelations but the sensation is secure) a person with an unremarkable life. It certainly feels that way. He is, by a happy coincidence, a schoolteacher, as I am: teacher of French, both literature and language. Hardly a coincidence, if we are one; so far we coincide, at any rate. Now I can feel my Alec-mind working a mile a minute, frantic. What more are we? A bachelor, ageing, that's clear, and yet—this is the most peculiar thing—he and I both feel as young, as tentative as... as a child left among unfamiliar adults. Absurd—indeed, we are the *senior* French master. No hesitation here at all. My work, my classroom, the term's set books are all perfectly, tediously sharp in his head, erupting at the least excuse like a horde of jostling schoolchildren into a vacant corridor, my empty classroom is present to view right down to the writing I left chalked on the board and the placing of each book, pencil and rubber on our desk, as microscopically and unnecessarily clear as: as the horned thing on our suitcase.

But pray God more substantial.

(*Microscopically* clear... was it the phrase 'under the microscope' that set off my hallucinations? That *bloody* doctor!)

Sartre—and as it comes, this multifoliate memory, I know Sartre is *mine*—Sartre, as I sometimes remind my students when they're looking bored, first saw crustaceans coming for him across the floor while he was working on... on *what*?... it was his most abstruse, ambitious essay, the summit of his philosophical work but never mind because I can find its name quickly enough when I get home, and while writing it he was wolfing down some compound drug later favoured by wartime pilots, it's coming now: dexedrine laced with amyl. Yes, and for the rest of his life, God help him, the great thinker was liable to glimpse a pair of claws moving towards his feet. Also the poet Nerval took a pet lobster—a real one—for slithers on a lead, along the Paris boulevards... it occurs to me that the rest of my memories might start coming back if I addressed them in French.

To calm himself down, Alec turns to the side window of the little car. The lights are red. The shops, the street, look quite familiar. Is it Wembley? Willesden? he wonders: do I know the damn place?

Beside me Norma with her lean capable hands on the wheel. Her dark hair frizzing, her straight nose. The nose *very* straight. Straighter than I remember it, in profile. Has she lost weight, altering the lines of her face? I don't like to ask, in case this isn't so and I betray the tricks my memory, our memory, is playing me, remembering her perhaps from some long-distant, plumper period. Norma taking off her earrings to make love. It comes to me that she's wondering how I feel, in a car.

Promptly, 'Would you rather drive?' she asks.

Oh it's amusing to be psychic, but I'd exchange it for a simple packed lunch of memories.

'You're sure? You look nervous.'

'Not about being in a car,' I say, and remember in a rush: a road, a stretch of woods. Why I'm here. How could I have forgotten? How have I functioned, till this instant, without asking myself how I came to be here, what brought me to the cottage hospital? But Alec knew; yes, Alec was functioning *for* me. 'If I could remember what happened, I might have something to be nervous *about*.'

'You know you'll probably never remember it.'

'It would help if somebody could tell me *how* it happened.' I must not panic.

'What *do* you remember?'

Searching, I don't even recall feeling tired, if that was it, if I dropped off. Suppose I veered off the road to avoid a child, an animal? A wobbling cyclist perhaps, a car shooting out of a side road without looking. A stretch of woods, I can picture it but it could be any stretch of birchwoods. No sound, no car. What if I had a blackout, would it have shown up afterwards, would anybody know? 'I *was* alone, wasn't I?'

'What makes you say that?'

If I'd picked up a hitchhiker.

'Of course you were alone.'

Picture the boy running off, terrified, into the dark. I see him running off into the woods, stumbling.

'I've never known you to pick anyone up. You're so protective of the Alvis.'

Alec looks away to avoid the tender smile that accompanies this. Will the lights *never* change?

'Nobody was hurt. You were shaken up and you've lost a few minutes of your life. Think how much worse it could have been.'

He leans over to hug her lean body. She engages the engine and he releases her, my burden lightened; and, yielding now to the need for solace, I hear myself say, 'I thought it would clear up in a matter of days. I've been waiting.'

'You shouldn't be going back to work.'

'If not to work, where?'

'I could take a few days off,' Norma says.

'I've just got to get used to it.'

She watches the road. Can she tell there are two of us, watching her?

I see on a lamplit page the words (mine?... it's my writing): *my fiftieth year is ending, if I am not ripe for solitude now I never will be.*

'Was I getting a bit slow-witted recently? I mean, have I been this distracted for years?'

She shrugs, smiling.

'I have?'

'You're suffering from post-clinical amnesia, that's what the doctor said.'

It sounds odd and I make her repeat it. 'I didn't know there was such a thing.'

'Didn't he tell you?' She studies me.

'He might have done, I don't know.'

Norma looks anxious for the first time. I must try and make her understand, before the tears come.

'Now look—don't worry. He said it would pass... it's true I do seem to have less information than I should have, in some respects, but in other ways—this is the odd thing—I have more than I want. Or sooner than I want it. At times it's like getting the answer before you've finished framing the question, if that makes any sense.' Try again, she's still looking pent-up. 'You know how it is when you hear the first bars of a song and you don't recognize it yet, but all kinds of emotions flood in, feelings you've attached to it, in the past...' (where is this fluency coming from, these welling words?—not mine—Alec's!) 'or—it's the same thing—you're reminded of someone but for a moment the name, the face eludes you... it's coming, it's so close that you can already sense what you feel about the person, what you *really* feel, uncensored. And you're aware that this could be a little too instructive. That when you realize who the person is, you might rather have remained in the dark.' Saying it, I know this is true. 'That's how I feel all the time.'

She braves it out. 'And when you think of me?'

'Oh, I remember lots of things. I don't forget who *you* are, for goodness sake.' Immediately I hear myself add, 'Mostly fragments, but that's how memory is.' Seeing something in her eyes.

'Yes,' she says. This is the woman I haven't married. That I know, and it's clearer, in a rush of feeling, than I dare tell her.

'I'll ask the head to give me time off,' I offer cheerily. 'Though I've told you how he is, often enough.' As I say it, I know it's true, I *have* told her. 'He hates malingerers.'

THE HEADMASTER IS young, not as young as the doctor but so young that I expect him to show some concession to the difference between our ages, some embarrassment even, a touch of deference, but instead his gaze, his smile, are man-to-man, almost paternal, perhaps he *is* embarrassed at being my junior, it occurs to me, that's why he's trying not to acknowledge it.

He says something, very softly and indistinctly I think but I must be going deaf because I can't make out the words. When I replay the murmur in my head, I feel increasingly sure from its tone that he is saying something about my health, the way I look.

Is his hair pomaded? It comes to me that I've never previously stood over the headmaster, a man a good six inches taller than myself and now seated before me. Or is it just naturally slick and wiry? Does he slick it back to stop it falling youthfully across his face?

Take the rest of the term off, the headmaster is saying, and I can hear him now, 'It's only three weeks till Christmas. We can cover for you.'

Is he trying to get rid of me? Does it show in my eyes that I know this, or have I said something?

Because what the man says now is, more distinctly still, as if in answer: 'You know there'll always be a job for you here as long as you want it. You do know that, don't you? You're one of our pillars,' he adds, the word coming out sounding oddly like 'pillows', as though my chief function here were to suffocate people in their sleep.

I gaze into the eyes of this dark-haired boy, this dark-haired man rather, the firm neat eyebrows and dark eyes, and see in them, to my bewilderment, nothing but compassion.

ANOTHER HORRIBLE ENCOUNTER: descending the long winding hill through genteel suburbia back to impoverished suburbia and the underground station, Alec is no longing carrying the brown suitcase but instead a small grip, an overnight bag which I know contains fresh clothes, when he finds himself slowly catching up with a young man walking down the pavement ahead of us, unusually tall and thin, six foot six or even eight, wearing black drainpipe trousers and a grey sleeveless vest as if it were summer, a creature whose cropped hair, bunched on top in a greyish-brown mass, ends in a curious single rat-tail down the back of his head and neck, a thick thread coloured, as I see when we draw closer, pink, and to my revulsion I realize it *is* a rat's tail, cut off and worn like a trophy perhaps, but no, worse is to come. The grey-brown mass on the man's head *is* a rat, a live rat, no doubt a pet but all the same Alec slows down for fear the man will turn to glance at us, revealing the rat's head above his own. Our steady, clopping progress, his and ours, magnified by the silence of the fog, leaves me in a quandary. The rat-man's pace isn't slow enough to overtake, we're stuck behind him. What to do? Alec turns off down a sordid side street, and as soon as he does I know it's a mistake.

We pass a betting shop, a pub, a stretch of pawky grass littered with dented cars from one of which, some twenty yards away, a young man in his twenties smiles at us through a yawning door and emerges from behind the wheel, although from the look of the car it seems unlikely that he, or anyone, has been driving it recently.

He stands beside the car, stretching as if we'd woken him from sleep, a strange tall soft-faced boy with a running nose, not as tall as the rat-man but sinewy, feline.

Then, and I know he's going to do it because the nervous stretching motions have lie written all over them, he steps out into our path, stands square in front of us, causing Alec to stop dead a pace or two away from him. If we tried to continue round him between him and the beached car's front bumper we'd probably have to nudge him off the narrow pavement, or he'd nudge us off if we tried to pass to his left, where parked cars line the street, we'd bump and that's the last thing I want.

He wants to stop us and we've stopped.

His soft features have a melting look, it's hard to concentrate on them. An oatmeal-coloured jacket and a grey pullover, and beneath the chin a new cheap shirt, plaid collar sticking out, in fact the whole wardrobe looks new but inappropriate: beneath beige linen trousers the shabby black shoes give him away, the dirty hands. The face is dirty too, I see, as Alec looks back at it.

'I'm Danny,' he announces, but the name too, stiffly spoken, sounds as if it was acquired with the wardrobe, 'will you take charge of me?'

I stare at him, unable to believe my ears. The question is impossible, no-one can address such words to a stranger.

Incredulity clearly shows in my eyes, because he repeats the sentence, adding: 'Will you take care of me and look after me?'

Part plea and part command, hesitantly defiant, his voice betrays him. The formula has failed him in the past.

'No,' I say, trying not to sound shocked. My own voice has a calm enough ring, and I recover my bearings. 'But I'll buy you a cup of tea.'

I regret it instantly. Why didn't I say, I'll give you enough for a cup of tea?

'Don't want a cup of tea,' he says, a snarling Cockney whine replacing the previously careful consonants.

We stand staring at each other. All this is the rat-man's fault, I reflect vengefully, I wouldn't have turned off otherwise. I long for someone to arrive, to emerge from the pub or the betting shop to witness the scene and legitimize my escape.

Now is the moment to step round him, past the parked cars and out into the street but I don't move, I even think of turning round and returning to the school.

The boy begins to shiver. He stands there as if willing it to continue. The shiver turns into a prolonged shudder. Is he going to have a fit? But no, he's demonstrating cold.

'Give us your coat,' he says.

'That's ridiculous,' I say, knowing it isn't ridiculous at all.

He has both hands in his jacket pockets, trying, I take it, to control the shudder. Instead one hand has located something, brings it out, using the other hand to open it. A knife.

To my amazement the sight of the blade releases me from fear, a kind of lunatic merriment rises in its place. I'm being held at knifepoint for my tired blue overcoat: a perfect mismatch for the rest of his outfit. 'We're about the same size,' I say. 'Give me your jacket, you can have my coat.'

'No,' he says, 'that's old, this jacket's new.'

'It's only a jacket,' I persist, 'this is an overcoat.'

'But it's new, my jacket, look at it, it's *brand new*.'

'Then why are you begging?'

'What?'

For a moment I feel pleased about the way 'begging' seems to confuse him, erasing the presence of the knife; then his confusion passes.

'I'm not fucking begging, mate,' he says, holding up the knife, 'what do you think *this* is?'

But the initiative has already passed to me. 'I haven't got any money, and you're not having my overcoat.'

'Sod your overcoat then,' he says quietly, almost a mutter, and I watch him carefully fold the knife and put it in one pocket. I sense that he is oddly pleased with our exchange, as if stalemate flattered him, were a kind of intimacy honourably won.

Then I have to fight off a moment's dizziness as I also realize that the curious screen on which Alec acts my part has been absent since Danny began to speak.

'I'm Alec,' I say.

Danny is carefully cutting an untipped cigarette in two, with his knife, on a formica tabletop. We are sitting in a transport café, facing each other across our cups of tea. He offers me one half of the cigarette and, when I refuse, returns it to the packet. 'Learnt that in the army.'

'Goes twice as far,' I nod.

'Nah, more than that. You see the secret is, you get most of the pleasure from lighting up, right?'

I watch him as he does so with trembling hands, almost burning his face. His nose is running worse than ever.

'What do you do?' I say.

'I'm an architectural historian.'

'Is that right.'

'You don't believe me?' From under the table he brings out a couple of books, though I can't work out where he's kept them hidden, a battered paperback Pevsner, *Hertfordshire*, and a large hardback with a bright shop-fresh cover featuring Chippendale chairs.

'You're also an expert on furniture?'

'I'm teaching myself. I'm going to be an antiques dealer.'

'Good idea', I say as he studies me keenly. 'Antique dealer,' I correct, 'you don't say *antiques* dealer.'

Danny looks at the books, then at me. 'Will you keep them for me?'

'No thank you.'

'I don't want to lose them.'

'Then why give them to me?'

'I've read them twice. Now I need someone to test me on what I know.' He grins, and I sense that I have told him my profession. 'Someone to keep me up to the mark.'

I shake my head.

'I'm sick of carrying them. You've got a bag.'

'I really don't want them, Danny.'

He sips his tea, eyeing the Pevsner, then picks it up and opens it, studying a page at random.

'Who do they belong to?'

'They're mine,' he protests, 'I got them from the public library.'

'Stole them from the public library.'

'Not if you take them back for me, then they're not stolen, are they?'

I ignore this and we sip our tea in turn, amid the café din, while Danny eyes me restlessly, planning. It gives me a curious pleasure to watch his calculations, based, as my own are now in this intense, endangered present tense of shock (*post-clinical*... whatever that means), on a stranger's face. I don't have to feel guilty that I remember so much less than I should about the other person, or about myself, since we both start from nothing, from invention.

Danny's seems to me an extraordinary face, unlike any other I've seen. Unformed and almost wriggling to emerge, fighting to break a mask of skin. No matter how often I look at them, his features seem to melt when I look away, even seem to melt when I'm looking at them. Literally so, in a sense, thanks to the two transparent rolls of snot on his upper lip. Above them the formlessness of his nose, and eyes of a mesmeric lack of colour that I'd barely noticed in the street, yellowish, almost khaki; a catlike quality to his jaw and small, fleshy but pallid lips. Monkeyish perhaps. A thin face, but every feature soft, this was what made it hard to memorize, made the features seem to blend into each other. The snot has a yellowish tinge, the same tint as his water-spaniel eyes, irises from which the colour seems to have been drained.

And now for some reason I felt I had never been so aware of the person in the foreground, within a dim enclosing babel of place which at last I understood—acknowledged, that was how it seemed—as so much less important than the aura released by the encounter itself, its local mythology, the sense—yes, this was what I seemed to be acknowledging fully now—that each time a human being confronts another, whether in life, in dream, or in imagination, it takes place against a kind of living tapestry, the scene (as it might be) a terrace, the landscape beyond it launched by a protecting ha-ha into distant fields (woods, unseen lakes) patrolled by beasts from heraldry and, further off, barely more than a dot, a speck, a tiny mounted figure, spear raised and stabbing downwards from a rearing horse: in other words the masque of the heart, a vast receding backdrop of the heart's history, of possibilities evoked by memory or, if the person before us is a stranger, the clues their eyes, their face and manner (or their name, the precise shade of their dress) evoke from memories of others, a certain impatience or social discomfort, uncertainty or curiosity colouring the foreground, hovering around the face, with tender anxieties and desires lurking a little further off (white on white like obscure pieces of garden furniture against the marble balustrade), with sexual longing, fear, or rage behind this where the land suddenly falls away, and on the darkling plain beyond, murder.

As I begin to wonder how much of this morbid line of thought I have allowed into my face, Danny seems to anticipate me.

His first movement is swift, as if scalded: pushing back his chair.

He ducks out of sight for a moment and when he reappears his movements maintain the same manic rapidity, he is up and out of his chair and halfway towards the door when I notice he has my overnight bag in his hand.

A few faces turn, I too watch him with the same mildly startled expression as he barges through the door and sprints across the street and out of view. The faces have turned to me now, this is my cue to protest. Stop, thief! But no words come. I should feel angry or at least distressed... instead I feel obscurely ashamed: was it something I said?

My abashed expression makes it all clear to the watching faces, I can tell as they turn away: I must have made an obscene suggestion to my young companion, who has fled with his belongings. I look down at the forlorn, abandoned books, which now look like *my* stock-in-trade, a failed bribe. Titles directed at his empty place. For all the guff I've been telling myself about the easeful company of strangers I feel nothing but relief at Danny's absence. The loss of my clothes seems cheap at the price. Now I can finish my tea at my leisure.

I'M IN A house I don't know. But I do know it's my sister Jennet's house and I can feel my mind devising explanations. She's moved into it recently, perhaps. Yes, it seems from the way Jennet is showing me round that I'm right about this, and that the move is recent enough that I don't have to feel ashamed of being here on my first visit. 'And this is Eamonn's room,' I hear her say, leaving me to open it myself, so many emotions colliding on plump Jennet's round face that it goes completely blank.

I knock, hear Eamonn's polite 'Come in', and enter a splendid loft with skylights along one side and on the other a view over rooftops to a distant silhouette I recognize. Alexandra Palace. Eamonn lies on the bed, fully clothed, reading beneath a lamp that renders the room nocturnal, clinical. My nephew. (No hesitation, none, I know where I am now.) Nineteen, and dying. His old man's eyes are fixed on... no, correction: an old woman's eyes, gazing at me across a distance I can never bridge. His grandmother's, my mother's eyes. *Well, boy? Come to see how I'm doing?* But that was in hospital when she was scourging us all for her approaching death. Eamonn is staring at me open-mouthed as if I were the best present anyone had ever brought him. He starts to speak but tears of eagerness overtake him, he ignores them and scrambles off the bed into my arms as if he were still a child, and my mother's eyes are gone, drowned, sweet almond lids close over them.

He has to do the hugging, I can barely raise my arms, it's not a wraith I'm holding but the whole firmament, my drowned boy home, my joy, my child. As he crushes his waterlogged lungs against me I can feel the desperation lurch back into my heart, but I feel so much more alive now with him pressed against my chest. He hugs me harder as if to give me all the life he can.

Doesn't ask me what I'm doing here. As he shows me his room, I note how drastically he's changed, the sallow skin of his mournful Mediterranean face dominated by its long, intelligent nose, bonier now, eyebrows dark bristling loops, high-arched and creeping down towards the corner of his eyes like a Christ on a Byzantine icon. None of the pimply gawkiness of boys his age, he seems both older and younger, wiser and more innocent, and I feel the vertigo of losing myself and falling into this luminous being, knowing I have to lose him. For a time as he walks round the room explaining and describing, it's as though I am not here at all, the observer, but that

I am he, picking up this piece of machinery, pointing to that wall-chart.

I can still feel him in my arms, a part of me.

'D'you know where this is?' He is pointing at a row of colour photographs taped to the wall, but I can hardly see them I am so consumed with him, his gaze, directed now at me and not at the snaps. 'I only got them out the other day. Look. Don't you recognize it?'

Forcing my attention onto them, I see they overlap to form a panorama of a ploughed field, featureless, dipping into an unseen valley with a partly wooded slope beyond. On it a small white house that seems familiar.

'A hint,' Eamonn says, enjoying this. 'It looked a bit different before they put the field to wheat. Imagine pasture. Thistles.'

'It's Cornwall, isn't it,' I grope.

'I knew you'd get it! It's the view from the back bedroom window. Whatmough's field. Here's where I saw the plane come down, the German plane, right here...' he puts a finger on a spot, level and unmarked, on the harrowed field. 'I saw it all the way down till it hit and burst into flames. I heard it coming, I could see the whole thing from my bed. Really shook the window too, it must have nearly blown it out. I can *see* it come down *now*,' with two diving fingers he trails a low hedgehopping path along and down the wall towards the photographs, making a loud wasp-whine between his teeth, and, 'paughhh!', fingers spreading wide as they meet the ploughed earth.

'You really saw that, did you?' As I speak Eamonn is erasing a small dent in the central photograph caused by a dive-bombing fingernail. The nails are long and for an instant I picture his reluctance to cut them, as if each clipping were a remembrance of death. 'I'd forgotten that. What was a German plane doing near us?'

'They said he might have been coming in to land and give himself up, but he ran out of fuel first.'

Poor bastard, I make to say, the reflex wartime phrase bringing a host of images into my head, but I can tell from Eamonn's expression that it will be wasted breath; the images, though, airfield images, I'd like to linger with them and I can't, Eamonn's eyes are alive with something he has yet to tell or yet to ask. But he holds back. We look at each other in silence, as if honouring the German pilot, though our minds are elsewhere. 'When did you say you took these pictures?'

'About three years ago. Three years last summer.'

'And you,' faltering now, 'did you just... go in, and...?'

'No, I went round the back and took them. It's all right, there wasn't anyone at the house. I mean, it's lived in, but there wasn't anyone at home. I trespassed,' he enunciates happily. 'While I was there I even looked for the ball we lost under the hedge when you were batting.'

Threadbare, almost black, the tennis ball.

'Remember how we searched? Hours and hours. Somebody's dog probably got it years ago.'

'But... what took you to Truro?'

'I wanted to see the house.'

'You mean you went there just to see it?'

'How long is it since *you've* seen it?'

I shake my head. It seems to be exactly what he wants from me.

'We could go there,' spilling from him, 'couldn't we?'

'Where, to Cornwall?'

'Yes, to the house, I've been wanting to go for ages. I mean with *you*.'

'Well we must, we absolutely must, I'd like to see what they've done to it,' I say, lying, since it's the last thing I want to see, 'we'll go this summer.'

'No, let's go *now*.'

He means it. Light filling his face, until the sallow skin glows with consumptive beauty like candle wax lit from within.

'Your mother wouldn't hear of it, Eamonn. It's freezing cold out there.'

'No it isn't, I've been out today.'

He's an even worse liar than I am, and I let it pass. 'It's out of the question. You've forgotten how tiring it is, a long journey like that. It's at least two hundred miles.'

'Two hundred and forty seven, if you take the A30. Two hundred and eighteen by the A303, but it might be nicer to go through Stockbridge. We stayed there once, remember, at a bed-and-breakfast?

And it'll only be tiring for you, you're the driver, I'll just be sitting there tucked up nice and warm, we'll take plenty of blankets. And a thermos.'

'You forget. I haven't got a car. I crashed it.'

'Hire one then. Hire a nice new one.'

I stare at him. I've never hired a car in my life. '*Hire* one?' But already I can feel my own rising excitement at our mutual truancy. I realize without any sense of shame that I've always wanted to steal the boy. 'No. It's a delightful idea, the whole thing...'

'No it's *not* delightful, it's not a *delightful* idea,' he is quietly earnest, not mocking me, 'it's a dangerous idea but I want to see the house again before I'm too sick to travel,' and, forestalling me quickly, 'I know that might be years away, but I don't want to take the risk. I've been thinking about it a lot. When you came today,' his face seems even paler for an instant, 'I thought you must have known somehow.'

'I'd no idea you cared so much about the place. It's not... it wasn't particularly nice as a house, I mean for children.'

He stares at me as if betrayed. 'You taught me to bowl there.'

'Johnny!' Jennet calls from below, and for a moment I don't know which of us she's addressing, then Eamonn's face reacts, altered, a Johnny-face of reluctant obedience. The voice comes again. 'Lunch in ten minutes, you two!'

'What's for lunch?' I say brightly, hearing myself treating him like a sick five-year-old.

He shrugs.

'Aren't you hungry?'

'You go and talk to her, tell her we're going.'

Colour is entering his cheeks from the top, at the cheekbones, and I know I have to stop it now, before it's too late. 'This summer. I promise. Come hell or high water.' Seeing the disappointment in his eyes, 'We'll do a proper tour, go round the moors, the mines, the lot. D'you remember how you told me once you were a tinner in a previous life, a tin miner down a Cornish mine?'

Eamonn nods. 'First above, on the surface, then below,' he corrects, reluctant, eyes still pooling in despair.

'Working for the Jews, you said. And I tried to explain to you that you couldn't have been working for the Jews, down a Cornish mine.'

'But I was right, wasn't I?' glowing now with small, returning pride, 'the Jews were only sent out of Cornwall in 1282 by Edward the Confessor.'

'Edward the first, not the Confessor. Close enough. To the Cornish all English kings were pretty much the same anyway.'

I can see him begin to heave, holding onto the cough, and I don't know what to do. He masters it, but the flushed turbulence is still there in his face.

'I'll go on my own,' he says curtly. 'I'll go by train. What are you going to do, you and my mother? Lock me in my room?'

I want to hug him so badly. Instead I stand motionless in the dock.

'Don't be silly. If it's what you want, I'll talk to Jennet. Just calm down.'

I BLUNDER INTO the world of rental cars like a Bedouin confronting a shopping precinct. Eamonn wants a red Ford Prefect, and although I know he won't complain if I bring back something else, I want to get him a red Ford Prefect; as a result the search sends me into a blur of streets and shop fronts and connections made or missed with public transport; at each confusion I am losing Eamonn, chasing back and forth across the city towards red Prefects promised on the telephone, where only blue ones prove available, or else red cars of a different make, until I've located one at last, and at last a duffle-coated Eamonn and I are descending the stairs of Jennet's house, adjusting his woollen cap and muffler, and out the front door carrying his overnight bag.

The car is there, the red Prefect, outside the house.

Only it isn't empty.

There are clothes in the back seat, piled high it seems.

And then as I approach them the illusion of loose clothes reassembles into a person, clothed, sleeping in the back seat of the car I have just rented.

Eamonn and Jennet watch in bewilderment as I advance on the

car, fumbling through pockets for the keys. I knock on the rear window and the clothes, the all too familiar clothes, react instantly like a startled cat, the oatmeal jacket and grey pullover uncoiling and the beige-clad legs jack-knifing sideways to bring a bleary Danny-face to the window, smiling in slow recognition as though I were the surprise.

I stare at him, unable to repress an odd spurt of relief at seeing him again.

Rather than bellow at him through the window for all the street to hear, I begin hunting for the keys once more.

'It's open,' he mouths hugely, helpfully.

I open the front door and as I do so I remember the one reason I could possibly feel pleased to see Danny again: my grip, my bagful of clothes. It's there, sitting on the front passenger seat. What the hell is going on, I begin to say, but Danny is already speaking.

'It's all right, I was just keeping watch for you when you come back with the car and went in, you shouldn't go off without locking a car, you know, not in London. I brought you back your bag. See it? I haven't touched the clothes. All right? They're not my style anyway. Only kidding,' he grins. 'I'm sorry I ran off with it. It's habit, you see, and I only wanted it to carry my books, I get fed up with carrying books all round the place, and I mean, carrier bags, you know what they're like, the handles come off before you're clear of the shop.'

'Hold on a minute. What the hell are you doing here, in my car? How did you find me?'

'Look in your bag.'

'What?'

'What's sitting there inside it?' he prompts me as if dealing with a dull-witted class. 'First thing you see, right there on top of the shirts? Don't you know? Your address book.' He shakes his head in disbelief. 'You didn't even know you'd lost it?'

'This is my sister's place,' I say, and as I say it I can hear Eamonn and Jennet approaching. 'They've just moved. The address isn't *in* the book.'

Glancing up and back I see Eamonn's face as he hesitates, intrigued, stopping a few paces away. Jennet looks flabbergasted, as though I am revealing to her a secret life.

'I *know* it's not in the book,' Danny is explaining patiently, 'your school is, though. Right? I had to work to get it out of them,' he briefly wipes his eyes but not, I am sorry to see, his nose, where the snot has dried into ochre snail tracks on his upper lip, 'I said I was a relative,' the feline grin again, 'but I don't think they believed me.'

'Would you please get out of this car and leave me alone,' I say, slightly louder now, for Jennet's benefit. Unzipping the grip, I find that everything seems indeed to be in place. 'Thank you for the bag, though I don't really understand why you decided to bring it back.' Turning to Jennet, 'This character mugged me earlier today, in the middle of Northolt.'

'I told you, I needed it for my books.'

'*Out*,' I say firmly. 'You left the books in the café, if you remember.'

'Nah,' he says dismissively, without making any attempt to get out of the car, 'not *those* books, I'd done with them.'

'Shall I phone the police?' Jennet calls.

I shake my head. Her face, now placid as her voice, shows a grim fearless pleasure I don't associate with her at all, as if she were about to call for a rodent exterminator. 'No harm done,' I point out.

She stares at me. Meanwhile Danny, when I turn to him, is still sitting contentedly in the back seat behind me, and I wonder whether I shall have to try and manhandle him out.

'Well come on for God's sake,' comes Jennet's voice, 'are you taking the boy to Truro or not?'

'Truro? That's in Cornwall—that's where my daughter lives, my little girl.'

'Out! I mean it, Danny, just get out and get on with... becoming an antiques dealer or whatever it is. I'm not taking you to Cornwall.'

'*Why* not?' he says plaintively, and when I don't answer, 'You think I'm stupid, don't you?' I restrain myself from asking what kind of thief restores his booty to the owner, unbidden. 'You do, don't you? *I* can tell fake Hepplewhite from the real thing,' he is saying, '*and* tell you what year the real one was made, what's more I can speak six languages, and I should think that's more than you, right? But, you see—*you* think I've already forgotten. I haven't: it's *antique* dealer.'

He mimics my voice and intonation uncomfortably well. Then, winningly: 'If you took me to Cornwall you could teach me lots of things like that.'

'And then you'd run off with my bag again. Or maybe the car. Out of habit.'

'Christ,' he explodes, and his rage makes me recoil, suddenly it's like being caught with a clawing, spitting cat in a travelling car, 'I brought you back your fucking bag, and this all the thanks I fucking get. Listen,' and he wrenches the back door open so viciously I expect to see the handle in his hand as he squirms out, 'you can stuff your fucking bag, *and* your clothes and the rest of the cheap crap *and* your trip to fucking Cornwall. I could have taught *you* a thing or too about antiques, mate,' he is standing on the pavement now, shaking with righteous fury, 'but now you'll *never* fucking *know*, will you? Well you won't fucking forget *me*, I'll tell you that now, I've got your little black book all memorized, I know where to find you. As for you, missus,' he turns on Jennet, 'you can go and call the fucking police for all the good it'll do you, I won't be here when they come but I *might* be along tonight, or some other night when I'm not busy.'

'Come along, Johnny,' Jennet hauls at Eamonn's arm, 'I think we've heard more than enough of this.'

'It's all right,' Danny relents benevolently, suddenly calm. 'I've said my piece.' He spreads both arms to include us all in the gesture, bows his head briefly and, taking a step back, declares, '*Buona notte, tutti*,' before turning and marching off, jacket flaps swinging. His unimpeachable Italian accent leaves us all in disarray, even though it is broad daylight and 'good night, all' makes rather less sense than the rest of his tirade.

I look at Eamonn, and see that he is still watching the departing Danny with a dazed expression on his bloodless, dark-eyebrowed face. More than dazed; dazzled—and I realize that he is still adjusting to the outdoors, to air and city smells, let alone to Danny. He looks like... like a desert hermit emerged from months of pious meditation in his cave to find himself on a battlefield; like a Bedouin in a shopping precinct. Between us if we make it to Cornwall unscathed, I reflect, it'll be a miracle.

SLEETY RAIN LIKE meteor showers popping little moonscapes onto the windscreen, as we sit stationary, wedged in traffic. Eamonn seems utterly content. The journey west stretches ahead of us; while I try not to think of how the strains will show tomorrow on the boy's face, of the long drive and at the end of it a peep over the hedge perhaps, at someone else's snowman—I dread this part, and can't fathom my own disinclination; for the moment the drive lulls me as it lulls Eamonn beside me, our cabin warm and isolated, free-floating, a time-capsule where no-one can catch me out. Eamonn is talking, holding forth about Grail quests and Arthurian legends, about the Islands of the Blest. Erudition he supposes wasted on his mother. My hands on the wheel seem more liver-spotted than I imagined them to be, a rash of a dull, evil, khaki colour.

At last a wider carriageway between strange factories set in gracious isolation, with lawns before them and pennants flying, oddly gauche and touching in their optimism. I study their friendly faces for the first time and find them charmingly various, united only in their suburban pride. At the crest of the hill a campanile with a green head tops the Gillette building. At that instant a burst of rain brings corrugations rippling down the edges of the windscreen where the wipers jerk back as if electrocuted, and I see a sodden, familiar figure by the roadside. Eamonn breaks off in mid-sentence and cries:

'It's him!'

As the figure steps out into the road, flailing urgently at us with both hands, we've passed him and Eamonn has turned round in his seat to gape through the back window.

'That *was* him, wasn't it?'

'Yes.'

'How on earth did he get here ahead of us?' I search for Danny in the rearview mirror, then the wing mirror, but can't see him. 'Do you want me to turn round and pick him up?'

'Not really.' Eamonn is still gazing back. 'Bet you he came by Undergound.'

'I didn't see a station. Did you?'

'Bet you he did. Or else,' he smiles, 'he got a lift with someone who avoided the North Circular.'

'Yes, I'm sorry, that wasn't very clever.'

Eamonn shakes his head. 'I don't want to get there fast. Do you?'

Moments pass and I still haven't slowed down.

'I don't mind,' Eamonn murmurs. 'Do *you* want to go back for him?'

'No.'

I brake now, for a junction, and as we emerge again onto an empty avenue the signpost greets us.

'See, there you are, we're on our way: the Great West Road.'

But as we drive on our journey seems curiously blighted, as if Danny's ghostly presence will be with us all the way to Cornwall now, and under my breath I curse the image of him flailing at us in the rain.

'It *was* him, wasn't it? Why is he chasing us like this?'

'Just a whim,' I say, but Eamonn looks at me doubtfully. '*I* don't know. He just seems to have taken to me.'

'You don't think he'd really go back to the house tonight? To burgle us?'

'Because we didn't give him a lift?'

'It's what he said.'

'That was just talk. And he got a good look at your mother in one of her fiercer moods.'

'Because... I was just thinking, he couldn't, could he, if we went back and picked him up? We could put him out somewhere *really* far from anywhere.'

I glance at him in surprise.

'Just an idea.' Switching smoothly, 'What happened when he mugged you? What did he do? Grab your bag?'

'Actually it was my fault, I bought him a cup of tea.'

As if this explains a good deal, Eamonn gives his mother's grim nod and turns away.

We both stay silent for a while. Arthur and the Grail seem to have retreated into the mists, as we head towards Staines.

'The best galloping ground in England,' I hear Eamonn pronounce slowly, studying me as though I, rather than he, should somehow be proud of this piece of information. 'That's what the coachmen used to say, wasn't it.'

Grunting to hide my puzzlement, I see we are crossing a dismal, level piece of heathland, with clumps of low birches, here and there gorse. Bagshot Heath perhaps.

'You told me that. You taught me the whole history of this road, the Roman bits and, later on, the riders and the coaches, and things called Russell's Fliers which were carts that went really slowly...'

Russell's Fly-vans, I correct him, as the memory returns.

'You see, you *do* remember! You were going to write a book about it, you said that once.'

'A *book*? About Russell's Fly-vans?'

'Not just them, about the road, the Great West Road, you said it was the old road west before the Romans, then they built the Old Sarum Road on top of it, then all the coaching journeys later, and you were going to follow it all the way down the A30, all the way to Land's End. The longest lane in England.'

'That's right, that's what it's called.'

'Who called it that?'

I shrug, helpless. I trust this seems like normal adult forgetfulness; I'm in no hurry to tell the boy that my memory has become one of the shorter lanes in England. I have no recollection of dreaming up this so-called book. Or of ever planning to write a book of any sort.

'You said we could write it together, if I did the hard work,' he grins, 'reading old books and finding mentions of the journey west. That's what we were going to call it: The Journey West.

'When was this, Johnny?'

'Oh ages ago. I must have been about fourteen, we were driving back from Truro.'

'And we never did anything about it?'

'It was just an idea. A game. I've got my notes, we could still do it.'

'I think I've missed the moment. It's years since I read all that stuff.'

'Too much like hard work, eh?' Eamonn chuckles. 'D'you remember when we went to look for the site of Vindogladia in a place called Gussage Cow Down? Vanished Vindogladia...' he revels in the romantic sounds.

'Yes,' I lie, 'yes.'

STOPPED, WHY HAVE we stopped? In a filling station, to get petrol must be. I'm standing here on the cement as if jolted awake, without even the bursting bubble of a dream. With no idea how I got here, where we are: nothing falls into place, the strangest feeling, why am I entire? Entire in space: my legs below. And everything around me stripped of time, or rather is it I where I am in my eye that's lost in time?

Give in. Trust it.

Familiar now, like waking blindfold on a high wire, the nausea gradually retreating, I could laugh now with relief. Like an old horse asleep on its feet, then suddenly the field again: nothing to be afraid of.

Good freezing cold assails my brain, my legs. My name is Alec, Alec Simmons. Cold recalls it and I shiver gratefully.

Only an instant lost perhaps, enough to wipe the whole board clean behind it—not even sure which is my car until the red, the rental car, red brings it back. Can't be petrol, started off full up. How long have we been going?

Eamonn is in the toilets, that's why we've stopped. And perhaps, it strikes me, his absence from view precipitated my instant of crisis. I am by the shop door, supposed to buy something... or just waiting?

Calm down: I *can* say to the boy, 'What was I supposed to buy? It's gone clean out of my mind.' Silly old uncle. I step into the shop to try and jog my mind, wondering if I've filled up with petrol anyway, now that we've stopped, glance round for Eamonn, no sign, and as I do a van pulls into the service station, beside the bearded driver a passenger leaning forward, pointing, pointing at something. Pointing at my car. Well before I recognize him all the feelings are there, ominous: fear, resignation, tenderness.

Now I can see Danny thanking the driver as he opens the van door, turning back again now as if putting something into the man's hands. A library book?

Danny sees me behind the plate glass of the shop and waves.

I gaze back at him, watching Eamonn approach around the

building, Danny greeting him like an old friend, coltishly charming. Accorded one of Danny's fantastical, courtly bows, Eamonn stares. His glance finds me. He grins, helpless, and I smile back. Perhaps if I look away there's still a chance none of this will be happening, clench my eyes and wake up in my bed, even my hospital bed will do. But they're still there, talking now, now *both* waving, Eamonn beckoning me out but calmly, unthreatened, I see. Come out, uncle. Danny beams at me as I emerge.

'D'you know I've never been further west than Brentford? This is Indian country.'

DANNY'S HEAD NOW poking forward from the back seat, thrusting like an eager dog's between mine and Eamonn's. One restless hand switching on the radio, which I switch off again.

'I'll take you to the nearest railway station,' I say.

'Oh come on,' Eamonn pleads, 'let him come. We can show him the moors.'

'I'd like that,' Danny says.

'And Truro, and the house. It's where we used to live.'

'Oh yes?'

'And we could see lots of things while we're there. Restormel, and Castle Dore. And Fowey. And we could go to Land's End, couldn't we?'

'Yeh, why not?'

Stop this now. 'We'll do the full tour this summer. We're just going to the house this time, Eamonn.' And for Danny's benefit, 'Where I grew up. It belongs to someone else now.'

'I'm sure they'll be pleased to see you. At least I hope so. I appreciate this, you showing me the places you lived.'

Neither of us says anything.

'I'm not really a villain, you know, I'm just a tearaway. You don't have to be afraid of me,' he grins. 'Not when I'm on holiday.'

I could hear it in court, Danny listening and nodding in approval: m'lud, my client is simply a tearaway, not a hardened villain, and a gaol term at this point would only...

'Ever been in gaol, Danny?'

"Course not. I told you..."

'Borstal?'

'Thass not gaol.'

'What were you in Borstal for?'

'I've never been in Borstal, so there.'

'Juvenile Court?' I can tell from Eamonn's stillness that this is making him uncomfortable, but I feel I have to warn him somehow.

'Listen, you can wind up in Juvenile Court for sticking your tongue out, if you're in the wrong place at the wrong time. You can be walking home completely innocent and on the other side of the road some prat's mucking about...'

'What were you in court for, Danny?'

'I don't have to answer that.' He grins. 'Unless you're offering me a job, in which case you might check up on me, see if I was telling the truth.'

'I'm offering you the chance to stay in this car. By telling me the truth, something about yourself I can believe.'

Danny sighs. '*Vaffanculo*.'

'Start with your Italian. How d'you come by that?'

'Italian family took me in when my Mum died. Speak Italian, do you?'

'Enough to know what you just suggested I do with myself.'

'No offence, it's just something Italians say.' He reaches forward, rumples Eamonn's hair. 'No offence, kid.'

But Eamonn sinks lower into his coat, staring ahead.

After a silence Danny speaks again, 'All right, I'll get out, I know when I'm not wanted. You can stop here, if you like.'

'I'd rather hear about your life.'

'You'd rather hear about my life.' Danny sighs again, theatrically. 'I was born in Tottenham,' he begins with studied weariness, 'actually I was born in Egypt if you really want to know, but I don't usually tell people that, 'cos they call me a wog. I was *raised* in Tottenham. All right? This is the truth. My Dad was in the Army and then he got out, and I've no idea where he is or what he's doing and if I met him I'd shove my fist down his throat because my he's never sent my mother nothing all these years...'

'I thought your mother was dead.'

Danny seems to be considering this for some time, and when I glance at him in the mirror his face is expressionless.

'All right, my *step*mother then. She's not my *real* mother, all right? Satisfied?' He sulks. 'Will that do, then, teacher?'

'It's not a whole lot.'

'All right, I've got a brother lives in Los Angeles, he's in the film business he *says* but I don't know what he *does* because I've never seen his name or nothing. I've got another brother married a Turkish tart when he was seventeen, a Turkish *girl* from Cyprus, all right? He's got two kids already and I think he's going to move out there, thinks he'll be better off. That's what he reckons. I'll be the only one left when he's gone.' Danny pauses. 'That's it, that's everything. That's more than I tell most people.'

'And what about you? Do you... do you work?'

'Oh Christ, here we go,' he singsongs, mocking: 'Have I got a trade, to see me through life? I've had more bloody trades than you've had hot...' My wellfed face seems to make him think twice.

'...pasta,' Eamonn murmurs, and it's a moment before Danny picks it up, starting to grin.

'What you say? Hot *pasta*? He's quick, this kid. Aintcha,' he adds, rumpling Eamonn's hair, and this time the boy doesn't wriggle away. 'I could be the best bloody chef in London if I wanted, I'll tell you that. I learnt when I was tit high to a grasshopper—begging your pardon, all right? Okay? Can't help the way I speak. I was *this* high, I could just see over the table. This woman, she... when I was with this family, I told you, right? She spread the dough out on the morning paper, then she took the rolling pin and rolled it till you could read the headlines, that's how thin she rolled it. You could read the bloody sports results.'

'You can make lots of money as a chef,' I interrupt, and instantly regret my tone.

'I *know* you can make lots of money as a chef,' Danny echoes witheringly, 'I'm not talking about making *money*, I'm talking about making bleeding *pasta*.'

Glancing round the landscape to orientate myself, I realize it's the gigantic conifers of Windsor Great Park, all around us now, that have caught my attention. For a moment I'm bewildered, not sure if we're going from Truro to London or London to Truro, this is Virginia Water, and I thought we'd *been* through Bagshot Heath, many miles farther on. Unless we're going round in circles.

'Eamonn... where are we? Haven't we been through Virginia Water?'

'No, this *is* Virginia Water. Only we're not quite there yet. Shrub's Hill next, isn't it?'

'Don't ask me,' Danny says cheerfully.

'Yes, look, there it is!'

'There *what* is?'

'Your favourite building,' Eamonn cries, 'Holloway College!'

I stare. It *is* Holloway College, and we're in Virginia Water, miles to Bagshot Heath. Eamonn is telling Danny the history of the College as if he were Pevsner himself; and I can hear my voice, my tones and phrases, in his. But if I ever claimed it was my favourite building it must have been in a moment of exaggerated mockery, this bloated pink château with pseudo-Jacobean ornaments, built by the self-important Dr Holloway in...

'... Dr Holloway in 1887, he made his fortune out of pills and ointments, with horrible advertisements showing suppurating limbs.' Turning back to point at the College, 'And that's what he did with the money.' Eamonn glances at me, 'You said it was built on bad legs and medicated grease.'

As we laugh, I restore my attention to our route and let Eamonn play the guide, happy to have found a pupil. Old, familiar territory. At intervals, preposterous houses. Agincourt, Toad Hall, The Paddocks. Evergreen Virginia Water glides by in gloomy Victorian laurel and fir, as if the Imperial age had sought to dress the world in mourning. But for what? For contrast? The lakeside with its fake ruined temple evokes chaste romances; ancient, happy London coach parties, come to the country for a weekend picnic. Eamonn's voice:

'This used to be called the Devil's Highway.'

'Flippin' 'eck,' says Danny with restraint.

SNOW ON THE ground, snow in the air too, now coming at us in sleety flakes growing drier and firmer, as we get our first glimpse of southern downland, with a file of tiny black overlapping trees on the horizon, like a millipede stranded in the snow. The sky has cleared around a single mushrooming cloud. Snowflakes falling against blue sky as we enter a dark tunnel of overarching yews, high on a ridge above the snow-filled valleys, and a pigeon hurtles over us and out at the end of the tunnel, in an ecstasy of flight.

'... called Egypt Mill,' Eamonn is saying. 'Why is that?'

'I haven't the first idea,' I say.

'Because the gyppos were there,' Danny puts in. 'It's obvious. There was a sign to Egypt back there,' he adds, 'three miles, it said. You could have let me out. I'm home.'

'You're the most unlikely-looking Egyptian I've ever seen.'

'I know. That's why I keep it dark.'

Danny's cheerful friendliness is such that my heart has gone out to him entirely, though I feel sure his benign humour won't last. Eamonn too watches him with intent pleasure from under his eyebrows, dark eyes glistening, mouth open, as if we'd captured a large alien bug.

'I knew this bloke once,' Danny begins, 'proper gyppo, taught me to ride on Hackney Marshes, his mum told fortunes and he knew how to read palms. He said I'd got the knack.' Something told me to intervene, but I hesitated. 'I've got a book on that too, palmistry. Only not with me.'

Eamonn says nothing.

'I'll have a go all the same, if you want me to. Left hand first.'

'It's all right,' Eamonn demurs, 'I've had it done before.'

'Not by me you haven't.'

One tentacle of hand reaches out and grabs Eamonn's left wrist as he tries to hide it, and breaks free from Danny's grip.

'I'll do the right one, then. Half price.'

'I haven't got any money,' Eamonn protests.

'Ask uncle,' Danny grinning. 'It's okay, I won't charge you this time. Free of charge, just this once.'

Eamonn holds his fingers closed over his palm.

'What are you afraid of? You don't actually *believe* in this stuff, do you?'

'That's just the trouble, he does,' I laugh, trying to defuse the situation.

'Christ on a crutch,' Danny says, opening Eamonn's fingers, 'there's no lines here at all!'

Eamonn and I glance down together in involuntary alarm.

'That gave you a fright, didn't it,' Danny smiles at our suscepti-bility. 'Sorry, must have been something in my eye, 'course it's got lines on it. All over the place. Heart lines, head lines, life lines, luck lines... you've got 'em all.' He gives a dramatic pause. 'There's illness here,' waiting us out, 'danger to life and limb, I'd say. Just about when you're... ninety-three, I'd say.' Now Eamonn looks up at him for the first time. 'Give or take a year or two. Know what I think?' Danny says, cocking his head and raising Eamonn's palm closer to his face. 'You're going to be a professor, a teacher like your uncle here. You're going to be a memory man.'

'I believe it,' I say.

'What about love?' Eamonn asks.

'Ball your fist.'

'What?'

'Ball your fist. Now turn it sideways. No, little finger towards me, that's it. Three... no, four! Four kids. And all by the time you're twenty. Nah,' says Danny, grinning apologetically, 'I've got it wrong, that's not four kids, thass four *wives*. That's four marriages, you dirty dog! That's what I call a love life.' He restores Eamonn's hand, and Eamonn studies it in fascination. 'Another satisfied customer. Uncle, what about you?'

'Let's see yours first,' Eamonn says to my relief.

'You don't want to see mine,' Danny says. 'It says I'm dead. Died as a child.'

'Be serious,' Eamonn says.

'I am being serious. I'm dead. Haven't you heard of the phantom hitchhiker?' He grins. 'That's only my left hand, mind. I was born with bad luck—but I made my own. Look at *that*...' he proudly offers us his right palm, dirty enough to read almost anything in. 'That hand will take you anywhere. That's the hand of a man reborn. It's a millionaire's hand. Watch this.' He turns his hand over, making a fist. When he turns it up again and opens it, a five pound note, folded into matchbook size, uncurls on his palm.

Eamonn laughs, delighted. 'And I can do that any hour of the day or night.'

'You had it up your sleeve,' Eamonn reaches for Danny's arm.

Danny withdraws, easing back on to the seat behind us. 'Takes practice, that does,' he grins. In the rearview mirror I watch the note, refolded but re-expanding as he stuffs it back into a little hole in the torn lining of the oatmeal-coloured jacket I had thought brand new when I first saw Danny. Now it looks slept in, crumpled, already fraying.

Beside me, Eamonn hunches and sinks lower into his duffle-coat.

The drive down into Stockbridge is alarmingly slippery, snow falling harder now and the sky dark, by the look of it there's been a lot more snow here already and I can feel the car sliding downhill out of control into the roadside slush, for an endless moment I rotate the steering wheel in frantic impotence as if piloting a child's toy car without linkage between steering wheel and tyres, the car with a quiet will of its own, somehow it chooses to avoid the ditch and I pretend control once more.

'I don't want to get caught in this snow in the dark,' I say, still resonating with the panic of the skid, but what worries me more is that I can tell from the way Eamonn's eyes bulge intermittently that he's holding in a cough. 'I think we should pitch camp in Stockbridge, if that's all right with everybody.'

'The bed and breakfast?' Eamonn cries excitedly.

'Suits me,' says Danny.

Eamonn turns round in his seat. 'Will you teach me to read palms?'

'REMEMBER WHEN I went to Italy?' Eamonn asks.

We are lying in the darkness of the guest house bedroom, our beds a few feet apart. His question takes a moment to sink in, since Italy puts me at once in mind of Danny peering over the table at the pasta covering the sports results; when I replay Eamonn's words I feel doubly in the dark. Eamonn in Italy? His face fits it, I see him in a black robe in the dusty street. But no memory comes. Shall I risk admitting it? At worst another avuncular lapse, nothing alarming.

'You've never been to Italy.'

He chuckles. 'No, I never got there. And it wasn't really Italy. Didn't you hear this story? Perhaps Mum never told you. I was about five, I think. We were in Cornwall, Mum and I together. Remember the Italian prisoner-of-war camp just the other side of Truro? Somehow I'd got it into my head that this was Italy, and I decided I'd go and see it. I got up early, took some food out of the larder, some slices of bread, I remember, and an apple, and set off for Italy. That's what I thought: there was another country down there, and I was going to see it. I walked along the road, I can remember how far I got, I can remember the whole thing. Eventually a car came past, it was the doctor, d'you remember? Bald and speckly. Anyway he stopped and opened the car door, said, where are *you* going? I must have said, to Italy. He told me to get in.'

We're both laughing in wonderment, and I can hear him fight back the cough. 'Your mother must have been livid. And scared witless.'

'I don't remember getting back at all, or what happened. Perhaps she wasn't even up yet. It was very early.'

'You don't think you imagined all this?'

'No,' Eamonn says, amused. 'I didn't do it in a previous life. I did it in this one.' A long pause, then, 'Do you get frightened in the dark sometimes?'

'Sometimes. Not so much these days, I suppose. If I do I just turn the light on.'

'It's all right, I don't really need it.'

AFTER A TIME Eamonn's voice comes.

'You know when I said about being a tinner. I never told you this, but when I went below, when we started working underground, I knew I was going to die there, and I did, I think, I don't remember it but I was always afraid of the mine filling up with water. It wasn't the ceiling caving in, it was the water coming through.'

He speaks calmly, but the horror of it vibrates in his voice.

'That's what I remember, when the water breaks through the wall.'

'It's over, Johnny,' I say helplessly. 'You don't have to think about it.'

'Yes, it's over,' he repeats.

We lie in silence.

'Sometimes I wonder if it really is a memory. If it isn't still to come. But it can't be, can it, as long as I don't go down a mine?'

'That's right.'

After another silence, 'D'you think we do remember past lives really? Or is it just like a bad dream?'

'I couldn't say. It's real to you.'

'It's more than that. More frightening.'

'All right... but you've done that now, you've lived it, in another life. You won't have to suffer it again.'

I can hear his wheezing from my bed. And when he thinks I am asleep he allows himself racking, muffled coughs.

I LIE IN the dark trying to nod off and when at last I do I take my anxiety into my sleep with me so that, asleep and dreaming, I am still anxious about getting to sleep. Finally I get up, the light is on at my desk and I find I am writing the book Eamonn and I have planned to write together, the book of the road. But what I am writing is called *The Autocar Book of the Road*, and I feel sad about this because I know that in consequence I cannot have it published under our names. Then I wake in relief, thinking: I don't have to write *The Journey West*, I've lived it. And I hear what has woken me. A banging noise from below. Now a kind of yelp, and a door slamming, muffled shouts.

I have a vision of the light snapping on in the dining room and Danny frozen in place as the lights come on, standing by the mantlepiece beneath the Relief of Lucknow, Danny with the family silver filling both hands, dropping it and swinging at the owner with one of the long-handled copper warming-pans off the wall, slinging tulip-decorated Love From Holland sabots at the owner's yelping dog, at police filling the room, seizing the Caribbean conch from the centre of the dining table and using it as a knuckle-duster...

But the house has gone silent again.

I WASN'T SURE we'd even make it out of Stockbridge through the snow. More has fallen overnight, is still falling, and I know the sensible thing is to turn back.

But Eamonn's eyes—he knows it too—hold me, they run through me like a spear. More than pleading, they say: don't refuse me *this*. With that expression on his face I'd have carried him to Truro on my back.

Once more his skin has that treacherous luminosity, his nose seems sadder, longer, and his eyes devour his face. He looks barely strong enough to speak, but he regales us with more Celtic tales, darker ones, spells and revenges and ritual kings each slain by their twin at the six-month solstice.

'Bet he had a good time, this bloke, while he *was* king,' Danny observed. 'The Tongs do that, you know, the Chinese Tongs. It's an old tradition. They give you a night of bliss, all the booze and girls you want, or the hashish rather, more likely heroin these days, then they send you off to kill someone and be killed. I don't know why they have to be killed, but the idea is, they do.'

'That's not quite the same thing,' Eamonn said.

'No but what I'm saying is, d'you want a long life and a boring one or a short life but a happy one, like your kings? I know you're not in the best of health, anyone can see that,' Danny begins and without moving my head I glance in the rearview mirror in alarm, hoping to catch Danny's eyes.

Have I said something to him? Did I tell him something in the café? Please God I didn't. Eamonn says nothing.

'I'd pick a short life and a happy one, myself,' Danny continues, and with a cheeky stare, 'What about you, uncle? Too late for that, is it? What I'm saying to *you*,' my terrors revive as he turns to Eamonn again, 'what I'm saying to *you* is this: if you decide you want to blow it all out one night, you come to me. The Seven Sisters Road may not *seem* like the Garden of Earthly Paradise to most people, but let me tell you, it's what you know and who you know that counts.'

'We believe you, Danny,' I say firmly, trying to tell him with a glance that we don't need to hear any more. He ignores me.

'You've got four girls there on your hand, I told you, didn't I?

Four girls in one night... it's not beyond the bounds of possibility. If you've got the money. And it helps if you like dark meat,' he mutters, apparently more for my benefit than Eamonn's.

My second vexed and warning glance now seems to provoke Danny, because a sly expression comes over his face, and something in it abruptly restores the vision I had of him caught thieving in the bed-and-breakfast in the middle of the night.

We study each other for a while, and when our eyes lock I feel we're daring each other, I can feel the sheer force of my desire to surrender and to see where it will lead me, but with the accompanying certainty that I don't have to yield to that.

Then to my horror he reaches into his pocket.

His hand comes out with something bulky, shiny. A tall metal sugar sifter. 'Now this,' he says, with an air of triumph, 'is not the sort of item you expect to find in a humble bed-and-breakfast.'

I see Eamonn staring at it, then looking up at me, but the road demands my attention.

'Oh come on,' Danny says as I look away, 'don't tell me you've never nicked anything from a boarding house, or a hotel. This is Georgian, genuine Georgian, and those bloody idiots put it out under our noses.'

'You may have noticed,' I say, 'you're not their usual run of clientele.'

'Oh, it's the Queen's bed-and-breakfast, is it?'

I hear a stifled giggle from my left, from Eamonn.

'They probably don't even know what they've got,' Danny continues. 'They'll be relieved to replace it with plastic.'

For some reason—I dare say Eamonn's complicitous snigger—this enrages me, and I turn and wrest the sifter out of Danny's hand.

'This,' I say, 'is going back, with us, on the return journey, to be returned by *you* in person, if you're still with us, and those are the conditions on which you *will* be still with us. With an apology.' I feel absurdly pompous, and my heart isn't in it, but I persevere, 'Otherwise I shall return it myself and apologize for you.'

'Oh *dear*. But you won't ever go back there again after, I can tell. *Mi fai schifo, tu.*'

'Danny... what I don't understand is this. You steal my bag, then you bring it back. You steal this, which you say is valuable,' I hold the thing up, 'though it looks like a piece of twentieth century tin to me, and what do you do? You go and show it to me, knowing I'm not going to let you take it. So this too goes back to its owners.'

'What about the rest of what I've got stacked in here?' He raises one jacket flap and shakes the lining. But no chinking noises follow. He grins. 'Nah, you're right,' he says, pleased, 'I'm not a thief. I don't *want* these things, I just like taking them.'

Eamonn giggles openly now. 'You're an exhibitionist.'

'What's that mean?'

'You're a flasher, Danny,' I explain, 'you're a flasher of stolen goods.'

'You saucy person,' he says to Eamonn. 'I'll tell you what I am,' Danny crows with a dramatic flick of his jacket, 'I'm a matador of crime!'

We start laughing helplessly, Danny joining in.

'Just don't call me as a character witness when you get caught, all right?'

'You never saw nothing,' Danny says cheerfully, 'I'll say you put that what you say is useless tin in your pocket by mistake, being a forgetful old sod, and you wanted to pass the blame off onto me.'

'I'm not thinking about this one, Danny. That's being returned anyway. Some day you'll get caught with something else, before you manage to give it back.'

'Oh look, I'm not *stupid*. I don't *always* give 'em back.'

'But you prefer showing off. I'd say you were doomed, as a criminal.'

'I was doomed before I was a criminal,' Danny says with a grim twist to his smile, an unconvincing twist but I sense that he means it. 'And don't you give me that all-knowing look.'

'I don't know if you were doomed or not, Danny, and neither does anybody else, including you. But I'll give you the benefit of the doubt. Just don't do it again, I beg you. We're going to have to stop somewhere if the snow goes on, and I don't want to be worrying about whether you're downstairs nicking the silver.'

'It's not your responsibility. I'll pay my way, like last night.'

'It *is* my responsibility, Danny, I brought you here. If you get caught, the police are going to wonder what the hell I'm doing, why I haven't turned you over to them already.'

A man in heavily bundled clothes is standing in the mist and snow further along the ridge. As we get closer he turns into a yew tree. Danny is sulking in the back seat.

EAMONN WANTS TO show him Stonehenge. 'Especially in snow,' Eamonn insists, though I dread any detour onto higher, exposed ground where drifting snow might trap us, I can visualize it, unable to go forwards or back. Hedges, built high with snowdrifts, have kept our winding lane free from the worst but now, as we head north from Salisbury, slow files of cars pick their way round frozen tidal tongues of white, above invisible valleys.

In the grey light Eamonn's intensity of will shines in his face, his mouth half-open, breathing shallowly, his eyes pushing the fog back, forging a way for us through the oncoming snow that seems to spark from a single, receding, vanishing point at the centre of vision, hypnotic: we are plunging into the invisible heart of the atom through a blackboard galaxy of racing, dying particles, till vision blurs, the sparks freeze into streaks, and the universe ahead is nothing but a great white dahlia sucking our humming craft into its maw. All three of us are silent, concentrated, an accumulation of desire. And it works: the fog and snow begin to yield, and sweet rounded thighs of hill come into view, snowy, recumbent hips in a blue haze, a few motionless, sentry sheep; and we descend into a busy, dirty town full of boarding houses calling to us. Abbotsbury, Lamorna, Sunnybrow, hot and cold in all rooms.

Then in the trough of a valley we come to another junction. 'This is it,' Eamonn urges.

But when I look across him at the long hill west, the climb is a mass of yellow ruts scrawled in the snow where cars have lost their purchase, sliding back, and several still sit stranded and abandoned at the roadside halfway up the hill. I slow to a crawl and we stare at the debris, the ice and beached cars.

'On the way back,' I say.

Eamonn hangs his head.

'He wants to see it. We could walk from here, couldn't we?'

'*You* could,' I say, finding Danny's eyes in the mirror, trying to make him understand.

He shrugs. 'On the way back then.'

BACK IN OUR winding lane I jerk awake in the choking heat of the air vents, my hands are piloting us safely down the centre of the road, steady enough and slow, but I have no idea how long I was gone. And before my first rush of alarm is over, the thought comes: was this how the crash happened? Dropping off at the wheel? But no, that was *before*, before this started. Even so I have to shake from my mind the sense that I am driving *towards* the crash. That there *was* someone in the passenger seat beside me, sitting as still and pale as Eamonn.

No-one speaks, it seems that I've done nothing to alarm my passengers. But am I blacking out more often? Better stop, plead tiredness.

And then the bus slipped into view.

Almost at the same moment I know where we are. Windwhistle Hill. We hear the sounds first. From somewhere beneath the towering crest of beeches, screams come, bottled wasp-rage capped in polythene. Then, emerging from the bend, we see it, the blue and white bus sliding downwards infinitely slowly, broadside to the hill, straddling the road as if sweeping it, as if under infinitely tender, well-judged control. But the faces at the windows have the look of the damned in mediaeval frescoes, motionless, falling unbelieving to their doom.

Sliding down, still broadside, the whole bus wobbles once, twice, like a toy, as the wheels mount roadside ridges and stumble on. All it will take, as the the slide gathers speed now, is one big ridge to send the bus over onto its side, glass shattering. And each jolt fills the air with a fresh stab of screams. Whether it topples or not it will sweep away everything in its path, including us.

I draw to a halt at the foot of the hill, protected by the bend. 'Go on! Go on! Don't stop!' shouts Danny suddenly in my ear. It sounds like a madman's voice, and a madman's advice, as I sit frozen, watching the appalling spectacle ahead. Then I hear the back door wrench open, and Danny is tumbling out, scrambling towards the hill, falling and getting up again.

'Oh God,' the words spilling at last into the silence of the car, I can't tell if they're mine or Eamonn's.

The advancing bus suddenly rises at the back like a ship tossed up by a wave, and now the screams come like a sigh of indrawn breath, like surf, as the wheels hang in mid-air, the bus arching towards its side, poised. Then the lower front wheel lurches rapidly downhill, the bus dives forwards like a whale and we can see the driver madly spinning the steering wheel against the skid, but it's too fast, the passengers fall back like space travellers pinned back by gravity, the bus bucks down, veering off the road, rises once like a happy thing at play, then disappears, the windows vanishing in a great spume of roadside snow.

The hill is suddenly empty again as the snow-spray settles, featureless and white with only Danny moving on it, scrambling crazily uphill, feet splaying wide like a speed-skater's. 'Stay here,' I bellow at Eamonn as I prise open the door.

Out in the snow only my nostrils register the cold, I'm running but my feet sink leadenly, wearing gigantic clown's shoes.

I can see Danny clawing at the snow around the bus, pummelling it as if releasing all his rage.

Then to my horror the bus shakes itself abruptly, without warning. An irritable beast disturbed, it trembles, snow cascading off the roof onto Danny, and settles again in disgruntlement a few feet further downhill. The roof and windows are visible now and I see Danny too emerging, shaking off the snow and kicking at the snow beneath the door of the bus, wrenching at the door now.

I can hear him shouting to keep back, as one by one he lifts people down into the track his feet have beaten to the bus.

Panting, bent double and breathing in the searing agony of the frosty air, I hear footsteps behind me. Eamonn's duffle-coat, flapping open around his thin body as he hurries up behind me. Other people are climbing the hill, too, from a file of cars now parked beyond our own, and I wave a furious arm at the boy, too winded to speak; I point at the scene above us, the passengers dispersed, dazed, around the road, Danny hauling them out of the bus with furious, disciplined intensity. At last the driver, and the ordeal seems to hit him now as he trips on the step and takes Danny with him into the snow. Both lie invisible for a moment, and then a single sound comes, breaking the silence. Danny's high-pitched, gleeful laughter.

A hand tugs at my arm. 'Come on,' comes Eamonn's voice. I grab at his arm and hold him tight, we totter like two novice skaters on the steep incline. His eyes are glowing, fixed on the scene above. It's pride I see in them, pride at Danny's prodigal efforts.

Both Danny and the driver rise, sticky with a cracking paste of snow, they pat themselves down, then each other, still grunting and shouting with relief. Voices swell now as they join the passengers in the road, welcomed like goalscorers, like men returned from the dead. I almost expect a wave of applause. Some of the passengers wave joyously at us in reassurance.

'Will he get a medal?' comes Eamonn's cracked voice from beside me. 'I bet he will. You'll see he gets one, won't you?'

But Danny is already breaking away from the throng of arms, ignoring calls, now he's skating back downhill, sideways as though mimicking the bus, showing off, skimming on one foot then the other, slaloming.

'Waahhh!' he yells, unstoppable, arms out askew but balancing him perfectly, mouth wide in ecstasy, and in his shout I can hear, 'Alive! Alive! Alive!'

THE WEATHER HAS closed in again as we skirt an invisible Dartmoor, the light as thick and gloomy as the shrinking pool of the visible world that encloses my feet as a dream fades to blindness, a fifty-yard treadmill of hissing slush we seem to carry down the road for hour after hour—but to us it seems the very opposite of a shroud, it's a little space of dim light we alone bring with us through the encircling fog, this is our aura, one we grant to other cars in passing, before they recede into the night: the Windwhistle elation is still with us, we're a winning team, and when Eamonn covers his mouth and with the other hand grips the car door for dear life, to stop the coughing from shaking his soul out of his body in blood and phlegm, I see Danny's grimy, bony hands come up from behind Eamonn, one settling on either shoulder to hold and calm him.

Launceston comes, I'm driving faster than I should and almost miss the hand-scrawled sign propped up against an oil drum. Black letters: A30 BOLVENTOR ROAD CLOSED, and in red, AVOID MOOR.

'Which shall we try, north or south of the moor?' I say, trying not to let slip how disheartened I feel, knowing what's to come: by either route a maze of lanes easy to confuse for each other even in clear weather and with a detailed map. 'North or south,' I repeat when no answer comes.

'West,' Eamonn says quietly. 'Straight on.'

I shake my head.

'Straight on where?' Danny asks.

'Bodmin Moor. But you saw the sign, the road's closed, we can't go straight on.'

'We might as well turn back, then, and go home,' Eamonn says savagely. 'You know we'll never get round the moor in this weather, we'd take all night.' And when I can find nothing to say to this, 'Don't say we've come all this way with just the moor to cross and you don't even want to try and see what it's like? What's been the point of it all then?'

'Hush,' I say.

'You know the moor backwards, I bet you could cross the moor without lights if you wanted to, you *know* you could.'

'How far is it to where we're going, then?' Danny asks diplomatically. 'I thought we'd have run out of good old England long before this.'

'Less than an hour, straight on.'

'In decent weather,' I put in. 'Look, there's another one,' I say as a further sign, A30 BODMIN CLOSED, offers us minor roads to left and right.

'Yeh but what's *that* mean, *closed*? They have to put these signs out with every sort of driver in mind, don't they, that includes little old ladies. It *might* mean snowdrifts ten foot high. But we don't *know* that till we see 'em, do we? It could mean snow like we've already got through. I vote we go and see. What do you vote, uncle?'

'This car is not a democracy, I'm afraid, Danny. It's a one-party state and I'm Leader for life.'

'Ah but I'm the ju-ju man,' Danny says. Singsong now, 'You can't survive without the ju-ju man, I'm saying *go*, *go*,' one bony hand snakes past my head to point at the darkness of the moor ahead, fingers splaying as if to rebut the snow still squirting at us from the dark, 'I'm going to magic this car all the way to Truro. You've seen my magic. You know I can do it.'

'*Go! Go!*' Eamonn is echoing, imitating Danny's gesture with both hands now like a tic-tac man flashing 10s at the snow; until they're both rocking backwards and forwards, chanting, and I too want to give it all or nothing, damn the signs, we've come through worse, and conquered.

At every instant I expect to see flashing lights, a police car parked across the road, or at least a line of oil drums, warning cones. But none appear. All traffic has ceased. We are alone on the climb to Bolventor with darkness falling, I am alone with two crazy exhausted boys at my side, urging me on, seemingly prepared to chant us all the way to Bodmin.

Eamonn is right, at least this much: my headlamps are on but I know every bend before the beams find it. A slow climb out of Altarnun, half right, half left, then long and straight until the first right-hander, and on the long straight climb I feel as safe, as certain in the unseen contours of the moor around me, as one lover tracing another's body in the dark.

Even inside the car I can feel its weight, the way the moor lies on the earth's crust, its smell almost, its musky peat-scent, odours of bone spiced with decaying sheep-turds, rank hair, bird-kills, sweet tormentil and ling hidden in the springy turf, fused by the sun and mingling like incense on those rare days when the Atlantic wind declines to comb the moor with its salt breezes; I know its rough pelt skinned bare and grey like shaggy ape-skin over knee and elbow, over granite bones; as now my headlamp beams pick out its orangy sedge-hair poking through and shaking off the snow; I feel it bristling on the black hide of the moor.

And all around us, invisible, the ruined mines once full of men toiling in the rocky deep of the shafts—I see a kerchief-headed

Eamonn with a pirate's face, splashing around in an echoing engine room, through water-logged galleries. Sailors in stone, trapped in the hold of the mine.

Now I sense the moor around me as a cemetery, as death. Through the tyres, the accelerator, through brakes, the steering wheel, through every straining nerve and sinew of the car like a skittering, frightened vole I can feel the road turning to ice beneath the thin cover of falling snow. We're still going, uphill but not too steep. The boys chanting triumphantly, they don't know what's to come. I do. I know the long slow S before the dip, before the hill up to Jamaica Inn and Bolventor. Its lights are just visible now, dimly, ahead and up above us, on the crest opposite ours, but as soon as we swing out of the S and down into the dip, my first cautious touch on the brakes sends us slewing sideways, wheels locked up, overtaking ourselves in funfair derision as the headlamp beams sweep wildly across a landscape as forbidding as the sea.

Everything slows now, the boys' chanting too dips an octave and ends in a moan as we skate downhill at an angle of 45 degrees to the road, something oddly sedate about it, it's a tango, our wheels facing in different directions yet somehow acting in consort to carry us forwards. Right-hander at the bottom of the hill—when we get there will that serve to correct the skid or fling us out and off the roadway to spin our wheels deeper and deeper in the unforgiving mush on either side of us? Is it a right-hander we want? There seems plenty of time to work it out. The boys have ceased their squalling, but I know I don't really *want* to work it out. *I want to see what happens.*

And I do; I get to see it. It's not a right-hand, it's a left-hand bend we needed, as it turns out, but as we start to slip-slide off the road into the nearside ditch I correct the problem inadvertently, through sheer panic, hitting the brakes and sending the Wolseley into a counter-skid, neatly reversing our tango-pose and sliding off into the left-hand bend, uphill this time, until we come to rest on a featureless slope, the beams picking out nothing but snow... under some of which is road, and under the rest... ruin. But the choice between the two is taken away from me. When I make to move forwards, accelerating cautiously, I realize we're moving back instead, the wheels aren't gripping and we're simply sliding back downhill, not a car any more but a heavy object sliding back and forth between two steep slopes till eventually we come to rest or fall off the road. This takes no time at all. Within ten feet of rolling back a crunch announces that we've found the ditch, and we settle, at rest at last.

'Good work, uncle,' Danny says with what sounds like unaffected admiration. 'I haven't seen four-wheel drift like that since Fangio come to Silverstone. Time for a push, is it?' he asks as I rev the engine ineffectually.

'I think it might be.'

Danny gets out, braces himself against the ice, pushes. Once more the wheels spin in an icy groove.

'One of you better lend a hand,' comes Danny's voice.

I glance at Eamonn, then switch off the engine. 'I don't want you outside in this, understood? Sit here,' I say, 'where I am, hold the handbrake, just keep your hand on the handbrake, you don't even have to steer. We're going to push you out, with the engine off, then when we shout, you pull the handbrake on. Then I'll come back, and start the engine, and off we go. All right? All you have to do is keep the handbrake off until I tell you, till you hear us shout, then pull the handbrake on, that's all.'

Eamonn nods like a wartime pilot high on Dexamyl, he grins a frantic death's head grin at me: 'This is *great*!'

With foreboding I step out into the freezing night, watch Eamonn slide across into my seat, and wait until he has his hand on the handbrake before moving to the rear of the car to try and get some purchase on the fender or the rear wing. Danny says something to me but now that I'm outdoors and across the car from him the wind is deafening and I can't hear a word. We're six feet away but I can't even see him clearly, the fog so dense it's like breathing gruel. All the headlamps show is fog and snow and, in the snowfield of the road, our skid marks. The lights of Bolventor have vanished, if that's what they were, and not a mere reflection of our own lights in the fog.

My first shove produces nothing. Instead my feet slip out from under me as my arms push me back across the ice, and I wind up on my knees at each successive attempt. It's like trying to push a boulder up and out of one of the freezing rings of hell. The cold is excruciating, and now the falling snow begins to sting my swelling hands and face. From what I can see of Danny by the faint light of the car interior, he looks blue already.

It comes to me that we're going to die here.

We could die here within a few miles of civilization—I can picture Danny surviving, making it, shuddering and jigging with his fingers tucked beneath his arms, arriving at Jamaica Inn; but as the snow descends no-one can reach us, Eamonn and me, from either end, Bolventor or Altarnun. We've stayed together in the car, because to lead the boy through half an hour of this would kill him as surely as an icicle in the heart. We sit there as the snow descends, running the engine and the heating till the petrol runs out and the batteries expire, then we in turn freeze quietly to death, our arms around each other.

Danny is staring at me queerly across the faint steam rising from the back of the car, turned suddenly red now as the brake lights come on and Danny turns to yell across the gale at Eamonn, 'No! Don't the touch the pedals!' Then he turns back to me. 'What is it?' he shouts. 'You want *me* to say the word? All right, come on then, one two three *heave*, right? One, two, three…'

We heave, and to my astonishment the car lurches out into the road.

'Handbrake!' Danny and I yell together, and make our way in the teeth of the snowy gale, to the car doors.

But as I get in, triumphant, I see that the excitement has been too much for Eamonn. His face tells me that I have finally pushed our luck to its limits, and he stares at me, as the coughing begins, like a man drowning behind glass, that I can't save; and once the spasm comes I know he can no longer feel the comfort of my arm around him.

The terrible sucking inhaling noises between coughs are like the skid only worse, at any moment it seems as if the body will shake itself to death, that the heart cannot take this despairing, longing shout of sinew, muscle, nerve and bone, and still survive.

'Christ,' says Danny from the back seat, his own teeth chattering, 'doesn't he have one of them breather things?'

'They're no good, it's the cough that does it, not the breathing in.

We'll have to get him somewhere warm and quiet. I'm going to try and turn the car. Just shout when I get near the ditch.'

THE SPASM RAGES on as we pick our way back to Altarnun and blindly south below the moor towards Liskeard, the nearest town, every tiny unmarked junction in the dark forcing a guess, a prayer, the child coughing his heart out in the seat beside me just as another identical junction of high-banked lanes appears before us, and the recurring sense that we've been round and round in circles brings me to the edge of hysteria. Life has no right to be like this, *ever* to be like this, I hear myself think in childish fury; as if it weren't my own fault that we're here in this labyrinth of icy, storm-swept lanes, headlamp beams profiling every bramble, every stick of dead grass now encrusted with snow and frost. Which way now, damn it? Which way? Which way?

And then the strangest thing happens.

Sudden alarm about how much petrol we have left directs my eyes down to the Wolseley's polished wooden dash and round-faced dials. Only they aren't there, and I'm gazing at a foolish plastic dashboard with rectangular dials, American-style. The Prefect's dashboard. By now I'm so used to my lapses that at first this switch from delusion to reality, from past to present, seems the least of our problems at this instant, I make to shrug it off and push it out to the back of my mind; but something stops me. It *doesn't* feel like a switch from past to present.

Until a few moments ago we *were* in the Wolseley, all three of us, amid coughs and panic and the cacophany of our conflicting theories, Danny's and mine, about which road to take, it *was* the Wolseley I controlled through skid and counter-skid, familiar with its ways, its sways, its balance on the road; it was the Wolseley's rounded rear wing I pushed out of the ditch. If this was an illusion, then... so was what I was seeing now. Yes: now I *knew* I was dreaming, the whole thing *was* a nightmare, round and round in a hell of frozen circles and repeating spasms. *None* of it was real, I'd caught it in the act this time!

And all I had to do was... what? Defy the thing? Suppose I say out loud: *this is a dream*, I'm *dreaming*: will it end?

But the words wouldn't come.

'Go left! Go left!' Danny is shouting.

I sat there staring like a fool, feeling (and I knew this meant it was already too late, I'd missed my chance) like an apprentice wizard, spell at the ready, but—say the words, and if the visible world fails to dissolve I shall have made myself absurd; worse, if it's not a dream at all I'll have to live with the absurdity of my behaviour. As if it mattered! Anything! to save us from this horror. But it does matter, even *in extremis*: no less than I might blush for shame to find my flies undone when standing on the scaffold. I can feel my courage fail me, and its absence feels like sanity. Which it *is* of course, I tell myself: who could stand up in a public place and cry, This is a dream! and, when the place remained intact, all startled faces, not flush with shame for ever at the memory?

I HAVE NO idea how we emerged from the lanes into a town, and whether we took twice as long, five times, ten times as long as we would have with a map to guide us to Liskeard. I only know that the cold, silent streets and their snow seemed bathed in an orange glow of salvation. It was the golden city pilgrims seek and every stone of it was precious, I could have kissed the ground outside Webb's Hotel, adored the icy pavement lit by its neon sign.

As we pass under the granite portico to push at the huge grey door, Danny and I supporting Eamonn between us, I feel as if I am seeing the place through Eamonn's eyes, in appalling detail, as if these were the last things his eyes will ever see; or my eyes, rather, because his are shut in exhaustion. I stare for him, I am the memory man now, recording every detail, behind the door the faded ochre-brown velvet curtains twelve feet tall, tired old drapes that look to have emerged from some travelling theatrical skip: we have to force our way through them into the lobby, a huge disconsolate room decked out with filthy imitation-leather chairs. And I find that I love every particular, every item in that room from the ghastly red-on-gold brocaded wallpaper down to the giant flowers on the red-carpeted floor, the internal telephone booth, the sign proclaiming LADIES

POWDER ROOM, the spacious six-sided glass cabin and the unkempt old man inside it, reluctant to receive us.

While Danny signs us in I carry Eamonn in my arms up the grandeur of the stairs, where an immense landing dwarfs a banquet table with a silver salver on it, also a superb barometer and a brass letter-weight on a wood base, the tabletop itself large enough to shelter a litter of full-sized billiard tables. On the landing an eight-foot tall mirror shows us our figures by an open neon strip above it: Chamber-of-Horrors lighting. Astonishing wallpaper accompanies us to the next floor, a mottled snake-skin, dirty yellow, almost colourless though dark with age (or could it be the aftermath of fire?) but smeared with thick bands of brown, a whorl design that looks like smoke-stains or the signature of a retreating flood, yet strangely uniform, consistent. Here and there a battleship-grey hue overtakes the whole paper, and all faintly showing a former gloss. On closer inspection this was once gold, but sprayed over, in thick relief, with meandering, faded bands of orange, cream, and grey. It is unique, this wallpaper, a work of art—and many hands. At a touch it feels like forcefully impacted cobwebs. To my amazement we pass a bat lying full-length on the stair carpet, either stunned or dead, a young one, perhaps. I step around it, trembling uncontrollably.

Our room is twelve feet tall. The wall above the window has a line of moulding that would have graced Nonesuch; but the other walls are partitions. Eamonn lies in his bed, like mine an iron bedstead with a simple bedhead of dark wood; he lies perfectly still and pale, but breathing. I know he will sleep now, tomorrow too, most of the day. On the table beside his head, a tray, a teapot, four sugar cubes, cup, saucer, spoon, a small cardboard pyramid containing milk, and an electric kettle: all identical to mine.

I am a pair of eyes, *his* eyes, and if I stop, if I stop even for an instant I know my heart will break with shame and fear, and he will die. The carpet is threadbare and cheap, as cheap as the dark wooden furniture but blue with whorl designs a paler blue, profiled in a darker, petrel blue. The basin, on tubular steel legs, is by Superior of Bristol, and as I bathe my hands and face in luke-warm water, still trembling, I fall hopelessly in love with the plug, it is a curiously lovely object which I know I shall have to steal, wrinkled like snakeskin as the wallpaper is, but still firm and holding its wide, flat flying-saucer shape, with a strong metal hasp at the centre, on a gently sloped boss. No chain. It has a name inscribed around its white circumference. Its name is Treasure.

'*DON'T TELL MUM*, you haven't told her, have you?' are Eamonn's first words.

'You're worse than I am,' I sigh.

'I've had attacks like that before and not told her. There's no point, it only worries her.'

'What do you think she's been feeling, seeing the weather reports? Of *course* I've told her. I phoned her last night.' From the glass-walled phone booth in the lobby, feeling like a bottled exhibit. But today the hotel seems a little less grotesque, and something of my sanity seems to have returned with Eamonn from the land of nightmares.

'You told her the *truth*?' I nod. 'What, *everything*? Danny, and...'

'No,' I admit. 'I seem to have forgotten to mention Danny.'

He grins, and takes a sip of his tea. 'Are we in Liskeard?' I nod. 'We don't have to go back, do we? *You* know I'll be all right. I'll be up today, it'll be weeks before that happens again. I mean, Mum could come down, couldn't she, if she's really worried?'

'No-one's going anywhere. Look out of the window.'

The snow lies so thick that the town square is deserted, with only chimneysmoke and the distant sound of a spade striking sparks off the pavement to show that its inhabitants are still alive.

'*Yn llys Cerridwen*,' Eamonn breathes, gazing at the feather-bedded roofs. 'That's where the name comes from, the name Liskeard, it's old Welsh for the court of the white sow.'

'The white sow, eh?'

He smiles at my bemusement. 'That's only one of her faces. Sometimes she's a swan, a mare, a ship, a grain of wheat even. She's a pure and holy moon goddess, the oldest of them all.'

'Did you worship her underground?'

With a pitying look, 'Of course not. We had our own spirits.' He looks tired again. 'We will make it to the house, won't we? It's only a few more miles.'

'When you're ready and not before. And when the roads are clear.'

Eamonn studies me as if trying to preserve whatever it is he's seeing.

'*YOU LOVE HIM* like he was your own, don't you.'

The words come through so faintly to me, so delayed, that I don't know if I answered or not. The first floor library, so-called, is dark and still, we are alone in it.

'You may think I don't know what that's like,' Danny says, 'but I've got a kid. A daughter.'

'So you said. You're married?'

'Me?' He smiles at me, and as he does so his monkey face looks a lot older, barely a rim of yellow eye around the enlarged pupils, greenish in the shadowy room, more human than its customary dead-leaf colour. I watch him reach into his pocket, bring out cigarettes and light one. 'I haven't seen her mother in a year and a half. She's in Wales somewhere, the slut. That's what I heard.' His face closes off.

'And your daughter's there with her?'

He gives a faint nod.

'You could go and visit them, we're not all that far from Wales.'

He struggles for a moment as if holding onto his temper, hand open in mid-gesture.

'Yes but I mean, *Wales*.' Danny lifts his eyes to me as if I am a geographical idiot. 'It's a large place, isn't it. I don't know *where* she is, in Wales.' The rage is still there. 'In her wisdom,' he says, pausing, 'she never told me. In case I put the law onto her.' From his expression I suspect this is more for fear of Danny than the law. 'Yeh,' he says after studying me for a while, '*and* she knows what I'd do to her.'

'Well, I take my hat off to her.'

'You *what*?'

'I don't know how she managed it. You're a hard man to get away from, Danny.'

'I didn't have her address book like I got yours,' Danny grins, 'that was my first mistake.' He muses. 'See, I don't like to lose people. Same when I was a kid. The last time my Dad came to visit I screamed the whole afternoon. Locked myself in the toilet and screamed the bloody place down.'

In the half-dark of the room it's easy to picture Danny bawling, the small face slack and bloodless, as now, as if some trace of it remains imprinted on his features.

'I know what *you're* thinking...' Danny's eyes wrinkling, worldly-wise again. 'No *wonder* he never come back! I don't much go for screaming kids myself.'

His face sets and I leave him to his thoughts. Between the seagull screams above the town, their chorus of limitless amusement, I can hear the grandfather clock on the landing and I think of Eamonn in his room, asleep, God willing. Flock wallpaper of a faecal brown surrounds us, interrupted only by the portrait of Ambrose Truscott, Benefactor. Builder of Webb's Hotel. Anno domini 1847. Books line the shelves to either side of him, and I find myself visualizing Danny stuffing them into holdalls to distribute in transport cafés from here to Bristol. When I look across at him in his armchair he is studying me again with that feline, possessive expression I remember from the café.

'What's the matter with the kid, Johnny is it? Is that his name?'

'That's right. They christened him Eamonn, but that was his Dad's idea. My sister never took to it.'

'You can tell it's not the flu. Not cancer, is it?'

'No, it's not cancer,' I say. 'It's worse in a way—you can ask him, he's read all the books on it and he's not afraid to talk about it. It's a weakness of the lungs, like asthma, except that it can kill you. You saw what happened yesterday.'

'Shouldn't he be in hospital?'

'He'll be all right now, until it happens again. Even if he *lived* in hospital, I'm afraid it wouldn't save him.'

'Christ, that's not fair, a kid like that.' We sit in silence for a while. 'I knew a girl looked just like he does. She had a hole in the heart.' He reads something in my face and I can feel the tears rush to my eyes as he says, 'You did the right thing, bringing him here. It's what he wants. I wish I'd had an uncle like you.'

But as he says it, even as I feel myself seizing tearfully at absolution regardless of its source, the enormity of what I've done, the risk I've taken, settles on me like cold sweat.

'You take your chances in this life,' Danny is saying. 'I'm only here by the grace of God. And the good folks at the Soho shelter, they had something to do with it as well. When I found Marie was gone, that's my kid, and I couldn't get news of her, I drank everything I could get my hands on. Went and stepped out into the traffic. Only you bounce off, don't you, when you're drunk? One time I got some news of her, the only time, they said she was calling another man Daddy, that was to tell me not to bother looking for her. I did it properly that time, swallowed a lot of pills, only I couldn't stop yelling when I got the cramps, I thought you just lay down and passed out but you don't, it's like you've swallowed knives. So when they took me to the shelter I had to drink some black stuff, not coffee, I asked for coffee but they brought me this other black stuff, then they made me drink a bucketful of water. That was the worst part, I could feel my stomach bursting but I still couldn't be sick. I fell asleep in the end.' He grins at me. 'So here I am. In... what's this place called?'

'Liskeard.'

'Oh yeh. No, in this hotel, I mean. I've never stayed in a hotel before. What's it called?'

'Webb's,' I say.

'Webb's Hotel,' he pronounces it with relish but there is something else in his eyes. 'I bet the rooms here cost more than a fiver. Right?'

A small movement of his wrist neatly exposes the torn lining where the banknote rests.

'Keep your fiver, Danny. It's on me.'

'Much obliged, uncle.'

EAMONN'S SLEEPING FACE is so utterly filled with hope I want to reach into his dreams to join him. Little by little the expression

56

changes, or perhaps it's just the light; or my over-anxious gaze. And all I see now is the pallor of his cheeks. A word comes. *Owl-blasted.*

As I watch, small shadows, blotches appear on his face, and terror grips me, I want to brush them away but as my hand moves I stop it, noticing that the blotches continue across the pillow. Behind us snow is once more flecking the window, the dim pock-marked light falling across the bed. All the same I want to touch his face, having granted myself permission. Unable to suppress the urge to rid him of the snow-shadows.

But in that same instant I know I can't. I'm still in the library, watching Danny light a cigarette, for an instant the flame clears his face of the diseased light from the window and I recall—as if my Eamonn-reverie had never been—what it is I want to say to him.

'In London you told me your daughter lived in Cornwall.'

'Nah, that was just... I wanted to come with you, didn't I.'

I nod. He always has an answer ready.

'Go on, you're not sorry, are you? That I came with you?'

I shake my head sleepily, 'I wouldn't have missed it for the world.'

I feel momentarily ashamed at this glib answer, and I want to tell him that I'm glad he's here, grateful indeed, I wouldn't have made it off the moor without him—till the thought comes that, without him, we might not have strayed onto the moor.

'I have told you a few fibs,' he is saying earnestly. 'But I reckon you knew better than to expect the gospel truth.' I nod. 'I mean, who's to say what the truth *is*?' I keep nodding, hoping he won't pursue it. 'What *is* truth? That's in the Gospels. I'll tell you something, and this *is* the truth, if I'm stuck in a little place like this for too long I get whatchamacosis.'

'Claustrophobia.'

'That too. Same when I was a kid.' I see him locked in the loo, bawling. 'Cabin fever, that's the word,' he says, exhaling smoke. 'So don't you worry if you find me gone. Won't be for long. I told you, didn't I: I hate to lose people.'

BIRCHES AND GORSE, a scrubby landscape the same on both sides of the road, I'm driving fast and already I can feel a dread, unfounded in anything I can see before me, an ache as though regretful of myself at the oncoming bend which *is* myself as much as I am, and the car is, travelling at undiminished speed.

It's time to turn the wheel but nothing happens and the ache persists, the sadness, even though I know with absolute and serene confidence that I shall not be crushed when the collision comes, I'll bounce, and now the road has gone from view, the birches rush at me. My hands are not turning the wheel. The car launches into the air, it seems to stop, still travelling, because my thoughts have ample space to spell matters out clearly, though it's not me but the moment, the travelling car in space and the trees ahead, that speaks, spelling it out: that my sadness isn't the sadness of this strange surrender to the murderous power of speed and the machine I'm sitting in, this—my mind baulks at the word—suicide; no, my sadness is a longing to be back in Webb's with Eamonn which it now seems I never can be, as the car hurtles, airborne, towards the birches; and still there's time, as I advise the place, the car, the birches, that I am *remembering* them, that I know they don't kill me, so why can't I return to Webb's? And still there's time: because, as the scene and the airborne moment patiently explain to me, you *can't* remember this—remember? What am I doing then, I ask, if not remembering, but my own answer comes, from within me this time, before I've even finished asking it: You're re-living, not remembering, and if you want to *keep* the memory of this, then you can never go back to wake up at Webb's with Eamonn. One or the other, either or. And I realize, as the airborne journey proceeds, a yielding newsprint birchwood rising at me black and white, blurred monochrome, with a sound of splintering, that if I want to keep this memory I shall wake in my hospital bed, never to find my way to Webb's in the same manner, never to wake with this memory in my head—unless there, in my hospital bed. I jerk myself out of the dream and into blackness an instant before the splintering, too, comes to an end.

Have I made it? Have I made it out in time, did I eject from the dream or was it the instant of collision and forgetfulness? I *am* in Webb's! Awake, I stare into the darkness at the tall window, shaking with the reassurance of it. Clock ticking, distantly. Bedstink. Everything is here.

And—but puzzlement descends at once: did the dream lie? It *is* all here inside me. I still have the memory of how the crash occurred, *and* I'm in Webb's, in Webb's, safe in my bed with Eamonn and the journey to Liskeard mine and not erased. So why did the dream lie? I *have* got both. Then it comes to me: I haven't got both at all. What I have is no memory of the crash, but a dream about it: that's the price of waking at Webb's. The evidence I have is safe in memory, yes, but it's only dream-evidence, formed in fantasy. *Still* not remembered.

Yet the overwhelming feeling is relief, relief at being back in the musty-smelling room, within earshot of the landing and its grand-father clock; relief, now that I reflect on it, that this bizarre dream of a passive surrender of the reins (I still can't bring myself to seriously think of it as a suicide attempt—why try to kill myself?) isn't a memory, only a bad dream (there wasn't even anything in the dream to tell me *why* I was behaving like this, other than a terrible sadness that the dream itself, as truth, was mutually exclusive with the unquestionable, precious truth, the daylight truth of my journey to Webb's and the dream itself); relief that I now *have* something, no matter how wrong-headed, to fill the void of memory about the crash, a something that belongs, I remind myself, to the pathology of dreams. But it'll do.

Then it comes to me at last, and in the darkness of the room I nod, absurdly, I can't stop myself because the joy is such—at realizing *why!* and I bless language for its innocence, for being unable to prevent its speaking: I know, I *knew*, in the dream, that I was going to *bounce* when I landed: that meant *survive*—Danny's words in the library, *only you bounce off, don't you, when you're drunk.* I have been dreaming my crash as Danny's abortive attempt at suicide.

Tears fill my eyes, I shake my head now, sitting up in the dark in my bed, to think of my curious insufficiency of soul, of self, how I collect the agony of others, to lodge in my heart; more, to *fill* the lodgings, in case my own drab, uneventful inhabitation is inadequate in The Inspector's eyes.

'*JUST LET YOURSELF* go,' Danny says.

We are all three of us in the room, Danny on one bed, Eamonn on the other, and I lie on the blue carpet, facing the opposite way, my head level with their respective pairs of feet.

'I learnt this off a bloke in hospital, did I tell you I was a porter once? Worse than the army, that was. But one bloke, this other porter, taught me this. What you have to do is, first you close your eyes and blot out everything except my voice, then *imagine* you're opening your eyes but don't open them *really*, just imagine it, you're looking down, and where you're looking from you're going up towards the ceiling, just picture the room below you, you don't have to think about floating or what it's like to float, you never have to think about that, just picture the room beneath you as you rise up, first a few feet, then a bit higher, then up towards the ceiling...

'If nothing's happening, just let go of it, let yourself settle again, where you are.'

Nothing *is* happening. I hear a stifled giggle coming, I think, from Eamonn's bed.

'Start again,' comes Danny's voice, 'slowly this time, eyes closed, now *imagine* you're opening your eyes and you can see yourself, where you're lying, you're seeing yourself from just a few feet up, you're still lying there... now leave yourself behind, you need to leave yourself there so you can come back to where you are, that's your safety lying there. Keep seeing yourself, the whole room now, the three of us, you're going up, the beds, the carpet, looking down now from the ceiling.'

The silence is interminable, no-one speaks, nothing is happening, though it's easy enough to picture the room, the three of us lying prone, eyes closed.

'And now just keep going up, that's right, you can't see yourself any more, what you're seeing is the roof, you're looking down at it, now keep on going up...'

It's the strangest sensation. I *can* see the roof. A moment ago I could see the three of us, I could see the iron bedsteads and myself between them and the basin, and the blue carpet with the pale blue whorls profiled in a darker blue, now they've gone and I can see the roof beneath me and I'm still rising, I can see The Parade beneath me and the dip with its ruined houses and the Pipe Well where it all began, it's bright sunlight and there's no snow left and I can hear the seagulls all around me laughing and screaming, I have a seagull's-eye view of the town, it looks strange seen from above and unfamiliar, a few people opening shops and splashing water on the pavement, Muchmore the grocer outside Ough's disappearing again into the shop, and I'm still going up and up, above the seagulls. And to my alarm I realize that Danny hasn't told us how to come back down again, and now the view is terrifying, a scooped-out bowl of vision with a town, receding, in the middle of it, and somewhere down below...

I WAKE AS though stabbed, writhing to be free of the pain, sitting up violently then trying to be still, to see if...

But the pain is not in me, it's not in my chest where I feel it, it's in Eamonn's death that I've attended, and a rush of images comes with it, I am sobbing over him, he's warm and dead at once, the room is crowded with people but my eyes look only for Danny, Danny who understands and has forgiven me, and he isn't there.

It's still dark.

Still dark thank God.

Grandfather clock ticks on the landing, unperturbed, as if its time were timelessness itself. I push back the sheets and blankets, go to Eamonn's bed.

I hug his arms, I kiss his cheek, his forehead and his eyes. But I can't hear him breathing. And he doesn't wake.

WE ARE IN the car together, driving across the broad plain that leads to the house, and there are memories calling us from either side of the road, too many to keep up with and now we're so close to the house, all that's left is in our eyes, watching for the moment when the house comes into view.

And there it is, distance pressing it flat against the hill. There it is, so deeply set into the steep hillside that it looks shoehorned into it, as if peeping from a giant foxhole guarded by bushes, the stone facing beneath the roof streaked dark today with melting snow and gleaming like a miniature mansion with its two windows above and two below. The road up to it hidden by the frozen hedge.

Now we're in the lane, invisible, approaching. Traversing the hill. The house slides up beside us like a ship into dock.

And all the changed and unchanged things are one, I can't tell which is stranger, the new door with its unfamiliar contours or the old path up to it. New flowers, trees gone, but nothing that matters has changed; or can.

Alec is standing by the low wooden gate-post with its little wrought-iron gate, still there, his hand on the gate-post's rounded head: I can feel its soft, eroded wood under my palm—bringing a sudden dizziness as the post moves in its socket, as infallibly, as far and no farther, as ever.

I so wish Danny were here, but I know he has fled for good reasons. He warned me; but now I know too, I've guessed it, what he is: yes, an army deserter. The sense of scandal that surrounds his disappearance creates a dark patch in my mind. Yet I'm quite sure I shall see him again.

I know he is tracking us, ahead of us even, watching us approach, watching us now from the edge of the woods where the breeze comes, and the boughs lift, leaves rising like a swarm of starlings.

Eamonn is waving triumphantly from the hedge, a ball in one hand, and I can tell from here where Alec is standing that unless it's shrunk over the years it's not the one we lost, it looks like a squash ball but I wave an Alec-arm joyously back at him anyway. A woman is approaching me along the red-tiled path, walking as carefully as if the grass on either side were ocean, a thin-faced woman, a preoccupied face, she's trying to smile but it looks as though the mere presence of strangers troubles her like a long-anticipated hour of dread.

'Yes?' she ventures.

I've never seen her before but she is suddenly so dear to me, made so absurdly dear merely by walking from the door I set out from to go to Italy with three slices of bread in one hand and an apple in the other, the soft bread yielding till my fingers almost met through them, walking down this path, so dear to me that I smile at her with all my love in my eyes; and she stares back with a sweet, willing, deluded smile, broadening in surprise as though she were about to recognize me.

'My name is Alec. Alec Simmons,' I say. 'I was born here.'

What joy to taste the stillness of the moors!
I feel afraid to shake their holiness
By breathing freely. Silence, beating heart,
And let me listen to the feet of God.

—John Harris, *A Story Of Carn Brea*

MY NAME IS HANBURY.

It's been Hanbury most of my adult life. A few old family friends still call me by my given name, my first name, John, but these days just about everyone, even members of my school staff (those senior enough to call me by name), calls me Hanbury. The boys call me Creeper, behind my back. To my face my mother used to call me Humphrey, but that's an old and foolish story.

Quite recently, following an eventful day, I think perhaps a decisive day in my life, I had a dream in which I was called Alec (no-one actually addressed me by that name, but *I* knew I was called Alec), a troubling passage of dreams that haunted me for days and left me grieving for a totally imaginary death—two of my colleagues even asked if there was something the matter, and I could hardly tell them it was a dream bereavement. The death of someone close to me, a child. And I was driving back to the Ark, although in the dream it wasn't the Ark, it was my family home. That's to say: in the dream my family home turned out to be the Ark.

There *was* a death in my family, for which we all grieved, but it happened before I was born. Nonetheless we continued to grieve, and I suppose it's true that I grew up in an atmosphere of permanently suppressed mourning. I too mourned, for something that never happened to me at all. Perhaps this explains why in my dream I gave myself another name, though it's also true that I know two Alecs, one of them an Alick: Alick Penby-Stiers, a fat man who teaches Latin to the younger boys, and Alec Thurgo, our MP for

Liskeard and Launceston since the war, an absurd person who insists on being called 'Major' to remind us of his skulduggery in foreign parts. He was a commando, much decorated. I mustn't be rude about the Major, especially not if in the dream it was in *his* honour that I re-baptized myself; he brought his ward Egon von Lützow-Brüel (rumour had it that Alec adopted the boy, an orphaned German child with English forebears on his mother's side, in order to burnish his image as Tory spokesman for German affairs) into my life, changing it for the better and for ever. Frightening my life, I sometimes think, into being.

It all began with the boy's grandfather, 'Mad' Trimble, a well-known cleric before the war, who had a kind of fit while standing on The Parade in Liskeard. At the time—this was in '52, when Trimble was a few months short of seventy—he was on his way to an ecclesiastical gathering in Truro, and stopped in Liskeard, nobody quite knows why but most likely for one of the few reasons anyone ever stops in Liskeard, to buy a newspaper or have a pee before resuming their journey. According to subsequent eye-witness accounts, he emerged from his car, an unmistakable figure with his height and white hair, his dog-collar and the ostentatiously plain wooden cross he wore at his chest, and looked around him at the unremarkable affairs of the town until his gaze fell on Webb's Hotel, hitherto a similarly unremarkable chunk of granite, though it is a listed building and, for what this may be worth, one of Liskeard's more august pieces of architecture. It too featured in my fateful dream, somewhat transformed, grotesque. In reality it's a dull grey cube, as I say a chunk of granite, a squat thing defaced by a neon sign, with a pleasant portico and good mid-nineteenth-century windows. One of these now caught the Reverend Trimble's attention. I'm told he stood there for some time, staring open-mouthed at the window (which is currently, for other reasons, one of the more curious features of the town), gave a cry, and fainted on the pavement of The Parade.

His own description—I should add, perhaps, that he was known as 'Mad' Trimble *before* this happened, long before, for reasons unassociated with fits or visions—of what he saw in this second-storey window has been immortalized in print. *VICAR SPIES VIRGIN IN TOWN CENTRE, FAINTS...* declared a cynical headline in the

Liskeard and Launceston Gazette, and several other papers speculated, only half in jest, about Liskeard's prospects as 'the new Lourdes'. I myself have heard Trimble tell the tale on more than one occasion. But even in his own accounts, as in the succession of oil paintings which have filled (filled to the inch) the fatal window since 'Mad' Trimble took up permanent residence in the darkened room behind it, details vary. What is certain, at least in Trimble's mind, is that he saw a girl, a woman, behind the closed window, someone whose lineaments were at once virginal and spoke of sacred motherhood; dressed in blue, though the blue certainly varies, as indeed does the shape of the dress. And the features, to judge by Trimble's painted evocations, vary radically—deriving each new incarnation, in the view of town wags, from the vicar's latest passion in the town, each new amour inspiring a fresh canvas to replace the last.

There was, I suppose it's fair to say, no self-evident *model* (except in scripture and imagination, realized in different fashion by religious artists over the centuries) for Trimble's madonna. Because when the poor man recovered from his initial faint, was helped to his feet by a throng of shoppers, broke free of them and staggered into Webb's to ask who it was at the window, he was firmly told that the room in question was unoccupied and that no member of the staff could be said to resemble the person Trimble had seen there. No girls, nubile or otherwise, were employed by the hotel. The few guests did include one young mother, visiting a boarding school son with the flu (I know, because the child was mine, that's to say in my *care*, not *mine* of course but at my school). This was the lady my chap Edmonds called his mater, Mrs Edmonds, quite attractive, always very well turned out but in her stiff twin-set and pearls hardly a ringer (even Trimble could see this) for the Virgin Mary.

At first the old boy simply refused to accept the hotel's information. Sceptical—he claimed—of his epiphany, he promptly booked himself into the vacant room, to await the stranger's return or reappearance. The pregnant room I was about to say, for so it was in several senses, giving birth to a larger family than Trimble's own (he had four daughters): a family of cognate paintings. The Virgin herself never returned, to my knowledge. The days and weeks went by while Trimble waited, scarcely leaving the room even for ablutions. Supplicants arrived to try and prise the vicar back to his family—wife and daughters came, together, and singly in turn, departing again unaccompanied; and to his pastoral duties—a bishop was heard shouting in the corridor outside room 26, the staff reported gleefully—and to reality: several psychologists sent by the Bishop and by Trimble's own diocesan masters were reduced to calling calming questions through the locked door, without reply.

It was only after a year that the first painting appeared in the window, hailed in The Parade with gasps and pointing fingers, almost with a cry of *Habemus Papam!*, such was the effect. But unlike Rome's triumphant puffs of smoke, the painting was really, I suppose, a sign of defeat, of mourning. A confession that the Virgin would return no more; indeed, the numinous figure *could* now never be seen again from The Parade, since her two-dimensional image perfectly filled and blocked the window. Henceforth Trimble lived by artificial light, which may account for the curious tones of the subsequent paintings. Besides, these were his first attempts at art, he'd never even been an amateur dauber, which speaks much for his courage. The more so since he gradually began making forays into the town, where he could look back up at Webb's, see his own handiwork and, more perilously, hear people's opinions of it.

I would say—not everyone agrees—that as a painter he's improved over the years, and I particularly like a recent portrait known as 'Lizzie' to the locals. It has a certain flatness (Modigliani comes to mind), but the face... the unknowing 'sitter', and reputedly old Trimble's latest infatuation, was the daughter of the man who now runs Ough the grocer's, Elizabeth Muchmore is her name, of an old Liskeard family, a lovely girl... the face is... well: tranquil, grave, at once desirable and serenely remote. No mean achievement, in my opinion, for an artist self-taught at the age of seventy. Her dark hair and dark complexion are probably more appropriate to the Virgin's original (I don't wish to make quasi-theological or historical assumptions here; I just mean a Middle-Eastern lady, out of David's line) than the wan, fragile blondes beloved of Renaissance artists. But Lizzie's high colour marks her as unmistakably English, an English virgin whose feet Blake might have gladly pictured walking with her son on England's pasture green. (For all we knew Lizzie's feet, like those of her predecessors, may have been shod or unshod, there was no telling since the windowsill terminates each figure on the unframed canvas just above the knee, the better to give the impression of a person standing in the room beyond. I often wondered—having never been inside the room, nor with one exception met anyone, Trimble aside, who had—whether the canvas itself continued to the floor, with sacred knees, calves, ankles, feet...)

And where were the old, discarded canvases? In room 26, it was reasonable to assume. As Trimble's fame grew and spread, bids came from sources far and wide, from galleries, collectors, religious foundations, millionaires and nuts of many nationalities, offering Trimble untold sums (estimates abound) for individual paintings, for the entire Madonna-sequence, or even a loan, a travelling exhibition to be heavily insured and guarded round the clock before returning safely to Room 26, Webb's Hotel, Liskeard. Substantial bribes to beg a glimpse, with or without a camera—even these were refused. Perhaps Trimble had burnt the old ones, he wouldn't say. Perhaps they were all stacked in his room and we would see them one day. To their eternal credit, both Dawson, the owner of the hotel, and the local council have resisted all blandishments, including cash in hand, to threaten Trimble with expulsion from the room, in exchange for a deal over the paintings. Besides, on what pretext could they evict him? The old man pays his bill—or so the hotelier claims. Town gossips maintain that no rent is required of him at all, indeed that Dawson would pay a small fortune, if necessary, to persuade Trimble to stay, given the way the old boy's labours have filled the hotel with pilgrims and sightseers for nigh on fifteen years.

One thing's for sure, though, there's been no need to bribe the man to stay. The tourists have vexed him on his ever-rarer excursions from his room, where even in his growing deafness the knocks on his door must have maddened his seclusion, but the place is holy to him. Just as much to the point, perhaps, he's had one beloved companion here (here, that is, as long as he remained at my school): his grandson Egon. Egon was the only human being familiar with room 26 since Trimble entered it (it's said the hotel's friendly, one-eyed cat, now dead, was sometimes seen to be furtively admitted), but one who would rather die than betray its secrets.

Having said it all began with 'Mad' Trimble, his vision and his subsequent tenancy here at Webb's Hotel, I see that I am talking of the train of events that led to Egon's presence in my life, with its joys and disasters (the very joys and disasters that, like the hotel itself where I write these words in the so-called 'library', were twisted and translated in my dream). But there was a kind of prologue, a premonitory one, eight years before Trimble's arrival, ten before Egon joined him here.

It was the summer of 1944, I had recently taken holy orders and thrust myself into battle (as I saw it) as a padre attached to an RAF station, Alfriston in Suffolk. At this point I was still rather startled to be addressed as Reverend. It was hard to keep a straight face. I was all of twenty-six and wondered, much as a rashly new-married man might wonder, if I would ever fit my new role. I'd shown no excessive piety at Winchester and had barely left the school when I was summoned back to stand in for my housemaster while he had his appendix removed. I never left; but fell instead under the spell of the austere, imposing Bishop Garbett, whose unworldliness enabled him to believe, mistakenly, that Winchester schoolmasters knew everything (including goodness). Years of Theological College were quite unnecessary, he said, for a chap like me; at his behest I spent two successive Augusts at Westcott House and emerged a priest. Strange as it may seem I thought of it as a natural extension of schoolmastering, pastoral rather than evangelical. It was the war that changed me from a would-be shepherd into a thief of souls. Peace swiftly restored my senses, but for three years I was like a drunk on a bender.

At Alfriston my flock divided sharply into two groups, much more sharply than they do these days, into believers and unbelievers, those who flew with God (or gave the fliers ground support with hands and prayer) and those who flew with grit and curses. In the air, in combat, I dare say the two groups blurred into a mass of terrified daredevils mingling God and curses; the airwaves were a lexicon, I gather, of the sacred and profane in many languages, English, German, Polish, and the rest. But on the ground you either came to chapel and prayed like a crusader between bouts of slaughter, or you stayed away and gazed at dog-collars with a kind of sneering defiance, as if they offered a fraudulent evasion of the solitary battle to be brave.

In all truth I doubt if even my most devout air-crew-parishioners evaded this battle, no matter how often they prayed, in public or in private, or visited me to share their terrors. But evasion (in the literal sense) there was, for those who could stand it no longer. And when it took the form of mental breakdown, rather than taking leave without permission, I was called on, along with the station doctor, to help determine whether it was fraudulent or not. There were no psychologists in attendance in those days, no-one believed in it, or they pretended not to, for fear of slackening the stiff upper lip which alone, and unaided, would save us from the Hun. This was my true battlefield, my front line: the world of lost souls. Lost not to the Devil or to unbelief, but to chaos (which some of my confrères would call synonymous with the Devil; this only means they've never been to war, Satanic work if such indeed exists, from which the flight into chaos was nearer to the search for God than many a conversion I have known). As I say, this was my combat zone. Leading the men in prayer or coaxing them, privately, through their terrors, was a routine business by comparison. Perhaps it could have been otherwise: I might have dealt with the LMF cases (that sick and cruel stigma, Lack of Moral Fibre) with routine efficiency, preserving my distance, or inspired to it, perhaps, by self-preservation. Instead I had my first, vertiginous glimpse of who and what I truly was, of my compulsion to replace my own interiority with another's. And the more painful that other's world the more I wanted to ingest it.

(Like all too many of my dreams my recent Alec-dream bears witness to this continuing need. And yet the day that preceded it, that inspired and fed the dream—did it not herald my freedom? Enough of dreams; I shall leave the reader to judge.)

At the time I was both terrified and gratified by this discovery. I thought it was the proof, at last, of my vocation. Lucky I (who knew so many doubtful brother-priests) to be called to that which I already am, I told myself: a shepherd and a lover of mankind. An altruist! And of the strange, heady surrender it brought with it, of the dizziness at the parapet of self, what did I think? I rationalized it, I was full of subtle, existential explanations. After all, what *was* altruism but a paradox, since to care for others demands, does it not, a substantial self with which to care? And that self would be tested to its terrifying limits by the exercise of love, it would be pushed into a corner, puzzled and protesting, struggling to establish its own territorial rights, its *need* for a ground on which to cultivate that very love that threatened to consume it.

Ah, but that was the lie. Or rather that was truth, as a description of the tug-of-war of love, the danger of giving entirely; the lure of giving all in the hope that this alone will make us entire. The lie, the lie I told myself, was that this described *my* inner battlefield. When in fact it omitted from it a figure barely human, a fire-breathing dragon that scorched me daily, but whose eyes I couldn't face. That love I felt, that altruism that was like a joyous succubus within—and oh the sensuality of yielding to it all one's self and all the desires that torment the hours of the day, yes it was time itself that love supplanted—that sweet safety of vocation: I *didn't* struggle with it to preserve my foothold in myself, I fed it like a tumour, in a ghastly dare with God. If I could swallow others (their grief, their trials, *their* desires in place of mine), how many, Lord, could I swallow without being full? Without touching the walls of my soul's cavern, my capacity? Could I ingest the world's souls, each and every one, and *still*, bloated with a titanic love, a vessel with all humanity in my hold, contain them? Not explode? Then, of course, I would *be* God.

Not that I told myself any of this. Wish to be God? No thought could have been farther from my mind, drunk as I was on my own humility. But I *knew*, and this was the breath scorching me, one I dismissed as nothing more than the exhalation of the void, climbing that parapet where I stood cleansed of all my private wishes; I knew that as I listened to poor Denis Towle, a Squadron Leader obsessed with the idea that his own wing were trying to shoot him down, and consequently confined to barracks, I was feeding on his tearful delusions like a gourmand on pâté, I *wanted* them inside me to squeeze out my own troubles, even his memories became mine as I listened: *not* to avoid myself, not that—though it might have seemed like it to any other rational being privy to my soul—but in order to touch at last the true retaining wall that *was* John Hanbury; and not the everyday illusion of that Hanbury, that little Humphrey, dog-paddling in muddy confusion in the empty spaces of me, but the true, the resistent substance at the edges of temptation and of terror, a circumference I would locate only when the finite muddle-void within was filled to brimming with an epidemic mass of others' muddle-worlds; *then, then* when I'd got enough of them inside me, then with the cry of Enough! I would know my self by its limits.

Does this sound crazed, obsessional? It's little different—a priest's version, that's all—from the spirit of the frightened warrior who deliberately puts himself at greatest danger, in a wager against God: do Thy worst! Or in redeeming me, letting me live, grant me that knowledge which unites me to my mortal self and to my immortality at the same instant, the sense of who I am in utmost peril, of how close I can look death and dismemberment in the face, before flinching.

I knew this soldier's temptation well from airmen's tales, and understood it partly (with proper charity, I thought) as a disguise for simple suicidal urges, in the face not of battle but of fear too prolonged; courage's twin; also, though I kept this analogy to myself, a version of Christ's own temptations. And that was how I explained to myself my greed for others' sufferings. I was testing myself. I would identify myself through the limits of my capacity for *caritas*. And I would come to rest, not in flaccid resignation, accepting these limits, but with a sense at last of *where* the fire-fight was, on the perimeter, the fight to stretch and better myself. So I thought then.

I had all I could desire, there at Alfriston. If anything, I wanted *more* Denis Towles, I'd have colluded with Field Marshal Goering and his Luftwaffe into scaring the entire squadron, broken and shaking, into my vestry. And how I loved that vestry! I can smell it still, its incense was unlike the musty smells of any vestry I have known, since it fell from the roof, from the great beams of Canadian pine that spanned my airfield chapel and filled it with the breath of forest sap. But the LMF cases passed on and out of my vampiric grasp, to hospital and back to other wings, or to demotion and the disgrace of working among backroom Johnnies.

Denis himself ended up as one of these, interrogating his former duelling partners—the real ones, that is, captured Luftwaffe air-crew; until his second breakdown when to my gratified surprise he asked for me. For Hanbury.

By the time this happened I was no longer at Alfriston. My messianic sense (and oh I was *so* humble, such a devoted young shepherd, that those who knew me would no more have thought of me as the megalomaniac I was than as a spy for German High Command) had driven me to resign as station padre. Too many sceptical servicemen held up the garlic of self-protection when I approached, slavering after their souls. No, what I wanted was a flock entirely composed of emotional and spiritual haemophiliacs. I couldn't quite think where to find this willing crew. Until it came to me: recruit my own. I had a patron in the cloth, then Dean of Wells, and with his encouragement I formed a community of walking wounded, pacifists, conscientious objectors, Bolshies and the like. Quite small at first, but it grew. Premises were also found for us by the good Dean, a house on a wooded hill near Dobwalls in Cornwall, less than an hour's walk from Liskeard; a refuge which one of our community immodestly named The Ark.

And to the Ark it was that Denis came when, seemingly, too much proximity to German heroes had brought him low, and restored the poor man to the ghastly haven of chaos. So it was explained to me; in the weeks to come I learnt the real causes of his second collapse, and they were very different from the first. They had to do with the fellow-interrogator who accompanied him to Dobwalls, his gaoler, as it were, since the RAF were anxious to be sure that Denis didn't flee into the countryside to spread whatever paltry secrets he'd gleaned of Luftwaffe strategy. Or rather his collapse had to do with his gaoler's wife—something of which the gaoler, a man called Richard Thurgo, was blissfully unaware.

Their sojourn at the Ark was a feast for my vampire-self, since few of my flock needed to unburden themselves as much as Denis did; and a nightmare, since his attitude to his friend and escort, Thurgo, swung from weeping self-abasement to homicidal rage and back again. Denis, still shaky from his previous breakdown, had found his salvation in a secret, unrequited passion for Richard Thurgo's wife. It was mortal torment to him; amongst other delusions he was convinced Thurgo was trying to kill him. A grain of humour would have saved the day, but Denis was a man of incurable honour and untainted by irony. I had to advise both Denis and his baffled friend. At last Richard retreated, still bemused, to his interrogation games in Buckinghamshire, and Denis, after several escapes into penitential solitude on Bodmin Moor, was removed to hospital by his parents; where he took his own life.

I stayed in touch with Richard Thurgo, we were bound for ever, it seemed, by Denis Towle's agony and death. At any rate I had no-one else to turn to, since this was my first and for many years most mortifying defeat. I couldn't let go of it. Denis's parents wanted nothing of me, indeed they seemed to blame me for his suicide. Richard wrote to me, at intervals. And he, in turn, seemed to welcome my answering divagations on grace and the Holy Spirit, my attempts to make sense of Denis's pain. He always said—Richard, this is—that his stay at the Ark was one of the most nourishing periods of his life. I even have a letter in which he asks to be buried there one day, and I've kept the letter, though the Ark itself has long since burned down, and its author vanished, pursuing his fate into regions beyond our correspondence, where not even his brother the Major seems to be in touch with him. Last heard of as a maker and purveyor of pornographic films in Hamburg, I still picture in Richard's soul an unspoilt place for the Ark and its inmates and our innocent (ah, innocently murderous) friendship of summer 1944, united in our love for Denis.

And this, this love, was how I met the Richard Thurgo who some years later walked into Soviet German woods and rescued a child who'd been living on his own, for several years, in the forest; how my life became ensnared with the demented race of Thurgos and led, in time, to my taking charge of Egon, the wolf-child, from Richard's brother Alec. And brought us all here, to Webb's Hotel.

'DON'T BE A Humphrey *all* your life!'

Live it, I've come to think she meant, *live* it: but as a child it was a double aggravation to hear my mother say this to me, since it was she who'd dubbed me Humphrey, and since I wasn't even called Humphrey, except by her, damn it, I hadn't been christened Humphrey but John. Worst of all my father, whom I did not care to hear insulted, *was* named Humphrey and had been a rather fearsome and successful Humphrey all his life, at least to my child's eyes: few and far between were the people who called him anything other than *Doctor* Hanbury. Clearly my mother had another view.

The problem was with the name John. It was my brother John, my elder brother drowned and gone before I was born, who had been *John*, the real, proper John. He had been the firstborn, three girls had followed in an attempt to generate another boy, and by the time I arrived, belatedly, the original John was almost far enough in the past to have been one of those countless uncles lost in the Great War and after whom so many sons were named. At least... I say this in attempted exculpation of my parents, who should never have had the foolishness, or risked the ill-luck, of naming one live child after a dead one. This, in time, they realized; neighbours' cruel tongues told them so, turning what they had taken for a pious act of thanks to God for finally rewarding them with another boy, another John, into an embarrassment; worse, an inadvertent curse. True, there were plenty of precedents, especially in Victorian times when children died in droves and only a recourse to the family bible prevented parents from running out of names. Indeed it happened—I know of one actual case myself—that a late arrival was given the same name as one of the earlier, now long since grown-up and departed children, before the parents actually noticed that they now had *two* Freds or Marys. But in the 'Twenties when I was growing up, such prodigality was frowned on. And the embarrassment wouldn't go away. Distant friends of my parents would stare in puzzlement and steal a glance at each other, on being introduced to me, thinking (and I could see it in their faces), isn't he *dead*? And they would study me where I sat in the front room with them, beside my sisters, trying to decide whether it was their memory or nature that was at fault for enabling me to return from drowning. My parents grew wise to this in time, my mother deflecting it by introducing me as Humphrey, which only compounded the problem since if there weren't two Johns here there were two Humphreys, and *either* way the Hanbury family seemed to suffer from echolalia; and my father by introducing me as John the Second. 'King of England,' my sisters would promptly chorus sourly, bowing. It was their mocking revenge for my privileged role of only son, and I begrudge them not an instant of it. But still, and despite all precautions, the same moment arrived, recurred. 'No, not the one we lost, this is his namesake John, our youngest.'

Not the one we lost. *I* never lost him, that's to say his death was no part of my life, having preceded it by a dozen years; and yet I never could lose him, his shadow. We are occasionally one, administratively speaking, when a government department informs me that I died in 1899, that my request for a new passport is denied, my bills all paid already, my account settled. I have my 'No, that was my *brother* John' letter down to a fine art, but fraudulence still hovers round it. Indeed when Alec Thurgo revealed to me that his brother Richard, whose burial in Highgate cemetery I had attended (I'd even asked, in vain, to officiate at it), was very much alive and kicking in Germany, I felt a curious stab of kinship. Even a sense of wasted opportunity—since who could be better placed than I, John Hanbury, to vanish into a new life, leaving the unquestionably dead John Hanbury behind me, once and for all?

But I can't imagine disappearing, much less starting a new life which in my case could only be identical with my present one; the only life I could possibly lead and one which I love with undiminished appetite. And whereas the Thurgo family was one which I too would have fled at the first opportunity, my own dear loving, grieving family is an ever-welcome companion, almost my second career.

Most large families produce a priest—in or out of the cloth. Large landed families, of course, usually squeezed one into a dog-collar in bygone days, and although you will read that the son who ended up in the priesthood had been deemed unfit for anything else, I think there is a factor social historians ignore, one that has nothing to do with what passes for *realpolitik* among the rural gentry. A psychological factor, if you like. On the children of any family devolves a kind of psychic cake to be divided up between them, the cake of responsibility for the family vessel, its balance, its seaworthiness, its guidance—irrespective of the actual cargo, which may be, almost certainly will be, a shipful of fools. The cake (I seem to have made it a floating cake, or perhaps an edible ship—on second thoughts not so implausible: a family birthday cake in the *form* of a ship, with a St

Elmo's fire of candles burning at the end of every spar) is the cake of *family* itself; as distinct from the cake of genetic inheritance, which may well divide up among the children along quite different lines. Indeed the various responsibilities for the family's fate as a family may be assumed, or rejected, by children whose temperament has outfitted them for a role quite other than the one they end up with. I often wonder whether John the First would have proved the leader, the guardian of his sisters and the consolation of his parents' old age that the rest of my family believe. Perhaps he would indeed have turned out to be a golden boy, as golden as their memories of him—but with no interest at all in the family. And built an empire overseas. As it was he fell overboard, all too literally, before we could ever know. So I took on the role, the priest's role, of family pilot. Now, I know that plenty of people assume this role, willingly or not, without taking holy orders (though many of them deserve sainthood). Any of my sisters could have done it, and let me take the second watch. But there are families so doom-struck that within them nothing short of the cloth, of total sacrifice, will hold the rending beams together and quell the mutinies. Which is why, when I read of clerics past, or when I meet one today, I think ah *ha*... a fellow-spirit, not in God or in theological disposition (least of all in that), but another poor unfortunate who felt called to hold the family-world together, or who, like those single ants you see providing a living bridge across a chasm for other ants to walk across, just happened to be in the wrong place at the wrong time.

My father Humphrey was a GP in Truro and subsequently—it was John's death that provoked the move—in Reading, and I have every reason to believe he was a good and dedicated doctor. Too much so, perhaps, or too consumingly so, because he left himself nothing to come home with. It was like having dinner with a grimly burdened ghost. I think he was a kindly man. I say I *think* he was, because he was never *un*kind, to the best of my recollection. He was elderly, and eyed me warily, as if too close inspection might cause me to vanish like my brother. When he touched me his cautiousness filled me with a sense of my insubstantiality. I was all of fourteen before I finally recognized this emotion, one I'd been living with all my life, as humiliated rage. For a few guilty years I'd thought it was failed mourning, a resistance to grief or an incapacity for it that, if I ever confessed it, would exile me for ever from the family. Certainly from my mother, for whom mourning *was* life. And my sisters had learnt, in differing ways and degrees to mimic this. Happily, it was against their temperament and, when we were alone, we frolicked. Sometimes I think it was against my mother's temperament too, and that she wasn't mourning John the First at all but protesting, in the only way her unconscious mind had come up with, against her husband's absence from the home in all but body.

We lived on the outskirts of Reading in a large early Victorian house close enough in spirit to a vicarage to have ensured me a lifelong sense of continuity. (I too, it occurs to me from time to time, have become *Doctor* Hanbury, that's to say Doctor of Divinity, a title I've never used, and never will use. I make sure no-one *ever* uses it. *The Reverend J Hanbury, Headmaster*, it says in the school prospectus—oh, the joy the day I first saw that, the sense of *docking*, coming home—and God knows *Dr Hanbury, Headmaster* would only evoke foolish thoughts of Dr Arnold.) In Reading, yes—a true headmaster's upbringing—we had a croquet lawn, and splendid trees around it. We had Dotty the cook-cum-housemaid, whose attempt to introduce me to sex almost put me off it for life. We had evening recitals at the piano, lengthy games of cards, and endless summers out-of-doors. It was a great area for gardens, though neither of my parents was much interested in cultivation. Only the other night I came to, in the darkness of my bed, with my mouth full of the taste of raspberries gorged in a neighbour's fruit cage one afternoon when I was ten or thereabouts, so sharp and clear on my tongue that my own mortality seemed perfectly absurd. Can such things *vanish*? I might, perhaps, I felt at that instant, but my palate would surely haunt the headmaster's bedroom for ever.

I should add that I was gorging our neighbour's raspberries without permission, furtively. In the family cake there is also the slice of delinquency, rich and heady but essential to the balance of a family; somebody must always eat it. Several members of the family may share it, sometimes the entire family may nibble pieces at night, in secret, but it can't be left on the plate—which is why, when I come across a delinquent child, I find it hard to feel the requisite outrage on behalf of the rest of his family. Instead I think: Oh, *you're* the one who got that slice, the poisoned one (or who seized it greedily; it hardly matters), who served the family in this most necessary of ways, maintaining and completing it precisely *as* a family. For what inheritance, what genetic pool is without its murderers, its defilers, its vindictive ones? Which of us could have got here without the violence coursing in our ancestral blood? So I honour the ones with the mark of Cain, to me they're something more than the prodigal son or the lost sheep of Christian charity, they're the very founders of the flock—avatars, if you like, of foundation itself. You will have noticed that violent men (and women) are usually active breeders.

In childhood I thought *I* was the delinquent one, the sin-eater. I munched on this in secret, ruminating guiltily in the midst of our sombre, contented family. Drowned John was dead; I was alive, but was there anything I could do or be that would draw as much love and attention as dying? My first feeble attempts at crime were mostly thefts—I once, aged nine, stole half a crown from my father's trousers as he lay snoring in his study bed at night, to buy a school magazine for which I was convinced he wouldn't give me pocket-money—but these forays distressed me so much that I soon desisted. The cost in fear and misery was too great, at nine I was already a burnt-out delinquent, clearly past my best, and this puzzled me. In time I realized why there was so little on my plate, barely a crumb of criminal satisfaction: my father himself had eaten the rest, though his was the delinquency, the vindictiveness—invisible to our childhood awe of him, father the *doctor*—of absence. So I turned to a new crime: goodness, the sweetest of revenges against the family and my failed criminal self, because it was a false goodness. I would have sworn to it. Later, at Alfriston, I turned this on its head. My kindness-mask had been, I decided, God's double bluff to fool me into His and my own way, since beneath it I actually *was* kind, but could never have believed it, or found my way to grace, unless I thought I was the bad child vengefully pretending to be good. God, I told myself, was even more devious than I was; he had to be, in order to be God. These days, now that my messianic past is long gone, thank the Lord, I have a rather simpler view: I don't believe in goodness at all. In the *practice* of it, by all means. In God: as and how you may (and if, gazing round at His tortured creation, you can believe in *His* goodness, you'll believe anything). As for me, when I perform what I hope is a good action, or what I fear is a bad action: I'm just eating my slice.

IT'S NOT, I think, an exaggeration to say that the two people I have loved most deeply in my life I loved at first sight, or at least, as the glimpse deepened and the eyes held, at second glance.

I'm not speaking of my parents of course but, in the first instance, of Egon von Lützow-Brüel, a fourteen-year-old German Count. The second was Chrissie Wolfe; but that must wait. I say Egon was fourteen, but no-one knew his actual age. When his father Count Peter was arrested by the Nazis for complicity in the failed July '44 bomb plot against Hitler, how old was the child Egon? Three-and-a-half is my guess, based on conversations with psychologists; and for reasons I shall explain in due course. On the same day in 1944 his mother Maggie, old Trimble's daughter, Hampshire-born but now a German Countess, was also arrested and taken east to die, on a train, Alec Thurgo says, between concentration camps. The train was carrying armaments as well as prisoners, the latter perhaps as a disguise for the munitions; but these were spotted from the air and strafed, incinerating hostages and arms alike. By the time this happened the boy was already, to all intents and purposes, an orphan. His very existence as Count Egon von Lützow-Brüel was denied by the Nazis, who kidnapped as many offspring of the July conspirators as they could find and had them adopted under new names. Egon escaped to the woods and was saved; though I've often wondered whether during his four-year woodland exile he didn't inadvertently carry out one of the Party's aims by losing track of his identity, forgetting his former name and titles and assuming in their place the sounds of his adoptive forest.

From this point on I only had Alec's word for it, and he his brother Richard's who retrieved Egon from Mecklenburg in 1948, that Egon was raised alone in the woods, fed partly on nuts and roots and berries and the like, but also on bread and other civilized foods left for him by his parents' servants. They were still there; his family home was still there; why did the child not return to them? The clue seems to lie in one particular family servant, whom Alec claims dimly to remember from visits to Count Peter's family schloss in the late 'Thirties. Alec went there with Maggie Trimble—*his* girlfriend, he lets me understand, promptly stolen from him by the egregious, courtly, over-educated Hun. The servant in question, a girl, seems to have been of limited intelligence, perhaps an idiot; but during the war, when Egon was born, she became his boon companion. It was she who frequented the woods, and lived there in a kind of treehouse which had become Egon's second home—perhaps his true home, if he was closer to the servant girl than to anyone else—by the time his parents were taken from him. And as I understand it, Egon and the girl continued to live there in the treehouse until the Russians came, and took her. Thereafter, three years and more, Egon refused to come out of the woods—this in itself is less puzzling, to judge by the many stories I have heard and read of the bloody Russian irruption into Germany. Many people, singly and in groups, remained in remote woodland hiding-places for periods of several years, praying the Russians would leave; which in Mecklenburg's case they never did.

But this is also a tale of the family cake, and fraternal rivalry. During the war, Richard Thurgo had succeeded where his elder brother failed, in marrying a Trimble: Maggie's sister Molly. It was he who traced his nephew, alone and on foot in Russian territory (and I must say Alec speaks somewhat disparagingly of this heroic mission of mercy, perhaps to make sure nothing clouds the superiority of his own commando antics). How old was Egon held to be when he came out of the woods with Richard? 'Looked nine or ten to me when I first saw him,' Alec says of the day he first saw Egon, in '52, 'behaved like twelve.' Evidently he decided to split the difference, because when Alec brought him to me three years later, Egon's 'official' age was fourteen.

And his real age? Egon had no birthday, I was amazed to find, that's to say he celebrated none, and when I offered to share mine with him, he refused. He wanted no birthday. 'Every day,' as he winsomely put it, 'is my birthday.' I wondered who had taught him this egregious phrase; I could tell it wasn't what he really meant, or what he wanted. Egon wanted none of birthdays, it was his mark and he was proud of it. He was in all apparent respects a perfectly unexceptional child, and if I'd been quicker on the uptake I might have noticed in this one piece of obstinacy the sign of something larger; of a greater need which would in time consume his life and mine. But I was overwhelmed, as was everyone who met him, by the seeming normality of the boy. Any quirk was a kind of relief, noted but easily dismissed again, from the chap's *absurd* normality. How could he be so... ordinary? Manners perfect, English excellent; both faintly aristocratic, though no more so than the average English boarding school child—and why not, in his case? Wasn't he a genuine German aristocrat? We failed to ask ourselves how this seigneurial air had survived in the woods, while the child was scratching for roots. Also his German seemed to have vanished oddly fast, it was perfectly idiomatic and authentic, indubitably German, yes, but halting. Seemingly it had retreated, like his other past experiences, into oblivion. For this he clearly had a knack: he had, he insisted, no memory of the forest at all. Again, we paid little attention. We were all the more grateful, if a little puzzled by it, for his speed of assimilation. We reminded ourselves that other savages of deeper stain than Egon's had become no less civilized in short order, not to say *plus royaliste que le roi*—like the natives retrieved by early seagoing voyages of discovery, who became darlings of the European courts, in ruff and lace. At our first meeting I even had the impression that his good manners made Alec Thurgo, MP, feel uncomfortably vulgar.

The boy I met that day had one exceptional thing about him, which captured my soul before I understood why: his eyes. At fourteen—or thereabouts, he was certainly small, even small for fourteen—the rest of his face was still so unformed that it contained no guarantee of his later handsomeness (attested by one and all, not just my tender eyes). But his eyes were the grave adult eyes you sometimes see in children, in Egon's case with something more in them, eyes as old—this was my immediate romantic thought, since I already knew of his background—as the forests he'd grown up in. Green they were not, but they were pale and grey and strongly flecked with something of a darker, indeterminate colour, gold in the light but probably brown since in shadow the greyness of the iris faded to something closer to a warm ochre on the rim around the expanded pupils. More compellingly still, his eyes were dissimilar, not in colour but because in his left eye, on the right side of his face as you looked at him, stood a small black dot as perfectly round as a second pupil though invariant in size, floating in the north-east quadrant of the iris like a small planet halted in orbit.

Who could look into such eyes and not keep staring at them? This Egon clearly knew, and he held my gaze, giving me as long a time for study as I liked.

'This is Egon,' said Alec gruffly. He had his full county MP regalia on show that day, I remember, natty tweeds, waistcoat, club tie, carnation buttonhole. Egon was wearing the grey school uniform of his previous school, well pressed as I was pleased to see, though it was hard to imagine Alec Thurgo overseeing this in person; I had yet to discover Egon's own obsessional neatness.

'Pleased to meet you, Egon.' Along with his polite smile of response came an almost imperceptible movement of the head, I thought I'd imagined it for a moment, a vestigial German bow performed only in millimetric form as though for his own benefit alone. A private compact with his origins. But I think Alec noticed it, or was watching for it, and I saw his lips tighten.

'What shall we call you at the school?' I asked, 'Von Lützow-Brüel might be a bit of a mouthful for some of the staff, let alone the boys.'

I omitted to say that anything which would reduce the aggressively Teutonic effect of his name would be to the good, consumed as we still were—the boys worst of all—by triumphant and vindictive wartime myths. Why provoke them with a 'von'?

'People will get used to it,' he said quietly. Then with a shrug, still smiling into my eyes, 'I don't mind. What would you like to call me?'

'"Egon Lützow" would probably do the trick.'

Egon nodded. 'Is that all right?' he asked, turning to Alec.

''Course it's all right. And none of that "Count" business, d'you hear?' I saw Egon flush, as Alec glanced at me. 'I think some of the boys at his last place didn't fancy calling him *Herr Graf*.'

'Nobody asked them to. It was *their* idea.'

'I'm happy to leave that up to Egon,' I said, avoiding Alec's glare. 'I don't think my lot are over-impressionable. We've got a Sultan-to-be and a couple of fledgling Maharajahs.'

Alec said nothing. But he didn't forget my rebellion. As we emerged into the drive, out of Egon's earshot, he turned to me. At fifty-one, fourteen years older than I, he was still handsome and imposing, and he knew it; the face hadn't gone yet, the leathery drinker's face with its beady eyes, dark cheeks, and fine, composed lips beneath the salt-and-pepper moustache; a few years yet, before he let that grow into his trademark flourish, and let his weight go at the same time.

'You'll keep a close eye on the pompous wretch, if you've got any brains in your head. And kick the airs out of him, with my blessing. What you do with your Maharajahs is your affair. But in my book being a Reverend doesn't entitle you to be an idiot into the bargain.'

Any more than being an MP entitles you to be a bully, I thought and then, as intuition overcame timidity, said it aloud.

Alec gave me the full benefit of the Thurgo glower, veins glittering purple on his cheekbones. 'We'll get on all right,' he grinned, and sauntered off towards the Alvis. 'Just keep an eye on the boy.'

OF COURSE THE first thing I want to do, like everybody else, is get Egon to talk about the forest.

I knew the outline of the story, many people did, it had been written up in the newspapers on a number of occasions. Certainly schoolmasters in the South-West knew about Egon, and tales from Beale in Somerset, his former school, were passed around at school matches; but like the newspaper articles, they all concentrated on his bewildering normalcy. No mention, even, of the 'airs' Alec attributed to Egon. He was said to be popular, a good student, a passable batsman-wicketkeeper, very keen. A year or so before he came to me, a foolish, publicity-seeking policeman, charged with investigating the slaughter of several sheep in Taunton Vale, got it into his head to interview the former wolf-child at the nearby school, and duly made the local front pages as a result. If he'd done his homework first he'd have discovered that Egon was no prowling nocturnal carnivore. In fact he avoided meat like the plague and had been violently sick and bedridden for days after one of his schoolmates had forced part of a corned beef sandwich down his throat, to test the German boy's vegetarianism—a creed Egon shared (though I doubt if the schoolmate knew this) with the man who had had his father hanged; with Hitler.

Boys are curious creatures: like the German nation, who after the war managed to revile both Hitler *and* the 'traitors' who had conspired against him, Egon's schoolfellows were unimpressed by the sacrifice his father had made in the very cause of freedom for which their own war heroes had fought and died. Indeed—and I know this not from the newspapers or the gossip current about Egon, but from Winterson, the Beale headmaster—they taunted him as a Kraut, a Jerry; some, for all I know, may have insinuated that his father was a *cowardly* Kraut. Even before I met Egon I admired him for his courage in the face of this. And there... I too had fallen for the lure. Perhaps boys aren't so strange. Like Germans, like the rest of us, they admire heroes (I can picture them queuing up humbly for a peep at Count Peter's Iron Cross, had he won one and passed it to his son), and even the Germans' equal contempt for Hitler and his would-be assassins follows a cruel logic—they all failed in the end.

'How much *do* you remember?'

'Only Hamburg, with my uncle Richard. And the old woman who taught me to write in Gothic lettering. Nothing before that, sir.'

'Nothing?'

To have him sitting before me, in my drawing room, is like harbouring a mysterious electrical device, improbably housed in grey flannels and Aertex shirt. He's all containment, coiled; but you can never catch him out. Not a hair out of place—literally, since I'm sorry to see that like many of our boys he uses Brylcreem on it, so that in his case his formerly sandy hair, now darkened, no longer matches his eyebrows and coarse, reddish eyelashes. Still, he's a perfectly charming boy, with his round, polite face, the great animal eyes, small nose, and merry, lipless smile. More like a man playing, with perfect skill, a child. I sometimes wondered if he was born at the beginning of the war—yes, what if he's a shrunken nineteen, not fourteen, what if he knows it and he's laughing at us all? Meet Egon

Lützow, one of our brighter fourteen-year-olds. But if he *was* laughing at us, he never showed it, only listened with complete attentiveness, smiled modestly, chose his words with grace and deference. I must have sensed already how possessed I was with his improbable calm, and the great dynamo of fears my instinct told me lay beneath it, waiting for its moment. But I told myself my interest was purely scientific: here I was (I with with my well-honed emetic skills, trained by vocation to enable others to confide in me), faced with a miraculous being compared to whom the best-travelled explorer was a crashing bore. He was, after all, the very thing they sought, the Abominable Snowchild sitting here before me in my patched pink armchair. He'd been a man-animal, he'd pushed to the very confines of the brain until nothing human remained and all was leaf and wind and branch, forest floor noises, danger, smell of food; just as I hoped one day to reach the very confines of my spirit, filling it with memories; with *his*. But scientific, scientific... I saw myself in a long line of clergymen with historic hobbies, engineers, inventors, naturalists. I would be the Gilbert White of Egon's inner, German Selborne, articulating for the world a wolf-child's bestiary.

And I would take as long as it needed.

'You remember *nothing* of it? Not your parents? Or where you lived? Not even the tree-house?'

'I know there was a tree-house, but only by being told. I can't even imagine living in a tree-house.'

'You can't *imagine* it?'

'Not really.'

'Not even in your dreams? No trees, no forests?

'No. I don't even like them very much.'

'Well, perhaps you've had your fill of them. Do they frighten you?'

'No.' A shrug. 'But there's nothing to do there, is there, really? It gets boring.' He suffers my gaze for a while. Then, 'I must have been bored all the time, when I lived there. Perhaps that's why I can't remember.'

'Perhaps. But then again, I wonder why you chose to stick it out for years, even in winter. If you were bored.'

Egon gives a puzzled half-smile, mimicking mine, as if he shared my harmless curiosity. Could he really remember nothing of those years? Was there a key, if I searched hard enough? I'd often wondered how it was that Richard Thurgo, the most unprepossessing specimen I've ever laid eyes on, had lured the wolf-child down from the tree-house and out of the forest. Richard of all people—how would an ogre lure Jack *down* the beanstalk? What was the secret? Richard, it occurred to me now, would have spoken to the boy in English: in his mother's tongue. A thread at last—so Egon might have thought—to lead him back out of the labyrinth.

'And now? Where d'you feel happiest? In town?'

He ponders.

'Where d'you feel most at ease?'

'I don't know. Playing fields, I suppose.'

'You like the open ground.'

'I like cricket.' Glancing up and catching me, 'Why does that amuse you, sir? My father liked England very much. Alec says they went to Lord's together.'

'Did they? That's interesting.' But for some reason the image irks me. 'Tell me about your grandfather. You get on well with him?'

Egon chuckles, a pleasantly deep, adult sound. 'I think so, sir. He seems to like me. Has he said anything to you?'

'No, not a word. I don't think he trusts many people now. But he confides in you, I take it.'

'Oh yes, sir. He's tremendously interesting about all kinds of things.'

'Such as?'

'Well, he talks about scripture a lot. You'd like that, sir, but I can't follow half of it. And when we go out on the moor, he knows a tremendous amount about plants, and geology, that sort of thing. He makes the best bird noises.'

'Does he? Well I'm damned.' I try to picture crabbed old 'Mad' calling to buzzards. 'D'you like it out there, on the moor?'

'Oh yes.' Then as if picking up *my* word, my idea, 'In the open.'

'Yes.'

We look at each other through a long, unconstrained silence, and I realize that Egon has the almost American knack of holding an unblinking gaze without giving offence; I always thought it was part of their business training rather than a national characteristic, but with Egon it has another quality altogether, that of looking quite openly at you, seeing you, and not seeing you at all.

'D'you ever watch him paint?'

'Yes, sir. Only I'm not supposed to talk about it. Or about his room. He made me swear.'

'I understand. How did you meet up with him again? He didn't write to you, did he? Was it through your Aunt Molly?'

'No, sir. Aunt Molly and Alec don't get on. I never hear from her.'

'Well, then? How did it happen? I understand you visited him once or twice, from Beale.'

'I saw it in the newspapers, about his vision.'

'Oh, not the Vicar and the Virgin, all that stuff?'

'Grandfather has all the clippings. Sometimes he reads them to me, and he laughs like anything.'

'That's good to know.' But something has clouded Egon's face.

'I'm not sure... I'm not sure he knows I'm his grandson. Not all the time anyway.'

'I suppose that's only to be expected. Who on earth does he think you *are*, then?'

'Well, the first time I went there I kept on knocking on the door, softly because I didn't want to frighten him, I suppose, and calling out who I was, and he did open the door to me. Mr Dawson said he's very deaf and when I kept on tapping at the door he might have thought I was the cat. When I get there now I always call, "it's Egon, it's your grandson," and he lets me in, but he's never called me that, he doesn't call me anything.'

'Tell me: did you ask to move to this school?'

'Oh yes, sir.'

'It was *your* idea, was it? To be near your grandfather.'

'Why?' Suddenly childish, 'Isn't that all right? I *can* go and see him on Sundays, can't I?'

'Of course you can. It was just for my information.' Silence falls and I see that he is waiting for me now, watching me. It makes me aware that danger signals have been going off in my head, a sensation that I've been manipulated, led away from the nest. 'And that was the only reason you wanted to leave Beale?'

'Yes.'

At this instant I know he is as poor a liar as I am, and I thank God for it. His expression freezes, suddenly blind to everything before him.

And then I realized that whatever it was he was thinking, it had nothing to do with me or with the school. At that moment it was death I saw in his face. I tried to shake this idea away—for no good reason it flew into my mind that he'd come here for a suicide pact with his grandfather, out on the moor. This was ludicrous enough to break me free of morbid imaginings, but when I looked at Egon again with what I hoped were fresh eyes, I saw the same death's head, the eyes dull, the face peaky and oddly emaciated.

'I like it much better here, sir,' he said, evidently to reassure something he mistook in my own expression.

Once more we sat in silence, a guilty one on my part. I felt disappointed at the way I'd handled the interview, and ashamed of my wild suppositions.

I must have frightened him, the last thing I wanted to do. I watch colour returning slowly to his face.

'D'you think you'll ever remember?' I say at last, and he knows without hesitation what I'm talking about.

'I'd like to. Really I would.'

But that too rings false, I note, this time in rising hope. He doesn't want to. That's why he will.

'Would you like me to, ah, inform the school, in a way that... well, we could work it out together, but it needn't be melodramatic,' I see him looking strangely at me, 'no no, I don't mean about your childhood, if you want to tell them or they hear about it from some other source, I'm sure you can deal with that, no, I meant about your father. I don't want any Nazi nonsense directed at you. I'm sure you're very proud of your father, and rightly so, and I think the *school* should be proud to have you here.' As I say this I feel myself losing control of my tone. Am I going too far, indeed should I be addressing this to him at all? Egon does not seem discomposed. 'Shall I say something?'

'No, sir. Thank you. I'd rather do it myself.'

'Well. Well, new school, new start. I'll leave it up to you.'

We smile. Good night, I say, and watch him rise obediently, noting the moment when his head turns and the current goes dead that has connected me so vividly to his eyes, as he walks to the door.

'Good night, sir,' as he goes.

EGON IN THE corridors: none of the boys pays him any special attention, no-one notices him, in assembly no-one studies him with curious or hostile eyes. Not yet. Lawton, *Here, sir*, Littlejohn, *Here, sir*, Lützow, *Here, sir*. Same cut-glass tones. Funny name, that's all. Unless... unless someone were to recall it from the Chard Gazette, *Sheep found slaughtered, wolf-boy questioned*. Do the kitchens know you like your meat raw, *von* Lützow?

But inside his head, no aboriginal designs. Only this: will I make the cricket team?

...but that doesn't entitle you to be an idiot into the bargain.

Sometimes I wonder whether if I'd taken the bull by the horns and done as I'd offered, spoken to the school at assembly, the whole sad train of what ensued would have been stifled at its source. But is it sad? I must leave it to you to decide; it depends on the outcome, after all, and I don't know that myself as yet.

I was hooked, that much I knew; from our first meeting, really, and once more from our first interview, and each meeting was like the first, not only because of the gentle parries but the sense of an undented surface which made every meeting the first. Nothing in his manner or his words acknowledged the frequency of our conversations, he never offered routine thanks for my interest in the events that had shaped him, traumatic as these surely were. Nor did I think he should; and I recognized that many people before me had probed and prised at his soul. Neither did he display impatience, no matter how long I questioned him. 'Good night, sir,' came as politely as ever from the door, without a backward turning of the carefully Brylcreemed head. If this was what it was to become human after a savage past, then our own human future was one to tremble at, it struck me, snake-pit coils of memory and instinct only made more dangerous, more combustive, as the shellac of civilization added each new, translucent coat. When would they erupt, in Egon? His was the face I looked for at assembly, at school Corps parade, on the sports field. I knew the movement of his flapping arms, the sleeves always kept rolled down no matter what the weather. Knees never dirtied. Shoulders high and tight. I was keeping an eye on the boy, as Alec had asked me to; and after all, this was no ordinary boy.

But of course there was more to it than that. He seemed to have fitted seamlessly into the school, his head turned with the others, hissed and cheered with the others, he was always in the middle of the throng, never at its edge. But the more oiled and precise his movements, the more he seemed to me at risk. I lived on tenter-hooks for no discernible reason. Without knowing it, I was growing to love him.

And how *could* I know it? *Saints don't love.* Love individuals, she meant; don't love like other men. These mocking words, sweetly not mockingly delivered, kindly meant—no... not entirely—these foolish words were spoken to me when I was still in my twenties, by a woman who loved me. I thought I loved her too, but she disabused me: I was very fond of her, and it made her miserable. June was her name, her boys were in my care, and she lived in Winchester, in the town. Our meetings were furtive at first, and pastoral—her husband was dead, she felt the boys slipping away from her, becoming ruffians. And I was the soul of sympathy, always vigilant, a listener whose maddening tenderness extended to the smallest, trifling worries, a patient refuse-collector in the park of love. How people glowed at the sight of my chubby, tolerant face! Here's Hanbury, to bless the feast! But did I really want June? I was relieved when she turned against me; yes, barely ashamed to be a bloody saint. My life seemed full.

Less and less I wondered what it was that made a bachelor of me. I found my colleagues endearingly childish when passion entered their lives; at Winchester we had a boy called Wagstaff who shed fierce tears, as though playing at adult pride, when he left the field a member of the losing side, and it was Wagstaff's eyes I saw in my friends' faces when they confided in me their raptures and their lovers' tantrums. I was touched, without envy; nor could I envy the impenetrable yet unfriendly-seeming bonds of married love as I witnessed it among my colleagues. They too, the married ones, were my friends—yet the very word makes me anxious. At Winchester I'd made many friends, both as schoolboy and 'Don' as the jargon or 'notion' termed the masters. Easily made and easily discarded; friend to all. Only my wartime conversion from shepherd to wolf had brought consuming, throttling friendship into my life: the Ark with its mad tangle of possessiveness—I couldn't move without feeling the skeins, I woke aching with others' pain and when Denis died it all but strangled me. I told myself I'd cared too much for Denis; like John the First he'd gone under. A convenient excuse for a soul too timid—so I feared—to embark on the waters himself. Now Headship ensured distance; confessor without intimacy—or rather no, there was intimacy aplenty, but without loss of control. Precisely what I sought when I'd joined the priesthood in the first place, no doubt. Until I met Egon I never knew what loneliness was.

If this was homosexual love, then homosexual love passes my understanding; it certainly doesn't resemble in any outward way what everyone insists goes on behind my cricket pavilion (I'm still not convinced), or in any inward way what I take to be the agony of Alick Penby-Stiers, who frequently confesses to me, and in appalling detail, his frustrated yearnings for this boy or that. Sometimes, in the throes of misery when tears distort his consonants, he cries out in defiance, 'I'b a hobosexual, not a *queer*!' and I picture poor fat Alick wandering the hedgerows in forlorn rags. (He confesses to me doubly, at once to his pastor and his employer, I believe: to the former in order to unburden himself and to the latter as what he thinks, and what he hopes *I* think, is a guarantee against his actually *indulging*—his word—what it is he may have partly expiated and forestalled by telling me aloud. Or does he think I'm enjoying the details, and by sharing his imaginary pleasures, vicariously, will feel obliged to forgive him if he *does* indulge? Oh confessional, dear confessional, I've long since ceased to believe in your purifying fire.) At any rate, I find it hard to think of my feelings for Egon as homosexual, least of all pederastic; though if, as a man, you love another man, or boy, and I love Egon to the point of sometimes thinking I live through him, is there a word for it? Paternal, filial, brotherly love... these are respected, of course, but are they

95

supposed to be so intense? It does disturb me a little to think that I dubbed myself 'Alec' in my dream, but I'd rather believe (encouraged by the spectral presence of his precious Alvis) that this was after Alec Thurgo, a doughty bachelor but without a taint of sexual perversion, rather than by secret identification with Alick Penby-Stiers, that somewhat less than doughty bachelor. In any case my love, whether for men or women—no less intense—has always been a kind of surrogation, possessive only in the most ghostly fashion. One of transferral of my self into theirs; one I can control.

I will not say I loved him as my child, because he wasn't that. The term is both too large, and too small, to describe it accurately. And in a sense I loved them all, the boys, as though they were my children. Yet that too is untrue: they were *not* my children, and neither with them nor with Egon do I believe that it was like loving your own child, whom some part of you has to repel for their own sake, as well as protect and adore. Their separateness (admittedly I speak as one who never has had children, though I still hope to) is surely part of what we have to teach our body's children. I loved Egon as myself: I know no better way to put it. I could scarcely have put a name to it then, but I knew he was a child in danger, even though he pretended not to know it, and his unexpressed need moved me—roused me, in my heart—to love.

THE CUBICLES, AT night. Egon lies straight and still under the covers in the iron bedstead: a ship, a plane, a pocket submarine. On either side of him rise green-painted wooden partition walls, ending a few feet short of the dormitory ceiling. The paint glows with a faint luminosity as torchlight from neighbouring cubicles bounces off the ceiling, slanting down the walls, throwing into sudden relief inscriptions all but erased by the layers of pale green gloss. Egon makes discreet contributions to the harsh-whispered wires of talk filling the darkness overhead; gossip about the staff, boasts about girlfriends, Talbot is measuring his erection to universal scepticism. Others are ignoring this, their torches focused down on books evoking dogfights in a Hurricane, or tunnelling under the bedclothes with descriptions of daring escapes from Stalag 17. We seem preserved, the staff no less than the boys, in a wartime amber, seemingly all the easier to indulge now that the danger's past; when will the world jolt forwards, leaving these scenes behind? Will it ever? Egon's own torch plays across the carvings on the partition walls, names only, no remarks, no limericks, just a litany of Anglo-Saxon surnames, teams of them as if in batting order; scores even, once you assign a number to the different letters, by alphabetic order. A wicket for each letter. Evans, M.F.J., 88 for 8. Peterson, W., 130, no, 131, for nine declared. Demands a recount. *Tell us about German girls, Lutzow.* Peterson, W.; 16 for 1, 21 for 2... A different voice: *Come on, Fritz!* Ignore, begin again. Peterson, W. Peter... *son*; that's when he sees it, heart pounding in disbelief, and looks away, furious, the game ruined; his own mind a gaoler, an enemy against him. Spoiling everything.

FORTUNATELY, INSTINCT IMPELLED me to phone Winterson, the Beale headmaster, and quiz him more closely about Egon's last few terms there, or rather make an appointment to do so.

I knew Winterson as a guarded man where psychological matters were concerned. There were things he might not tell me on the phone, aspects that perhaps reflected on the school or on himself, that I might more easily coax from him face to face. Even then if he suspected an impending interrogation, he might clam up. This was the politics of schoolmastering: a feint was required, followed by a surprise attack. At Beale Egon had begun to take an interest in fencing, a sport in which we were poorly equipped, and though I'd ordered masks, foils and the rest, we were still waiting; it occurred to me to ask Winterson if he would lend us an item or two from his singularly well-stocked armoury. Beale was rich, it would be a friendly gesture to a poorer-heeled fellow-academy, and above all a gesture towards Egon's relocation and his pursuit of a sport taken up at Beale; potentially an enduringly happy memory of the place—this was the line I planned to take.

It was Egon who drew my attention to a Saturday afternoon fencing contest in Exeter. I agreed to take both him and our only other fencer, Fishburn, to see it; we could turn the trip to further profit by dropping in on Beale, where Winterson, as it turned out, was both happy to lend us some equipment and glad, he said, of the opportunity to see Egon. His voice on the phone left me in doubt about this. Yet all in all it seemed a good plan. I didn't feel it was appropriate—with regard to the other boys at the school, not to Egon himself—to take him on such a treat alone; nonetheless, though I was happy to take Fishburn, a gangling, friendly fellow, I regretted the fact that I would be diminishing a first chance of a tête-à-tête with Egon away from school premises and school uniform. At least the whole thing now had the air of a normal excursion.

As we entered the sumptuous grounds leading to Beale House, a bomb went off. I don't think this much surprised any of us. It was a home-made bomb, in a galvanized metal rubbish bin, or what had once been a galvanized bin. Now it was a smoking thing of blackened strips like a metallic cactus. Ignoring our car, outlandishly dressed boys charged whooping from the rhododendrons to examine their handiwork.

'Chemistry?'

'Physics,' Egon said, and we drove on.

Beale is a different kind of school from mine, and is justly famed for accommodating 'troubled' children. It treats them well; too well, in the view of certain educationalists and many of the public—but this was no doubt why Alec Thurgo had first chosen Beale for Egon, and also why, in turn, he would have assented to Egon's request to move closer to his grandfather and to my school, on the face of it a more old-fashioned place which might discourage 'airs'. To be fair to Winterson, when he arrived at Beale he began to transform the old *laissez-faire* Summerhill approach into a novel way of dealing with the various advanced, retarded, and otherwise eccentric boys and girls drawn by Beale's reputation: he would find them each a sport, no matter how exotic. The neurotic son of a Finnish diplomat might find his heart's desire in jai alai; an anorexic heiress, therapy in mud-wrestling. England was after all the home of sports, the inventor—if not always the ruling champion—of more internationally favoured games than any other race or people. With considerable ingenuity, it seemed to me, Winterson extended the normal range of school games, soccer, rugby, cricket, tennis, boxing, swimming, squash,

squash rackets, fives and handball, hockey, golf, table-tennis, and the usual track and field events, in most of which Beale had dominated the South-West for many school generations, into a host of obscure sports among which no child, however cross-eyed, bandy-legged and ill-coordinated, could fail to find one at which he excelled. Or at least one he or she enjoyed enough to pursue with vigour.

In the six years since Winterson's arrival, Beale had produced an international pole-vaulter, judo champions galore, four National Hunt jockeys, the national real tennis title-holder, a leading kayak specialist, and most of the British skiing team at the recent Winter Olympics—in addition to their usual haul of track and field records at junior and senior levels. Winterson was himself a former hockey blue, quite corpulent now; *mens sana in corpore sano* was a tag he no longer illustrated, except through his pupils. Under 'Sporting Activities' the school prospectus offered twenty pages illustrating everything from tug-of-war to tiddlywinks, including the most esoteric varieties of martial arts. Since my own, much smaller school also followed in its headmaster's footsteps by being feeble at games but good academically, I should like to be able to report that Beale's university entrance figures suffered as a result of this exaggerated emphasis on sport. In fact—no doubt since its 'difficult' or disturbed pupils largely came from educated, well-to-do families, the kind who could afford Beale's fees—most of these passed their exams without being overly distracted by tuition (as might, I fear, all too many of my own boys).

We were now climbing the landscaped hill towards the Georgian pile at the top, always a splendid sight. Where my school is purpose-built, and remains a huddle of Victorian buildings within an encrustation of new extensions, sheds, and army huts, with playing fields on three sides, Beale was, and still resembles, a small stately home. The new buildings hang well back in respect, and they themselves are quite presentable, sometimes even inventive, examples of modern architecture, lorded over by Beale's domed observatory, the gift of a wealthy amateur astronomer who had attended the school in the 'Twenties. In terms of amenities Egon had moved back into the dark ages of boarding-school tradition: all I could offer was the charm of ancient desks and dormitories, a basin of warm water each morning in the senior cubicles, and cold baths for the brave. I wouldn't have begrudged the boy a look of regret, faced with the pleasure-dome he'd left.

But I could see none; instead I noted that he exchanged no greeting waves with any of his former friends and classmates that we might have passed among the roadside throng. He was gazing ahead, impassive. And though several boys leaned forward to peer into the car, then stared as we went by, none of them gave so much as a smile of recognition.

My plan had been to locate Winterson, and once the hand-shaking was over, despatch Fishburn to fetch the fencing equipment, along with Egon, who knew where to find it. It worked to perfection, the more easily since neither Egon nor Winterson seemed to find much to say to each other after the usual polite enquiries.

The boys left, and we faced each other across Winterson's imposing drawing room. His big head with its broad mouth and flattened nose jutted at me in the familiar way, but there was sweat on his balding, shiny head, and he looked curiously puffed up. Then I realized he'd put on weight again, but without doing anything about his clothes: the blazer looked full to bursting and the tie was about to garrot him. When he spoke it was in his usual skittish, jocular manner, 'Got time for a little confab, Reverend? Of course you have.' But he seemed genuinely nervous; and I was surprised at his taking the initiative. 'Cup of tea?'

'You've lost a rubbish bin to a science experiment,' I said. 'You may have heard the bang. Otherwise the school looks in...'

He didn't even let me finish. 'Damn it, Hanbury, it's not my place to tell you your job, and I'm no psychiatrist, you know that, but I hope you know what you're doing, bringing him back here.' To calm himself he walked over and poured the tea, while I stared. 'Milk, sugar, three lumps, right?' he muttered.

'Well remembered.' He handed me the tea, while I tried to fathom his mood. 'Was he *that* unhappy here?'

It was Winterson's turn to stare, raising the eyebrows that flew in little feathers above his blue eyes.

'Didn't Thurgo tell you? Oh God,' his face was rigid, 'I assumed that's why you...' He made an angry gurgling noise in his throat. 'For Christ's sake, I assumed he'd tell you.'

'Tell me what? What are you talking about?'

'You don't know that the boy tried to hang himself at the end of the summer term?' Winterson looked away to avoid my eyes. 'Poor kid. You mean that bastard Thurgo didn't tell you *anything* about it? That man's an absolute bloody menace. Did you vote for him?'

'What?' My mind was spinning.

'For Thurgo. Did you *vote* for him?'

'Well, I... No. As a matter of fact I didn't. What do you mean, tried to *hang* himself?'

'What I say.' Winterson fled heavily towards the tea-table. 'Well, *I* don't know, he probably does less harm in the Commons than he would crashing about here. Kind of man they should have rounded up on VE-day...' and shot, I thought he was about to say, judging by his face, 'and sent to bully the colonials.' Pouring his tea, 'Eh? Some people are no damn good at peace, the same way *other* people...'

As his gaze returned to mine, he broke off, mortified, remembering whom he was addressing. A man no good at war, who'd harboured 'conchies' and other malingerers.

'Well, I warned you the boys had been giving him stick. *Not* just because he's a German, we've got every nationality under the sun here. Because he's stuck up. That's the one thing we don't tolerate here. They can be loopy, lazy, walk round in a dream, that's what their parents pay me for, to let them dream, to *give* them dreams. But not to be stuck up about it, that's the whole point. That's what I'm trying to teach them.'

'What *happened*, Winterson?'

'I'm trying to tell you,' he growled, wedged by the table like a cornered boar. 'Here's what he did, if that's what you want to know.' He gave a sudden snort. 'D'you know we've probably got that idiot Thurgo to thank? I mean that the boy's still alive. Assuming he's responsible for the boy's clothing. Second-hand, most of it, though you wouldn't know it was, the way the boy looks after his stuff. Perhaps you already do know, if you've seen his pyjamas. Must have seen service in the first war. Anyway, that probably saved his life. He took the cord out of the trousers, looped it round a beam in the washrooms and of course the thing snapped when he jumped. Standing on a bath, in the middle of the night. Old one-eyed John sleeps on the same floor, or rather doesn't sleep much, by the look of him. The porter, you must have seen him. Looks mad, but he's utterly reliable, and he's the only one who knows, apart from me. Heard the crash, and found him, lying bleeding. Bashed his knee.'

I was too appalled to speak, but Winterson must have taken my silence as continuing criticism.

'It wasn't that he didn't fit in, nobody has to fit in here, you know that, half the county are baying for my blood because I *don't* make them fit in, and they go off into the countryside with their stink bombs, or cause trouble in the village shops. They're loners, and I'm proud of it. But, damn it, they don't *look down* on anyone, inside or outside the school. He couldn't get the hang of that. It wasn't what he said, it was just his manner, damn it. Even got me riled.'

It made no sense. This wasn't the boy who'd sat in my drawing room, unfailingly polite, the boy whom I watched mimicking his fellows to the point of self-obliteration. But then... *new school, new start*, I'd said it myself. And with a child's chameleon skills...

'For God's sake, Winterson, this summer when you told me he'd been bullied... why didn't you tell me the whole thing?'

'Bullied? Did I say he'd been bullied?'

'Ragged, then. Persecuted. What's the difference?' I regretted this; to be sure, there was no 'bullying', not at Beale.

'You haven't had time to get to know the boy, then. You can't bully a chap like him. He's too cold-blooded.' Winterson brooded for a moment, staring at me. 'All right. The fact is I told Thurgo I wouldn't talk to anyone about it. Said he'd speak to you himself.'

I sighed. 'Afraid it would harm his reputation, was he, if it got out?' I didn't add: and yours, your school's. You were just as afraid you'd be the one who mishandled the wolf-child. But my expression must have said it all, since Winterson flushed white with fury.

'Look, man. We did our best with him, believe me. I'm not sure he belongs in a school, quite frankly.'

You're wrong, I thought. And once more Winterson's fat, angry eyes saw through me.

'Some other institution, possibly. Yours, eh?' ne grinned. 'I wish you luck.' And he downed his tea.

The rest of the day was a blur; the boys enjoyed the fencing match, I think. I'm not even sure of that. It's a sport which in imagination evokes Errol Flynn as Scaramouche, but which in practice never failed to remind me, less appealingly, of marionettes attached to their cord. And of course that afternoon it was worse, it looked like a mad dance of death, the white-clad figures like masked phantoms plunging at each other, quivering for a long moment of animal rage, then sudden, frantic and ungainly, almost falling over in their rush to impale their opponents.

Egon was quiet and composed as ever, but now all I saw was the child raising himself from the tiled floor of the washrooms, the rope burn—invisible, but I could picture it—at his neck, picking himself up, shocked, bruised, alive.

Before we'd set off for Exeter, Winterson had tried to patch things up with me—I suppose he was afraid I'd put the word about, and make him look bad—assuring me he'd had lots of 'good talks' with Egon after the suicide attempt. I shuddered to think what these had been like. 'Could have brought in the psychiatrists, obviously,' he said, 'but the thing was, the boy absolutely denied having done it, insisted he was just down there for a pee, and that his pyjama cord had broken when he tried to do it up and he'd flung it on the floor, then tripped and hurt his knee. And knowing him, I think he'd have maintained this in the face of the good doctors, don't you? If he wanted to? In any case there was no *mystery* about why he'd done it.' And when I tried once more to probe about anti-German feeling towards Egon, Winterson just shook his head pityingly. 'For God's sake, man, when will you believe me? They wouldn't have cared if he was Goering's son as long as he shared his tuck with them.' He was protesting too much, I thought.

'Do they know how his father died, d'you think?'

Winterson shook his large head. 'I asked him that. Said he hadn't told anyone. Pride, of course.'

I wasn't sure how he meant this. 'Well, he's got every reason to be proud, I mean of what his father did.'

'That's what I'm saying. Too much pride.'

But I wondered.

I was so distracted I managed to run the tank dry of petrol on the way back, in the middle of a pitch-dark Dartmoor. I had a spare can with me; to my disgust I found it dry, all but for a few drips, with which we couldn't coax the engine into starting. Happily the second driver we flagged down did have a half-gallon to spare, so we weren't stranded for long. But I felt foolish, and at one point while we were waiting for a car to wave down, Fishburn wandered off without permission into the cold October night, to demonstrate—I took it—his contempt, though nominally at least to take a leak. 'Coming?' he called to Egon out of the darkness. Egon glanced at me. 'I'll hold the fort,' I nodded. I was too overwrought to want to talk to the boy now. And it was Alec Thurgo I wanted a word with.

But Egon loitered. 'No, it's okay,' he called to Fishburn.

I could tell little of his expression in the dark, but from the way he was turned to me, steadily gazing at me, I knew he was waiting for me to speak. He could hardly have failed to notice my change of mood after we left Beale, but unlike Fishburn, he must have guessed why.

'Winterson told me what happened your last term there,' I said. 'I'm terribly sorry.'

Egon said nothing.

'If you want my personal opinion he's a stupid man,' I blurted, 'and the school is…'

No, this was the wrong way to go about it.

'The school's all right,' said Egon quietly.

'Maybe. Maybe. I want you to tell me the truth about it. Not now, you don't have to tell me now, but I want to make sure it never happens again.'

There was a long pause, and a distant yelp from Fishburn.

'It won't, honestly,' said Egon at last.

Mutters out of the dark reassured us that Fishburn had only slipped and fallen.

I knew I should stop now, but I was brimming, unable to contain it, and I heard myself say, 'But to try and *hang* yourself…'

Egon continued to study me in the dark, for a long time. Behind him I could see the first faint flare of an approaching car, still some way away.

'My father didn't hang himself,' came Egon's voice, hard, this time falsely adult—and I realized with an unpleasant shock that it had a touch of Alec in it. It could have been, as a remark, a kind of tribute to his father, who after all didn't hang himself; but was hanged. I heard it differently, and couldn't yet place the emotion it expressed.

'And neither will you, d'you hear me? D'you hear?'

The car was coming nearer. I felt conscious of being brightly lit, for Egon, by the advancing beams, and had to shield my eyes.

'Say that whatever happens, no matter how black you feel about things, promise you'll come to me first. Say it.'

Egon's silhouetted head gave a small nod.

I shook my head, fierce now, one hand raised to halt the approaching driver.

'*Say it!*'

IF YOU GROW up with three older sisters, your childhood tends to be surrounded with dolls. You may be going rat-a-tat with your imitation Browning (I had one), making model frigates and Spitfires, and squirting your sisters with your water pistol, but what your siblings are doing, day in and day out, is dressing and undressing dolls; which has muddied many a growing boy's sexuality. I was, it's true, the boy my parents wanted. John—and you will understand my uncontrolled feelings where Egon's suicide was concerned—had drowned. And here was I, at last, to replace him. But since my parents lived in daily terror that I too would die, they coddled me, of course, and discouraged riskier if manlier pursuits. That fear went into my own soul and I've cursed them for it. Each time I step into a vehicle (much less a plane, which I had never done and swore I never would do) I make my peace with my Maker but remain petrified from one end of the journey to the other. I think, if I'm honest, I positively try to run out of petrol. Even going to sleep requires an act of courage: I see no reason (did my parents instil their own fears in me?) why I should wake up the next morning. During the day the fear passes. Indeed I sometimes verify this, by asking myself how I would feel, were I to be obliged to face a firing squad, now, standing on the touchline in the middle of a school match, or sitting silently at my desk, watching the class complete a written exercise. Or walking up the nave to read the lesson. I'm gratified to find myself resigned, unpanicked. I walk to the wall, wave away the blindfold and stand there, my mind empty. (A small voice says, oh no you wouldn't, if it was really happening. Yet what matters is that the *thought* doesn't make me panic.) I once knew a man who actually had been put up against a wall to be shot, which is perhaps why my fantasy takes this form. He was a Polish boy who fled to the West during the war, and tried to enlist in the allied forces. What had happened to Zbiggy was that he'd been caught in Klagenfurt, on the run with blatantly false papers, during a bombing raid; that same day he'd already jumped off a train to evade capture, and survived other adventures. The military patrol were in no mood for arrests. It would be only one more body in that rubble-torn street. So they stood him up against a house, and he fell to his knees, unable to stop himself pleading hysterically. To no avail. The officer levelled his pistol, Zbiggy shut his eyes, the explosion came and he fell away into darkness.

When he came to it was with a tremendous weight on top of him, and Zbiggy remembers thinking sadly that this, then, was to be his eternal punishment: weight, a crippling weight on his chest. Then, as he was dragged free of the fresh rubble where the bomb had landed, he slid past the black-uniformed arm of the German officer whom weight had punished instead, with a falling building.

When Zbiggy reached Britain he enrolled with the Polish fliers, less to fly than—since he shared my terror of the air—to find, or so he claimed, the bomber crew who had inadvertently saved his life. He never did, indeed his nerves were so shattered by his pass with death that he was found unfit for duty, joined my ranks at the Ark, and now, I'm glad to say, runs a successful motor parts business in Bristol, with a son, Matthew, who is also my godson.

Given Zbiggy's experience of execution, which for our joint therapeutic value I made him tell over and over again, I don't know why I think I'd face the bullets peacefully. But as I say, during the day I do. At night a rattling windowpane brings on incipient heart failure, and the suspicion returns that when I was an infant—I always feel like one, in bed—my parents looked in on me unceasingly to make sure I was still breathing. These days I can hardly blame them for having done so, I make my own nocturnal rounds of the school dormitories and I know my parents' emotion too well (even if it was they who bequeathed it to me) to be able to reproach them for it.

How was it that John the First actually drowned? I'd give much to know it myself and put an end to the multiplicity of images that circle in my mind, the different versions I've invented for it. It took place on a Sunday trip into the Cornish countryside, during the period of my father's practice there; beside a towpath. It was at a lock, I believe, but I'm not sure I haven't invented this—the steep concrete sides the five-year-old couldn't scale once he'd slipped in, the cries, my father's unavailing attempts to rescue him, nearly drowning himself in the process, since he could not swim. Perhaps there was no lock but only reeds and murky water. The tragedy had taken place at some distance from Truro and the family home, but now the house seemed doom-laden to my parents, the neighbours and their friends burdensomely solicitous, and they soon moved away to Reading. They would never talk about the afternoon of John's death, refusing even to specify its exact whereabouts, so I haven't even been able to visit it in later years, to verify my childhood version of it. Like my sisters who also were not born when John died, I've had to put my own pictures to the event that branded our lives.

Once, as an adult, I met the Cornish girl—she was a woman now, big and brawny—who had been John's nursemaid in Truro. She told me that on the very evening after John's death, the Sunday evening, my mother had walked into the nursery where the girl sat sobbing her heart out, and said quietly, 'Come out now. I'm going to put away his things. And we shall never,' spacing out her words, 'refer,' another pause, 'to John again.'

We did of course, that's to say we children did, and we made it impossible for our parents to avoid all mention of him. But no matter how often he was named, some element remained of Mother's first, fierce resolve which served, far from suppressing grief, to ensure that it could never end. And from the day the Cornish girl, Maria was her name, told me the story, its image of my mother is the one I shall carry to my grave, one I never saw but only conjured from

Maria's words: that small, courageous face (my face, if you remove from hers the lipstick, rouge and eye make-up, and most of the hair), standing in the nursery doorway, saying calmly, 'We shall never refer to John again.'

ALEC THURGO'S HOUSE was not in his constituency but on the edge of Padstow, in the north of the county, and the drive took me the better part of an hour, through winding Cornish lanes and towns with purported Arthurian connections, Camelford, Tintagel, Boscastle. It was a long, slow drive. His constituency party had at first, I believe, tried to persuade Alec to live closer to his loyal voters, and then were no longer heard to complain, once they discovered that the Major's idea of man-management derived, and would always derive, from his days as a commando.

I was of course coming by invitation; to arrive unbidden would be like kicking a sleeping bull terrier. I had forced the invitation on my host by telling him I could no longer be responsible for Egon if Alec continued to withhold essential information from me. Getting up the nerve to say this had cost me a night's sleep: what if the man's response was to call my bluff and remove Egon from the school? But my first attempt to cross swords with the Major, when he'd demanded that Egon make no mention of his aristocratic origins, had produced the only grin I had ever seen on Thurgo's face (and I include a number of television appearances), as well as the only pleasant remark he'd directed at me. So I steeled myself, made my pitch, and was gruffly invited. 'A bachelor's lunch, if you're content to share that. Save me getting the woman in from the village. Cold roast beef all right?'

His directions, as meticulous as if we were planning to re-mount the raid on St Nazaire, brought me along hedgerows to a modest cottage hemmed in by fields, a broad plain which gave no indication of the sea barely a mile away. Only the air, as I emerged from the car, told me we were at the island's edge.

'My mother's place originally.' Alec had come out to greet me in the same resplendent tweeds, but without the buttonhole. He gazed around, past the house, at harrowed earth all the way to the horizon.

'She didn't care for people much. She was an artist,' he rasped, with an expression that defied me to find this improbable, or even shameful. 'Glass,' he said tersely. 'I'll show you some of her pieces.' And as we passed through the cottage door into the well-ordered interior, 'I'm just the tenant, technically. She left the place to somebody we'd never heard of, Irish fellow, supposedly, by the name of Donovan. Old childhood flame, so we suspect. Fortunately,' he disappeared into the kitchen, leaving me unsure whether to follow him, 'the Irish can't locate him either. So until he comes to claim the place, I'm sitting here, paying no rent. Have a seat at the table.'

I decided he meant the dining, rather than the kitchen table, and found my way into a pleasant front room lined with oak furniture and neat, framed prints, and with his mother's glassware ranged in double-fronted cabinets. They shone so fiercely that I felt for 'the woman from the village', picturing Alec's military inspections of her dusting. 'You *are* ready to eat, I hope,' came Alec's voice through a serving hatch, followed by his head. 'Unless you're one of those types who insists on a filthy glass of sherry first.' It was a hard offer to refuse but I succeeded, studying his cropped, vigorous hair, bristling with health and reproach to my own hairline. 'Good-oh. Whisky's on the sideboard. I shall drink mine with the meal.'

He did, while I wondered if this would make our conversation about Egon easier—and whether indeed this was its purpose—or harder. Over the roast beef we gossiped about Liskeard and those who passed for its leading citizens; it was a ground on which I was relieved to be able to hold my own with Alec. I waited for him to switch topics in his own time. He knew why I'd come.

'So Winterson told you about Egon's escapade in the lavatories, eh?' Alec had chosen an odd moment to say it; he was behind me, picking up my empty plate. But it certainly stifled my answer. 'Fruit salad any good to you?' I nodded and Alec headed for the kitchen with our plates. 'Yes,' he called, 'he phoned me in a panic last weekend, the silly ass. As soon as you'd left. Afraid you'll tell the newspapers. I said he'd got the wrong man. Anyway,' once more he lowered his head to the serving hatch, 'you don't believe this suicide nonsense, do you? That's just Winterson's way of getting back at me for taking Egon out of his clutches. He can say he had to get rid of the boy, instead of the truth, which is that *I* got him out of there before Winterson's bloody school ruined him.' Seeing what I suppose was my unyielding face, he took a conciliatory tone. 'I mean, think about it. The boy's found with a bloody knee and a bust pyjama cord. He says himself it broke, the way they do if you pull them too hard like a silly young fool, and he fell over. Where's the suicide in that? You don't believe he'd try and kill himself, surely.'

'He as good as admitted it to me.'

'The boy did?' Alec looked at me with a trace of consternation, soon rescinded. 'Well, I dare say you led him on, did you? Tried to console him? Boys love that kind of thing, a bit of drama.'

We said nothing, until Alec had returned with the tinned fruit salads in two shallow glass bowls, set them down, and sat again, facing me.

'What?' he grunted, as though there had been no intervening pause. 'You don't believe it, do you? Why would he do it?'

'That's what I came to ask you. You said yourself that he put on airs, and the other boys didn't like it, teased him about it.'

'So I should hope. He's always put on airs. *I* tease him about it.' He raised his spoon, glanced up to see if I was doing the same, and caught my stare instead. 'Oh for heavens' sake, next thing you'll be saying *I* drove him to top himself. If he can't stand a bit of teasing, then...' I could see him struggling to control himself, 'then he's too bloody sensitive for *this* world, that's all I can say. Don't you *like* fruit?'

I raised my spoon, and we ate in silence.

'Christ knows, I didn't *have* to become his guardian,' Alec muttered at last through a mouthful of the stinging mush. He pushed back the unfinished bowl, stood up and poured himself a stiff refill of Scotch. 'It was either that or let him grow up in the gutters of Hamburg, with my benighted brother.'

'Why *did* you take him on?' I said, watching him light a cigar and shake the match furiously in the air before throwing it into the fireplace. 'You didn't *have* to save him from the gutters—if that's where he'd have really ended up. I would have thought there were too many German psychiatrists who'd have wanted to get their hands on him.'

'Dare say you're right.' He wandered to the fireplace, military pride getting the better of him, bent to pick up the spent match, and carried it to a waste-basket. 'But that's a pretty rotten fate too.'

He met my eyes, and a smile began with a down-turning of his lips. I smiled back; his suddenly merry face had such charm in it, I could understand at once his lady-killing reputation. 'Those bloody Germans,' he said, and started to chuckle. 'They certainly wanted to keep him, from what Richard said.'

His faced turned serious, but without shutting me out. 'You want to know why I did it?' There was a pause, and he seemed to think better of whatever he was going to say. Alec turned away, staring blindly at one of the cabinets, only a foot away from his face, full of incised bowls and goblets. The loneliness in his face was dreadful to see. Then he appeared to notice what was before his eyes, raised a finger to point at the glassware, then dropped it again without comment. 'My mother's efforts,' he said at last. 'What do you think of 'em?'

'They're very fine,' I said sincerely.

'Really?' He studied me, touchingly direct. 'D'you really think so?'

I nodded.

'I'm going to show you something no-one's ever seen,' he said abruptly, and strode from the room.

I was expecting him to return with a piece of glass in his hands. Instead it was a sheaf of letters.

He sat down in an armchair, holding them in his lap, not looking at them but at the same time ignoring me, so that I wasn't sure whether to rise from the table or not. When I did, and he looked up at me, it was with a curiously furtive schoolboy smile. He raised the letters a little way and dropped them again, still holding them tightly, into his lap. At that moment I knew who they were from.

'I loved his mother,' Alec said. 'I've loved her all my life.'

I DROVE BACK in a state of confusion. Had I been snowed, I wondered, had the Major, the political Alec, manoeuvred me by showing me his emotional side, all the more overwhelming for being unexpected? Leaving me unable to confront him thoroughly about his responsibilities where Egon was concerned; unable even to tell him how much the boy was at risk? No doubt it was a trick Alec had used before. And yet I felt guilty thinking of it as a trick. I didn't doubt Alec's feelings for Egon's mother, nor that in showing me Maggie's letters—which is what they were, letters written to him from Germany in 1937 and '38—he was indeed showing them for the first time; I may even have been seeing something more interesting to me than the letters, a side of Alec he hadn't shown anyone for many years.

To my intense embarrassment he had insisted on my reading Maggie's words, and wouldn't hear of my protests.

'It may get up your ecclesiastical nose,' he said firmly, 'reading another man's love letters, I mean the ones another man *receives*, but if you'd been in uniform during the war...' a low blow, this, but he was determined to get my consent by fair means or foul, 'you'd have got used to it. We all passed round our love-letters. It gave the other chaps something to dream about.' Yes, I thought, but their authors may have guessed this, and amended their letters accordingly; unlike Maggie. 'I remember reading my sergeant's wife's letters to him, and bloody salty they were too, lying in a paddy field in Burma, and trying not to laugh at some of it while a Japanese platoon marched by six feet from my face, closer than you are to me. Go on, read 'em. There's nothing indecent in them, for crying out loud, she was a vicar's daughter!'

Oh yes, I thought, thinking of vicar's daughters I'd known; and of Maggie's father 'Mad' Trimble, notorious, in the days before his vision and transfiguration, for possessing a large pornographic library, reputedly the best in the Home Counties. His nickname had been derived from this, less from the books themselves than from the tone in which Trimble declared that he had the Devil under lock and key—but always available to those who felt they could touch pitch and not be defiled.

This was on my mind as I began reading his daughter's letters; members of the clergy who regularly sampled old Mad's lending library had been referred to, in the old days, as the Know-Thine-Enemy brigade. Was I about to join, belatedly?

I started reading, but came across nothing obscene. Far from it.

Instead I saw to my distress just why it was Alec had forced the letters on me. It wasn't as some kind of nostalgic proof that Maggie had returned his feelings, though there was ample evidence of this. No, what the letters declared were Maggie's doubts about her future husband's character. To wit, his courage, his resolve, his sense of urgency in the face of barbarism.

Alec studied me as I read the letters, with an expression of vindicated pride on his face. Indeed there were real tears in his eyes. I was ashamed for him. The letters infuriated me with their querulous disloyalty, the way they played on Alec's affections while merely keeping him on the line, on the bench, a perpetual substitute if she ever actually changed her mind about marrying Peter. Doubtless she had been playing no less fast and loose with Peter's affections at the same time, living there in the schloss, forever planning the wedding... and showing Peter a face we never glimpsed in the catty, fretful letters.

I gave them back to him, not knowing what to say. Against the Peter she described, lofty, distracted, dabbling in dissent, I had to picture another, if only to give Maggie herself some credit for loving him; and Alec too, for loving her. And Egon—would I now be forced to see him as the child of the petulant bitch who had signed these letters with kisses to a half-discarded lover, and of a vacuous German dilettante-prince whom she was morally betraying on the page? No, I saw someone else through the letters: a troubled, educated man, cosmopolitan, Anglophile, yet too proud of being a German to be able to believe his countrymen could cast off their passion for civilization like a convenient mask.

'Do you talk to the boy about his father?' I asked when I'd mumbled something about the privilege he'd bestowed on me, and the thin, crackly paper was safely back in his lap.

'Not unless I have to,' Alec said. But he nodded at me as at a bright pupil, pleased that I'd grasped his intention in showing me the letters.

'He has good reason to be proud of his father.'

'What, for dipping his toe into that futile abortion of a rebellion?'

'Why d'you put it like that? They very nearly killed Hitler, in fact they maimed him for life, as I understand it.'

'Better if they hadn't, frankly. Turned him into a mad dog. Cost God knows how many Germans their lives, not to mention our boys.'

'You're saying they shouldn't have tried to kill him?'

'I'm saying they shouldn't gone off at half cock, damn it! They were ditherers and they muffed it. They were the wrong men at the wrong time—some of them only wanted a different *Führer*! Idiots.'

I didn't want to argue history with him, or the ethics of revolution for that matter. 'I wouldn't be ashamed of it if I was a German.'

'That's as may be. What I'm telling you is, as for Count Peter and *his* role in it...'—the title was an uncalled-for sneer, and instantly brought to mind Egon's words about Alec and his father at Lord's together—'he barely got himself involved in the affair, such as it was, and I know that for a fact. The man was an out and out coward.'

I had no knowledge of Egon's father, but the rival's jealousy in Alec's voice made me seethe. 'He died the same death as... as the heroes of that conspiracy,' I heard myself bluster.

Alec gazed at me. 'Don't be fooled,' he said quietly. 'The man was a dreamer, a prevaricator. He was an ass.'

'I don't think you'll be doing Egon any favours if you tell him that.'

I watched Alec's face go from its even ham colour to purple rage in seconds.

'God *damn* it, Hanbury, d'you think I'd insult the boy's father to his face?'

'I think he's not quite sure,' I said, 'how to regard his father. Granted that Egon's not the only boy of his age trying to deal with that—but for him, in his present circumstances, it must be especially painful. Your silence on the subject is probably as damaging as anything pejorative you could say.' Alec turned away in fury, but I kept going. 'At least he could hate you for that. But as it is... if he admires you, he can't admire his father.'

'Christ on a *crutch*,' said Alec slowly. 'I thought I'd got him out of Winterson's clutches into a pair of safe hands. Sensible hands, not... this... God, *you* were talking about German head-shrinkers. And now I have to listen to all this claptrap from you, pejorative this, painful that. Have you all gone mad, in your profession? Look, the boy's father had the *nous* not to fall for Hitler, but he joined up all the same and then he got caught up in a half-baked *coup* that never was, and paid the price for it. That's not easy for Egon to bear, I'll grant you that, but other kids have recovered from their fathers' failings or we'd none of us be here—and it's a damn sight easier to bear than having you or me telling him his father was a bloody hero, and then finding out what an ass he was. Can't you *see* that?'

I could see it. And yet the unacknowledged residue of Alec's jealousy seemed to me to poison his argument. Egon needed support, and the kind he was getting from Alec, 'brace up, don't be a milksop like your dad,' would crush him quicker than if Alec were Egon's real father and no less of a bully. At least the boy would have something to try and live up to, or to reject; but a dead coward father, and a live unsympathetic substitute: it was a recipe for disaster.

And it hardly helped that Alec loved the Maggie in the boy as deeply as he loathed the Peter in him. Was it my place, my duty to explain this to Egon? I wrestled with this on the drive home, knowing it *was* my place if no-one else would do it... but knowing also that what frightened me was *my* part in this paternal action, yes, an assumption of Egon's paternity almost; I'd done it before, like all schoolmasters, where it seemed necessary and unavoidable; but there was another residue here, no matter that unlike Alec I could acknowledge it. It was my own love, that might as easily blind my judgement as Alec's rage blinded his.

I took it slowly on the way home, and drove the smaller roads across the moor, including the track down to Dozmary Pool, a favourite place for reflection, where I got out and circled the lake. Though the water is little more than four foot deep, and with no evidence of ever having been deeper, it's here that Arthur is supposed to have hurled the sword Excalibur to its last resting place. Nothing about Dozmary Pool evokes this, yet this is one of the calmest and eeriest spots I know, in a setting so barren, so featureless and flat that the pool seems less a lake than a thin sheet of troubled glass fallen upon the moor, a space of saturated marshland eddying in the breeze. It's as dull and empty a scene as you could wish, but it vibrates with terror. The moor itself was in its late October splendour, when the hair on its rough pelt has turned to old gold, with orange and russet patches, and the skin worn bare in places to reveal the black, peaty hide beneath; like a great mangy, sleeping orang, I always think, with a few distant sheep and here and there a miniature human—like insects on the old beast's side we are, like lice; and in the distance rise hairless knees and elbows of mounded grey skin, lined, soiled, ridged, where the moor's granite bones press up towards the sky. I thought of Egon with old Trimble, botanizing, slow-footed, in the wind. When I'd fretted enough I returned to the Wolseley and drove in slow circles to Minions, where I parked beside the Hurlers, an unprepossessing group of monoliths, dwarfish and clumsy, some fallen. I often came here to think of Denis Towle, poor Denis Towle the tormented flier I'd nursed at the Ark as long as I could. When he ran away that summer he'd slept in the shelter of a ruined wheelhouse near the gap-toothed stone circle and during the day, he said, completed it by standing in an empty place among the Hurlers until he too fell, sunstruck, starved, exhausted, into the grass. The moor attracts madmen, as I know only too well; and mourners.

I still had no plan as I drove back to the school.

TORCHLIGHT. TORCHES PLAYING, in the dormitory—familiar, for an instant. Then the terror comes. The cubicle walls have vanished, all of them, and the torches will find him, any moment now.

Egon sees himself scrambling out of his bed to hide beneath it, quick, as the hunters shout strange guttural words. Then come the victim's screams, but not from *his* throat. From a woman's. He can see her now between the trees, held by her feet, her skirt, her hair, screaming, her face distorted in the torchlight beams. A language without meaning for him rages above him and he surrenders to his hiding-place, eyes closed, in tears of shame.

Behind his lids the torch-tracks remain, scoring the darkness. Then as the starfire fades, a metal door opens before him: opens without movement onto another, blacker darkness. He dare not go forwards, or back, and as he teeters and loses his balance he knows he is lost, fainting, falling towards the ever-opening door.

OLD TRIMBLE RISES abruptly from his bed, in darkness, fully clothed. He lights a candle—I don't know how it is that I know he doesn't use electric light, but as I see him light the candle I understand the strange light in his canvases—and gazes once more at his gallery of unframed Virgins of Liskeard filling every inch of wall, canvas jammed next to canvas.

Through Egon's eyes now: Trimble on the moor, 'Now *this* fellow...', plucking a minute yellow flower with extraordinary care in his old fingers...

ONCE YOU'VE TRIED to end your life and been given it back, is it harder to try again, or easier? They say no-one ever fully recovers from a nervous breakdown, never quite the same again: unlike the rest of us, they know where the edge is. The membrane of belief can never be restored, the illusion of insuperable sanity no matter how often you flirt with letting go. Now you know how close it really is, the chasm. And for the suicide who survives, cliffs and high windows, open razors, guns, all these sing their old siren song, but you're no longer chained to the mast. They're friends. Even pain has been a friend.

Again I try to picture Egon in his narrow bed, carrying the secrets of his exile and survival in the forests. The other Egon that he carries within. What could bring it to the surface? Always with him the fear of his own violence; using his *teeth*. Seeing himself jumping at another boy, hissing and growling. Demon-strength. He has felt it inside behind the fencing mask and in the boxing ring. And shaken it off since once unleashed it can't be stopped, it only knows how to kill.

Was I deluding myself that I knew where Egon went in his mind, to escape? I think not; I too fled to the moor.

Even there, on the moor that afternoon, I was drowning. Now I knew what it felt like. I wanted to hold Egon against the day, the buffeting, against veiled hostility, against nightmares too. I felt him disintegrating without me. I saw him dragged down by the weeds, fighting for breath. But it was my breath that was short. I could bring him back with me from the depths, he was my Lazarus and my whole life crowded in on me to choke me with this one godsent impossible hope of salvation, drowned John and stifled Hanbury and reborn Egon—my creation—drawing me on and up into a bottleneck where only one of us could pass, only one survive.

When I summoned him that Sunday evening after returning from Padstow, it was to find that he had been sent to the sick bay with a temperature; the usual October flu, I was told, he's only the third but there'll be more. I could hear their hacking coughs on my rounds that night. My father, rather surprisingly for a medical man, was of the opinion that you coughed your lungs strong. So far he seems to be right, in my case, since for many years I've been proof against bronchitis and, thank goodness, the ghastly asthmatic spasms of my childhood.

While Egon languished with the flu, news reached me that a small, select gang had been formed among his contemporaries. Marshall and Vanstone, two louts, were its leading lights, but nothing else was known. Had Egon been invited to join before he fell ill? Would he be, when he was out of sick bay? I wondered whether I should ask him, in due course; but if he had joined, wasn't the whole function of it, if it had a useful function for him, precisely to be secret? Even if I didn't probe, the very fact that I knew it existed might spoil it for him. Gangs and secret societies there had always been and would always be, at school. Some, as I remembered from my own school-days, were a matter of pure exclusivity, and served nothing more than to seal friendship in the face of others; some had a sexual significance, which might vary in the daringness of its rituals, as in its sexual orientation; some were exotic, some were intellectual elites, some were criminal, with thieving rituals. It seemed to be at least worth finding out to which of these categories the new gang belonged. But it would have to be done without exposing my informant, a boy called Ball who was his generation's snitch (perhaps still is; a talent for disloyalty can get you far).

By the time Egon was on his feet again the worst of my frantic anxiety had passed; we resumed our evening talks, and they became altogether more relaxed as I abandoned interrogation and we discovered common interests. Thanks to old Trimble botany was one, a curious hobby for a boy who professed to hate the woods, but

I refrained from pointing this out; that year a hot summer and a wet autumn had raised outlandish fairy rings, horse mushrooms, circles of shaggy ink caps and other rather more exotic fungi, on the summer's now deserted playing fields. Here, well out in the open and free of Egon's fear of claustrophobic foliage, we foraged and saved specimens, and in the evenings, compared notes. As the term drew on into November I discovered his other esoteric passions. Among these were astronomy and Egyptology, and he needed little prompting to begin a written project on the pharaoh Akhnaton, a true loner if ever there was one. Yet he seemed as obligingly sociable a creature, when I watched him among his fellows, as he had in the first few weeks. I hoped they'd had the good sense to invite him to join their gang. He was so biddable, such a conformist both in and out of class. Whatever the gang's function, I couldn't suppose it malevolent, and, foolishly perhaps, I let the matter ride.

I had, however, spoken to him about Alec, and as so often in these cases when you prepare yourself with an elaborate brief, your intended victim is there way ahead of you, with arguments you never anticipated.

'He wanted to marry my mother but she wouldn't have him in the end and she married my father instead,' said Egon as if reciting a particularly obvious and tedious passage from Caesar's Gallic campaign. 'I sometimes wonder what it would have been like if she'd married Alec,' he mused, and if he saw me gaping at his calm even-handedness, he pretended not to show it. 'It might have been more sensible really. Though in a way I think it was brave of her to stay in Germany, she must have known war was coming and she'd be on the wrong side. Don't you think?'

'Very much so,'

'Alec says she didn't really make up her mind till the last moment, but I don't see why that's so bad. They were probably both very attractive then,' I bite my lip at the 'then', 'and it wasn't an easy choice at all. I'd have waited till the last minute too.'

This time, happily, he doesn't ask me if I agree.

'And I think she knew she'd have been happy with Alec too. At least during the war, because he *was* a frightfully brave commando.' This is spoken with a sweet and delicate touch of irony that leaves its tenderness and genuine admiration intact. I am boggling.

'He was indeed,' I murmur.

'And then he started drinking too much. And she might have stopped it...' he is gazing dreamily, not at me, but out into the darkness beyond the windows, artfully showing me his fantasy at play, 'or she might not. And she might have left him. If he didn't stop drinking.'

'Who knows what might have happened. Do you ever talk about it with Alec?'

'Goodness no. He jumps at the sound of her name, and clams right up.'

'And about your father... does he...?'

'Pretty much the same. I don't think they got on.'

And he gave me a small man-to-man smile in which, behind the convoluted psychological scaffolding I had recently erected, the whole edifice of my anxiety collapsed. I could almost see Alec laughing in my face.

Coming back late one night from Liskeard, it was a clear November night and I was driving slowly, enjoying the sight of the school buildings ahead, their bulk and their curious excrescences like a mediaeval citadel, when I caught sight of a torch in Tupholme Wood, inside the grounds. I parked the Wolseley outside the gates, put on my scarf and hat, buttoned up my overcoat and made my way through laurel and rhododendron, along paths through the undergrowth made by generations of boys.

When I emerged, now with only a stretch of lawn to cross between myself and the mounded pine-wood, I could see that there was more than one torch, shielded by fingers that glowed red across the lens. A lesser pin-point of light glowed gold, faded again, then glowed once more like an impetuous glow-worm: a cigarette.

I had never come across a nocturnal gathering of this kind, and was tempted to retreat and leave them to it. Spying only made me feel old and foolish, and the behatted adult who might shortly step among them from behind a pine-tree struck me as little more than an envious spoilsport. I did envy them; but without spite. I was happy for them, and having decided I wouldn't interrupt them, I let my enjoyment of their game draw me closer, for a better look.

It was only when I saw that one of them was Marshall, a boy in Egon's year, and another his sidekick Vanstone, that I remembered the 'gang' Ball had mentioned. I moved closer still, now curious to see if Egon was among them.

He wasn't.

And even then I was peering at their faces, looking more for a vicarious taste of their activities than seeking to identify them any of them, other than the boy I doted on. It was a while before I noticed anything about their clothes.

Unsurprised, I thought: it's uniform. A military game, the most likely kind. Then I saw that if they were borrowed from the school Corps it was with major transformations, it wasn't the night alone that showed up hands and face above dark clothes, the uniforms themselves were black. With silver insignia. I was still taking this in as one of the boys produced the last few cigarettes out of a packet, and made to cut them to give everyone a shortened smoke. It was no knife he drew to do it, as the boys gathered round a tree stump to light the operation with their torches. As the long, broad blade came into the light I saw it was a ceremonial SS dagger. Or at least a passable imitation. The watching boys softly stamped their feet and hugged themselves against the cold, and for a heady moment I had a sense of being transported in time to the last days of the Reich, to a spot where youthful, shivering recruits kept watch in a pine-wood they'd been ordered to defend to their last breath: 'Werewolves', as these tragic units were dubbed. Nazi decorations dangled in the torchlight as the uniformed children bent over the tree stump and the freshly cut butts; then as I heard Marshall's familiar chortle and a hiss of 'Tough luck, Fenwick, you creep,' I saw the whole charade for what it was, my children aping Nazis, and I had to restrain myself from charging in, enraged.

At that moment I wanted to kill them. And perhaps even if I hadn't had Egon in my charge I would have felt the same. My pacifist days were long over; so much so that I often ask myself how real they ever were, in the days when I welcomed 'conchies' to the Ark. I had my own reasons for doing so, and they were never expressed in idealistic terms. War-scarred veterans were just as welcome for a respite between battles. I didn't try to discourage them from going back. But I loathed the xenophobic code that ruled the military life and nourished itself at its roots in civilian bigotry. Since then I'd grown more cynical, I thought; but no, that too was a convenient mask; I wanted to spray Tupholme Wood with bullets.

Then I heard brisk, authoritative footsteps behind me, crunching across the frosty ground. And saw the boys stiffen, swiftly extinguishing their torches and grinding out their cigarettes beneath what looked distinctly like School Corps boots from the armoury. Tough luck indeed, you little bastards, I thought, someone else has gone and spotted the torchlight, and I looked round to see who it was. Now their goose was cooked.

But the boys weren't running. When I glanced round in the darkness, they seemed to have formed up in a line, and their stiffness was a parade posture, not terror.

The figure they were waiting for strode past me, barely ten feet away, all I saw was a peaked SS officer's cap; and heard a voice I didn't recognize bark low, authentic-sounding German orders.

'*Zu Befehl, Herr Hauptmann!*' came Marshall's hiss, in an execrable accent, which for an instant broke my rage.

Then the *Hauptmann* switched on his torch, held in black-gloved hands, and by the faint light that reached his face I saw that it was Egon.

I HADN'T SPOKEN to Alec Thurgo since our 'bachelor's lunch' together, though I'd written him a note of thanks, and heard nothing further. Now I wondered whether to contact him immediately or not, with my unpleasant shred of news. I dreaded it, and thought up reasons to defer telling him; the man who had kept Egon's suicide attempt from me could hardly complain if . . . but no, no, tit-for-tat was no justification.

If I'm honest, there was another aspect to it. I was in Winterson's position, and the laugh was on me, after the sneers I'd treated him to. I was afraid Alec would remove Egon from a school where his fellows were apparently so eager to join him in Nazi games.

But damn the risk, either I believed in being open with Alec about the boy, as I'd demanded he should be with me, or I didn't. I phoned him.

To my bewilderment, when I told him about the Tupholme Wood brigade he hooted with glee.

'What, all crying *Jawohl mein Führer!*, were they?'

'That sort of thing,' I said, adding feebly, 'I didn't see any Nazi salutes,' as if this were a sign of hope.

'You know, there were some damn good units in the German army,' Alec said, 'I'm not talking about the Waffen SS, mind you. Of course if I was a boy I could see the appeal of the old black and silver. Couldn't *you*? Given that the Wehrmacht uniforms weren't much to write home about. I warned their Chief of Staff about it in '37. Beck. Hopeless man. I *told* him, if you dress them like stewardesses, they'll fight like stewardesses. But of course *he* didn't want to fight at all.'

'I thought you said some of their units fought rather well,' I murmured to gain time, confounded by his whole approach.

'So I did. Well, if you've ever got into a fight with a stewardess, you'll know *they're* no pushover either.' Alec chuckled heartily into the receiver.

'You're saying you don't mind Egon dressing up in full SS regalia?'

'That's your business, Hanbury. I can't say I'd be thrilled if I were you, though it does show a certain inventiveness. Eh? I suppose you can find the decorations at a souvenir shop, but the uniforms must take a bit of tailoring.' He paused, waiting me out, perhaps listening to my silence. 'I mean, keep a sense of proportion, man. He'll grow out of it.'

I was too choked to answer.

'Here's an idea for you,' he continued cheerfully. 'There were some damn fine skirmishes in Normandy, why don't you get the whole school to recreate one, sounds like you wouldn't have much trouble recruiting chaps to line up for the other side and get killed. Boys love playing at being killed, it's the best part of it. What do you think? Bloody good history lesson. Make it a Sunday and I'll come down and hand out the medals.'

'It's a thought,' I said glumly.

'Look,' he sighed, changing tone, 'if you want the honest truth I never much fancied the idea of turning Egon into a little Englishman.

There was already too much of that in his father for my liking. Wanting to be English, when he wasn't. Boy's German. Try and remember that.'

'Half German,' I said, hoping there was no need to remind Alec of the emotion he'd shown when admitting me to the written thoughts of Egon's British parent.

'And proud of it, by the sound of things.'

'I don't believe what I'm hearing, Alec. You don't think it makes any difference that it's precisely the SS who took away his father *and* his mother?'

'Hold hard,' he said, 'I know that voice. If you're going to give me more head-shrinker talk, you can save it for the boy. Or point a real psychiatrist at him, with my blessing, as long as you don't send me the bill. Bright chap like him can run rings round them, you know that.'

I said nothing for a while. Then his voice came again, in parting.

'Don't lose your sense of humour, Hanbury. War's over.'

For a time I toyed with the idea of putting Alec's suggestion into practice, and mobilizing full-scale World War Two manoeuvres, in the hope of exorcizing the school's obsession. But would it exorcize it, or only feed it? And if I understood anything at all about Egon's motives for forming a resistance movement against the nostalgic 'Got you, Jerry!' jingoism of his schoolmates, then the last thing he wanted was to bring it out into the open.

Underneath it all, I knew I was still angry. Angry with Egon; betrayed, hurt.

Like Alec I could see the appeal of the uniform to boys like Marshall, Vanstone and the rest; it disgusted me, but once my rage at them had subsided I could give them a kind of perverse credit for going against the herd, and even, if I had to, for locating the brutal charm of the Devil's party; to deny it could only increase its appeal. But that was as far as Alec's suggested sense of humour got me. I didn't think it an amusing game for Egon to strut proudly in imitation of the men who'd murdered his parents. For some reason it was the black gloves that sickened me most of all.

When I summoned Egon that night and told him without preamble what I'd seen in Tupholme Wood, he gazed at me in silence as if I were the enemy.

Half of me, the sentimental half, had hoped for a tearful collapse. But the other half had anticipated this stony reaction, and the pain of seeing our past evenings go for nothing. To assure him that I hadn't been spying on him, I explained how it had come about that I'd noticed the torchlight in the wood as I drove home, and the glow of the cigarettes—to my own frustration I heard myself sounding like an officer reproaching an NCO for his men's sloppiness. As I spoke it occurred to me that they must have seen the Wolseley leave, and picked their moment, not expecting me back so soon.

And still he said nothing. His small, disciplined figure had adopted precisely the look of defiance, erect yet casual, that we'd all learnt from interrogation scenes in war films. I wanted to shake it from his body, I felt all the interrogator's lust to smack the smirking victim's face from side to side. I loved you, you little cretin—didn't you understand that? How dare you treat me like this? My wounded rage, banging stupidly in my head, restored some sanity: at last, I thought, I know a parent's fury.

'If you don't want to talk about it, I can't make you,' I said. 'But I want to know a little more about what happened at Beale. They got at you for being German, didn't they.'

He wouldn't speak, and the flecked grey eyes stared right through me.

'How can it harm you now, to tell me? You'll never have to see them again. I promise you that.'

Something wavered in his face. But what? I had his attention, and groped in vain for the right move, till anger overtook me again.

'Can't you trust me, for God's sake? You'll have to trust someone sooner or later. Is there someone else you'd like to talk to?'

He looked me in the eyes, and I could feel the astonishment in my own face, at what I saw there.

'You mean you're not going to throw me out?' he said.

'I'm never going to throw you out,' I heard myself say. And came to my senses again. 'Unless you go round telling people what I just said. It would make things rather hard for me. But as long as it's our secret, and you want to stay, I promise you won't have to leave until you're ready to.'

I saw the tears begin, and wanted to hug him now.

I let him cry until I saw him searching for a handkerchief he didn't have, then I rose, dropped my handkerchief in his lap, and went and poured myself a Scotch, something I'd only ever done to keep visitors company. I stayed at the sideboard, listening to his sobs. *I didn't have to become his guardian, you know…* How often had Egon wondered, in the past, whether Alec would send him back to Hamburg?

'There was a Dutch boy,' Egon said. 'He was the worst.'

I returned to my chair as he began to enumerate the age-old, pitiless cruelties. Ostracism, sneers; no need for beatings, there never was. Swastikas drawn on the wall, on his desk, his clothes. Once even a hanged man. 'I thought you were taking me back there, when we went to Beale.'

'You thought *what*? That I was going to leave you there?'

He nodded. 'The whole Exeter thing, with Fishburn, I thought it might be just a way to get me to go.'

'What did you think you'd done wrong here?'

He said nothing.

'I mean… our talks,' I blabbered.

'Everyone wants to talk to me,' he said drily. 'Adults, I mean.'

'Damn it, they don't all care as much about you as I do. I know I've asked all the obvious questions—and of course I'm fascinated by what happened to you, you'd feel the same if it was someone else, someone you came across. Don't you think?'

He nodded.

'And it's not because you're an orphan. You're not alone in that, there are other boys who've been through hell, we had a French boy here before your time who'd seen both his grandparents killed in front of him.' Under his gaze I feel an inward shudder—*what* did I just say?… *care about you as I do?* How could I have said it? Flushed with shame, as if I'd caught myself trying to steal the boy, 'To be honest with you I don't know why I care about you so much, it isn't pity and it isn't simply curiosity. I've never experienced anything that remotely resembles what you've been through, I didn't even fight in the war, you know that. Perhaps you're helping *me*. I know I wish all my life I'd been as brave and resourceful as you.'

He'd turned stony again; it spurred me on.

'It was you that formed the gang, wasn't it, not Marshall and Vanstone and the others.'

Still the bazilisk eyes.

'I have my own ideas why you did it. You can tell me if they're wrong. I think it wasn't enough just to fit in, though you had to make the effort—it hadn't served you well at Beale, to try and live up to being who you were. So this time you thought you'd get in first, you chose the likeliest bully, Marshall, and used what you knew you could impress him with, to recruit him. Before he turned on *you*.'

Egon shook his head.

'No?' I said. 'What, then?'

'It wasn't anything like that. But if I tell you...'

'It's all right,' I said.

'They know I come here and talk to you.'

'No-one will know I was in Tupholme Wood, only you and I. You have my word.'

'It was Marshall's idea,' Egon said. 'I thought if I didn't join, they'd turn on me. But I knew all the right things to say, I mean in German, so...'

'You took over.' I paused. 'And you enjoyed that.'

He shrugged.

'I saw you. Remember?'

He was silent for a time.

'I make them fight the Russians. What's so bad about that?'

'Egon, a man wearing that uniform put a noose around your father's neck.'

The light in Egon's eyes died.

'It's not true,' he said.

'You know it is.'

He seemed not to have heard me. For a moment I wondered whether he'd put the cord around his neck, that night at Beale, to discover... but then he was speaking again, words I couldn't take in at first.

'He wasn't my father,' Egon said.

I stared at him, but he wouldn't meet my eyes.

'Egon, you're not suggesting...'

He looked up. 'I'm not suggesting *what*?' he said. 'I'm telling you he wasn't my father.'

'Wasn't your father?' I still couldn't grasp what he was saying. 'What makes you think that?'

'Because she wasn't my mother either. My real mother was killed by the Russians and I saw her being dragged away.'

'What *real* mother?'

'She was called Herta. I don't remember anything about her, but I know her name.'

'Egon, who told you this?'

He ignored me. 'I know she was taken away by the Russians. I don't remember it but I must have seen it, I was told I saw it.'

The tears were coming now, but they were different, fiercer.

'For God's sake, what gave you this idea? Did Alec say so?'

'He doesn't know. He wouldn't have taken me if he knew. If you tell him I'll kill myself.'

'I won't tell him, nothing you tell me will go outside these walls. Nothing! You understand?' I couldn't tell anything from his expression. 'Now, where did you get all this?'

But he'd clammed up.

'If it's true,' I said, 'who *is* your father?'

'I mustn't tell you.'

'Look,' I said, 'you've got to help me, you've got to tell me where you got this from.'

'It's my business. I shouldn't have told you.'

'All right,' I said. 'You're right. It's your affair, and I've no right to pry.'

I waited him out, but nothing came.

'I want you to disband the Nazi thing.'

'Why?' All the old defiance was there.

'Because it's loathsome, Egon. Because the SS killed innocent boys your age without a second thought. I forbid it, d'you understand me? I want you to tell me you won't do it any more.'

'And if I refuse?'

For an instant I was staring into the *Hauptmann*'s eyes, trapped in them like the ominous black dot of a moon that floated, captured, in one iris. I watched the pupil flex like a spider's sac when he blinked.

128

'I'm going to set you some reading, Egon. What's more I'm going to quiz you on it. And as long as you can continue to describe to me, accurately, based on the reading I've set you, the conditions in Auschwitz and Ravensbrück, Treblinka and Belsen, you can keep putting on the uniform and meeting at night in Tupholme Wood. I'll have the books for you tomorrow.'

WAS IT REMOTELY possible that Alec was the boy's father? That's if there was any truth in what Egon was saying. He clearly believed what he'd told me. He hadn't said as much, yet—Alec: it was the thought that had jumped into my mind... yes, from the very way Egon had refused to say who his father was. Egon had also said that Alec would never have taken him, if he'd known the truth. Yet that too, perhaps... even that was not entirely incompatible with Alec as the father. If Herta had been the serving girl, the 'idiot' as Thurgo had described her to me, whom he'd met in 1937 and '38 at Peter's schloss, who he said had looked after Egon during his childhood... would he disown a child of his by a German 'idiot'? With that man anything was possible.

I had to find out.

And if it was true, then Egon was, what—seventeen? Perhaps all of eighteen, nineteen even, a thought I didn't want to address. If it was demonstrably true, I might lose him from my care.

But I had to know, and the only person I knew of who could tell me was Alec's brother Richard. Alec had said he'd had no news of him for several years. Last heard of in Hamburg making pornographic films. Would I be able to locate such a man, in Hamburg? I'd never even been abroad, and the whole idea filled me with terror. Even the smallest impulsive action, when I find I'm considering one, restores my childhood fears: I'm planning to steal half-a-crown from Father. And yet it's always the impulsive actions, the ones that make me groan inwardly, *why* am I *doing* this? that have brought me the greatest rewards.

Above all I wanted to do something practical for Egon; and this was surely it. Whether it was what he wanted was another question. Perhaps, if I was able to learn anything, that would vary according to the outcome. No, I had to believe that in Egon's situation the truth, whatever it was, would be an improvement on the nightmare he was living at present.

SO IT WAS that during the Christmas holidays that year, Christmas 1955, I made my apologies as best I could to my mother and to my sister Ellen, with whom my mother had been living since my father's death, and took a boat from Harwich to the port of Hamburg (anything not to fly; I'd rather have swum).

It was the first Christmas I'd spent away from Mother in my forty-three years of life, and the prospect, I have to admit, rather delighted me. I saw myself spending it in a raucous, smoke-filled *Bierhalle*, being slapped on the back by beefy men in *Lederhosen* crying (rather like Alec though in a very different accent), 'Ze war iss over, yes?' *Another schnapps for my friend!* And seeing the New Year in, outdoors, beneath what my guidebook assured me were the finest fireworks in Europe, during 'Hamburg's famed *Silvesterabend*.'

In this latter fantasy the gigantic figure of Richard Thurgo stood beside me in the dark with one gorilla arm looped round my shoulders, his face (God, what a face it was!) intermittently lit by the starbursts above us, as he solemnly recited the truth about the Thurgo family. I'd found him—somehow—hunched in a porno-graphic cellar (small, dim? With flickering black-and-white *Mädchen* undressing coyly on the wall?—all I could picture, I realized, was Victorian erotica jolting mechanically through seafront viewing machines) or no, better... suddenly hailed by him in the street: *Hanbury?! My God, it is you! Hanbury!*

How I was really going to find him I had no idea, short of becoming an *habitué* of pornographic cellars. Alec had told me that, so far as he knew, Richard would be entirely unknown to the British Consulate; let alone the telephone directory, since he was living under an adopted name and hadn't vouchsafed it to Alec.

Nonetheless I was going with Alec's blessing, and a letter to his brother. 'If you ever find him, kick him up the rump from me, then stick this in his hairy hand,' was the fraternal salutation. Needless to say I hadn't told Alec I was going to Hamburg to try and discover

Egon's true paternity, but merely that I hoped to fill in some of the gaps in the boy's memory where his origins were concerned.

'And dally in the fleshpots, for research purposes...?' Alec had gleamed. 'I'd come with you if I had the time.'

He'd studied me, more seriously.

'Come on, Hanbury, why *are* you doing it?'

'I'm fond of the boy. He needs every bit of past I can locate for him.'

Alec nodded, negligently. 'They said you weren't queer. I checked. Board of Governors said they *thought* you weren't queer, just limp-wristed by nature. That wasn't how they put it, of course, but it was what I gathered. You're *not* queer, are you? I mean, you're not going to fall in love with the boy?'

'Depends what you mean by love.'

'Don't prevaricate, man. *Are* you bloody queer for him or aren't you?'

'I'm not.'

'You'd better not be, or I'll come and cut it off myself. If you find Richard, tell him Donovan hasn't put in an appearance and that I'm still in the old cottage. And that...'—an appalling attack of Thurgo sentimentality was on the way, I could see it in his eyes—'that... he can always come and stay here, if he cares to.' He cleared his throat. 'Until Donovan shows up.'

I wish I could say I had Egon's blessing too. 'Don't,' he'd said when I told him I was going, 'please don't,' as if I was proposing a painful injection. But something in him—or perhaps I only wanted to believe this—contradicted his words. I had to believe some part of him was as curious to know the truth as I was, even if he had to have it forced on him. He sat very still; I told him I would only disclose as much, or as little, as he wanted to hear of any discoveries I made, and only to him.

Our relations had been muted for several weeks. In the event I'd questioned him very little on the death camp books I'd given him. Enough to know he'd been reading them. I didn't even ask him if his gang had been disbanded. But I'd seen no more flashes of torchlight in Tupholme Wood; I kept close watch.

My first glimpse of Hamburg, as I emerged on deck that December morning, made me wonder how on earth we'd won the war. The port seemed to go on for ever, the Elbe barely narrowing as an interminable line of ships and gantries, ancient dockside storehouses barely touched, it seemed, by our bombing, loomed on either side. Thriving, too, alive with clanging blows and shouts; between container ships from Valparaiso, Cape Town, Tokyo, I saw a dozen half-completed tankers, naked in their freshly gleaming boiler-plates, awaiting paint but already pointing threateningly towards the river, on their slipways. That's when it first came home to me: perhaps we hadn't won the war.

I'd hardly slept at all, during the crossing; I was too excited, I suppose, as eager as a child on his first trip abroad. But I dreaded the prospect of a day half asleep on my feet, in a busy German city. I'd lain stretched out on my berth in the dark trying unsuccessfully to sleep and when at last I did, I only took my anxiety into my sleep with me, so that, asleep and dreaming, I was still anxious about getting to sleep.

Strangely, the first sound I heard when I awoke took me back home, to Liskeard I mean: seagulls crying in the same international seagull-tongue, scabrous and cynical as any sailor's, that screeched and laughed above Liskeard's Parade; that, as I write these words, is screeching and laughing now above Webb's, as though the seagulls can see it all, and know better than anyone the mocking twists of the story I have to tell.

Thereafter, the languages I met on my first day in Hamburg were incomprehensible to me, whether dialect or *Hochdeutsch*, of which I later taught myself a smattering. They were the most unfamiliar thing about Hamburg, which to my disappointment had a curiously English air to it, beginning with the air itself, the weather, and the British suits and overcoats—the *Lederhosen* I'd pictured clearly belonged to Munich; I didn't see a single pair in all my time in the city.

Where to start? Assuming I knew the answer, I'd belaboured Egon about precisely who had told him that Maggie and Peter weren't his parents; Richard, I took it. But when at last the boy spoke up it was to say that he might as well tell me since it wouldn't do me any good: he didn't know her name or her address. Yes, a woman, a very old woman he'd visited a few times, a psychiatrist. Richard knew her, he said, and called her the crone, *die Alte*, or when he was in a jocular mood, the dodderer. How many ancient, doddering psychiatrists would there be, in Hamburg? A needle, if ever there was one, in a Freudian haystack.

Richard held both the keys I needed; to the psychiatrist, and to what he knew himself—if he would tell me. 'Try the Reeperbahn,' Alec had said blithely, 'find the most disreputable joint, have a couple of beers, he'll be along, you'll see.'

If it was going to be as easy as that I didn't have to plunge into the utmost squalor immediately on disembarking, I decided, and treated myself to a wander around Richard's adoptive city, thinking about the meeting to come. As I've mentioned, for a time he and I had traded letters occasioned by Denis Towle's suicide. This had been during the post-war years when Richard was practising as a solicitor in London, before his own bizarre 'death' and disappearance in 1948. I hadn't seen him in the flesh since his visit to the Ark with Denis in '44; in eleven years I'd changed somewhat in appearance, fuller in the freckled face and with a lot less of the carroty hair I'd never much liked anyway—I looked a little more distinguished, I thought; he, on the other hand, couldn't but be unmistakable at this or any stage of his life. I'd knew I'd recognize him at a hundred yards and more, in any crowded city in the world. I'd guess that he was six foot six or seven, and looked bigger, since unlike those who grow tall and spindly, his body was a giant's, well proportioned apart from those gorilla arms and the lardy, club-like hands he was forever trying to hide. Not a man who could easily engineer his own disappearance, you might think; but he did. More than anything, and despite his size, it was the face you remembered: a face like shiny plaster, shaped like Mr Punch, all jutting forehead, nose and chin, but without the puppet's traditional red lips and gleeful smile. In the great jaw the mouth was uneven, sunk over bad teeth; the eyes were small and piggy under his huge brow, and the thatch of hair that sprayed up above it was more like a tuft of coarse black grass than anything that usually grew on a human head. This ogre's appearance—which surely served him well in the stews of Hamburg—hid a gentle, wary disposition, apparently unable to accustom itself to the effect his physiognomy had on others. He must have known how fearsome he looked; but it takes a mirror, or the expression on another person's face, to remind us of that exterior that fails to correspond to our intention.

When he'd arrived unannounced at the Ark with Denis, who was every bit as handsome as Richard was ugly, I'd unthinkingly assumed from his expression that Richard was the one in need of care, brought here for recuperation by the classic military type at his side, my old friend Denis, erect, gold-haired with strong, fine features and an air of invincible nobility; they might have stepped out of a fairy tale together. Indeed if I hadn't known Denis from his Alfriston days I'd have thought Flight Lieutenant Thurgo was having me on when he said it was his companion who was having the nervous breakdown. Most bizarrely of all, one of Denis's chief delusions was that Richard Thurgo was his missing twin. Denis, it's true, feared and sought to dismiss his own beauty, but an unlikelier pair of siblings you could never have found.

It emerged that Denis had long believed that he was one of twins, that the other had died at birth, and that his parents had kept this from him. In later years I've discussed this particular delusion with psychiatrists, who nod wearily as if all too familiar with it; more than once I've had the impression that what seems like the bewildering diversity of madness is as finite and predictable, to the initiate, as a row of dress uniforms lined up on tailor's dummies. To me in my innocence Denis's confessions were a breathless adventure through a constantly shifting mythological landscape I never knew could exist in a single human mind; with Proteus as my guide. Denis had always felt himself crippled by his beauty, or rather spiritually—if that's the word—eviscerated by it; it denied him to himself; and the twin, he had always supposed, had carried with him into death not only his own substance, his self, his soul, but his portion of ugliness as well. He'd stolen Denis' birthright. Only now Denis had discovered that it was not true that the twin, Derek, had died. No, Derek had been adopted (the twin's repellent looks, Denis now believed, had driven his parents to this, since they worshipped beauty—and this was also why Derek's survival had been hidden from him); adopted and re-named by a family called Thurgo. And they had met at last.

This was purest fantasy, as I learnt from Denis's parents. There had been no twin. The truth was that at the interrogation centre where he and Richard had met, where they worked side by side interviewing captured German air-crew, Denis had fallen deeply in love, for the first time: with 'Mad' Trimble's daughter Molly, Richard's wife. A love requited, or so Denis claimed. Yet loyalty was strangling him: it was, Denis said, like being 'at full throttle, with the brakes jammed on'. Fresh from the breakdown I had witnessed at Alfriston, Denis foundered again.

It was a sad story, *Beauty and the Beast* recast in an unpromising form and rendered comical by the fact that these two decent, upright men, profoundly fond of each other, were unaware of the murderous fuse that connected them. Meeting with them separately and in turn, it was I who knew that Denis, in his moments of derangement when he was no longer himself, thirsted to kill Derek. That's to say to kill Richard Thurgo, his supposed 'evil twin' and rival in love, before Richard killed him. I also knew, as the lumbering, puzzled 'twin' did not, what Denis was up to with his wife, for which Richard would, I think, have wrung his neck without breaking sweat. There were no brakes on Richard. I must have seemed the most anxious confidant either of them had ever met.

And the least successful. It all came to a ghastly end in the hospital the Towles had chosen for Denis, at Horsham. In one of his letters Richard assures me that in death Denis found not only a longed-for quietus but a wholeness he could never have known in life. Without knowing for sure what lies in wait for us beyond the grave—all I can do myself, as I tell my own flock, is pray that being united to God is no less than the soul's promise of a return home—that wholeness Richard speaks of is a matter of individual apprehension. At times I have felt, I think, as riven as Denis; and yet find it hard to accept that I or anyone should abandon the search for atonement in this life, and return the buck to God. I see that this sounds unforgiving. I salute all tortured souls, including those who put an end to their torments themselves. But for me our wager with existence can only mean, I suppose, that hope lies at the heart of things (fear and uncertainty, even despair... don't they all derive from thwarted hope?); indeed that time, the fall from grace, *is* hope.

Or perhaps I've never been in sufficient pain to feel capable of mocking existence itself, like Denis.

Egon's suicide attempt brought it all back of course, and now when I thought of the boy it was no longer as he was in the washrooms at Beale, picking himself up of the floor, sentenced once more to life; but rather as he must have been during the nights that preceded it, lying in his narrow bed. I tried to feel out in my mind the flaw, the failure of will that finally drew him to the act—or is it precisely the force of will, and courage, that pushes you beyond self-pity into action? And the wolf-child, the aborigine in Egon, what part did he play in the decision? His silence in memory, his oblivion, was perhaps already a kind of suicide. The aborigines themselves were said to lie down and die if incarcerated, forcibly enclosed.

Richard, the most aboriginal-looking person I have ever come across, escaped from his own incarceration by subtly different means. Fed up with 'small claims courts and that fat cow of a wife', as Alec put it, Richard used the opportunity of a car crash in Spain, which nearly killed him and incinerated his travelling companion, to begin a new life, in Germany; leaving the victim of the crash to be identified, by circumstantial evidence, as himself. And to be duly buried as Richard Thurgo in Highgate cemetery.

'Why Germany of all places?' I asked Alec.

'He loved it. Absolutely bloody loved the place. He's a scatter-brain, you know, behind all that peasant brawn. So are the Germans. Dreamers: it's their downfall.'

It looked to be anything but their downfall, that day in Hamburg. The *Wirtschaftswunder* was well under way, the city was full of prosperous citizens wearing the best foreign cloth, it had broad streets and new buildings bristling with glass. London seemed a drab, defeated place by comparison; we were the ones with the debilitating dreams, flying Spitfires and Hurricanes into a vanished sunset.

When I'd had enough of this humiliation—disgusted to find what an envious little Englander and jingoist I was—I asked a passer-by firmly for 'das Reeperbahn', to be rewarded by the kind of smile that, I take it, greets tourists all over the world when they ask for the red-light district.

I wasn't sure the Reeperbahn would be a modest strip of seamy clubs and film shows, easily scanned for Richard's towering figure. I really didn't know what to expect of it, but I was taken aback by the sheer length of the street and its remorseless trade, 'the mile of sin' as I now know it is justly called. In the warren of side-streets even more perverse activities than on the Reeperbahn itself, to judge by the graphic art on its painted-over windows, awaited the decadent visitor. I couldn't believe I was here, that it was my eyes staring at it, at them. This was somebody else, not the Reverend J. Hanbury, Headmaster, somebody who had temporarily taken over my body and overcoat, and wafted me away in time to this world of Arabian Nights. Or rather Arabian Nights were far too coy, there were no veils to be seen here. These were what my father would have called 'Turkish tarts'; irrespective of their nationality all tarts were Turkish to him, for some reason I never fathomed. I'm almost ashamed to say it, but I had never seen pictures of naked coupling before, not even confiscated from my boys at the school—if they circulated there, they circulated without stopping at me. I would have stood longer in front of the photographs outside the Grand Théâtre Comique-Érotique and such places, if it wasn't for the incessant pestering of the doormen. 'Come in, you want girls? *Entrez, monsieur! Fatevi a casa!*'

I have to say I did, in time, 'make myself at home' at René Durand's Grand Théâtre Comique-Érotique—though not at my own instigation—and met the famed René, a fierce fellow in a short, sharp Spanish beard. But at first I simply gawped, unable to think how I was going to scour these dimly lit, cavernous places their barkers revealed, raising heavy plush curtains in invitation. If I'd had the German or the nerve, I might have swept through flashing false credentials, crying *Polizei!* and even (based on films set in POW camps) *Raus, Schweinhund!* ... or, more sensibly, whatever the German was for 'Fire Inspector!'. How else would I ever flush out a Thurgo from these labyrinths?—and as yet I didn't know that Richard's empire lay in real tunnels beneath my feet, miles and miles of former wartime bunkers, enough to hide the Red Army, never mind a single Englishman in German disguise.

But I was far from despairing, that first day. The shock of mingling with porno-tourists and pavement girls, who also accosted me incessantly in a variety of languages, was quite enough to hold me in a daze; I got lost several times, but the bright lights of the cinemas kept hauling me back into the Reeperbahn's orbit. *All Hands On Dick* was the title, I remember, of one ostensibly naval saga, but if the dick was Richard's—and I was well past the point of averting my eyes, I was looking everywhere for a sign of him—the close-ups were too intently anatomical to reveal it.

Utterly exhausted, my head full of entangled limbs, I resorted to the Alec-strategy and sat drinking beer in a sordid café, where a quarrel in a North African language which sounded like camels spitting erupted into a full-scale brawl. It may have been an everyday transaction to them, but to me it was life in the raw as I'd never seen it. I watched every instant of it with what I hoped was an expression of world-weary insouciance.

I thought of my mother and Ellen, decorating the tree in Ellen's bungalow, from boxes I had unpacked and repacked and returned so often to the crowded roof space that I could have done the honours blindfold. At that moment it was as though I had been blindfolded for forty years, and I identified intensely—or thought I did—with Richard Thurgo, the man who had encountered this other, furious, untrammeled world and never gone home.

Would my sense of identification help me find the man? No, I decided. I was too scared, that day, even to enter one of the clubs, much less ask anyone if they knew a man *this* high, *sehr gross*, *sehr hoch* (I'd got these from the phrasebook but they both sounded suspiciously like *Sieg Heil* to me), and I retreated to a hotel in a more respectable quarter of the city, to fall into a sleep that, though I remembered nothing of it, must have been full of the most exotic dreams of my life.

'BITTE, EIN SEHR grosser Mann, sehr hoch...'. In the next few days I got thoroughly fed up with saying this. If Richard was as famous on the Reeperbahn as Alec claimed, they must have known whom I meant, most of them, the greasy barman, the one-armed walrus in an astrakhan hat, the girls on the street. Why were they protecting Richard? Did I look a threatening figure, someone who was looking to settle accounts with him? I, a small balding fellow with a freckled face and little beaky nose? But they either continued working, ignoring me, treated me to blank stares or else, to my embarrassment, interpreted my request as a statement of sexual preference and started discussing amongst themselves whether Hans or Georg would be *gross* and *hoch* enough to meet my requirements. Indeed it wasn't clear to me that when I said the word *gross* on the Reeperbahn it was understood to refer to any part of the body except one. Hans and Georg's measurements in this department were shown me by hand-gestures, amid loud disputes. I was back in the junior cubicles with Talbot.

Englisch Mann, I said a few times, but this had no effect at all. When I made faces to simulate the ferocity, even in repose, of Richard's features, it only made them laugh. In the end I had to remind myself that Egon hadn't wanted me to come at all, that he didn't want me to probe and would be far from disappointed if I came back empty-handed. Very well then: this was a holiday, a well-earned albeit a bizarre one.

Once I'd decided this I could have toured the churches and the sights, I suppose, the canals, the countryside, but I kept returning to the Reeperbahn, partly because I felt if I stayed there long enough I was bound to bump into Richard; partly, to be truthful, because the Reeperbahn was more fun. Now that I was here, I was determined to sample the wares. I got duly bilked, paying a fortune on champagne for girls who had no intention of entertaining me with anything more than their poor English; saw pornographic films including the aforementioned *All Hands On Dick*, a 'multi-lingual' production (the word was never more apt), which left little to be desired in the way of carnal fantasy, was poorly lit and abominably acted. Richard did not appear in it, even in name on the credits, and I began to wonder if he'd gone out of business. Or if Alec's description of his career was merely scurrilous and false. Or if he'd left the city altogether. All were possible.

Finally, having ogled the streetwalkers for days, I got up the courage and approached one. Propositioned one, I was going to say, but in truth she propositioned me. She was very large and very blonde, with a bullcalf face—but something about her, I was damned if I could say what, appealed to me.

For the equivalent of a fiver I didn't expect much in the way of amorous delights, it was the novelty that intrigued me, the whole idea of seeing whether a casual attraction in the street, a feature of my life as much as anyone else's, could be converted into gratification at the exchange of a banknote. It seemed improbable to me, and her behaviour once the banknote was handed over con-firmed this. In the street her manner had been *dolce* (if a Valkyrie can be *dolce*), wooing, even tender; I'd watched her approach other potential clients, and it was the promise of sympathy that drew me to her, I think. But as soon as money changed hands, her ensuing brusqueness seemed designed to send me back out of the room without further ado. I suppose I should have insisted on paying afterwards, but I didn't fancy a tussle with her; she was larger and stronger than I was. Sadly, the gorgeous blonde hair was a wig, a cheap one, and when I saw its lifeless filaments by the bulb that lit her sparsely furnished room, my lust expired with a sigh. How to escape? I didn't want to offend her and was still sifting through possible excuses when she led me by the hand to the basin, ignoring my protests, undid my trousers, pulled down my underpants and, when I'd stepped out of these, proceeded to wash me. This was done in silence, with none of the cooing endearments whores are supposed (by me at least) to trot out. Then again, such obligatory *tendresses* might have made the moment even more dispiriting.

I'd once been washed in this manner before. Other than as an infant at my mother's hands, I mean. And that was by Dotty the cook, Dotty the cook-cum-housemaid as my mother always described her, an oddly slighting appellation that on my mother's lips always sounded like a pretext to pay her less, rather than more, for combining two jobs. During one of my bronchial spells, it was the winter holidays and I must have been about twelve, the housemaid part of Dotty was dispatched to give me a kind of dry bath, a brisk rub with a flannel as I lay naked on towels. Looking back I think my mother was either unaware of the propensities of growing boys of twelve, having previously raised only girls; or, and perhaps this is more likely, she hadn't really taken in the fact that I *was* twelve. Least likely, though the most pleasant hypothesis, is that she knew perfectly well what she was up to, and this was my Christmas present. Doubtful, given my mother's personality; but I think my father would have been amused.

In the event my twelve-year-old genitals reacted, vividly, to Dotty's flanelled hand. So did Dotty. She was a tiny, wiry person with crabbed features and black hair so metallic and yet ungovernable that hers *looked* like a wig, although it wasn't. Not someone for whom I'd felt the slightest sexual attraction. When she saw, or rather felt, what was going on, her reaction was, to say the least, unfortunate. She removed the flannel, gazed down, and began to laugh uncontrollably. In retrospect I'd like to think this was embarrassment rather than contempt. At the time it wounded me to the core.

My erection remained, however, indifferent to humour, scorn or any other form of comment.

'Can't you get it any bigger than that?' cackled Dotty in her boozy, hoarse North London accent, and proceeded to rub me briskly to orgasm with the flannel. Briskly doesn't quite describe it; so roughly, in fact, that by the time she, and I, had finished, I was crying tears of pain and uttering barely suppressed groans—trying not to draw my parents' hair-trigger attention, though they were downstairs—and other noises which I dare say Dotty mistook for ecstasy. It was anything but ecstasy, however. It made me wary of the experience for years (for all I know that may have been Dotty's intention), and even now when ladyfriends are kind enough to reach down to take me in their hands, they hear an involuntary cry of 'Go easy!' burst from my lips before they've even touched me.

Somehow I restrained myself from telling my Hamburg bullcalf, I never discovered her name, to go easy, perhaps realizing that she wouldn't have understood and that by the time I'd explained what I meant it would be too late, since her English consisted of a strict repertoire of phrases—chiefly 'Come darling, we make love,' in a growl which would have made Marlene Dietrich envious.

As we went over to the bed I felt no prospect of an erection (though neither had I with Dotty, until it happened). We lay down together. There was no sign of improvement. I was beginning to feel thoroughly embarrassed, when the girl leant over to a bedside table, opened a drawer, brought out something I couldn't see and, turning back, goosed me sharply with what felt like an extremely blunt instrument indeed. Then I heard a whirring noise, and as she brought the mechanical dildo into action on my testicles, I was amazed to experience an almost instantaneous erection—which then carried us through the act of love; still in silence.

Now it was she who washed herself, seemingly indifferent as to whether I did or not. And she grew quite voluble. Where did I come from? Did I like German girls? Did I come often to Hamburg? Her charm, when it came, had a brittle quality but it was perfectly endearing and it wasn't her fault that I felt abruptly disheartened, lying there on the bed. For the first time I was an English school-master on holiday, a middle-aged bachelor doing what he was supposed to do; and what I'd enjoyed about the trip so far was that I wasn't doing anything that the Reverend J. Hanbury, Headmaster, was supposed to do.

We parted amicably enough, and by the time we were both back on the street and mingling with the furtive and the bold, I even managed a brief spurt of masculine pride, ludicrous as it might be. I was a cog that had not failed, in the great machinery of the Reeperbahn that drew so many from so far and wide. Was I to feel ashamed of this? Then I threw my casual truck-driver pride overboard and got arseholed drunk to celebrate.

For a time that night I went in fear of myself, wandering the streets mumbling like a stranger. What was I doing here anyway? Hunting down a family tree? Hardly. If John had lived and I had died… perhaps this was John's life I was living at last. I tottered chuckling round knots of Reeperbahn visitors, on and off the pavement. Some of them English. All it would take would be for one of them to recognize me and I could join Richard Thurgo in limbo for ever.

I'd given myself a week in Hamburg. Christmas Day had gone by, half-heartedly celebrated with toasts in bars, a phone call to my mother, and an afternoon spent in my hotel wrapping the presents I'd bought for everybody. I'd found Egon a daunting tome of German Egyptology; and an elaborate German penknife with nothing Nazi about it that I could descry. For my mother and Ellen the kind of knick-knacks I thought they'd like best—things that could be displayed, cheerful cups and wooden figurines and a couple of decorated aprons. For my colleagues, worse: beer mugs, they wouldn't have settled for less. I toyed with the idea of a souvenir for Alec, but given the doubt he already harboured about my sexuality, I decided a present might be pushing my luck too far.

On my last night in Hamburg I strode down the Reeperbahn feeling at once foolish and elated. I was a regular now, I headed for the bar of my choice without looking to left or right; I even thought a few of the doormen recognized me with a curt nod. What's more, I'd survived. I hadn't been knifed or mugged, hadn't fled the place in panic, or been found wanting in the heat of battle (the mechanical dildo would not, it was true, get a mention in despatches, but all heroes are entitled to their professional secrets). Perhaps the oddest thing about it, as I got rolling drunk that night, in solitary state, was that I no longer hoped Richard Thurgo would appear. Enquiries had failed or been stonewalled. I wanted to escape with the balance of my memories intact. I couldn't think how to begin any more, how to explain myself. Too tired to talk, in shock even after so many unfamiliar sights and smells, the last thing I wanted was a cry of 'Hanbury!', that self I'd left behind. The stale pong of revelry, sweat and booze and sex, hung in the Reeperbahn air, even in the streets, no matter how much cheap perfume and disinfectant were splashed around to hide it. My head was thick with it. I wanted to get out on the Elbe, out to sea again, and let the salt smells and the seagulls' laughter clear my mind.

If Richard Thurgo had passed me as I made my way to the Millerntor to catch the U-Bahn train, I might have let him go and walked straight past him. But he didn't. I have never been so drunk in my life, I said to myself, alone in the hotel lift, clutching my room key. I let myself fall full length, face down on the coverlet. With a final burst of energy I reached out for the telephone directory on the bedside table. This is your last chance, Thurgo, I said, you miserable aborigine. Either you're in this blasted book—which I hadn't bothered to consult, since Alec had told me I'd be wasting my time—or you can go to hell. You can keep the Reeperbahn and everyone in it. I've seen it, I've done it—I was fumbling through the Ts, Th, Thurmann, Thurow, go back—and I've... Thurfeldt. Thurmann.

No Thurgo. There.

No Thurgo: ergo, no psychiatrist, no 'dodderer'. No ergo. As a joke against it all, I turned to D. You see, damn it? No Dodderer.

But there it was, staring at me.

Doderer. Not Dodderer, admittedly, but *Doderer, von, A.-M.*

I stared at it; only one Doderer. Could this be Richard's dodderer?

It wasn't late, I was a cheap and rapid drunk, but it was well past office hours. Only one number, though, perhaps home. I dialled it.

Two rings sufficed.

'Ja?' A military bark. A man's voice, I thought, and nearly put the phone down. But I was drunk and slow, and lying on my front, and before I could move the voice returned, less aggressive now, 'Wer ist da?', and I recognized it as an old woman's voice, deep and throaty.

ENTERING ANNA-MARIA VON Doderer's apartment was like being transported to turn-of-the-century Vienna, as I imagined it. With its dark, heavy wooden furniture, its oriental figurines and rugs adorning the couch as well as the floors in the room where she received me, it may for all I know have been a replica of Freud's consulting room; at any rate its tone was close enough to photographs I've seen of the original to bring tears, I would guess, to faithful neurotic eyes. The furniture polish brought tears to mine; and that was before I'd tasted the Dodderer's schnapps.

When Egon had said 'an old woman' I had allowed for youthful overstatement, and expected a woman in late middle-age; but the Dodderer was extremely old indeed. She may have been all of ninety, more perhaps, and I could not in all conscience be more flattering than to say she looked no more than eighty-five, by lamplight. Some old people shrink (in size I mean); most do, I suppose. A few swell, and Anna-Maria was one of these. Two perfectly well-equipped faces could have been carved from her great handbag of a face—I admit they would only have had one eye each, but ample cheek, brow, and chin; and her wattles would have supplied a full council of the Veterans of Foreign Wars. As for her ears, I couldn't take my eyes off them; elephantine was hardly the word, they were like the speakers that come hinged on either side of certain record players, except that in her case they seemed hinged forwards the better to hear, rather than to play, the smallest sound you made. Thanks to heavy, jewelled earrings, they stretched almost the full length of her face; it made you want to apologize for coughing in case it had deafened her. I wondered what Egon—what any child—made of such a face bending down towards it like a falling Buddha, or like one of the great ships I'd passed, poised on their slipway, angled down, and whose vertiginous height had sent a tingle of fear straight to my scrotum; I could imagine a child screaming at the approaching mass. But I must have been wrong, for she was, as I discovered, a child psychiatrist.

Perhaps it was adults who were more alarmed by her looks, because she greeted me at the door with what seemed like exaggerated zeal and friendliness. Her features were as large as the expanses they had to fill; as a result her every facial response seemed histrionic.

'My dear Mr Henbury! Or is it Doctor? Or Professor?!' Her English was more than adequate, but her vitality was staggering. 'You have no idea! This is the pleasure of my last ten years, to meet my Egon's teacher! Come and have something to drink with me at once, and something to eat, and tell me all about the little monster. If you tell me he is no longer a monster I will whip you!' With a dramatic gesture she pointed at the wall of the lobby, where indeed a huge dark bullwhip of African origin hung menacingly among drums and spears. 'I say this to my patients, even the little ones: if you do not misbehave,' her huge old eyes sparkled with glee, 'I will *whip* you! How long do you stay in Hamburg? Come! This way!'

My taxi ride had done nothing to clear my head; I was still drunk, and so overwhelmed by the Dodderer that I assumed she had misspoken, or I had misheard, what she said about whipping her patients unless they *mis*behaved. But I was quickly disabused of this.

'You must understand,' she said as she filled my hands with what looked like a plateful of cold cuts on pumpernickel, and a lavish glass of schnapps, 'you must understand... sit now, this is not a buffet!' I sat. '... that I am famous for encouraging delinquency. Parents bring me their children because they make trouble,' she sat at her desk before an even larger selection of sweetmeats, 'and I say to them, you don't know what trouble *is*. Wait a few weeks. So, Mr Henbury, if you have come to tell me how good Egon is at his studies, I will listen like this,' she leant her great head across the food at me, 'and pretend I am deaf. I am old enough to do this, I think.'

Not with those ears you aren't, I thought, but nodded obediently.

'Good!' she said. 'We understand each other. Adult delinquency I do *not* encourage! It is to prevent adult delinquency that children must explore their own and find how boring it is. Yes? It is difficult to be a child, I think, don't you? It is *infuriating* to be a child, don't you think so? You must have been a child once, Mr Henbury. Come, don't you agree with me?'

I couldn't even begin to imagine disagreeing with the Dodderer, and nodded once more, trying to digest something that tasted like anchovy.

'So!' she grinned with a mouth that could have accommodated an entire slice of bread without effort. 'Now *you* speak. And I eat.'

'I can assure you,' I said, 'that Egon has been exploring his own delinquency to the full. He left one school where he didn't... particularly... fit in, and the first thing he did when he arrived at mine was to form a schoolboy group of Nazis.'

Even the Dodderer, as I'd intended, gaped at this summary.

'A schoolboy group of...'

'Nazis.'

'And you permit this?' she said, expressionless.

'Reluctantly. I tried to forbid it. In the end... I permitted it as long as he read about the death camps at the same time.'

Her frozen expression eased. 'Ahhh,' she sang softly, 'you are a *good* teacher.'

'No; that is, I'm not being entirely honest with you. He was removed from his previous school after an attempt at suicide.'

The Dodderer's full-lipped clam of a mouth snapped shut. Above it the long upper lip was like stone. She studied me.

'Then I am glad he was removed from that school,' she said at last. 'For the next holidays you will send him to me, please. I will pay.'

'Frau von Doderer,' I began.

'Ach!' she erupted. 'I am Frau Professor Doktor von Doderer, but

146

if you don't call me Anna-Maria...'

'I will, I will,' I said hurriedly. 'Alec Thurgo is his guardian. It's he who must decide such things.' She stared at me like a sandstone Egyptian cat out of Egon's books. 'But of course I'll certainly... suggest it to him.'

'Thurgo...' she said, as though the word were a lament. 'What sort of name is this? I have tried to find the name, but I think it does not exist. I think there are only two Thurgos in the world, and it is enough.'

'I was hoping you might lead me to one of them,' I ventured; and began to explain why I'd come to Hamburg.

She listened, often perfunctorily, nodding and cramming her mouth with the delicacies until they were all gone.

'Richard Thurgo I can find you easily,' she said at last. 'He is a worm, a very special worm, a big worm wriggling underneath the city. Yes—don't you know what he does? He has made the old underground air-raid shelters into a Valhalla for the living, with cinemas and night-clubs, and there they all wriggle together, the worms. Are you interested in such things? No? Why not? You don't have to be afraid of worms. You simply ask for *Reinhard*. He is Reinhard now. But he knows nothing about the boy. For him Egon was a troublesome pet, to be thrown out after Christmas when no-one wants to clean up the mess any more. About the boy's mother and father... I have no doubt. He *is* the father.'

'Who?' I said.

'Richard, of course. He raped the little serving girl, here in Mecklenburg, what was her name?'

'Herta?'

'Herta,' she nodded, leaning forward menacingly. 'Little Herta. You didn't know this?'

'When did it happen?'

She shrugged massively. 'That I can't say. In '38 perhaps? Before the war. The boy's true name is Franzl, but we shouldn't disturb that,' she said authoritatively, 'Egon is nicer, and I wouldn't give up *my* name to be called Trudl. Would you?'

'Certainly not.'

'The real Egon was killed with his mother, on a train between

Konzentrationslager. Richard knows this but of course he won't admit it because he doesn't want a *Waldmensch*, a wolf-child, as his son. He doesn't want a son at all. He doesn't want any family. The Reeperbahn is his father and mother, and he likes it. When he got to Mecklenburg the old servants brought out the wild boy Franzl from the woods and told Richard he was Count Egon von Lützow-Brüel, and they had been hiding him. Of course they did. I know these old servants. They would have brought out a pig in a sailor suit and said this was Count von Lützow-Brüel, if they thought Richard would believe it and pay some money for him. And you know who the ringleader was? From these servants? Herta's grandfather. Now he thinks, I am a peasant but one day my great-grandson will return and live in the schloss and everyone will call him Count Egon, although he is only Franzl the little bastard my granddaughter brought up in the woods. You see? You follow?'

'But... I thought in East Germany you couldn't be a Count any more, with a castle...'

'East Germany,' she sneered. 'This is Mecklenburg, and it will always be Mecklenburg. Go and see it, Mr Henbury. Then you'll understand who Egon is.'

She smiled at me, and it was such a loving, seductive smile that I saw all the tenderness behind the bluster, and how well the bluster served to give it contrast—she was more like Alec Thurgo than I would have dared point out. I had no difficulty believing in her as a child psychiatrist, while she wore that smile.

Then the steel appeared once more, behind it.

'But first send me Egon, Mr Henbury.'

THE DODDERER HAD said she could find me Richard Thurgo easily; and she was right. 'Don't think,' she'd roared at me, 'that I am a *connoisseur* of such things, it is only that I have spoken to Richard twice already this week, and so I know that after midnight you will find him appearing in a *show*,' she lowered her brows to accentuate the word, 'at *Monsieur* Durand's theatre, I don't know how your stomach is for such things, perhaps it's good,' she gave me a doubtful smile, 'perhaps you will enjoy it, it is called *Trümmer-*

bumsen, which means doing it in the rubble, except that these people only pretend to be doing it, I think. Or perhaps they *are* doing it. You will come and tell me, yes? You will tell me who was doing it and who was not. Tomorrow six o'clock?'

I explained that I was leaving tomorrow, though she frowned as if I were lying, and promised to write to her, 'all the details' as she insisted. And I fled.

I had little desire left to hunt Richard down, and even less appetite for the 'show'; but I reminded myself I was doing it for Egon's sake, and told the taxi driver where to go, ignoring both his grin and subsequent sallies in *Plattdeutsch*, none of which I understood. It was after midnight already and if Richard's Reeperbahn 'show' was as quickly over as mine had been earlier in the week, with the bullcalf, I might have already missed it. What was I going to do, confront Richard with his paternity? Hardly that. I was a weary, drunken, rather soiled and browbeaten traveller, on the eve of my departure, and the bellowing Dodderer had drained from me whatever spirit I had for the fight. What kept my curiosity alive was to see Richard again, not to meet him or talk to him, but to try for a moment to see in that gargoyle face some lineament of Egon, however distant. I couldn't imagine it.

I had underestimated the Reeperbahn. René Durand's establishment was still going strong at one ack emma, and I could hear the audience's roars of approval from the street.

If there's a theatre in hell, I expect it to resemble the auditorium of Hamburg's Grand Théâtre Comique-Érotique—though not because of the nature of the entertainment. Indeed, an exquisitely choreographed orgy would hardly be a disappointment in heaven. It was partly the dim red lighting, and the smoke drifting across the stage from dry ice in the wings, that suggested the other place, as did the gilt ornaments and the faded red velvet drapes, the red carpets and red-upholstered seats. But it was the performers' faces that best invoked the tortures of the damned. Oh, they were trying their best to look at once lusty and casually elegant, as they humped; it was precisely the strain of this unlikely combination that showed in their eyes. The fun, for the rowdy, talkative audience, seemed to be the business of guessing who really had an erection and who was not, as

149

the Dodderer had put it, actually doing it. One of the actors had an undeniable erection, of which he was evidently and justifiable proud; when he waved it at the audience I recognized the roars I'd heard as I bought my ticket. This gargantuan figure I knew (apart, that is, from his proudest member) well. If the Dodderer was to be believed, it was Egon's father; it was certainly Richard Thurgo.

The plot, if that's the word I want, of the show seemed to involve whores and their customers, and a prancing pimp whom I recognized from the photographs outside the lobby as René Durand himself. The whores wore rags, for some reason I couldn't grasp except that it served to expose more of them, and their customer-partners wore what looked like Wehrmacht uniforms, dyed green or yellow, except for Richard, whose uniform was dyed bright red, in keeping with the theatre. None of them looked like stewardesses to me. My seat was comfortable, too comfortable, I felt my eyes begin to close and forced them open again. You can't go to sleep at an orgy, Hanbury, I urged myself, look at what you're missing. The décor seemed to be rubble; dozily I recognized the tableau now, it was a ravaged post-war Hamburg, seen through a crazed nostalgia. Richard was waving his penis again. We had come far, Flight Lieutenant Thurgo and I, I thought as I drifted off. At least I've got one friend in hell.

A furious, sharp-bearded face was staring into my mine.

'*Raus!*' it said.

Somehow I knew this wasn't a dream, and gave a start. The place was ominously quiet.

'What?' I said

'It is finished, sir,' he said in menacingly precise English. 'It is done, finished, we are three o'clock in the morning and we wish to go home to bed.'

'Oh,' I said, unable to shake the drowsiness out of my head. I felt drugged. 'I'm sorry.'

I stared. The stage was dark and bare, the auditorium was empty. No, not quite empty, in the shadows behind the fierce little man—I remembered him now, from the show, he was the dancing, demonic pimp—loomed a larger figure, much larger, much taller. For some reason I was unable to move and simply sat there, nodding my heavy head.

The bearded man briefly followed my glance into the darkness of the aisle. 'Rouse yourself,' he barked like an order, and stood up, with a dramatic gesture at the stage. 'You see? These our actors,' he declaimed, 'are all spirits, and have gone home, for some *serious* fucking. What's the matter?' His face was right up against mine again, smelling horribly of drink, 'Why did you sleep? You don't like our play?' Before I could answer he had swept away and down the line of seats. '*Schmeiss' ihn raus, Reinhard,*' I heard his voice come, then a thump as the auditorium doors opened and swung shut again.

'Come on, old *chep,*' came the voice from the aisle, approaching now, and as he did I wondered why on earth he too spoke English with a German accent.

Richard put a hand on the seat in front of me, to steady himself, and peered down into my face. The great papier-mâché face was livid, shining, and I flinched from it. He gave a ghastly grin and for a moment I thought he was going to fall on top of me.

'You heard the man. Time to go.'

'It's Hanbury,' I heard myself croak in a voice I barely recognized.

'Is it?' he said without a flicker of recognition. 'Well done.' He nodded affably, and once he'd started he seemed to be having trouble keeping his head upright. 'Hope you can remember where you're staying, old bean. Come along now,' he said it with infinite gentleness, and to my alarm he bent down, put one giant arm under my knees and another round my shoulders, and lifted me clean out of my seat into his arms. 'You'll find your sea legs in the street.'

Held tight against his barrel chest like a baby, my head swam, and as we tottered along the line of seats I thought I was going to be sick all over him.

'Please put me down,' I said, my eyes clenched tight shut.

He was breathing a terrible stench of spirits down on me, panting with the effort, and despite his strength his legs gave way as we climbed the aisle. Together we fell against the side wall and I slithered awkwardly to the ground, pawing at him to stop from falling.

'There you are,' Richard grunted as I hauled myself upright, my fists clenched round his sleeves.

I looked up at his face, the huge chin bright with sweat, his head leaning back against the wall, eyes closed. We were both grunting with effort. At that moment the auditorium doors seemed as far away as Liskeard.

'I'm *Hanbury*,' I said after what seemed like an endless, panting silence. *Hen*bury, I almost ventured, wondering—in view of Richard's German accent—if that might help to clear his mind.

He opened his eyes. 'Knew a chap called Hanbury,' he said tenderly. 'Little dancing vicar.' He looked at me. 'That's not you. Is it?'

'Of course it's me, Richard.'

His head reeled exaggeratedly at the sound of his name, as though he intended a smaller gesture but couldn't control it. His small eyes squinted as he tried to look at me out of his swinging head. 'No!' he said dully, 'Good God man, it's not you, is it? God how you've changed. *God* how you've changed! What's happened to you?' His voice blurred as he attempted conviviality. 'What're you *doing* here? This is my... my... ach...' the phrase seemed to escape him, then return, 'my home from home: what do you think? D'you like it? You look...' he began to shake his head, then thought better of it, and tried to stop. 'Bad shape. You still a vicar?' The ghastly grin was back.

I was still afraid I might faint, if only to stop myself being sick on him. When he lifted an arm towards my shoulders I realized I was still clutching his sleeves like a child.

'Bit of air,' he gasped. 'Do you good.'

We began slowly up the aisle, an arm round each other, like men wading in waist-high water.

The street came at me all at once as if I'd blacked out for an hour, I was standing apart from Richard and there was a man lying on the pavement opposite us, legs extended, torso erect against the wall. Richard was waving to him. 'My good friend,' he was repeating, but I wasn't sure which of us he was introducing to the other. '*Ein alter Freund aus England*,' he called to the man opposite, who showed no sign of reaction and may have been asleep, it was hard to tell in the dark. I caught Richard's hand and pressed it in both of mine.

'Egon's at my school,' I said. 'He knows who his father is.'

Richard gazed at me, trying to concentrate.

'Where's your hotel?' he said.

I searched my mind.

'Well, what's it *called*?'

But at that moment I couldn't have remembered if the Inquisition had been asking.

We stared at each other. 'What did you just say?' he asked.

Had I said anything? Assuming he meant what I'd told him about Egon, I repeated it.

'Egon's father,' said Richard solemnly. 'He's dead. I loved him,' he nodded, and began to cry soundlessly.

'No,' I said. '*You*. He knows you're his father.' Richard looked at me, making no attempt to wipe away the tears. 'I've seen the Dodderer,' and I felt myself shaking my head as if at a bereavement, 'she told me.'

His mouth fell open as he looked at me without expression, and I saw the full awfulness of his teeth. The tears were rolling harder, but now he was laughing, a mirthless soundless laugh, and shuddering.

'*Verdammte Sau!*' he bellowed suddenly at the top of his lungs, and even the drunk on the pavement seemed to twitch. 'She got him while I was away, the interfering bitch!' He was still shouting. 'She made him steal a Focke Wulf!'

'A what?'

'A Focke Wulf!' his huge arms were extended, wobbling as he made aeroplane noises like a child. 'Annhhh,' and then a crashing noise, '...paughhh! Ask him,' he said, seeing my bewilderment. His hands grabbed my lapels. 'Listen to me,' he began with terrible, growling urgency, still loud, as though he couldn't turn the volume down. For a moment I saw that he couldn't remember what he was going to say; and I couldn't help, I couldn't remember what I'd been asking him, if anything. We stared at each other. Then recollection dawned in his eyes. 'I *have* no *son*,' he bellowed, 'she's a demented *bitch*! She doesn't know a bloody thing! *One*... person knows! Ludolf Bote!' I stared at him, and he saw my incomprehension. Using me as a support, he pulled himself up into military bearing. 'Brigadier Bote!'

'Brigadier...?'

'I gave him Alec's British Warm!' He relaxed again, panting. 'Ludolf the major-domo.'

'Where?' I said.

'Where d'you think? Schloss Brüel! *He* knows, you see. *She* doesn't know a thing! Look at him,' he roared into my face. '*Look*. Can't you *see* him?'

Confused, I tried to see Egon in the gigantic, piratical face glaring at me, and couldn't.

'In Egon!' Richard was still shouting. 'Can't you *see* him in the boy?'

'See whom?'

'Peter!' Then he convulsed, took his hands from my lapels and clasped me to him in a hug which I could feel squeezing the life out of me. I was too tired to struggle. Content to die, I rested my head against his shirt-front. '*Peter*,' he sobbed, and it was the last thing I heard before I passed out.

CRAMP WOKE ME, daylight, and a panic I couldn't fully understand told me to look at my watch. The movement of my head made me so nauseous I never saw the dial. This time I was going to be sick. I swung my legs off the bed, knowing without looking where my hotel bathroom was.

I had to put out a hand quickly to stop myself walking into the grey plaster of an unfamiliar room. I stared round in a daze at a desk in disorder, armchairs, litter. They've gone mad, I thought, puzzled and angry, they've changed my study round without permission. Looking down I saw the sofa I'd been sleeping on. Oh God, I said aloud; I was in Hamburg. I looked at my watch, closer this time. An hour till sailing. I was going to be sick. A door beside me. I opened it, onto a bedroom, Richard Thurgo's huge head on the pillow, and an open doorway beyond, into a bathroom. I plunged past the bed, wrenched up the toilet cover and retched at length into the bowl.

As the nausea eased I realized I was still wearing my overcoat. Steam rose from my body, cooling sweat. I looked and felt and smelt disgusting. I didn't care. All I could think of was the boat; escape.

Weak at the legs, I groped my way along the wall and past the door jamb into the bedroom.

'Got to go,' I said, but Richard never stirred.

I took a step, knelt on the bed, then as I leaned towards Richard, fell forward across it, my head and breastbone landing on his back. Without a sound he lifted one mountainous shoulder and shook me off like an insect, settling anew on his side. I put both hands on his shoulders and pulled myself up towards his ear. 'Richard,' I said, shaking him, 'Richard, I've got to go.' But he slept on like the ogre in Jack's beanstalk fairy-tale, as I crawled off the bed and found my way to the front door.

Happily, my hotel—the Sankt Georg, it came to mind without hesitation now—was close enough to the port for the taxi to get me there, wait while I bundled up my things and paid the bill, and to rush me through the morning traffic to the boat with just under ten minutes to spare; though I sweated every yard of the way, pleading with the man to hurry.

And oh the relief of seeing Hamburg shrink like a black ant heap into the distance, as we rode the tide into the marshy estuary, and out to sea! At some point I realized I'd never given Richard Alec's letter to him and, tempted as I was to read it, I borrowed a pen from the ship's purser and simply readdressed it, replacing 'Richard Thurgo' with 'Reinhard, care of René Durand, Grand Théâtre Comique-Érotique, Reeperbahn, Hamburg'. The purser offered to deliver it himself when the ship returned to Hamburg. He knew the Grand Théâtre well, he said, and I surrendered the letter to him in solemn complicity, avoiding his eyes.

I should like to say it was a changed Hanbury who alighted at Harwich early the following morning and sat, still stunned, on the train to Liverpool Street. But Hamburg already had a dreamlike aura in my head, the aftermath of the kind of intense, futile struggle that dreamers cast off when they wake. It wasn't that I was ashamed of having witnessed obscene acts, visited a prostitute, got drunk and woken in a strange apartment only to vomit in my host's bathroom, and now needed to reassert the person I'd been all my life until the last week of it. In fact I felt sad at my own fickleness, my thoughts returning to the coming term so easily and with such a sense of its reality and urgency that it made me wonder for the first time about dreams themselves—wasn't it possible, no matter how lightly we dismissed our dream-adventures by the light of day, that they contributed as fully to the development of our character as those waking experiences we were pleased to call formative? We dismissed our dreams as if they didn't count, once their affective power over us had evaporated; much as a criminal, I thought with my Hamburg-self in mind, might relegate atrocious murders to a self that had no claims on him as he washed up in his kitchen like everybody else, and carried his bagged-up rubbish down to the street for collection, greeting his neighbours as they did the same.

Then, like someone recollecting that certain events *weren't* dreamed at all, but were real, I addressed myself to the one strand in my life that demanded continuity with my Hamburg-self. What was I going to tell Egon?

That I had found the Dodderer, who'd corroborated his story that Maggie and Peter were not his parents; and that I now knew that Richard Thurgo (would I ever be able to picture him again as anything other than the penis-waver of the Grand Théâtre Comique-Érotique?) was his father? But *did* I know it? How, precisely, did the Dodderer 'know'? Richard had insisted she knew nothing, that she was a meddler, and that the only man who truly knew was at Schloss Brüel, a servant wearing, if I'd understood Richard correctly, Alec Thurgo's British Warm.

Then I knew what I had to do. At Easter—no, I could picture my mother's face, deprived yet again of her only son—no, this summer then, I'd find a way to take Egon back to Schloss Brüel with me. To Mecklenburg; to the forest, and the treehouse. Suddenly it all made sense: it wasn't just Egon's paternity we needed to resolve and retrieve, it was his childhood.

Softly, softly, I decided; and when term began again I said nothing to Egon of my summer plans for both of us. He seemed pleased with me in some way I couldn't quite identify—pleased to see me, or pleased to be back. Both, I hoped, but either would do. Though he didn't ask about Hamburg, I did sense that he was glad I'd been to see a place of which he had so many memories, and when we did talk it was about the city.

156

Given the contradictory signals I'd received there regarding his parentage, I said I'd uncovered nothing conclusive but that I'd traced the Dodderer and Richard, who'd sent him—I felt an idiot saying this, but I persevered, and he smiled indulgently—their fondest love. I decided to defer the mystery of the *Focke Wulf*, along with Anna-Maria's demand that I send Egon to her.

The index of how well I thought I'd succeeded in mingling half-truths with omissions, holding back the rest for a timelier occasion, arrived promptly during the first week of term.

Egon came through the door into my drawing room and instead of sitting down as he usually did now, unbidden, stood there nervously, halfway into the room. A needless jolt of anxiety on my part faded quickly as he said:

'Would you like to see a photograph of my mother?'

'Of *course*,' I exclaimed, thrilled to know he had a photograph of Herta the serving girl, and even more thrilled that he was showing it to me.

But oh dear God how I wished he never had! I can recall exactly the moment and the way he brought it out of his pocket with all the reverence of a pilgrim for a sacred relic, placing it in my cupped, open hands. I gazed down at it.

'I wrote to her from Beale,' Egon said. 'Uncle Richard gave me her address, and she sent me this.'

I was prepared, of course, for the 'idiot' Alec had called Herta, so I wasn't anticipating motherly beauty. What I saw was, I thought at first, as bad as I'd feared.

Very large, very blonde, with a bullcalf face.

It was infinitely worse than I had feared. I knew that face; it was unmistakable.

I had studied that face for days, then approached it in the street, negotiated with it and finally hovered above it while, with one bullcalf hand, she had tickled my prostate with a mechanical dildo.

I had been to Hamburg in search of Egon's parentage, and fucked his mother.

THE YEAR THAT followed was the happiest of my life. My only

157

complaint to God was that it went so fast, as such years will. I watched Egon become not only mine but the darling of others, and return to me all the happier and more devoted.

He was no longer the biddable, anonymous follower of school fashion, but a boy who could assert both his athletic and intellectual skills without fear of arousing spite. Admittedly they stood out more easily than they had at Beale, here he could operate at sixty per cent and still outstrip his peers; but more to the point he had learned to be English about it, and quite nauseatingly modest.

Without undue modesty of my own, I have to take the demise of the Nazi gang as a tribute to my strategy—since Egon applied it in turn to Marshall by handing on to him the books I'd given Egon to read. Not even Marshall, it turned out, could avoid being chilled by their contents. Whereupon Egon brought off a *coup* I hadn't anticipated. So as not to humiliate Marshall by rendering shamed and purposeless the gang Marshall himself had formed, not to mention the carefully made uniforms and their other expensive and painstakingly collected accoutrements, Egon incited the band to mutiny against their notional superiors. They would turn themselves into a revolutionary cell within the SS. At a nocturnal council Egon described to me in detail, he and Marshall outlined to the others their 'discoveries' about the death camps—the whole thing had a pleasing touch of historical plausibility about it—and the rest of the gang were suitably appalled by their comrades' misdeeds. Plans were laid forthwith to kill Hitler.

And who was 'Hitler' in this exercise? I asked tentatively.

'Well, you, of course,' Egon smiled, 'but you don't have to worry, we'll just make plans, we won't carry them out.' I was just about able to hide from my face, I think, my sense of how closely this fitted Alec's version of the July 1944 conspiracy, at least as regards Peter's part in it. Egon's thoughts were palpably elsewhere; because then he added, no doubt getting a little lost in the fantasy, 'And I mean if we *were* going to try for an assassination, I could always warn you, because the others don't know I'm a double agent.'

In the end virtuous revolution palled, it grew predictably too dull for the band, and meetings occurred less and less frequently, till the uniforms and insignia were finally retired to bottom drawers; like those of other former SS faithful. The war was truly over.

Post-war activities could now thrive. Egon overtook Fishburn at fencing, drawing several new enthusiasts into his wake, and in June we beat Beale at the sport: Egon's finest hour, and mine. It confirmed him as a school hero—and it even got me a pat on the back from the Governors.

But the outstanding proof of my happiness that summer was that it could survive, and help me overcome, the grimmest weeks of my life: my mother's death. She was seventy-eight, a ripe enough age; I'd settle for it any day, since unless I could be as vigorous an ancient as the Dodderer, which I think unlikely, I have no ambition to become an octogenarian.

Sadly, Mother wasn't ready to go. Perhaps she wouldn't have been however long she lived, we'll never know for sure, but it was a dreadful lesson to watch her fighting her death so bitterly. Father had succumbed to cancer ten years before, in his usual tight-lipped fashion, his face and his silence reminding us that this was a professional matter between him and his old adversary Death, and nothing to do with the family. He had saved others from their Maker for a time and in due course ausculted their silent chests, replacing the instrument in his bag without, I'm certain of it, saying a word, or needing to. His expression would have said it all. For a year he told us nothing of the cancer; if surgery could have saved his life I dare say he would have told us and embarked on it. But if it offered no more than an even chance of prolonging his existence, I know he would have dismissed it without hesitation. He'd never been ill a day in his life, he maintained, and even if this was an exaggeration he held the phrase aloft like the banner of his calling: he was the Doctor. He would be healthy till he died.

He was a strange, stern man, my father. Not once in his life, I realized with a shock as we were burying him, had I heard him mention his mother or father. They had died before I was born, and my own mother often spoke of them as charming people, both of them as shy as my father, yet who had welcomed her unhesitatingly as a daughter. For all that, and perhaps because of his reticence, he was as splendid as the sea to me, my father. Whether he was stormy or impassive, nothing deflected his mood; and I also knew well, from what he said to other people, how proud he was of me. I often wondered whether he unbuckled, unbent, when he was alone with my mother. He would have listened patiently to her every fretful word about the children, and modified—of this I'm sure—the worst excesses of her concern. He left me room to grow, and never once obliged me to measure myself against his expectations of me, only against my own.

Mother, true to archetype, was the tenderness in our family, the caress, the explicit encouragement. As I've said, even these were never free of grief, and John the First's shadow passed across our brows with her hand. If there *is* such a thing as cheerful tenderness I've never known it; perhaps I simply don't attract it, and there's something in my face that instantly makes people want to grieve, though for whom I can't say—even Richard Thurgo, when he raised me tenderly into his troll-like arms that night in Hamburg, gazed at me as though, dear as I was, I wasn't quite the one I was supposed to be. Perhaps that's it: I am the substitute, the eager back-up, number one reserve.

Or did I choose the role? Just as when Father died I chose to let Ellen take the brunt of Mother's widowhood. Admittedly she was the obvious first choice, she was divorced and living alone with a child who could nourish Mother's need to be a mother. For my part I could hardly have taken her on in '47, given my salary as a newly appointed school chaplain, my small apartment, and my precarious hold on a combined career of pastoral and teaching duties; cook-cum-housemaid, as it were; it was fully ten years before I lived down my 'war record' of giving comfort to cowards. (Even now I haven't really lived it down: the Governors only voted five to four to make me Head.) My other two sisters had put marriages and many miles between them and the family, Laura in New Zealand, Jennifer in Durban. I sometimes think a penguin would have stood a good chance with my sisters, as long as he'd promised to take them back to the Antarctic and away from Reading.

It wasn't really Mother's fault, she lived for mothering, that's all—and Ellen's little John came along just in time. Yes, another John; I prefer to take it that our family couldn't have enough Johns to replace the lost perfection of the first, rather than think I'd been declared a failure even as a substitute. 'He's the son Mother wanted from *you*,' Ellen said with more than a touch of our mother's tone in her voice: always finding something to regret. This John was a sickly boy, too, even sicklier than I'd been. But he was a tower of strength that summer after his grandmother's first stroke.

Out of the window went my plans to take Egon to Mecklenburg that summer. The stroke hadn't left her incapacitated, and Mother would be back in her old stride by Christmas, I hoped, when I could slip away to Germany; it wouldn't be the same as visiting the schloss and the forests in August, but a winter trip was still appealing. I had at least discovered that such a journey was possible to arrange, with patience, and after months of correspondence with the East German delegation in London. Hoping to seem less of a potential spy for taking with me a German boy on a visit to his ancestral roots, I gave Brüel as his birthplace and plain Egon Lützow as his name. As with boarding school boys, schlosses and '*von*'s would hardly ingratiate us with the people's republic. And I had a letter informing me in tolerable English that provided our lodgings were confirmed in advance, by us and by them, entry visas could be arranged.

The summer I passed instead was a gruelling one. Both in hospital and back at Ellen's, Mother griped and cried in turn as though mortality had only just been vouchsafed to her and she was the only one who would have to suffer it, we were all immortal apart from her. But for her of course we *were*; she hated anyone who would outlive her—she once admitted it to me, without embarrassment. She was too desperate for shame. Self-bereavement the doctors called it, and assured us that her behaviour was entirely normal; easy enough for them to say, they didn't have to live with her.

Ellen, with her florid complexion and Father's dark hair, had something of his stoicism too. She bore Mother's rages with fortitude: the tea was too hot, or too cold, the room was too hot or too cold, the blankets had been washed in the wrong solution and would bring her out in a rash, we made too much noise, or we made too little, she complained, tip-toeing about the house as though we thought ourselves angels of mercy... *Act normally, for goodness' sake!* What distressed me far more than her self-absorption—we'd probably have another twenty years of this, I thought, keeping my own fear of her death well under wraps—was something that Ellen could not share. My mother's face had begun so closely to resemble mine, not only its features but its grimaces of annoyance were mine, that it was as if I was seeing my own bad-tempered old age. The physical effects of the stroke had receded, leaving nothing more to show for it than a silt of slurred speech, and a rapid acceleration of the hair loss that had plagued her for years. We had the same little down-curved love-bird's beak of a nose, the freckles, the pale eyes in the round face, and now the same high empty brow with a flaming halo of carroty hair. The resemblance was so striking it was laughable. 'Don't blame her for looking like you,' said Ellen tartly one day when I'd been impatient with Mother, 'remember it's *you* that looks like *her*.'

The second stroke didn't take her, nor the third, though they followed mercifully fast upon each other. It was the third that left her paralyzed, her anger still blazing from her eyes at me as I read to her, hour upon hour, from her favourite books. Young John took spells too, and he was an excellent reader, I could hear him through the wall, dramatizing *Whiteoaks* with real passion. How I longed each day to find those eyes dulled! Nothing she had done in this life remotely merited being buried alive in her body. In her burning eyes I read: you're the priest, do something, say something! All I could do was stare, trying to understand her gaze. Demanding that I put her out of her torment—or furiously warning me not to?

All three of us who nursed Mother said the same thing to each other at one time or another, that summer: if it happens to me, for God's sake give me an overdose and I'll bless you with my dying breath. Would Father have done it? Ellen and I asked ourselves that too. He would have known how to do it without anyone finding out, but more importantly he would have known whether to do it, whether it was what she wanted. I wanted him back, more than I ever had before.

Just as it seemed it might go on forever, consuming our lives, she died one morning between the drink of tea we had to dribble down between her old lips, and the first reading hour of the day. I cried in relief and thanked the God I'd been cursing for weeks, for taking mercy on her.

EGON AND I set out for Mecklenburg that Christmas with all the excitement and fearful preparations of explorers bound for cannibal shores; I don't think he was any less nervous of setting foot in Soviet territory than I was. In fact he knew more horror stories than I did about Russian behaviour, first-hand stories too.

In the year that had gone by since my heady visit to Hamburg, much had changed between us, and for the better. Since acquiring hero status as a fencer (I was glad to see, with thoughts of Heidelberg fraternities and duelling scars, that the boy had chosen the épée and not the sabre) Egon had cast off winsome childishness, his defence against the adult world. He was now a resolute fifteen-year-old—or thereabouts, it was impossible to know *when* he turned whatever age he was. Though of course... one person would know. Herta; Herta would know. The memory plagued me incessantly: was it something of Egon in her face, her manner, that had led me to pick her out as a bed-partner? I kept remembering how often I'd assured anxious mothers that my staff could be relied upon to stand *in loco parentis*—with mechanical aid if necessary, I could now add, but it was not a formula I'd trot out with a straight face again. Yet I have to admit I was tickled (and I'm not referring to the dildo) by the situation. As long as Egon never found out.

And that was the problem. When I conceived the trip to Mecklenburg it was with an Egon in mind who wanted nothing to do with his old Hamburg connections, as he'd insisted. But now that my own journey had broken the ice—and now, perhaps, that Egon felt he had some real footing here in England, to return to—my new, strong, successful British Egon was keen as mustard to revisit Uncle Richard and other familiars, on the way to Brüel. And, of course, his mother. The address Richard had given Egon for her, two years previously, had been in Berlin, I was relieved to find. Hope sprang up briefly that it hadn't been Herta at all, in Hamburg, that my traumatized brain had imposed on a photograph of another, albeit similar Valkyrie, the lineaments of recently gratified desire. But I knew it wasn't so. The jaw, the smile, the horizontal Frankenstein's monster hairline above the bulbous brow, above all her expression with its curious mixture of servility and defiance, brought back a fearful, wondrous tingle of memories, as much in my body as my mind.

When Egon wrote to the Berlin address, announcing our impending visit to Germany, it brought—as I hoped, as I'd prayed—no
answer. In the circumstances, his proud attempts to hide his disappointment, and my hypocritical sympathy, sickened me. But what
could I do? I wasn't going to tell him where and what his mother
was, at any price. On the other hand, if we visited Richard... here
too grotesque memories intervened, I'd not only bedded the boy's
mother but observed his father's penis in ostentatious action, and
then been cradled like a baby in his arms. One night during the
autumn term I woke up in a muck sweat, the memories revived in
a garbled dream; lying there in the dark, remembering how my rear
had continued to ache and tingle on the ship back to Harwich, and
still feeling Herta's blunt intrusion, I prayed that she alone had
performed this office. That on our drunken return—of which I
could still recall nothing—to Richard's apartment, he hadn't vented
his lust on me. *These our actors...* René Durand's sweat-stippled
beard jutting at my face, I could remember that all too clearly... *have
gone home for some serious fucking.* Surely not in our case; since
although the activities on stage at the Grand Théâtre Comique-
Érotique had included real or simulated buggery with both sexes, and
though the way Richard had clasped me to his bosom, weeping
Peter's name, had struck me before I blacked out as something more
than tearful nostalgia, I couldn't recall Richard waving his member
at a male actor. No, and I'd woken next morning fully buttoned,
indeed overcoated. But for the first time in my life I thanked God
for oblivion, for having released me from the role of memory man;
Please Lord, I prayed, surely in Thy sight I loved Egon enough
already, without having to endure the most comprehensive initiation
in the history of surrogate parenthood.

But whatever had happened, Egon and I would now have to walk
or taxi our way down the Reeperbahn to find Richard, or rather
Reinhard, and unless the gods were with us we stood a good chance
of passing under Herta's nose, there on the pavement, perhaps
even—I pictured the worst of course—accosting a potential client.
At best if she pretended not to recognize me, or simply didn't, what
if she recognized her son? And he would recognize his mother; as a
Hamburg tart. *Oh look, here's your mater, Egon,—you didn't tell me*

she was an undercover policewoman, working the streets! I saw myself trying for this in clumsy German while alerting Herta with a dig to her ample ribs. No, it was hopeless.

Only when we'd embarked, in falling snow, at Harwich, and Egon was sleeping peacefully—or pretending to—on the bunk below me, did a solution came to me at last. I couldn't remember the look of the street where Richard lived, nor its name or even the look of the building I'd fled in haste, fearing to miss the boat; but the Dodderer would know. Her information could enable me to phone Richard and arrange to meet him there, with Egon, and to warn him in advance not to reveal Herta's profession or her whereabouts. I'd been hoping to avoid another harrowing encounter with Anna-Maria: I was obsessed with the idea that she'd steal Egon from me, kidnap him and carry him off in deep trance, hypnotized as I pictured it, to some von Doderer retreat deep in the German woods. *It is for his own good, Mr Henbury!* I heard her booming voice down the telephone, *if you are a good teacher you will know this. So go home now, Mr Henbury, and wait until I send him!* But I would have to beard her, if I wanted Richard's home address.

I was shaking inside as I once more looked up the Dodderer's phone number, this time with Egon at my side in our hotel room, unpacking neatly.

'Ja,' came the deep male bark once more, and its crispness instantly brought into my mind the bullwhip hanging in her lobby.

But I'd misjudged the Dodderer, though it seemed to give her pleasure to elude my blundering.

'No no no, my good Henbury,' she cooed; something had caused me to be stripped of my 'Mr' rank in the intervening year, perhaps my unseemly eagerness, the night I'd met her, to visit the Grand Théâtre Comique-Érotique, 'of course I will not give you Richard Thurgo's address. I hope you have been thinking while I talk, then you don't need to ask me why I do this, but I tell you anyway because I think you are more of a fool than I thought. Richard Thurgo is a pervert, he is charming, and I love him because he *is* a pervert. But an old woman like me is immune to his perversion. *Leider!*' she cackled, 'you understand? Pity! If I was younger it would be different. But he is a bad influence on the boy, and a great fool.' And more to the point he mistrusts *you*, I thought, though I hadn't counted on her knowing this; she would be afraid that he'd poison Egon against her. 'And I hope you have the good sense in your head not to take the boy hunting through St Pauli for him. Egon has seen enough of the Reeperbahn for one lifetime. So, you bring the boy to me at five o'clock this afternoon, and we begin from there. For his sake, and for your sake too, Henbury, I hope you have not left this too late!'

I groaned inwardly; now the woman was no use to us to help find Richard, she was simply a dangerous pest. Unbidden, and ignoring her orders, I said, 'I'm passing you to Egon, to say hello,' and handed him the receiver.

It worked. I watched his sweet smile—it was the dreadful, obedient, childish smile, returned—fade as he listened, politely answering in German what sounded to be a mixed tirade of sticky German endearments, well-my-little-fellow questions about school life and, ruining the effect, the touches of steel, the commands that in her heedless desire to get Egon back into her clutches she couldn't, just as I'd hoped, resist. I was not the fool she thought. Other kinds of fool, perhaps; but I knew ogresses.

Egon put the phone down slowly, and held it down, as though to prevent the Dodderer coming through it in a vast eruption of ectoplasm.

For once I didn't mind the childish tone in his voice. 'Sir, do I *have* to go and see her?'

I shook my head. And though I hadn't told Egon what Richard had said about his parentage, I added without explanation: 'Before you see the old Hamburg crew again, there's a man at Schloss Brüel I'd like you to talk to.'

MY AUTHORITY WITH him seemed to suffice. I glowed with the thought that he trusted me, as we spent our day in Hamburg harmlessly revisiting certain old haunts of his, the orchards south of the river, now snow-covered and still, the site of weekend visits when Egon was little; Elbe-side walks through Blankenese; two churches in Altona where Karin, one of Richard's girlfriends, had taken the boy for worship. Altona brought us, by my map, a little too near the Reeperbahn for comfort and put my nerves on edge, twitching whenever I glimpsed a tall figure, or a peroxide blonde one; and I was relieved when we went on to Wandsbek in the north of the city, to gaze through padlocked iron gates at the Gymnasium, Egon's first school. Nearby lived 'Mutti', Karin's mother, 'if she's still alive,' Egon said, and glanced at me in hope that I'd make an exception for this member of the Hamburg crew: this was the 'old woman' who Egon said had prepared him for the Gymnasium by teaching the wolf-child how to read and write, in Gothic lettering. No doubt an extraordinary old woman (and having met the Dodderer I now respected Egon's estimate of 'old', so she might well be dead) but I wanted no more possessive, interfering voices, gently told Egon we'd visit her on the way home, and offered instead to spend our final hours at the heartland of his Hamburg memories: Fuhlsbüttel airport.

He jumped at it. Before we left England he'd begged me to travel by plane with him to Hamburg, even—when I was adamant about my terror—boldly said, 'You go by boat then, and I'll go by plane. Alec will pay, if you ask him. Nicely,' he added, bringing a little realism to bear.

How could I tell Egon that not even his delight could compensate me for the night I would have to spend alone on the boat, picturing him white and staring among the screaming passengers as the aeroplane plunging downwards, 'Annnhhh!' as Richard had evoked it that night on the Reeperbahn, in a context I had yet to investigate, and '…paughhh!' out of control into the North Sea? The boy would have thought me an even bigger 'wet' than he probably did already.

'It's out of the question,' I lied sternly, 'I've already settled our budget with your guardian, down to the last chocolate bar. You know how he is.'

Egon had me that his happiest afternoons in Hamburg had been spent plane-spotting at Fuhlsbüttel; and now, though the very sight of the things landing and taking off made me feel queasy, we were able to do just that.

'Tell me,' I said once he was happily settled beside me on the terminal's observation deck and was reeling off the names and the most obscure specifications of distantly arriving aeroplanes, including, at last, a Focke Wulf, 'about *your* Focke Wulf.'

He kept his eyes averted from me for a moment, without reacting, and I could feel in my own head as surely as if I'd left it to take up residence in his, the old impulse to lie.

'Richard told me,' I said, though in truth all Richard had done was to impersonate a crashing Focke Wulf, with the mysterious remark that the Dodderer had 'made' Egon steal one. 'Was it something to do with the Dodderer?'

'In a way,' he nodded. 'I wouldn't have done it if she hadn't egged me on. I wouldn't have had the guts. I used to think she was brilliant, the best person in the world.' Then he remembered something, and I knew a moment later that it was the fact that I was not in league with the old girl, I'd let him off the appointment with her and he was free to confide in me. 'I really thought she was great, she said such awful things about everybody, Uncle Richard, and even Karin, *and* her mother. She's supposed to be Mutti's cousin, that's how I got sent to the Dodderer, but d'you know what she called Mutti? She said Mutti was a bitter old woman, because,' Egon fought to restrain a grin, 'because she hadn't been asked to run Auschwitz. I didn't know what she meant then, I thought it must be the name of a school because Mutti liked teaching so much.' He glanced at me. 'Until you gave me those books to read.'

'Anna-Maria doesn't mean to be malicious,' I pretended, 'she just has a very dark brand of humour.'

'I really used to like it,' Egon said. 'And the thing is, I had a friend called Gerhard Stolz at school, his father took me up in his plane, with Uncle Richard, it's the only time I've ever flown. So I cooked up a plan. I was a bit mad in those days,' he added in a rueful middle-aged tone I wondered if he'd borrowed from me, 'I mean I really thought I could fly a plane, just from watching Herr Stolz do it. My idea was to persuade Gerhard to steal the keys to his father's plane, make copies and sell one to me. I told him I just wanted to sit in the cockpit. Junker F-103,' he said without changing tone, puzzling me until I saw that he'd flicked his eyes to the horizon where a distant whine had alerted him, long before I even saw the plane, to an incoming aircraft requiring his identification. 'The Dodderer was always asking me to tell her my worst fantasies, I mean about nasty things I wanted to do. Most of them I invented for her, and they were pretty horrible. I mean, murdering people I didn't like and that sort of thing. From the way she listened, I often thought she was going to tell me to do it, but she didn't, until I told her my idea about stealing the plane and flying it back to the schloss.'

I stared at him. 'She actually encouraged you to try and fly the plane?'

'Not really, no,' he admitted. 'We sort of agreed it would be better if I just sat in the cockpit and, you know, *imagined* flying to Brüel. She must have thought it would be therapeutic,' he said sagely. 'The keys cost me a hundred Marks.' He looked away again, I assumed to identify another aircraft, but there was none in the sky, and I caught the edge of a blush on his cheek. 'I've never told anyone this, but I stole the money from Uncle Richard.' He turned to face my response, the blush gone and the face naked now.

Though I longed to do it, something told me this was not the moment to confide in him about my own all-too-similar theft, even if it was a paltry half-a-crown, from Father's trouser pocket. Egon needed me, not as a fellow-delinquent, not as a father surprising him with tales of his own childhood misdeeds; as something different, though I couldn't put a word to it. As a headmaster, I suppose, but at that moment the title was like a millstone dragging me under.

'Go on,' I said.

He seemed satisfied with my response, and took a breath. 'I only meant to sit in the cockpit, really I did. But I had the keys to the ignition, and I'd watched Gerhard's father do it. Start the propeller. Taking off was simple really, you just pulled out the throttle till you were going really fast. Then hauled the stick back. Someone half my age could have done it. I didn't really know about runway clearance, I suppose I thought Herr Stolz was just talking to the control tower out of politeness, to tell them he was leaving—perhaps I did know really, but I wanted to be airborne before anyone could stop me.' He grinned. 'And I was for a moment. I'd have been up in the sky and gone, I might have crashed and killed myself or I might have landed somehow at the Schloss, but I'd never have come back.' Egon must have seen something in my face because he added, 'I didn't ever imagine I'd come to England then. All the same, if I'd got properly airborne... I wouldn't be here now. What happened was, I pulled the stick back and the nose went up, and we hopped into the air like magic, just like in my dreams, and that's when I saw the other plane coming in to land. I actually think I saw the pilots' faces, or maybe I just imagined that afterwards—you know, with their faces like this,' he mimicked horror, 'and pulling back on the stick to gain altitude and clear the runway. I was so scared that at first I pulled the stick back further and nearly stalled, then I realized and shoved the stick forward a bit too hard and came down with a terrific bump,' he grinned proudly, 'and then a lot of bumps, I couldn't get it to take off *or* land, then we got past the end of the runway into a field full of cabbages. If it hadn't been for the mud I think I'd have turned round and tried to take off again. But we were stuck, and by the time I got out there were sirens going and they'd called the ambulances and the police and everything.' He paused. 'I made the headlines,' he said, mock debonair. 'But I don't think Uncle Richard was too pleased about it, he had to pay Herr Stolz for damage to the undercarriage, and the farmer for the damage to his cabbages. Even the Dodderer was a bit shocked, I think. She said...' Egon paused, collecting himself, adding, 'I used to be able to do her really well... she said: "you are a very disobedient little boy," or something like that,' he giggled, beginning to get into the impersonation, "and a very... also a very fortunate one. Now that you have discovered how stupid it is to try and carry out certain foolish ideas, you will learn to tell *vishes* from *fects*: yes?"

'Anyway, that was when Uncle Richard took me to England and told me Alec would be looking after me from now on. It was his way of punishing me, I suppose, but Alec thought it was a bit of a lark too, what I'd done, so really I got away with it. I just wish...' his eyes roamed the airfield, and now I was seeing it with him, the little aircraft with the even smaller figure in it, hopping and bouncing down the runway into the cabbages beyond. He glanced at me, saw that I was following his gaze. 'That's the field, over there,' he said. It was peaceful, unmarked, full once more of winter crops. 'I don't know,' there was apology in the voice, and something more, as yet I hadn't twigged to it, 'I wish I'd made it, really.' Then his glance clarified things, and before I could object, 'You could say *you* were a pilot and we could rent a plane, I'd pay you back somehow, honestly, I still know how to take off.'

'If I ever fly,' I said firmly, 'it's going to be with someone who knows how to *land*.'

'*Bet* you I could,' he brazened.

I shook my head. 'I'm afraid I'm with the Dodderer on the matter of *vishes* and *fects*. Sorry.'

'All right. If I promise not to fly the plane, can we rent one with a pilot, all the same? *Please*,' he wheedled.

'No.'

'If I blindfold you...'

'No. That'd be worse.'

'All right, two sleeping pills, and when you're fast asleep I'll get the pilot to carry you to the plane and strap you in.'

'No, Egon. We can't afford a plane *or* a pilot, much less one who'd be prepared to carry drugged passengers around.'

'How much would it cost?'

'*No*.'

'*Please*.'

'No, Egon.'

WE FLEW. THOUGH not to Brüel, which would have contravened in spectacular manner the minutely specified travel plans I'd agreed with the East German authorities. 'Oh gosh, so *what* if we get reprimanded?' Egon said. 'We wouldn't get the reprimand,' I pointed out, 'for the simple reason that we'd already have been shot out of the sky by Russian MIGs.' I too could quote aircraft when I needed to.

But I felt it was about time for me to grow up and jettison my fears, to share Egon's delight; until that afternoon at Fuhlsbüttel I had no idea how much it meant to him. So we rented an hour's nightmare in the neighbouring skies and our pilot Angelo, an Italian immigrant stout and merry and far more indulgent than I would have dared be, let Egon take the controls once we were high and steady above the snowfields of Upper Saxony. I must admit the little plane never wavered in Egon's hands. I wavered, however; it was the apotheosis of every dream-terror I'd had, implausibly suspended in a rattling hulk of metal thousands of feet above certain death. Every nerve-end screamed this out. It made no sense, only dream-logic kept us aloft, and when I allowed myself to close my eyes I gave us vigorously flapping metal wings.

'You're a good sport, sir,' said Egon, shaking my trembling hand once we'd emerged from our deathtrap onto a terra firma I swore I'd never leave again, unless for water and then in a very large ship. The boy was dazzlingly elated, still many feet above the ground, adding in a modest undertone, 'But you know, don't you: I could have landed it if he'd let me.'

As we returned to our hotel with Egon still rhapsodizing about the feel of the controls, the ease and freedom he'd experienced, I rejoiced to think that our perilous Hamburg day had turned into such an auspicious start to this voyage of rediscovery. Alas it was to be by far the best day of our trip, and had I known what was coming I'd've turned round then and scrambled us both onto the boat.

WIND, AND THE metal rattle-trap, familiar clatter, swaying in the dark. No hands to clear his eyes of sand, of burning sand. Ice-tears, dissolving now. Snow frees them, wet lids lifting to reveal bare struts and spars limned in silver, lit from below: snow on the ground. His hands are numb from gripping, climbing. In the dream the treehouse and the aeroplane are one as he inches along the wing of branch, mauled by the wind, towards the safety of the gaping metal door.

Before Egon's eyes the roof lifts, flies off, sheet by rusty metal sheet. Wind peels away the flaps of corrugated tin around the door, the door still opening onto a treehouse skeleton. Snow furs his face. Hugging the branch, he sinks his swooning head into its cold white pelt.

THE YEAR BEFORE, Christmas in Germany had been cold and dreary, sometimes even mild and dreary compared to Liskeard in the depths of winter; I was used to the cutting wind of the moor, and this Hamburg weather, I thought, was singularly tame and grey—I couldn't remember once seeing blue sky. It must have lulled me into

172

a state of false security.

Schwerin, the nearest town to Brüel with a hotel deemed suitable by the East German tourist authorities in London, was barely fifty miles away, our rental car was already booked, our hotel room awaiting us. Another twenty miles due east and we'd be at the schloss. The land for many miles around was glazed with snow, we'd seen that from the plane, but the weather was fine and even the smallest lane was clear and visibly in use, below us. Supposing as we did that we were heading for an even more remorselessly efficient state (it was certainly the impression the brochures gave, and our own prejudices reinforced it), we would both have been puzzled to hear that where West German snowploughs stopped, at the border, no East German ones took over. And no-one warned us. My only concern, as we set out in our brand-new German Ford, was what we might find at Brüel, and its possible effect on Egon.

'The man we're looking for is called Ludolf Bote,' I said as we drove through prosperous villages showing no sign, any more than Hamburg did, of the ravages of war. 'D'you remember him?'

Egon concentrated with furrowed brow and mouth half-open.

'He's Herta's grandfather,' I said. 'Your great-grandfather.'

At this he gave me an astonished look, then hunched his shoulders in a further effort to think.

'Yes,' he said at last. 'Ludolf. That's right, like the red-nosed reindeer, only not. That was what I thought when I heard the song the first time, I thought they'd got it wrong, to make it go better with reindeer. The name,' he nodded, 'that's all, but I can't remember what he looked like.'

'You don't think he was Japanese, as in Ludolf the led-nosed leindeer?'

Egon chortled, and raised his hands to his face to give himself slit eyes. 'You're talking about my great-grandpa.' He turned to me. I don't look Japanese, do I?'

I remember thinking we were merry as grigs, whatever grigs were; it was a favourite phrase of my mother's, and before I could prevent it her angry dying face came back to me in a rush, and I wished so much that she could see me now, at this moment. If it was true that Ellen's young John the Third was, as Ellen had said, a kind of

substitute for the grandson Mother had wanted me to give her...
even if I sired a tribe I couldn't repair that now, but if she could
have seen Egon and me laughing together, so happy in each other's
company, she would at least have known that fatherhood wasn't
foreign to my character. Some of my emotion must have shown in
my face, because I saw Egon working himself up to a speech as he
turned forwards to gaze through the windscreen.

'I know I haven't told you how much it means to me, you bringing
me to Germany—and everything, I mean, not just that...'

'It's all right,' I said, 'it's been the best fun of my life.'

He hesitated, still staring at the road ahead, and I wondered if I
should have put it that way. It was true—but from his point of
view, what had my life been like if this was the best of it, driving
along a dead straight German autobahn in a rented car? Then he
resumed, perhaps reflecting that a priest, let alone a headmaster,
probably didn't have much in the way of fun to compare this with.

'Going up in the plane,' he said, 'that was great. I'll never forget
you let me do that. *And* came too,' he added in an afterthought.

I was mainly glad that no 'sirs' had crept back into his thanks. We
were a long way from the school.

Indeed as far from the school as I ever wished to get. Huge,
repeated signs were now alerting us to the approaching border, and
warning us with many exclamation marks to turn back unless
properly accredited; the exclamation marks seemed to doubt that
anyone could ever be sufficiently accredited, and I wondered, not for
the first time, whether our entry visas and indeed the East German
Tourist Board itself, as unlikely an organization as an Arctic Tourist
Board, weren't a combined trick played on the gullible and the
unworldly, to bring them up against the reality of international
politics and turn them away with a slap. We'd both fallen silent.
Ahead of us our accompanying pine-forest terminated, and beyond
it, on the snowy plain, rose a series of gigantic wire mesh walls
topped with barbed wire, one behind the other, punctuated by tall
wooden watchtowers, heavily manned, their searchlights waiting for
the dusk. It was so unlike any landscape I'd ever seen that I braked
in alarm, and before I'd understood quite why it was so menacing, as
unnerving as a futuristic film, I felt the sweat break out under my

174

flannel shirt.   Realizing that my skid to a halt might look oddly suspicious to the guards, I accelerated again. But now it came to me, what I was seeing, and a glance at Egon told me he was seeing it too: photographs of concentration camps encircled by the same vicious walls of wire, and towers. It took an effort as if quelling vertigo, to enter the place of my own free will; and then with a terrible conviction that we would never be allowed out again. In my panic I even turned on Egon in my mind. You'll be all right here, you little German wretch, it's your home—what will they do with *me*? This was all his fault, he'd conned me into it and I would be led away—for what crime I couldn't imagine—to hard labour, making East German car registration plates.

This would have been fairly light duty, as I realized once we'd driven ten miles into the country, on what the map portrayed as a main road, without seeing a single car. Unless they were just too sensible to bring their cars out onto roads so poorly serviced. The villages we passed through had no cars parked on the street, though we saw a few, snow-covered, down muddy tracks between houses. They looked as if they might have been long abandoned. No inhabitants were to be seen, not a soul, no-one even peeping from a window; only the smoke rising from the chimneys informed us there were living people in this country. The houses themselves looked still in shock, as if they'd survived an artillery attack within the past hour. They were pocked with shell-marks, dirty, doors unpainted, here and there windows and roofs still smashed in. After the bright new toytown of the West, this Germany was like its mocking skeleton twin, an advertisement for before and after. Yes, that was it—it was a time-barrier we'd crossed, no wonder it was so alarming. We were entering the land of the dead. Even the forests looked as though their waxy burden of snow had been oil-painted on, each branch of fir hidden beneath an improbably large snow-dollop, and lacquered into place a generation earlier; the entire motionless landscape, battered houses, fields and trees, frozen that way since living memory.

The ten miles had taken us an hour, skirting laboriously round tongues of snowdrift and into hidden, snow-filled potholes, but despite our slow progress and the grim surroundings we were both filled with an exhilaration as hysterical as my earlier panic. We'd made it, we hadn't been stopped, we were *in* East Germany—I could imagine no equivalent for this rush of frightened exaltation, no setting, not Germany itself under the Reich nor the Sahara nor the jungles of New Guinea, that could have seemed so electric with threat as this harmless snowscape... it wasn't hell, where torments raged, but some chilly Plutonic underworld where time had died and would claim us too, the moment we stepped out of our timebound capsule. But we were here and nobody was even following us, we were invisible, we could go where we liked and talk to whom we wanted. At the border they'd searched our car for fully twenty minutes, and scanned our papers for as long again. But once the guards in their grey-green had returned the documents without comment and waved us on, once they and the death-camp wire perimeters were out of sight, the relief was shaming. What absurd fears—yet if a mere border post could inspire such feelings in a tourist, how numbing must their first glimpse of the real camps have been, for millions of apparently docile enemies of the Third Reich?

'Let's see your passport,' I said as Egon was putting it away, a German passport obtained for him, he'd told me, by Uncle Richard's 'friends' in Hamburg, to make it possible for Richard to take the boy out of the country and consign him to Alec. I hadn't thought to study it as we approached Customs in the port of Hamburg, just as well because I now saw that it said *Egon von Lützow-Brüel*, no 'Count' thank God, yet somehow the name seemed to have squared sufficiently with the 'Egon Lützow' on our documents to have satisfied the border guards.

It was the date of birth I wanted a glance at. 1941, it said; no month, no day; perhaps there were many such, in Germany. I could feel Egon studying me. I handed it back. 'We should be able to get that corrected, if your great-grandfather's still around to tell us.'

Egon nodded, restoring the passport to his inside pocket. 'Or if there's anyone still around who knows,' he said lightly. He sounded well guarded against disappointment; I hoped he was.

We hit our first full-sized snowdrift without warning, at the summit of a bend.

This time I had the good sense not to hit the brakes. We weren't going fast, but the road was in reverse camber, sloped away towards the outside of the bend, and on the slushy surface we'd have ended in the ditch, or broadside on into the drift. As it was we entered it head on, not with a quiet hiss as my reflexes supposed, but a jarring bang as if the snowdrift's base had turned to ice; at the same instant the front of the car jolted upwards, flinging us forwards at the windscreen where the jet of snow gave a sense of plunging into surf.

One of us had to push, the other stay at the wheel in case the car began to roll back through the slush and down the hill. We soon discovered that Egon was the stronger of us. After he'd heaved and pushed the Ford clear and we'd worked a wide enough trench through the snowdrift with our gloved hands, we managed to get across it, half an hour later, with further bouts of pushing. We drove on, carefully now.

It had begun to snow.

Twenty more miles to Schwerin, but neither of us had to say it: there was no turning back. My correspondence with the East German authorities had made that clear. Either we kept to schedule or our visit would be terminated. We were expected at the Albrecht Hotel in Schwerin, and if we turned back now we'd have to begin the months-long process of obtaining visas all over again.

I couldn't tell whether Egon, who was going home, who *was* home, felt less vulnerable to the danger I felt all around us than I did, I who was only on my second trip, and my first drive, abroad. We hit our second snowdrift, and our third, and as the sky gradually darkened I found I'd lost count of how often we'd climbed out to flail like madmen at the snow, carving a path through this deadly, insubstantial stuff as if it consisted of the fast-evaporating minutes of the day. Our faces were red with exertion and the knifing cold, as we drove on I could hear Egon wheezing, even after the panting had settled, and I wondered whether he was fully over his last term's bout of winter flu.

By now the danger was quite specific. One impenetrable snowdrift and we were done for. Behind us the snow filled our footsteps as we worked, just as it had no doubt filled the breaches we'd made in the snowdrifts behind us, hours ago. Even if we gave up on Schwerin and on Brüel beyond it, indeed on our entire visit to this windswept hell of ice, we stood no better chance of getting back than going forwards. Once or twice I thought I heard a hiss of wheels behind us, and waited, pausing, for some robust truck to appear. Anything, a tank even. But nothing came.

I prayed to God with all my might for some sign that I hadn't brought the boy back here to die. At that moment I saw Egon appear in front of me, emerging from the snow-swirling mist: his blistered face was crumpled, mouth wide, teeth bared.

Then I realized he was laughing, though the sound wouldn't come. 'It's clear,' he panted. A hoarse bark of a laugh followed. 'Can you believe it? There's another one ten foot away. Looks even bigger. Come on,' he said, 'let's do it now before we get back in the car.'

I wanted a rest, I wanted to crawl back inside the car and sleep, but Egon tugged and pushed me as he'd tugged and pushed the car itself, onto the next snowdrift.

'If we have to,' he gasped in my ear, 'we'll leave the car and walk.'

I glanced at him and I was looking at a boy I'd never seen before, an Egon I'd never met. There was snow on his eyelashes, but beneath them his grey eyes sparkled with glee; under the small, now bright-red nose, his mouth was curved in a perpetual snowman grin. I understood at last. He was the wolf-child in winter, he was in his element. It eased some of my terror, but none of my tiredness. *You* walk, I thought. I'll never make Schwerin.

And finally it came to just that: on foot, another ten miles, perhaps more, ahead of us. We put on virtually all the clothes we'd brought in our respective suitcases, crammed our pockets with the few remaining pairs of socks we weren't wearing, with valuables and toiletries, in case we never saw the car again. I locked the doors—as if anyone was going to steal and drive it away—and we plunged into the long drift that had finally broken our will to persevere as human snowploughs.

It was easier going for a short while, knowing we wouldn't have to scoop out any more snow with our exhausted, ice-caked arms. My face had gone numb. But soon the dead weight of my body felt like someone else's draped on top of mine, each limb encased in lead. When we were going downhill, or level, my legs kept going under their own inertia, like a jointed metal toy. As soon as we came to a hill or a snowdrift, the machine stopped. Invisible diver's boots seemed to be holding me fast to the road beneath the snow. Not one more step. Not if my life, or Egon's, depended on it.

But the boy himself was like a demented puppy discovering snow for the first time. Standing rooted, bent over, trying to cough the razor blades out of my chest, I watched him run, *run*, to the top of the hill to see whether Schwerin was in sight; not for his own sake but to give me comfort, I realized as he ran back to me and lied shamelessly that he could see the outskirts of the town.

As if it was all a game being played with a spoilsport parent, he went behind me, put two hands on my back and pushed me uphill, my feet stabbing forwards to stop me falling. I felt ashamed to be his burden; though God knows I wanted him to save my life. Some time later, I don't know how long, I knew that he had locked an arm around my waist, his shoulder firm against the small of my back, and his head wedged between my side and my arm like a second-row forward waiting for the scrum to form. I couldn't believe his strength and his persistence.

But by this time I was no longer a living, feeling thing, I was watching us in amusement from somewhere else entirely. I was a pair of binoculars penetrating the blizzard, watching a boy trying to force a broken wheelbarrow to the North Pole. Only it wasn't cold any more. I was watching him push an upright mummy through a sandstorm.

WHEN I HEARD the biscuit-crunching footsteps I mistook them for my own, until I stopped. Turned. Turned to see a shape, a figure stalking towards us out of the mist. His face was hidden by the fur-lined hood of his military parka, but salvation spoke out of the very way he walked, his steady untiring tread as if mocking the snow for trying to hold him back. Too weak even to call out, I watched Egon race towards him, feet throwing up a spray of snow; then stared in astonishment as the boy's headlong rush took him barrelling into the oncoming giant, almost knocking him over. And then—then as I realized it wasn't excited clumsiness that had sent Egon into the man's arms—yes then when they embraced, spinning joyously as the bear-arms closed around his victim and hoisted him into the air, I glimpsed the brutal Thurgo profile and made to croak my glee, though no sound came. Richard, damn it, Richard Thurgo!

Now they were talking, shouting, though all I could hear was a cackling laughter like gunfire, and Richard pointed a long arm at me, index finger extended from his great red paw. Pointing at me and laughing helplessly as if I were a lop-sided snowman Egon had made to greet him, complete with bowler, scarf and carrot for a nose.

'You ass!' he panted as he approached, his face misting and reappearing again through the explosion of frozen breath. 'Look at you—you're dressed for Sunday morning chapel!' And turning to quell Egon's amusement, 'Couldn't you have clothed him properly?'

'How did you find us?' I mouthed in blubber-words.

'What?'

He laughed as I shook my head in frustration.

'I followed you of course, what do you *think* I did? Border guards didn't like the look of me, they held me up for a bit of the old cat and mouse. They liked the look of my money well enough. Meanwhile you fellows did the road-sweeping, saved me a lot of trouble.'

But how... how did he *know*—Egon now grinning up at *Onkel Richard*—had the boy written to him, alerted him? But no address, no—only Herta's, in Berlin—

'For God's sake, Hanbury, you don't think you can wander round my city without being spotted? Think you're the invisible man, do you? You bloody innocent.' His gargoyle features shone with snow-blisters as he drew a wet hand across his eyes and turned to Egon, propelling him forwards. 'Lay on, Macduff!'

As Egon scampered ahead, Richard swivelled back again, replanting his feet.

For a moment only Egon's footsteps, as Richard studied me.

'Thought I was going to let you kill my boy, did you?' he muttered.

His eyes held mine, black they looked in the shadow of the fur. I couldn't find my voice. *I have no son!* he'd shouted that night on the Reeperbahn pavement.

'Come on! Keep moving! Or do I have to carry you again?'

THOUGH EGON SWEARS we never made a bivouac, it's still one

of my clearest memories of that terrible journey. From my half-finished igloo I saw the two competing in the snow-flecked twilight, snapping branches and beating the snow off them, spying more fallen branches, chasing each other, scuffling like dogs over a prize.

The fire was lit. We watched Egon curl up in the lower folds of Richard's parka. He was asleep at once.

'Why did you let him go?' I whispered through chattering teeth.

No answer came from Richard, bent over the boy. I couldn't see his face.

Had I spoken at all—made any sound? I said it again, but the great head lolled onto his chest and Richard slept.

Throughout the night I tended and coaxed the fire as if it was my very lifeblood, watched it compose the shapes and faces of delirium, saw them grin and dissolve. Before my eyes Richard and Egon were dying, I was sure of it. But when I shook them they moaned in dreams, like the living.

We were tramping through the snow again, the sun was up and glowing through a frosty haze, mocking our addled steps. Each in his cell apart now, automata amazed to find one more step, and another, without falling.

Egon is missing.

I have no voice to tell Richard, as he threads his own way through the trees.

I've stopped, content to stay, a tree among the trees. But when I look up at my fellows... Egon, Egon is climbing up hand over hand through the dark branches to the treehouse, and my mind swims. The treehouse! And Brüel, we're close, missed Schwerin altogether but we're there, we're home! Feet on the branch, Egon has pulled open the door and stands, one arm against the grey bole of the tree.

'Come up!' he cries, a strong voice resonating in the darkness of my head, joyous. 'She isn't there!'

A faint crashing sound, nearby, I turn and see Richard too gazing up at showers of waxy snow tipping off a fir tree branch that bows and shakes itself like a living thing, as the owl lands on it.

I LAY ALONE in a room so small that for an instant I was quite

181

sure it was the grave, equipped with a few small, ugly funerary ornaments to see me through the afterlife, among them what looked in silhouette like a small television set; it was dark, I felt quite numb but glad to find that everyone, not just Tutankhamen, awoke in the kind of funeral chamber whose images Egon and I had studied at the school. I wanted so terribly to tell someone, to tell the world—I would make it my mission—that the ancient Egyptians were right, that... but my dream had already shifted to another scene, on the industrial outskirts of a town, with Egon there beside me, and both of us falling over together in the tram ruts hidden by the snow. I wanted to tell him about the afterlife, but I was too busy wondering why I had never taken this road into Liskeard before, why I had never stumbled across these decrepit factories—and why Germans, by their names on the signboards, had ever come to Liskeard in the distant past to build these antique, satanic iron buildings.

WHEN I WOKE again it seemed to be because every limb hurt, my legs worst of all. When I tried to take a breath my lungs screamed and, as punishment, hurled me into an agonizing and humiliating coughing fit that forced liquid from my mouth and nose and eyes, and wouldn't stop, though every cough seemed to strip a dry patch of membrane off the bleeding wall inside my chest. I was able to open my eyes at last, breathing shallowly, still shocked by the abraded flesh I carried where my lungs should be, my source of breath.

Around me was the same damned tomb I'd glimpsed in the dark, it hadn't been a dream. I prayed this narrow cubicle was the Albrecht Hotel and not, as seemed more likely by its appearance, a hospital. Happily I was in my own pyjamas, having—as I remembered clearly—worn them under my clothes for the assault on Schwerin. But here there was nothing that suggested a hotel room, no card on the bedside table, nothing pinned to the door. Outside the window, a featureless brick wall six feet away. A hospital *where*, though? In East Germany? The television seemed improbable. Had I been returned to the West?

The room was so small I was able to switch on the television with one unsteady movement of my arm. Nothing happened at all on the screen, nothing to tell me where I was, though the machine hummed a faint whine and a light had come on somewhere in the back, reflected on the wall. Then an image blossomed on the screen, a black and white image, oddly flattened as though seen through a zoom lens; on it a man in a suit was standing in an alley between what seemed to be two bungalows, he was hunched over a line of metal rubbish bins, searching through them methodically, in turn. There was no sound at all. I watched in a stupor as the man in the suit rifled the rubbish bins. Was this socialist realism?

Suddenly a voice came, very loud, startling me, and I reached out to reduce the volume. The voice was oddly familiar, it was American, it spoke in English, and before I could find the right knob it had shouted at me: *I think he's beginning to doubt the existence of the real.* This struck a chord, I knew just how he felt, though it seemed an oddly metaphysical remark to make of a man searching through palpable rubbish bins. No further comments came, once I turned the volume down, and I watched the man abandon the rubbish now, looking round the alley in puzzled despair—then abruptly we saw two other men in suits, one of them watching the proceedings through a telephoto lens. With almost tearful relief I recognized in the man at the camera the hero of *Mission Impossible*. I felt as if he'd come to save me personally, he'd airlifted me out of East Germany to the place I was now, safe in the circuit of American television series. Perhaps an episode, given the only piece of dialogue I'd so far heard, specially written by Jean-Paul Sartre. Light dawned as the two voyeurs talked, at normal volume now: it was a *reel*, a reel of film, that the object of their espionage had been hunting for in vain.

I was ready to call out for help, to find out where I really was. But I had no strength to do it with, any more than I had to get out of bed and open the door. Instead I closed my eyes and tried to sleep.

A German voice woke me, a male voice.

It was coming from the television, I saw when I opened my eyes, where a newsreader seemed to be talking about the weather. At any rate he mentioned *Schnee* a lot. I wondered if he was going to tell us whether my body and Egon's had been found. Then I noticed a plaque behind him, on the studio wall, proclaiming: *DDR*. Despite

Mission Impossible I was still in East Germany, and I began to cry.

OUR VISAS PERMITTED us seven days in the country, each night to be spent in Schwerin at the Albrecht Hotel—where indeed I was, as I discovered to my relief, and not in hospital. I spent the first five in bed; and should never have got up on the sixth—but by then the weather had cleared a little, our car had been retrieved, and wild horses wouldn't have stopped me taking Egon to Brüel.

When he looked in on me that first morning I was delighted, overwhelmed in fact, to see him well. I couldn't grasp how he managed it. He was positively rosy with health. It seemed all he needed was a diet of blizzard-walks; it came as a shock to think that English boarding school life was too soft for him.

'You'll never believe it!' he said, bubbling over, '*Everybody* in this place knows who I am! I mean, the whole *town*. It's supposed to be a Communist country, but they all call me *Herr Graf*! Some of them even take off their caps to me. And their wives curtsey!' He was laughing, mocking it, but his pleasure was evident.

'How do they know,' I croaked, 'who you are?'

Egon shrugged. 'They just know. The hotel manager's got our passports, I think he spread the word that the *Herr Graf* had returned,' his grin spread wider and wider, 'on foot and through the snow...'

'Carrying his aged tutor,' I said. 'Thank you.' The pain of talking made it easier to keep things brief and to the point. 'I owe you my life.'

'Oh rubbish,' he said, embarrassed. 'You were just being feeble.'

I was content to nod at this, studying him. ...*Everybody in this place knows who I am!* I hesitated, then thought better of it: it was the wrong moment to ask the *Herr Graf* whether that meant he'd thrown over Richard and Herta, his 'real' parents, in earnest, in favour of Maggie and Peter; or just for a day or two.

And it was only then that I remembered how we'd got here; who it was that had risked his life to save us both.

'Richard,' I said, 'where's Richard? Is he with you?'

'Richard?'

'Yes. Is he here in the hotel?'

It was only then that I saw how Egon was staring at me.

'What's the matter?' I said.

'Uncle Richard?' Egon's face hovered between delight and disbelief. 'Are we meeting him here?'

'He followed us,' I said, 'don't you remember?' But the awful truth was already dawning on me; Egon's now disconsolate expression said it all. 'He caught up with us in the storm, and helped you build the shelter.'

'What shelter, sir? We never built a shelter.'

'Yes we did, you and Richard made it and you got the fire going...'

To ward off what I saw on Egon's face, all kinds of self-protective thoughts came rushing in: Egon was lying, he'd abandoned Richard in favour of his newfound *Graf*dom, Richard somewhere seething waiting to ambush me... but no—

'Oh God,' I heard myself sigh, 'are you sure?'

'I haven't seen Uncle Richard since he brought me back to England, sir.' A tactful smile had replaced his disappointment. 'D'you think you might have been hallucinating? I mean, I'm pretty sure we never built a shelter. Or a fire. Honestly.' The smile acquired a mournful tinge as he hurried on. 'D'you know what, though? I met two chimney-sweeps who used to clean the chimneys at the schloss. They say it's been pulled down. It's gone.'

'What has?' I was still trying to shake my head free of the palpable, audible Richard it contained. *Thought I was going to let you kill my boy, did you?*

'The schloss.'

Fever-demons, dreams. Very well; but dear God it was unnerving—no memory was clearer, no part of my history more authentic; and couldn't any piece of that be snatched away, just as easily, if Richard's frost-bitten face, his bulk, his voice... if...

'The schloss?' I echoed.

'Yes, *you* know, where I used to live. Schloss Brüel.'

...If that was dream, then this was not; but did it differ? I studied Egon's face. The schloss was gone, he said; and his quiet, amazed sadness—yes, it would have served the Queen well, in the event of a fire at Balmoral.

'I won't even be able to remember how it looked,' Egon said, 'unless somebody's got a photograph.'

'Somebody will, I'm sure.' Let Richard go, let the fever-dream go. 'And Ludolf? Did you ask about your...' I could have bitten off my poor raw tongue; it was too late, Egon had seen me stifle 'great-grandfather', but I battled on all the same, 'Does anyone know if he's still alive?'

Egon's voice was muted now. 'Yes. They say he was this summer, anyway. I've got an address for him.'

But I had the distinct impression that Egon wouldn't be heart-broken if the weather obliged us to stay here in Schwerin among his bowing, curtseying feudal serfs.

'I'll tell them you're awake. They've got a doctor waiting to see you.' He smiled a little awkwardly, not knowing how to handle this reversal of our roles. I'd been the one who visited *him* in sick bay, told him to take it easy, to sleep as much as he could. Now he nodded twice, firmly (was that what *I* did when terminating my visits?), and said, 'I'll be back around three,' heading for the door. 'I've been invited to lunch with some old friends of my parents. Cheery-oh.' Then, putting his head back in through the doorway, 'D'you know my grandfather was also called Egon? *He* was Count Egon. I never realized it was a family name!'

As he closed the door I felt a spurt of anger at his fickleness; and at myself—for goodness' sake, the kid was fifteen, and suddenly, from being a struggling alien, a despised Kraut at an English boarding school, he was being treated like a homecoming king. Who wouldn't trade in their parents for that?

So why did *I* feel betrayed?

Alone again with my fading fever-dream, I sank back into it, consulting Richard Thurgo's beady stare. Own up, Hanbury, it said, we're in this together. I was shamingly proud of having coupled with Egon's mother, that was the truth of it: I did *not* want to see Herta reduced to a Dotty-role of cook-cum-housemaid-cum-whore.

For a while I fed on envious images of Egon being fêted by the old guard, toasted with God knows what precious wines hidden from the regime, and leaving me to be entertained by *Mission Impossible* and

Ukrainian agricultural documentaries; until the doctor's admirably soporific drugs put an end to reveries. My vaunted lungs—clearly not 'coughed strong' enough, Father, unless you were talking nonsense all along—had given way, and having spent my first holiday abroad blind drunk I spent the second one largely asleep.

It wasn't till the sixth day, when Egon paused for long enough in his reports of revelry to mention that the car had been brought back to the hotel, that I felt strong enough to seize back the initiative. We'd come this far to find old Ludolf, and find old Ludolf we would.

'That means the roads are passable. We're going for a drive,' I said, swung my legs out of the bed, stood up, and nearly fainted.

'Not today,' said Egon, steadying me anxiously as I flopped back onto the bed.

'Today,' I said. Or else we'll never make it. 'It's twenty miles to Brüel, half an hour on a clear road. Dig out Ludolf's address. I'll see you in the lobby in fifteen minutes.'

I knew I was running a high temperature and shouldn't be up, let alone out of doors and driving, I felt weak and doped and hot and in a dream, but we were going to get at the truth, no more illusions, true kingship or bust. We would find it at the *Hof*, apparently a kind of old people's home just outside Brüel itself where Ludolf was not merely one of the inmates but, as Egon understood it, was the caretaker, the boss.

And Egon too began to get excited as we drew nearer to Brüel in the bright sunshine, recognizing woods and fields, occasionally houses; but I could see in his eyes that it wasn't the dwellings, it was the contours of the landscape that clutched at his heart.

I saw him steeling himself. 'If Ludolf will take me there, I'd like to see the treehouse. But I don't want you to come,' he added quickly. 'You mustn't. Please,' he smiled. 'I'm not carrying you home a second time. Let me go on my own, with Ludolf. I promise you I'll tell you all about it.'

In the event, I was so tired by the time we reached the *Hof* that I barely took in what was going on around me. A tribe older than God; somehow they all lived in an impossibly small bird's nest of a house, and the oldest of all was Ludolf, white-bearded, white-haired, every inch the prophet. His opaque blue eyes stared, seeing nothing,

I thought. But he wasn't blind at all. What his eyes said was that they would look if they wanted to—and he certainly looked at Egon with an expression I shall never forget—but that their owner had seen enough for one lifetime and now would see as much or as little as he chose, of outward things.

The old people saw my condition right away and I was hurried off to bed upstairs under the roof, barely protesting. 'Ludolf says you can rest as long as you want,' Egon said, tucking me in, 'we don't have to leave before tomorrow afternoon.'

I'd scarcely nodded before I was asleep again, carrying into it the extraordinary, motionless gaze Ludolf had directed at the boy, when the old fellow first emerged from the *Hof* and saw who it was. He'd stepped through the doorway an elderly military man, erect, head held high. When he saw Egon he stopped, his knees seemed to give way and he staggered for a moment, then recaptured his balance, legs slightly apart now, knees a little bent. His arms had fallen away from his body. He seemed to be murmuring an oath under his breath, but as it went on and he crossed himself at last, I knew it was a prayer thanking God. He looked at Egon with astonishment and yet as though he was the only real thing in an otherwise familiar, unreal universe; as if Egon were the sum of what little had survived the flood intact; his work, his treasure. Standing behind Egon I couldn't see the boy's expression, but the stillness of his body transmitted to me, to mine, I was going to say, to my body, how awed and moved he was. Then he was running to the old man, and I felt his arms hug me, flung around him as though around me. I'd never seen him hug anyone before, or be hugged; at that moment I was both of them, enfolded in their embrace. And their happiness filled me as I slept, in imagination I was with them in the forest as surely as if I'd been there in the flesh.

EGON FOLLOWS IN Ludolf's footsteps, no need for words now, just the sound of an old man's short steps in the snow.

In the low pallid sunshine the wood has lost its ice-forest glitter and weeps heavily into the slush around each trunk. Out in the open the shrinking snow is still solid but pocked, beneath the dripping branches, with pissholes by the dozen, by the hundred, as if a passing army had paused here to relieve itself.

Soldiers. Russians. They were here once but he can barely picture them, his dreams can find no footing here, not on this path, in these trees, not here or there in this landscape too real and too precise.

Oh how he wants to be at home in this place but he recognizes none of it, not a tree, not a gully or a clearing, he could as easily be in Cornish woods walking obediently behind a stranger in a faded camel-hair coat, a British Warm. A few sick leaves dangle above him, obstinate, reproachful. Farther off, the distant tree-line banks up grey and fluffy, soft and brittle as an old man's hair. What is he supposed to feel? Here Ludolf is at home, not he.

Egon remembers nothing. Nothing. Only he himself is here now, gazing dully round as if for the first time. He feels a fraud, relieved that Ludolf never turns to look at him.

Where are they heading? With a shudder he sees that Ludolf's footsteps have crossed fresh tracks in the snow, two sets in friendly parallel, animal tracks.

And then it comes to him, bubbling up gratefully like an excuse for being late to class: it's winter, the child he was must have been hibernating. Yes—hidden here or there, beneath those rocks, that cluster of fallen trees, in that dip overhung with melting icicles. Hunting for hiding-places. That, *that* he can imagine.

The small tracks lead towards a gully; fox and deer seeking out water. In place of ice he sees the gully flowing and alive with minnows against the clear sand. Water-flies swarm in the sunshine. Frogs basking on the banks, waiting for the water-flies to come closer.

A clearing blossoms in his mind, widens into a field ringed with firs. In the dawn light, the fox with his forepaws extended in the grass, rearquarters and tail high, yapping, the stag stamping and the fox retreating now, then both whirling round each other in the bright field like gladiators watching for an opening, till they're face to face and the fox stops, slowly extends his forepaws along the ground, yapping, and the dance begins again.

Standing still now, Egon lets the feeling gather the forest to him, tree-line and leaf and soughing branch. City of trees, where each has been arranged so that the wind plays a distinctive, familiar melody as it passes through: sounding its name.

Ludolf has stopped. High above them the beech tree parts into two grey limbs smooth as flesh, and there at the widening wrists, braced by no crossbeams but held fast in the twin limbs themselves, sits the rusting horror of the treehouse. Metal, tin, chicken wire, iron, patched and peeled and many-bolted. Windowless. *Metall*, Egon breathes as though he'd never known what it was when he lived in it. The treehouse calls with Herta's metal voice, Egon runs forward, starts to climb, the rope is long since gone but all the holds are there, they come to his hands and feet until he's almost running vertically up the tree, along the branch and pulling at the door. He opens it and...

Darkness, and a stench that makes him faint, drowned in himself. Light rapidly shrinks to a circle around my feet. But I can still hear for a moment. Metallic click, squeal of metal door on metal hinge.

He opens it, and...

I LEARNT THE story slowly, on the way home, driving back in a fever-trance to Hamburg. But had to be told again, when I was steady again, weeks later. The boat, and the return to Liskeard were a blur, I know Egon took my hand and led me shuffling like an old man through the crowds, a ghost led by a boy. For a time I had to let go of everything, even the school, and hear term start without me, all around me. Poor fat Alick stood in for me till I was pronounced fit to resume my life.

Sometimes I wonder if I ever have resumed it, whether I'm not at the *Hof* now, under the buoyant feather eiderdown, dreaming I'm at Webb's, writing these words; dreaming that I'm back at the helm of my swarming ship, the school. And that I've lost Egon for ever.

It's not the experiences of those days in Mecklenburg that have marked me; after the long snowdrift that defeated us on the way to Schwerin I had few experiences of any note, only one long experience of dreaming, in or out of the body, it's the same. It's the absence that's marked me, that waits for me daily, just around the corner. The day, which had always been safe territory, each morning a reprieve, is now as haunted as the night. One step, at any moment, from the abyss. Daylight itself is now the verge of sleep; and now during its dispensation, once so generous, I no longer own my body. Not when I wake, not when I sit at lunch lulled by the shouting surf of boys, not when I speak at evensong—once the most alive of hours, the last brightly lit act of day. If I could reclaim each moment of those lost days... but no, it wouldn't make any difference. I've entered the business of leaving, letting go, it's irreversible. It's night I long for now, bed greets me like a mother's arms; with its permission to depart. Then I can *be* a ghost. I can be Egon if I wish.

WHAT HE TOLD me of his day with Ludolf began, not with the visit to the treehouse, of which he only gave me the barest outline, saying the battered little metal house was still there, that he'd climbed up and looked into it; but nothing of what he saw there, even when I pestered him on the subject; no, despite his promise he began the story after he and Ludolf had emerged from the woods to visit the site of the schloss, now entirely razed, and the still extant gatehouse where Ludolf had once lived. From Schloss Brüel they walked to the village of Tempzin, where a startling sight awaited Egon in the churchyard: his own grave.

None of the three people memorialized on the headstone, Ludolf explained, were there in skeleton beneath the earth and the lovingly tended flowers. Count Peter's body had never been returned after execution by the Nazis, but his name was where it belonged, beside those of his wife and son, whose remains had been interred in Poland.

For a moment Egon saw his newly reclaimed aristocratic birth slipping away from him: who was it, then, that died with Maggie, if not his Egon-self?

'My great-grandson,' Ludolf said. 'Franzl was his name. My Herta's child by your uncle Richard. Don't you remember Franzl? You played with him often in the woods.'

But Egon could only stare. Nothing, no other child, no companion's cries filled the woods, in memory.

'It was before you *lived* in the woods, *Kleiner*. To save you, when the SS came, your mother took little Franzl with her, pretending he was you. He was a little older than you, but small and often ill. This was why they allowed him to stay with her. We hoped they would both survive.' Under Egon's eyes, the old man resumed, 'You hid with Herta in the woods, until the Russians came and took her. After that, you would never come out, although we begged you, yes, and tried to tempt you with clothes and food. Until Richard came and took you. You remember?'

Egon shook his head. His mind is on something else. He dares it: 'It *was* Franzl? It *was* Franzl who went with her?'

'You think I don't know my own kin? Come,' he took Egon by the hand, 'I have photographs of Franzl, and of you, with your father and your mother. Come.'

Before they left Egon stole another look at the headstone. It gave his date of birth, January the 15th, 1941. And date of death—but this was Franzl's, as Ludolf's family album was to confirm, Franzl whose strange porcupine quills of black hair and large, ungainly features greeted the world with a bewilderment Egon preferred not to dwell on. January the 15th, 1941: it was, it truly was, his date of birth. He was about to turn sixteen, and he was Egon, Peter and Maggie's son.

All this he told me with pride, happy to find he was who he was meant to be; whom it said on his passport. And I was happy for him. I'd missed his sixteenth birthday—spent by me in the headmaster's bedroom where my maddening weeks of convalescence, tormented by the muffled sounds of school lfe, had at last expired. But Egon assured me he'd celebrated with his friends.

He still wouldn't talk about the treehouse, and for some time I continued to brood on what it was he'd found there.

Then I let it go. What mattered most to me was that our visit had fulfilled him, had removed, as I'd hoped, the shadow over his paternity. I'd wound up bedridden for a time, but I'd escaped worse thanks to Egon himself; what we'd obtained was cheap at the price.

Yet how short-lived a happiness it was! I was so proud of him—and of myself—and so sure of my ground that the downhill tumble of the months that followed seemed the cruellest disappointment of my life. Already in February, as my own physical health improved, and even my day-hauntedness began to recede a little, I watched Egon's sickness begin.

He was entitled to a delayed reaction, God knows. But it wasn't physical, his symptoms were entirely in the mind, and it was the best part of nine months before I or anyone else understood it.

EGON AND THE gang are meeting beside the plane, in daylight. The Messerschmidt is their secret, a crashed German fighter lost in a remote quarter of Tupholme Wood, and apart from the vegetation that has grown up around it the plane itself appears to have been made of some rust-free metal, aluminium I decide, untouched by time or weather. Its tail is up, its yellow wasp-nose partly buried in the earth, and the boys in their Nazi uniforms are gazing at it with awe. Egon strips creepers from the cockpit, and finally drags open the cracked perspex cover to reveal a figure in a sheepskin-collared leather flying jacket, his head fallen forward on his chest, and the khaki-coloured hair covering his face. To my horror, and before I can warn him that the face will be a skull, Egon takes hold of the hair and pulls the head back up into the light. I gasp, but the face is young and fresh and unravaged and belongs to Denis Towle.

WHAT I REMEMBER most clearly about the early stages is how he fought. He wanted none of it, poor child. All I could see were the stratagems he seemed to be devising—I could only guess at what they cost him—to stay within the bounds of sanity; which for him were the school bounds; his room, the house, and finally the school grounds themselves. I had no suspicion of it at first. All I saw was the glowing, successful boy, come at last into his own. Now that he was indubitably sixteen, he had moved on from the cubicles into a room of his own, as did the other boys his age. I thought he'd be delighted. But within a week of my return to duties he asked if he could change.

'Of course,' I said. 'If you can find somebody to swap with.'

'Thank you, sir.'

I saw him hesitate. If it was about finding someone prepared to exchange rooms I didn't expect him to have problems with that; I'd shamelessly given him the best and largest room, and such was Egon's current status in the school that none of his contemporaries demurred.

'D'you think I could go back to the cubicles, sir? I know it's not usually done, but I really liked it there.'

'Back to the *cubicles*?' This made no sense.

'I liked it better, really I did.'

I studied him. There was a troubled look to him that night, one I didn't recognize, a dullness to Egon's eyes that contrasted harshly with the eyes that had revelled in our emergencies in Mecklenburg.

'That's a problem, you know,' I said. 'I don't mean because it hasn't been done before—though it certainly hasn't during my time here—but... because of the other boys. They'll be a bit puzzled, won't they? To see someone going backwards in... well, in rank. Particularly someone they admire.' His face was growing longer by the second. I grasped the nettle, thinking—oh, like an idiot—that I must preserve at all costs the place he'd achieved at the school, the very source, I thought, of his pride in himself. 'Won't they think it rather childish?'

'I don't care.'

'And what about the fifth form boys in the cubicles?' I smiled, 'They'll probably think I've sent someone to spy on them.' Egon was silent, and I played my most cruel shot. 'And your friends, people like Marshall—well, you know how they are. Won't they suspect you have a particular interest in the younger boys?'

Egon looked away, restraining tears now. Fuming, miserable; and I wished I hadn't pushed so hard.

'Look,' I said. 'Come back to me if you can't find anyone to swap with, anyone whose room you like. And we'll talk about it further.'

But he made no sign, not even a nod, and I knew I'd made my point all too forcibly.

'What's the matter with the room, anyway? It's always been the one people went for first.'

'It's got a funny smell in it,' he said sulkily.

'What sort of smell?'

'I don't know, I can't describe it. Keeps me awake at night.'

'I'll have it fumigated if you like. Give it a good clean, the whole house needs it, really.'

He managed a sour smile. 'That would make it worse, I should think.'

'You're probably right. I don't much like the smell of disinfectant either. Anyway, see what kind of arrangements you can make. We'll talk again. All right?'

But as the days went by he didn't revive the subject, and when at last I did he shrugged and muttered that he was staying put. 'It's not so bad if I open the windows,' he said. 'And put on another jumper.'

I nodded. After Mecklenburg I no longer fretted quite so much about his health. And when I thought about the matter, I quite misinterpreted the signs. I thought he was lonely for company; a school bedroom of his own was new to him, he'd always been in dormitories or cubicles. He'd get used to it.

It was one night in March when I was on my slippered prowl that I began to see how wrong I'd been.

As I rounded the stairs to Egon's corridor I saw his door was open, only slightly ajar but immediately noticeable by contrast with the file of closed doors beyond his. I walked to it, then stopped, unsure whether I should peep in or not; I could argue a certain right, but this was precisely where my prowls turned uncomfortable and made me wish I could abandon the habit. It wasn't just that I had no desire to invade their privacy, I wasn't really even spying on the boys at all; and although I knew I could never hope to convince them of it, I wanted *nothing* to be happening on my ship, with its tortuous passageways and small, sudden inclines beneath worn carpet that I knew so well I always walked it in the dark, without a false step. I *needed* nothing to be happening, and when I heard furtive activities I sighed and turned back, pretending to myself that I hadn't heard and didn't know whose room the sound was coming from. I never took action on it, not even later, not even covertly (I liked to think) in the way I behaved towards the boys in question; and almost invariably it only confirmed what I knew from other sources or had noticed myself during the day. I often wondered sadly why the boys didn't rescind my nickname, since I was evidently such an incompetent creeper that I never stumbled on a crime to prosecute; or did they take me to be a cowardly 'Creeper', or worse, so dedicated a voyeur I only wanted to continue spying? Because it wasn't that at all. That I couldn't sleep had always been my primary excuse, to myself, and secondly that I loved the humming silence of my ship, the faint throb of the boiler-room audible in different tones in every corridor, the smells of night like settled dregs of day, a distillation of every separate joy and anxiety the waking hours had brought each boy—I loved it as I loved no single moment of the hurly-burly day, at night I could recapture all of it at my leisure, it was all waiting for me, sifted, there to sniff and recollect for as long as I wished, as if preserved under glass. Now that I *could* sleep, and actually used my alarm clock to wake me at two a.m., my primary excuse had gone, but it only made me realize that all along I'd needed no insomnia to legitimize my prowls. I was addicted to the sleeping school. It was the only time I had complete control, unstinting pride in them and in myself. I was at home then, and I cursed any boys I could hear trying to share—as I thought of it—my hour of bliss. They were out of line, not for infringing discipline by the school rules, but for violating *my* privacy as surely as if I'd found them on my own bed. At night the school and everything in it was mine. But as I hesitated at Egon's door, I was face to face with the consequences of this: to violate their privacy was to violate my own, and I couldn't do it—not even to fulfil my responsibilities as a headmaster. That was only my daytime self. At night I wasn't 'Creeper' but Count Dracula, sinking invisible fangs into the lifeblood of the school.

With my hand on the doorknob, I thought of softly closing the door. It was what I really wanted to do: to restore untroubled night. Common sense told me this wasn't wise. If by any chance Egon was out of his room, and hadn't merely neglected to close his door properly before he went to sleep, he'd return to find it closed and suspect that I'd discovered his absence on my prowl. As I stood back, leaving the door ajar, and looked down the silent corridor, I saw a faint gleam of light, further down, where a doorless archway led, at a slight angle to the first, along a further corridor to the toilet at the end of it. When I stepped quietly to the archway, I saw a light under the toilet door and breathed a silent sigh of relief. No mystery, then. But as I backed away I realized I hadn't been quiet enough, the light went out and silence followed. Nobody emerged. Presuming that Egon was waiting for me to leave, I made appropriate noise—easily done without theatrical efforts, I knew the location of each traitorous floorboard—as I returned along the corridor past Egon's room and descended the stairs to the floor below.

No sound from Egon's corridor, and against my will some instinct made me pause and wait to hear the familiar footfalls. None came. The house had become suddenly alien, its pulse no longer beat with mine—it was a mutinous ship, and suddenly I needed to hear the careful slippered steps and the door closing on a body restored, my own body, to wholeness. I couldn't move until it was restored. Five minutes passed, then ten, and it came to me in alarm as I pictured Egon in the dark, silent toilet, that the little narrow room was the nearest thing on his floor to a cubicle, a cubicle all to himself at this hour. Did he spend the night there?

Then to my relief I heard the door open, no flush, only the footsteps coming slowly towards me, above my head. They reached me. Then silence. No sound, not even the faintest click, of the door closing. It was as if he'd disappeared, directly overhead. I waited, baffled. Waited longer this time than I'd waited for the toilet door. Then, as slowly as I'd ever moved, I stepped back towards the wall behind me, knowing exactly when my back would find it. The stairwell above and below me was lined with iron bars beneath the balustrade, and with my eyes adjusted to the darkness I could see, as I moved back, first the top of Egon's door, still ajar, then more of the door. Then, as my shoulders touched the wall, and I froze: the top of a rumpled, sandy head.

If I stretched up an inch or two and met his eyes, what would I do? Grin as if we'd been playing a game, both knowing it? It wouldn't ease my shame. Did he know I was there? As I hesitated, I saw myself standing motionless there in the dark, holding my breath, in the full absurdity of it: on one floor a boy, and on the floor below, at dead of night, a fully grown man pretending not to be there. It was a kind of madness, Creeper's come-uppance. I mustn't be so silly. I stretched and met, not Egon's eyes, but a sleeping face, eyes closed, head back against the door jamb; so low that I knew he was sitting on the floor, legs extended perhaps, or folded. As if guarding his room.

What in hell's name made him want to sleep that way? I ducked my head down slowly, carefully, and made my way soft-footed down the stairs and back to my room. No pleasure now in completing my rounds, however quietly. I had another hand on watch, duplicating me, and I couldn't fathom why.

TO TELL EGON what I'd seen would be to put at risk all trust between us, he'd think—or rather know, if it was true—that my friendship had slipped over into obsession and that I wasn't just doing my rounds, as he knew perfectly well I did, but breaking my own rules by lingering to spy on him.

So I had to wait. To accede now, for no apparent reason, to his request to move back into the cubicles would tell him what I'd seen, as unerringly as if I owned up properly; and would have the same effect, I decided selfishly, of making him wary of me, even if it gave him what he wanted. Besides—trying now to find less selfish reasons—it wouldn't help me discover what was at the root of the problem. I didn't believe it was the smell of the room. I have a keen nose and I'd sniffed the room, along with neighbouring ones, while the boys were all out on the rugby fields. The base smell was identical, a hundred years of coal fires, sweat, ink, dirt from the grounds trailed in and ingrained in the carpet, an indefinable smell of boy and, on top of it, depending on the room, a more definable one, as each current tenant exuded more or less of his personal smell. Marshall's was rank, Vanstone's sickly as his sweat, Talbot's stale with the incense of erotic experiments; and Egon's, no less unmistakable. It too was a sweetish smell, but an aroma less cloying than Vanstone's, a curiously innocent, child's smell like the top of a sweaty baby's head; as though, even now that we'd found him a birthday and a true, settled age of sixteen, this had done nothing to restore the four years lost to the forest, or the three-and-a-half before it, equally lost to memory and obliterated by his wolf-child self; as though, in fact, his glands had only begun their civilized olfactory life when he began anew in Hamburg less than ten years ago. It was the insuperably fresh smell, even at its sweatiest, of a nine-year-old. What was it then, about his own room, that Egon really hated? His own smell? Even if mingled with that of other boys, in the narrow cubicles he'd loved his own smell would have pressed in on him even more. It couldn't be the view from his room, I thought, a pleasant view of the sports fields he delighted in, since the cubicles had none at all. *What* then?

One night soon after the toilet incident I met him face to face, with a shock, in the kitchens, perched tensely on a chair.

We stared at each other across the dark tables, both of us in dressing-gown over pyjamas. Now there was no disguising the fact that we were both midnight prowlers, but at least I hadn't been caught spying specifically on him, and I switched on the light to make it all seem more routine.

'Hungry, eh?' I grinned, though there was no food in front of him, and all the cabinets and drawers were closed. 'I'm usually the one with midnight tummy-rumbles. What do you fancy?' I walked to the large refrigerator, opened it, and stared at a vampire's treasure-hoard congealed in fifty small, transparent plastic bowls. 'Looks like it's red jello or red jello.'

Egon said nothing, and when I glanced at him I saw with a sinking heart how much ground I'd lost in the months since we returned from Hamburg such friends. United for ever, I thought, by the way he'd saved me from the snow, nursed me, led me home by the hand. Linked by our plane ride, *I'll never forget you let me do that*; by what we'd found in Mecklenburg, to which I'd thought myself such a tender, discreet, enduring witness. Now his small figure sat before me, watching me, held in that same disciplined and erect manner he'd adopted eighteen months ago, when he first came to the school and we were strangers.

'Tell me what the matter is,' I said.

His gaze didn't waver. After a silence, I took a chair and parked myself across the wide table from him, conscious of the bitter smell of wood polish and old encrusted food scored black into grooves in the tabletop.

'I'm the world's leading expert on insomnia,' I said. 'As you probably know. Tell Dr Hanbury.'

It had been an involuntary adoption of my father's role, but now I saw in Egon's face much the same anxiety as Father's sternness must have evoked in his patients.

'Forget I said that. I don't know the first damn thing about insomnia. I just suffer from it and I couldn't begin to tell you why. And d'you know something odd? Since we came back from Mecklenburg I don't suffer from it any more. Perhaps you can explain that to *me*.'

As I said it I thought, fool, now you've undermined all the pretended innocence of your own presence here in the middle of the night; but Egon either didn't notice or hadn't believed me in the first place, because a little animation entered his face and he finally spoke.

'You're probably still catching up on sleep, sir.'

'Perhaps,' I said. 'What about you? You had a pretty energetic time yourself.'

He looked at me in silence, still erect, controlled.

'D'you mind if I get up, sir?'

He was scraping back his chair before I could answer.

'Not at all,' I said, and watched him walk round the tables towards the door, flexing his shoulders as if his posture had been an intolerable strain. 'Where are you going?'

'Nowhere,' he said breathlessly, passing the door to continue a circuit round the room, and I noticed for the first time that the sound of his voice seemed to distress him, as if in his own ears it didn't sound like his. When he reached his chair again, he seemed to force himself to sit down, and his hurried lap of the room didn't seem to have brought any relief.

His hands worked at his pyjama knees.

'Have you ever suffered from claustrophobia, sir?'

'Have I? Good Lord, Egon, you saw me in the plane.'

'But that was different, it was being up high, wasn't it?'

'Up high and enclosed. If you'd pushed me out the window, I promise you my first feeling would have been relief.'

He studied me, unsmiling. Without changing expression he began to cry. I waited, knowing better than to prompt him.

'I'm sorry.'

His voice broke on the word, and I searched my dressing-gown pockets; this time I hadn't got a handkerchief either.

When I started up towards the drawer where the napkins lived, his furious voice warned me not to treat him like a snivelling child any more. 'It's all right, it's all right,' he raged, and I sat back down again, waiting for him to regain composure.

'How long has it been going on?' I asked, and when he didn't answer, still angry with me, 'It's only this term, isn't it? Since we got back from Germany.'

'I try not to get out of bed,' he said at last. 'I try so hard, but the more I try the more I *have* to. And if I don't... if I don't my mind starts to play tricks on me.' He glanced at me, frightened now at what he was confessing as if this were worse than claustrophobia. 'I'll only tell you,' he said—yes, yes some kind of madness for which I might have him incarcerated—'if you promise not to send me to a psychiatrist.'

'When has anyone ever sent you to a psychiatrist?' I said, thinking of Waterson's refusal to do so; and Alec's contempt for the breed.

'The Dodderer,' he said bitterly, and I felt ashamed at my forgetfulness. 'Just don't send me to her.'

'Not if you went stark staring bonkers,' I said, and saw his lipless mouth tremble in a half-smile. 'If you're mad, then we're all mad—don't you know everyone's mind plays tricks on them?'

Egon shook his head, and gave a shudder. 'I can actually smell smoke. Every night.'

'Smoke? Why d'you think that is?' And thought I saw the answer at once. 'If you've got the window open, it's probably the fog filling your room.'

He shook his head again. 'It smells like burning. It only happens when I won't get out of bed, and the smell tells me the house is on fire.' He swallowed, and spoke slowly. 'I *know* that if I don't get out of bed right away, the stairs will have gone and I'll never get down.'

He paused to collect himself, and I saw again his crouched figure outside his door at night. Not guarding his room; guarding the *stairs*.

'I *know* it isn't true, I know it's just to get me to give in, and leave the bed, and once I'm up the same old fight begins, trying not to leave the room,' the tears were coming again but he ignored them, 'I'm sorry, I'm doing everything I can not to leave the house...'

'*Leave* the damn house,' I cried, unable to take any more of this, 'd'you think I want you going through this for *my* sake? Leave the damn house and run naked round the grounds if that's what you feel you want to do, who's going to know?'

'The mad wolf-child,' he giggled, but there was no relief in it, only rising hysteria, 'I bet someone... I bet they'd see me and sell the photographs to the newspapers.'

'Rubbish. I'll run with you, that'll really give them something to write about. Headmaster's midnight runs with naked wolf-child, round the playing fields.' His giggles increased dangerously, and I waited for them to settle. 'Is that what you want to do? If so I advise you to do it. I'm serious.' I felt a glimmer of understanding, a nascent theory. 'Or do you want something different from the playing fields? There's always Tupholme Wood.'

'I don't know,' he said. The giggles had passed and all at once he seemed sleepy, head drooping. 'I haven't let myself think about it.'

'Well *do*,' I said. 'And get out there and do it, I'll keep *cave*.'

He nodded. But I could see that somehow my home-made brand of therapy hadn't caught his imagination.

'You can tell me,' I said. 'Is it Brüel you want to go back to? Is that the problem?'

'I've thought about that,' he said. 'And the funny thing is, it isn't.' He looked at me. 'I don't know why. I *love* to think about it now, the woods and the...' he completed the sentence as if he'd trapped himself into it, 'the treehouse, and Ludolf,' he added quickly as though the name were a protective charm. 'But you see, I've done it there. I *know* I've done it there, even though I can't remember any of the details. I'd like to go back some day, but that's different. It's completely different.'

'Tell me what happened at the treehouse,' I said.

But his eyes stared through me in the old way, and I knew I'd lost him.

CLAUSTROPHOBIA: *I EVEN* went and looked it up in medical dictionaries, where a psychological illiterate could equally well have supplied the attendant definition. What it didn't even hint at were its possible traumatic origins, *etiology* was the dictionary word for it and the kind of word the greedy amateur 'head-shrinker' in me was now using in conversation with myself. This traumatic etiology was the kind of thing Freud had provided for almost everything, I supposed. I went to Freud. Freud was worse than no help. He was firm on the subject: claustrophobia derived from a compulsion to be promi-scuous; *or*, on the other hand, from a compulsion to be monogamous, itself a fear of promiscuity, which was, I gathered, a disguised attraction to it. I was bewildered by this rigmarole; he seemed to have all the exits covered, on the assumption that everyone was called to promiscuity. But why did only some of us suffer from claustrophobia? The answer lay, predictably enough, in childhood. His patients had witnessed—or imagined they'd witnessed, which we were to take as amounting to the same thing—their parents coupling, evidence of their mother's 'promiscuity' in that she was being unfaithful to her son; or of the father's unfaithfulness, in the case of a daughter, though the child-witnesses were largely male, as if the female sex had less to complain of in male promiscuity. But the point here was that it never seemed to be the child himself who had either witnessed or pictured the dread event—the child didn't remember anything of the kind, whether as dream or as reality, it was the Herr Professor Doktor who remembered on the child's behalf, by inter-preting his dreams. And here, for me, the ice gave way. Not even my newly found amateur status as a head-shrinker could equip me to interpret, as Freud did, a dream of staring wolves as symbolizing the parental genitals in action. My first Hamburg trip had shown me genitals in action (indeed as I thought then, Egon's parental ones), more genitals in action than I really needed to see in one lifetime, yet none of them had suggested staring wolves. I was out of my depth.

And for a time I thought my own more modest approach, practical rather then theoretical—indeed based on total theoretical igno-rance—was working. I'd counselled exorcism by indulgence (wasn't this the kind of thing the Dodderer had extolled?). And most nights Egon seemed to be acting on it. From one or other of the windows, on my prowl, I would catch a glimpse of him, not naked thank God but wearing running shorts with a sweater on his back and another looped tightly round his waist, jogging himself exhausted in the moonlit grounds. It seemed to do his daily classwork no great harm, and he was fit as a flea, he won the school cross-country championship at a canter, glancing in my direction as he crossed the line to innocent applause.

It was a false dawn. And the first time he ran away from school, at the beginning of the summer term, I finally had to face the fact that somewhere along the line I'd failed, as utterly as Winterson had failed.

The sin of pride, no doubt my foremost sin, had made it possible. I thought myself so much the better, kinder man than Winterson. Yes, I'd thought myself Egon's saviour from the Wintersons of this world; never mind his friend. Thinking myself generous, I'd hurried the boy into a return to Germany, about which I knew he had mixed feelings. It was *my* hand, in Egon's, that had opened Pandora's Box—that was how I now saw the treehouse. Whatever it had contained, this was its legacy.

I'd always restrained myself from checking that he was back in his room after his run, and not roaming the house—chiefly out of fear that he'd catch me doing it—but it never occurred to me that he wouldn't return at all. The morning he was found to be gone, it was too late and I had all the time in the world to reproach myself. I had ceased to be in charge—officially. Once the boy left school bounds, as I was bluntly informed, the matter was out of my hands. But I couldn't believe he was gone, and spent the first day searching every room, searching the cubicles, under the beds; searching the toilets, the classrooms, every last cupboard, storeroom, shed. Finally round and round the grounds, not caring that to the staff and the rest of the school I looked like a desperate dog-lover bereft of his pet. I felt Egon was watching me all the time. I even glanced up into the trees, expecting to see him at every moment.

If some bright spark hadn't alerted the newspapers (no doubt sold the story to them, if I knew Marshall) I think the Governors would have let the incident pass. As it was, *Wolf-Child On The Run, Sightings Near Bodmin* were headlines that did the school no good at all. And though my job would not be in any immediate danger—a sacking now would only compound the bad publicity—I knew it wouldn't be forgotten when my record came up for review. It only needed one old duffer to change sides.

I hardly needed it, but Alec Thurgo gave me a clear idea of what the old duffer would be saying in private. 'What the hell have you been up to, Hanbury?' he bellowed down the phone. 'All this hogwash you've been giving me about turning the boy into a star, these god-damned trophies he brings home—you should have left well alone, not tuned him up like a bloody racehorse. Nobody asked you to do that. He's already too highly strung, I've told you that often enough. And I tell you this now: if I find out when you get him back that you've been trying to bugger him, and *that's* why he's run away, I won't just have your job, my lad, I'll do as I promised you the Christmas before last. I'll have your *balls*.'

We got him back, after three days and sleepless nights, retrieved by the Cornish constabulary, and I was horrified to find him in a police cell in Bodmin, looking every bit as exhausted as I was. Clothes, hands and face filthy. I made him wash before we left.

'Not half as bad as German gaols,' he said cheerfully on the way out to the car, and revealed to me for the first time that he'd run away in Hamburg, when Richard had first left him in Mutti's care, and that the *Polizei* had found him hiding in a park. He told the story at length now, as if it were a delightful memory; and perhaps to deflect my questions for as long as possible. Proudly, 'I *bit* several of them. It took three of their biggest men to bring me in.'

'Are you as unhappy as all that, at the school?' I asked as we drove slowly across the moor. 'You can be honest, I promise I won't take it personally.' I smiled at him. 'I'm beginning to be unpopular there myself.'

He looked at me, stricken. 'I didn't mean to get you into trouble.'

'You haven't,' I said and, continuing to lie, 'I only said it to cheer you up. If the powers that be are going to panic at a thing like this, I don't want to stay there either.' And this I meant: 'We'll both leave.'

'But I *love* the school,' he said sincerely, staring at me in puzzlement. 'It had nothing to do with the school. Are you saying I can't come back?'

'Of course you can come back. It would make life easier if I could say I'd had some explanation. Why *did* you run off?'

'I wasn't running away from the school,' he said earnestly, 'I really wasn't. I just wanted... I just wanted a weekend by myself.' I studied him, waiting. 'And then it turned into, I don't know, a long weekend, I suppose. I wanted to see if I could live on the moor. Couldn't you say you'd told me to do it, as a survival exercise, you know, for the School Corps?'

'A bit late for me to remember that now. And were you able to?' I said. 'Live on the moor?'

'Well,' said Egon, gazing out at it, at the glorious hedgerows crammed with the purple and yellow of May, at the gorse-lit moor beyond. 'No.' He grinned. 'Actually I couldn't. Don't tell anyone but I stole a loaf of bread from somebody's kitchen yesterday. The police didn't mention it, and anyway I hope the people think the dog did it, I gave him a slice and left the wrapper by his kennel.'

'Cunning little swine.'

He yelped with pleasure.

'Seriously,' he said at last, without looking at me. 'Are you angry with me?'

'Not in the least,' I lied. Well, a partial lie; I wasn't angry with him now, not now that we were together. 'I'm just afraid that you're not telling me the whole truth about your escapade.'

'I am. Honestly I am. I just had a terrific urge to be out on the moor.'

'What about old Trimble?' I said. 'Didn't you feel you were letting him down? He must have been expecting you on Sunday.'

'Oh that wasn't a problem,' he said. 'If I don't show up at Webb's, we always meet up on the moor, by the Stripple Stones. We usually do, in summer. That's where we met on Sunday, and I left to walk back alone, that's all.'

I sighed. If there was more to it all, I wasn't going to get it from him today. 'I *am* aggrieved about one thing,' I smiled, 'without you we lost by an innings on Saturday. Against Drummonds, if you remember. They have a stupid man called Hartley in charge of cricket. He was gloating, and in a crummy German accent too: '*Vere iss ze demon bowler from Hamburg, Hambury?*'

'I'm *not* a bowler.'

'That's what I told him. Egon, if you really do like being at the school and you want to pick things up where you left off, will you give me your word you won't run off again without coming to me first and telling me what's on your mind?'

'Certainly,' he said, 'I promise.'

NOW, ALTHOUGH I left him, as before, to his nocturnal runs—I felt I could hardly forbid them without turning the school into his prison—I couldn't help watching him a little more closely during the day, to gauge his mood. Since our return from Mecklenburg our evening meetings had become rarities, they were less necessary, I'd thought, and for my part I imagined myself in almost telepathic communication with him, without need of confirming conversations. I'd been wrong, at least about my telepathic insights. And now he only came at intervals, usually bearing an unfamiliar plant for my botany books to help identify; and the treehouse mystery that lay between us put me all the way back to square one, to our first meetings together, as constrained by his obduracy as by my efforts not to turn them into interrogations.

To give some credit to my powers of observation, to my feeling for Egon, telepathic or not, it was only intuition, backed by a subtle change of mood I saw in him that day, that led me to anticipate the night of his second escape.

He was a little more silent than usual, a little restless, nothing to alarm even the interested onlooker, and I questioned my own suspicions. In my jittery state they were strong enough to make me break my own rules that night. I dressed warmly; waited till the house was quiet, and stepped outside. Feeling a fool, but telling myself that this time my living was on the line, I stood in the rhododendrons where I'd once stalked Marshall's SS platoon; from there I had a view of the door where, if he kept to his routine, Egon would emerge in running clothes.

Out he came on the stroke of two, and when I saw what he was wearing I knew I'd been right. Trousers this time, shirt and jacket, and outdoor shoes unfit for running in. 'You little bastard,' I breathed as I watched him saunter down the paved drive towards the open front gates. Keeping well back, I followed him on foot.

I dare say tracking a man requires expertise. I had no convenient crowds to cover my inexperience, and I assumed that if he heard me he would bolt at once; then I'd be done for—he was the cross-country champion, not I. So I stayed well back, and promptly lost him.

I'd guessed where he was going, though, from the direction he'd chosen, and though The Parade was empty when I arrived at the centre of Liskeard, the faint suggestion of candlelight, undulating behind Lizzie in Trimble's window, gave me hope that I'd been right.

Deciding I'd confront Egon when he came out, I took up a position in front of the Empire Fruit Shop with its blue neon sign (a fish, Christ's symbol, as old Trimble would no doubt be gratified to note, if Lizzie wasn't in the way; with a more secular *And Chips* flashing on and off inside the neon outline of the fish). I hunched there opposite the hotel, under the throbbing, humming sign, for all the world like a jealous lover staking out his adulterous mate. At least I could believe that when Egon fled to the moor, it wasn't done, as he'd assured me, against the school or me. Now I felt like a jilted confidant. What he wasn't telling me he was perhaps telling the mad old man his grandfather, in the flickering light behind Lizzie's back, and mine. Telling 'Mad' Trimble of all useless people. What would the man have to offer him? For all the intelligent conversation he'd get from his grandfather, Egon might as well be confiding in Lizzie.

At that a thought struck me. Lizzie, now a blotchy figure with the more thinly painted sections of her showing brighter against the light than the encrusted parts, oddly like a colour negative, a Virgin in colour negative... could it be that Egon was confiding in Trimble largely *because* the old man barely knew who he was, perhaps wouldn't answer him at all or even remember what Egon had told him? The idea eased my jealousy; it would mean Egon didn't want a wise, reactive friend, and I hadn't been singled out for slighting. Yes, and suppose it was precisely Trimble's blinkered obsession with the Virgin that gave Egon a clue to the heart of his own distress: here was the one subject, aside from botany and bird calls, on which the old boy was forthcoming... but if so, *what* clue was he supplying? A Virgin-clue. Had there been an altar inside the treehouse, an altar to the Madonna? That seemed neither especially likely nor, indeed, traumatic. Was Herta the Virgin? I knew otherwise, and now that Herta had been discredited as Mother, I could disabuse Egon myself. Except that I had not the slightest idea why a Herta-Virgin would be meaningful to Egon. His mother then, Maggie? For an instant I wished Freud could be standing next to me outside the Empire Fruit Shop so that I could apologize to him for my apostate sneers, and ask his advice. This was surely his territory.

As so often, the answer I couldn't come up with was so obvious I missed it altogether. It had to do with a virgin, I'd got that part right, but in all other respects I was hopelessly off course.

For some reason I lost my nerve that night, I still don't know why, and when I was woken from my trance by the sound of the gigantic hotel front door creaking open, I darted back into the darkness of the alley beside the shop. I'd failed to prepare a speech or even decide in what mood or mode I would reproach Egon; I knew, too, that I had time to hide myself—no matter how familiar they are with the weight and stiffness of Webb's Hotel's ten-foot-high grey door, I have yet to see anyone breeze through it at the first push or pull. By the time Egon did emerge, I was telling myself there might be some profit in seeing where he went next and, if it was back to the school, in ruminating on this lesser infringement than I'd feared, before deciding what to do.

This time I made a better job of shadowing him. It was easier: he went back tamely to the school gates, and into the silent dormitory buildings.

Now I was left with a fine dilemma. I knew I ought to warn him that I'd seen it all, because if he did it again it would only take a passing police car on the prowl and we'd both be done for. But if I made clear how closely I was spying on him—a lying hypothetical warning, 'I hope you're not thinking of visiting the town at night...' might just as surely give the game away—wouldn't it drain the last dregs of our trust? The options had been narrowing steadily, inexorably, I hadn't wanted to believe it but now I had to face the choice I'd been dreading all along: between Egon and the school. Which did I love more?

EGON OF COURSE. And of course that was the way to lose them both. His third and final evasion—I don't count where he is now, as I write this, because the word evasion is too absurdly small for it—broke the bank, at least as regards my running moral overdraft with the Governors. They didn't fire me, but they let me know they were considering it; and not because I lost control of a uniquely frisky young animal. I have everyone's sympathy for that, a sympathy that nauseates me in its dismissal of Egon's humanity. No, it'll be because I tried to be too 'pally' with the 'creature' as a former headmaster of the school termed him to me. If only I had Winterson's sink-or-swim attitude to problem cases, I'd be in excellent odour.

And if only Egon hadn't burned down the Ark.

It was an accident, he swears, and I believe him. I almost believe him.

The Ark, the premises loaned to me in wartime by the Dean of Wells to house our 'conchies' and other dazed miscreants, was church property, left to the diocese by a farmer's pious widow. Actually I understood her to have been chiefly interested in table-tapping, in a pagan attempt to contact her departed husband, so the vicar of Dobwalls assured me; either she returned to the Christian fold with a vengeance at the last, or arranged her will to slight her surviving family. Given the beauty of the place, I was glad I never came across the disinherited. I became hopelessly attached to the sweet Georgian-fronted doll's house, hard against a wooded hill, with its outbuildings below, fronting a stream; the remains of an old millhouse hid there beneath steeply sloping fields, too steep for grazing or for farming, full of oxlips and orchids; and in the wood itself stood a small long-disused chapel which not even the farmer's wife had tried to reclaim from the cows who now lived in it. They came to me with the loan of the property: chapel and cows and fields, the ruined millhouse and a section of the stream. Miss Platten it was—I remember now—who re-named it the Ark, a sanctuary for men and animals alike. How reluctantly I gave it up in '46! And was amazed to find the place still standing empty when I got the Liskeard job eight years later. The Dean of Wells was Bishop now, and though he's never admitted as much I'm sure it was his private canvassing that got me the post. He strongly approved of my return to schoolmastering. This is an ungrateful thought, but I've always thought he was glad—fond as he was of me—not to have to choose between his conscience and abetting my preferment within the clergy. My theological unsoundness tickled him in private; better to keep it that way. In the '50s his influence with the Cornish diocese seemed unabated, and when I asked to borrow the vacant house and grounds for school activities, he engineered it once more. I had in mind our many country boys for whom an afternoon in such surroundings, playing Farmer Giles with aged, patient livestock (mostly superannuated beasts belonging to a soft-hearted smallholder, who lent them to us during term-time) was preferable to school sports and certainly more functional.

So it began again, my tenancy of the Ark. In truth I tried to limit my own visits. Much as I loved my ship, the school, my heart was still in that little moorage outside Dobwalls, and each visit found me laying inappropriate plans to move the headmaster's residence there. It was unthinkable, in term-time; I was also afraid that if I spent the holidays at the Ark, as I longed to, I'd spend the terms yearning for it. In a perverse way, and once the first shock was over, I almost wanted to thank Egon for burning it down when he did.

There were only two weeks left of the summer term, and I was ready to breathe out, thinking that by a miracle we'd made it, Egon and I. I'd encouraged him to visit Alec as often as possible, and he did—or so he said, claiming that he and Alec met at Webb's, which explained why I never saw the Alvis roll up on Sunday mornings. Nor had I heard a word from Alec since Egon's return from Bodmin gaol and his assurances to Alec that he hadn't been fleeing my attentions. That Egon even had to say so had fractured my dignity, but at least it preserved my physical manhood. I had no reason to think Egon really was spending his Sundays with Alec, who'd shown little interest in weekend visits; but that was precisely my strategy—let him do what he liked with this escape valve, so long as he was back by Sunday night.

Indeed, on the Sunday night when he did not return and rumours began to fly around the school, I firmly calmed everyone by telling them that the boy was in London with Alec, and would be back late. It was a desperate throw, but by then, Sunday bedtime and no sign of Egon, I had little to lose.

Standing anxiously on the verandah outside my drawing room, as midnight approached, I actually heard the fire engines hooting their way out of Liskeard and down the Dobwalls road. But I made no connection. Egon wasn't a firebrand, to my knowledge.

An hour later the police arrived with Egon. So many lights went on at bedroom windows that it was futile to try and get them doused, or even shout from the drive that I knew each and every inmate by room; they'd only have watched in darkness, and I was busy dealing with the uniformed sergeant and my frightened, shivering boy.

Looking closer at him as I ushered them into the drawing room I saw that he wasn't frightened, he was just plain cold despite the black leather jacket he was wearing over school trousers. I'd never seen this garment on him before, yet he looked oddly familiar in it; and I realized with a jolt that it was the flying jacket around Denis Towle's shoulders in my dream that it called to mind. All through the interview that followed he appeared not to be hearing what the police sergeant was saying, but kept his eyes on me. I couldn't fathom the expression, it wasn't that he was sorry for *me*—that was what I thought at first, and instead of soothing it infuriated me—or that he was sorry for what he'd done. It looked as if for the first time our deeper roles had been reversed and he was haunted by me, drawing life from me.

'What do you want us to do with him?' asked the sergeant. To judge by his manner he was not unduly thrilled to have drama on his hands at one a.m. 'To be frank with you, sir, I'd rather have kept him in the cells, given his record. Can you lock him in his room or something? At least till morning. Then we can inform Mr Thurgo. Unless *you* want to ring him at this hour. The fact is, he wasn't too pleased the last time we put the boy in a cell, though we did treat him with kid gloves—what would you do if you had the MP's adopted son in your police station? He is the adopted son, isn't he?' he said, seeing something in my expression.

'No. Alec Thurgo's his legal guardian, that's all.'

'Same difference as far as we're concerned. The lads at Bodmin got a right ticking off, though I don't see much else they could have done. They were only holding him for *you*. I'm not making the same mistake. I'll get a worse wigging if you lose him, mind. Can you keep guard over him till morning?'

I nodded.

He'd already told me about the fire at the Ark, and my first reaction had been anything but relief—except to see that Egon had survived it. He'd admitted the fire had started while he was there, without permission; indeed it would have been hard for him to deny that he'd been there at all, given his singed clothes and features daubed with melted ash. But he could easily have claimed he'd seen the fire and rushed to put it out, I thought. A perfect alibi for his absence, even turning him into a hero. It required barely a fraction of his canniness to think of this. Why hadn't he done so?

It wasn't honesty, as I discovered once Egon had been bundled away in Matron's care, with instructions not to let him out of her sight until I joined them. 'What do you know about a motorcycle and sidecar,' the sergeant pulled out his notebook, and made a display of laboriously finding the page. 'Registration number... BDA 674. Familiar to you?'

I shook my head, visualizing the machine, black, Egon's hair streaming back as he revved away, and the departing number plate; an anagram for BAD.

'You were not aware that young Lützow,' Loots-oh, he pronounced it, 'was in possession of this vehicle and was driving it on the public road without a licence?'

'No,' I said. It was as I'd pictured it; and all too plausible.

'You don't seem very surprised, if I may say so, sir. He's had no lessons. You do realize he could easily have killed himself, *and* others in the process?'

I was past caring for the sergeant's opinion, whether or not he passed it on to Alec, or published it in Liskeard town square.

'I've seen him fly a plane,' I said, 'without lessons.' He looked at me as though I were clearly insane and the sole author of all Egon's misdeeds. 'Very ably,' I added. 'I'd bet good money that he was a better and safer driver than any man on your force.'

The sergeant had heard enough. 'I doubt that, sir,' he said, 'in any case the boy was breaking the law—and will be prosecuted for it in due course, Alec Thurgo or no Alec Thurgo. You have my word on that. Along with anyone, *anyone*, who might be regarded as his accomplice in this act. I shall pretend I never heard what you said about him flying a plane.'

'It's all right,' I said, 'that was in Germany. And I can assure you I had no idea that he owned a motorbike, much less drove it. Where did you find him?'

'Riding back across the moor, sir. Coming from Launceston. It was his face that made us stop him. He should have had the sense to clean it up.'

'From Launceston,' I said. 'Not from Dobwalls?'

'That's right, sir. But he didn't try to deny that he'd been at the fire. Says it started while he was upstairs. He'd lit a fire in the grate and forgotten to put the fireguard back, that's what he says. Says a log must have fallen out of the grate onto the carpet.'

'It's possible,' I said.

'Yes, sir. It's possible. We'll have a better idea when we get the fire department's report. Now if that's all you need from us tonight, I'll be back in the morning bright and early, and we can ring Mr Thurgo together.'

'I'll phone him myself, first thing,' I said. The tiredness was hitting me too now. 'You don't have to be involved.'

'I *am* involved, sir,' he smiled in grim politeness. 'Though if you'd prefer me to make my own call, from the station...'

'No no, come by all means. Safety in numbers,' I heard myself say, and changed this hastily to 'solidarity, I mean,' though I knew I'd forfeited whatever chance I had of obtaining this from the police.

I relieved Matron from her guard-dog role, and sat on the end of Egon's bed, gazing at the remorseful, newly cleaned face on the pillow. Despite the events of the night his expression brought nothing but a guilty ache into my chest, and I found myself smiling at him in weary complicity.

'You can lock me in like he said, it's all right.'

Yes, I'd earned this: now he was comforting *me*.

I wanted to leave the Ark till last, at that moment I still couldn't bear to think of it ruined, gone.

'Sorry we have to do this now,' I said, 'but that policeman's coming back first thing in the morning to phone Alec with me, and he may come before we get a chance to talk and... for you to tell me your side of it.'

From nowhere, and before he could answer, I suddenly felt myself fill up with rage, as though I was the Ark myself going up in a roar of flame, out of control.

'You stupid, stupid boy!' I heard myself shout, still vaguely trying to think what it was that had possessed me; Egon's face on the pillow looked far from startled, however. 'You promised me! You said you'd come to me first—and instead you went and stole a blasted motorbike—'

'I didn't steal it, sir,' Egon put in quietly, 'I bought it.'

'I don't care! You weren't supposed to be on the road with it, and now... unless Alec can do wonders for you, you're going to end up in court on two charges, that and arson.'

'It wasn't arson.'

'Oh Christ,' I said. 'What were you doing coming back from Launceston? Did you run away after the fire, or what?'

He shook his head.

'I had to take my girlfriend home,' he said, still calm and contrite, 'to *her* school. We tried to fight the fire, otherwise I'd have got her back in good time.' He must have seen me boggling at him, but he ignored it. 'I saw her climb in safely, though. I don't think anyone will have found out.'

'Girlfriend?' I stuttered at last. '*What* girlfriend,' my mind was reeling back through possible assignations at Webb's, on the moor, in Tupholme Wood, all over the grounds at night, encouraged by *me*, the stupid inadvertent pander, the patsy, and now the whole world of my amateur therapy was falling on my head along with Freud and half a dozen futile, idiotic dictionaries, 'how long have you known her? Who is she?'

I have fled as a grain of pure wheat
On the skirt of a hempen sheet entangled
That seemed of the size of a mare's foal
That is filling like a ship upon the waters;
Into a dark leathern bag was I thrown
And on a boundless sea I was sent adrift...

—The Song Of Taliesin

HER NAME WAS CHRISSIE WOLFE. I didn't know whether to be shocked or relieved when I discovered that she was just fourteen years old. Had I known that she was going to be—after Egon, indeed more in certain unavoidable respects than Egon ever could be—the love of my life, I think I would have been even more shocked, and certainly relieved when Egon rebuked my expression by telling me sternly that nothing more than tender kisses had been exchanged between them.

Of course I've asked myself, and always shall, whether I would have loved Chrissie if someone other than Egon had introduced us, if indeed Egon hadn't found and loved her first; and if she hadn't loved him with a love at least as strong as mine.

Sometimes it's clear enough to me: I can ask myself such things precisely because I know I would have loved her anyway, although eleven years have gone by, arduous years (whose story is properly hers to tell), before I felt ready to declare my love. As I am today; or as I shall be soon, when this memorial is complete. And if doubt creeps in, I've always read these old questions the way they probably deserve, back to front. In other words, by understanding that Egon's love for Chrissie, like ours—Chrissie's and mine—for him, only reinforces my love for her. It could never undermine it, no matter what happens now.

She was born in London and into a family of German Jews, recently naturalized. Egon seemed unimpressed when I remarked on this common Teutonic background; and, more surprisingly, he simply stared when I made to tease him about Chrissie's surname. I had to spell it out for him: the wolf-child had fallen for a Wolfe. Even then he only bridled irritably as though he truly hadn't noticed, and informed me that the name had been changed from the original Walfisch.

The Wolfes themselves had spawned daughters, three of them, and given them names which distanced them even further from their recent past. Resolutely English names: Joanna, Christine, Frances. The parents were not, as Chrissie put it, practising Jews. (All the same I found it a little hard to understand how they had alighted on the name Christine; but perhaps I am over-sensitive to such matters, since rather like Egon in his obliviousness to the implications of Chrissie's surname, Chrissie herself blandly insists that her parents simply thought Christine 'a nice name'.) Even her grandparents had no longer visited the synagogue in their native Frankfurt; all observances had long since been discarded. They were enlightened world citizens, free of cant and the bonds of history. In Frankfurt they had read Heidegger and discussed Nietzsche. Even Nietzsche, however, failed to give precise warning of the history that was shortly to enmesh us all, much less advise the Walfisches that their enlightenment would not save them from it. Jews they were, Jews they felt themselves to be (with or without a yarmulke), but they were Germans first. They swore by the greatness of the German nation, its manifest destiny and their share in it. So much so that Chrissie's Uncle Oskar, disguising his origins under a false name and address, actually joined the fledgling National Socialist Party. When Chrissie first told me this I took it for an atrocious and sinister joke. It wasn't. Like many of his fellows (and not a few of his relatives) Oskar Walfisch believed in national pride, in socialism, in full employment and in thumbing his nose at the Versailles Treaty which had so high-handedly penalized his country. Had he read *Mein Kampf* with its anti-Semitic ravings? Perhaps not, but his horrified family justly held ignorance to be no excuse, and excommunicated him. Liberal they might be—to the point where certain defiantly sectarian members of their race could be regarded as an embarrass-ment to loyal German citizenship, even as social fascists—but this was going too far. Unbowed, Oskar responded by changing his name for good, and disappearing.

Many families had a black sheep, some delinquent or crazed unfortunate who was rarely mentioned and about whom the children speculated, secretly. Oskar was something worse than a black sheep, he was a black hole into which the entire family might fall if he so much as surfaced in their thoughts. Would they not disintegrate with shame? Oskar was anti-matter. Even excommunication was a bond, a form of recognition by default, and wouldn't do; after all, Aunt Ilse had been banished merely for setting up house with a guttersnipe young enough to be her grandson, Cousin Josef for gambling away his parents' largesse and ending up serving in a sweet shop; and then there was Grandfather Jacob who, it was said, had been ostracized for ten years after bringing his mistress to a bar mitzvah. What punishment remained for a Jewish Nazi? What escape from him? And this—this gruesome dilemma—faced the Walfisches long before genocide was a reality.

Oskar could be written out of family conversation, and all but lost to memory. Yet not entirely, because... what if he reappeared? It was said that Hitler himself had Jewish blood and that his persecution of the Jews was an attempt to hide this—a case of over-compensation almost without historic precedent. Self-loathing Jews there had always been, and while not condoned their behaviour could be understood as a twisted by-product of persecution. In the mirror of self they saw themselves as others saw them; and hastened to beat the aggressor to the draw. But if one of these could rise as high as Hitler, how high might not Uncle Oskar rise?

When might he be heard of again—and as *what*?... not as a Walfisch at any rate, that was the saving grace, and no member of the family professed to know the name he had adopted. Yet what if he was seen, encountered, photographed? And in what dreadful guise? What—worst fear of all—if he were to be unmasked?

Like her sisters, Chrissie grew up with no idea that she *had* an Uncle Oskar. Her mother had no brothers; her father just the one, Gustav—or rather he had had a brother, for Gustav was dead. Poor foolish Gustav (faded photographs endorsed this, showing him fat and friendly behind his curly moustache) had refused to believe in the coming holocaust, and waved Father and Mother off at the train station, as they fled to Paris in 1934. He was the family martyr.

221

When the Gestapo came for him he jumped off the balcony of his apartment, dying instantly on impact with the pavement, so the Walfisches—or rather now the Wolfes—had been assured: a dreadful fate, but less so than that awaiting many who lacked his courage and resolution.

So the children understood it, and if Gustav was rarely invoked, neither were the Walfisch cousins, great-uncles and great-aunts who had vanished in the camps. The subject was too painful for recapitulation and, beyond a certain point, children should be spared.

But no matter how well locked, it is the destiny of cupboards to be opened; and of imprisoned skeletons to rattle their chains. The Wolfes had escaped their Walfisch-dom and with it most of the Frankfurters, whether friends or relations, who remembered Oskar Walfisch, fat and friendly, with his curly ginger moustache. And who would have been thoroughly puzzled at the mention of a Gustav Walfisch. This precautionary change of name (Oskar himself could hardly have complained) served as a first line of defence against the truth, along with the forbidding fate assigned to 'Gustav'; indeed the false name may have helped the Wolfes to believe their own lie. Better perhaps to have destroyed all photographs that showed the smiling renegade, using the hasty departure from Germany to explain the lack of family snaps, and denied Father any brother at all. Yet this too would have had its dangers. There were Walfisch cousins in Israel, others in Brazil, and one, a very distant cousin, who was by repute a heroic medical man, in Africa. No-one knew quite where in Africa; but the Brazilians wrote letters, and the Israelis visited. Shame to tell, it was the Israelis who let the side down.

They were Rosenzweigs, cousins of Chrissie's mother, and perhaps their loyalty to her father's Walfisch stock was not as great as it might have been. Father and Mother Rosenzweig would never have dreamed of mentioning Oskar, but their children were not so discreet. They knew little, not even Oskar's name; only that there had been an unmentionable crime in the Walfisch family, and they couldn't wait to discover what it was. It had been committed by someone their parents referred to grimly as 'Adolf'—another precautionary pseudonym, this time a bitter one. Chrissie, the middle child, less ambitious than her elder sister and less canny than the younger, was the innocent Wolfe: she it was who was elected by the gang of younger Wolfes and Rosenzweigs to confront the family. 'There's something we'd all like to know,' said Chrissie brightly over dinner on the eve of the Rosenzweigs' return to Tel Aviv, 'and it's this: *what happened to Uncle Adolf?*'

There was in truth no answer to this question. At least no answer that Chrissie has so far found, and I tell the story much as she told it to me. At the dinner table the Wolfes looked puzzled and the Rosenzweigs went white; despite the ensuing bluster it was clear that a juicy secret had been located, and could not be left undisturbed. Letters flew between London and Tel Aviv. Denials only provoked appalling speculation. The Rosenzweigs' mocking nickname for Oskar Walfisch backfired on both families: when gossip at the Wolfe girls' school reported that the girls believed they were secretly related to Hitler, Mr and Mrs Wolfe knew it was time to lay Gustav to rest and raise the dreaded Oskar from the shadows.

And the fact was, no-one knew what had happened to Uncle Oskar. The best that they could hope for was that he had slunk into obscurity—was he perhaps the African mystery cousin, the girls cried, curing lepers in lifelong atonement? But no, the Wolfes hardly dared indulge this pleasing hypothesis in case the cousin in question (it was true that no-one even knew his name) arrived to be accused of crimes he had never committed, much less atoned for.

The worst, of course, was the possibility that Uncle Oskar had never repented of his early allegiance; nor been exposed as an absurd impostor, a Walfisch in Nazi clothing; had joined the ranks (it was unthinkable!—no, it was thinkable, that was the awful thing) of those who murdered his own race.

And had survived?

One thing was sure. After such a past, if he had lived it and come through, there would be no knock at the door, no fat, friendly or gaunt and harrowed Oskar suddenly appearing at the feast to beg forgiveness. Of all the crimes humanity could boast, could any be as unforgivable? Oskar would know this, that was sure. Or was it?

In reality he was already there, among the Wolfes, present in every mind. Now the door had been opened, and he was inside.

But what was he, poor fat friendly Oskar who had thought himself so free of tribal cant, so open-minded that he could see virtue in his own oppressor? Was he a monster or an idiot? And should one be afraid of such a dreadful, tragic clown?

What was he, if not the spectre that haunted the Jews and turned the horror of the camps into an accusation? The spectre of their submissiveness to tragedy, even complicity with it.

Until further notice, Oskar Walfisch was alive. He was Mengele, he was Martin Bormann.

He was salvation too—these are not Chrissie's words but mine and I must stand by them—if only we (yes, and the Wolfes themselves) would take humanity as our standard, with all its evil indivisible from good. Distinguishable, yes; but wound in a molecular embrace that, even as it mocks it, spawns our moral, mental universe. That fearful universe, where Uncle Oskar is only a knock at the door away.

IN MY STUDY sits a photograph I cut from a magazine many years ago. It shows a young girl standing in a darkened room, with long straight dark hair and a pale thin face and all the responsibilities of adulthood prefigured in her sad, solemn eyes. For reasons shamelessly autobiographical I imagine that the dark house is a rectory. I feel sure there are quarry tiles beneath her invisible feet. The soft unlined face begs a caress, though it would shrink from it, and the best I could do was cut the picture from the magazine, I've forgotten which one or what the image illustrated, and keep it.

It's the story of a day I have to tell, a single day; though not the concluding chapter of our story, Egon's, Chrissie's and mine. Rather a day of transmission—if I stop writing this and turn to the window I can see, in a garden beyond The Parade, a fan of russet beech leaves rising above a laurel hedge like a wall of flame, as if the green laurel were untouched by its own funeral pyre—and renewal, the day, as I mentioned many pages ago, that led that night to the tormenting sequence of dreams in which I had become Alec (though hardly a Thurgo in nature, even in dreams) and presided over a death that seemed to be rescinded in the end, a death and no death, on a homeward visit to the Ark.

Regarding Egon Lützow, we the undersigned...

I woke already drafting the letter.

...concerned that Egon should not be deprived of vocational quali-fications and continuity of schooling...

It was the last Sunday in August, another Sunday, this one between terms. A lot of negotiation had gone into making this the chosen day, to settle Egon's future. By now the six-week-old furore over Egon's 'orgy of destruction', as the Liskeard and Launceston rag put it with typically heedless exaggeration, had died down. Indeed there was little substance for scandal, though that hadn't prevented it. The fire department's report was unable to disconfirm Egon's version of how the Ark had burned down. Of course the report was widely touted as a whitewash drummed up by Alec, but I know for a fact that it wasn't. However the fire had started—sadly it had spread to the woods, scarring the hillside—there was no evidence of arson. Nor any evidence, thank heavens, to suggest that Egon had been trysting at the Ark with an all-too-young lady. (And although people would have seized on it to literalize the newspaper's 'orgy', Chrissie's presence made it even less plausible, if you knew Chrissie, that together they'd torched the house.) Only the three of us knew she'd been there. Alec grimly paid the fine for Egon's vehicular misdemeanours. It would be a while before Egon was allowed to drive. In this, the sum total of the 'scandal', he was only one of many reckless teenagers; but Egon's notoriety ensured that the reports made him sound like the vengeful Hun cutting a blazing swathe across the Cornish countryside.

Alec complained a good deal about being out of pocket and growled a good deal at Egon both before and after the court hearing, a little over three weeks ago now. But he was surprisingly restrained with me, no doubt writing me off as an incurable ass, if he hadn't already, and yet... perhaps he thought Egon's crimes more manly, this time around, than merely running away from school. And something else, something quite different came into my mind: I had a mental image of Alec in the Commons, Alec among his cronies, many of them no doubt parents with 'difficult', rebellious teenaged children; in this vision Alec found himself to be the object of sympathy. I doubt if anyone had ever felt sorry for Alec Thurgo, from their heart. If it was happening now it would be heady stuff.

225

As for the school Governors, their conclusion was simple. Egon was sixteen-and-a-half and ready, like many another restive trouble-maker of his age, to leave. Ripe, as one headmaster of my acquaintance likes to put it, for the sedative of unskilled labour.

I could hardly claim that under my stewardship the school had proved a nurturing haven for the boy. During the last month of term Egon had worked hard to turn in a creditable performance as Puck in A *Midsummer Night's Dream*, the school play, but this was far from sufficient to reassure the Governors that his hooligan days were over. Indeed Egon's role only served to remind them (had I been courting this?) of his real-life pranks. And yet, even before I'd marshalled my own case, the Governors met staunch resistance from one influential quarter. 'Oh, you're throwing in the sponge now, are you?' Alec began briskly when I phoned to pass on the official recommendations. 'Think you can shrug off your duties just like that?' I tried to repeat what I'd already explained to him, that this wasn't *my* idea at all, but he was in full flow and I was a convenient whipping post. I didn't mind, on this occasion; it was like watching my champion in training, an unexpected one but no less welcome. 'If you reckon you can just offload him onto me, you've got another think coming. I'm paying you to produce a properly disciplined youngster, and a properly qualified one, and that's what you'll do till he's good and eighteen. Besides, the boy *wants* to stay. That's what he tells me.'

I hadn't seen Egon since the day of the court hearing. He was in Padstow, I understood, staying in the cottage while Alec beavered away in London. But I would see him today; both of them, indeed. I had convoked a meeting, with Alec as unofficial chairman, of all those who would stand behind me in my efforts to retain Egon for one more year, by which time he would have taken his A-levels and, I had no doubt, passed them with ease. If he was prepared to show up for them. Apparently To spite Egon's Aunt Molly, Richard Thurgo's estranged wife, Alec had invited both Trimble's other surviving daughters, one of them visiting from Canada and neither of whom had ever laid eyes on Egon. If Alec could have invited Trimble's long since deceased wife from beyond the grave, I think he would have, and the meeting was to take place at Webb's hotel so

226

that the boy's grandfather could also lend his voice to the plan. If ever Alec had heard 'Mad' Trimble's voice he might have hesitated. Irrespective of the individual prestige or even sanity of its members, a solid family front would, we hoped, emerge with a petition to the Governors to be drafted by myself.

...behaviour which though unruly and impermissible must be seen in the light of...

'I'll get the Secretary of State to sign it, that should do the trick,' Alec had said. 'Just write the usual guff.'

I lay in bed listening to the Teasmade drool and splutter, and shut my eyes against the light that would shortly come on with a heartless, triumphant hiss from its accomplice the kettle. Why keep the truth from myself? The minutes were running out on us; from the moment he told me about Chrissie I knew it was time to let him go. But I would go on meeting Egon's wishes as long as I could, and if they brought me another year with him, so much the better.

I'd been half awake for hours, my chest tight with excitement, roughing out the letter and telling myself it would be a perfectly straightforward day. Alec would bring the crew of relatives down from London—mentally I piloted them through evergreen Virginia Water and across the gravelled emptiness of Bagshot Heath—to tea at Webb's, whose antique splendours would hush them into quiet self-importance. And I would fetch Egon from Padstow.

During school holidays the abandoned buildings trouble me. Empty classrooms in the sunlight, so still and forlorn—as if night had been turned into day, and my ship raised intact from the depths. Or rather, filled as we were then with Armageddon terrors, like a vision of the post-atomic scene, devoid of people. The little separate desks with their built-in seats do not appear to be waiting for re-occupancy. I can't believe, to look at them, that they'll ever be sat in again. But I'm obliged to confirm the emptiness of each and every classroom. Also the grounds basking in an infinity of release, and the chapel, tidy as a museum. Today my own classroom so oppresses me with its finality that I turn the squeaking blackboard roller, spooling up clean-scrubbed spaces in search of unerased evidence, something uncon-cluded to keep watch over the desks. Possibly in French; Miss Rogerson, a pinched-looking girl charged with teaching this subject, had defected during the Easter holidays to marry a Breton hotelier and inflict her crabbed French (scarcely more fluent than my own Winchester brand, school-taught) on the shopkeepers of Brest; I'd taken over for the summer term.

But when script appears, it's in someone else's handwriting, not mine. Far too fastidious.

Aleximenes the Great, the peace-loving slave who rose to be satrap of Egypt, ruled the province with a lenient hand until, appearing before the people...

Here the blackboard eraser, or perhaps a tweedy forearm, had swept a windscreen-wiper curve across the board, over which ran more of Alick's copperplate writing—of course! I recognized it now, but what had Alick Penby-Stiers been up to in my classroom? Was this message for me? Across the smudged-clean curve the culminating phrase had been translated into furious chalk: *coram populo!*

Trying to picture Alick—Aleximenes the *Fat* would have been a more truthful *nom de plume*—appearing here before my own *populo*, I started like a sleep-walker aroused. The posters on the surrounding walls were all wrong, with their maps of the ancient world, their marble Grecian bums. I wasn't in my own classroom at all, but Alick's.

Now feeling like a spy I read on. Beneath the sleeve-smudge the fragments told a bizarre story, presumably intended for translation by Alick's Latin class.

...he refused to yield to them his favourite, Lustio the Wild Boy of Persia, that gladiator famed for his swordsmanship...

Behind my back, desks no longer empty rollicked with glee.

...whose crimes outside the arena had enraged the Egyptians. Recalled at last to Rome, the indulgent satrap was called before the Senate and stripped of his honours...

It was common practice to enliven prose translation with topical references, especially in the last, carnival week of the summer term, but this was too scurrilous by half. Recalled to Rome and stripped of his honours indeed! Erasing the offending stuff, I was tempted to replace it with a fable about Aleximenes the Fat and *his* swordsmanship, then thought better of it.

Recalled to Rome... suddenly the force of it hit me. Did Alick know—did everyone know except me—even the boys—that I was for the axe? Once Egon was removed, I could be dispensed with too. The image returned of Alick reporting to me when I was convalescing after the East German adventure and he'd acted as my stand-in, at prayers and in assembly: Alick overly apologetic, protesting his inadequacy too much. Did he covet my place?

As I made my way down the deserted staircase I found myself trembling uncontrollably and had to stop, holding onto the banister with both hands. In the silence of the building I felt more like an aged caretaker than a headmaster, and absurdly frightened. Was it really possible that I was on the way out? There had been rumours, but they were too far off-beam to take seriously, grumbles from town councillors who claimed to be concerned for Liskeard's 'standing' (this of a little market town supine for centuries, indeed fast asleep!) in the nation at large. According to them I was putting Liskeard on the map in the wrong way, as a byword for the new laxity; I was turning the school into a laughing-stock, a place where freaks were indulged (and would soon be ravaging the town): turning it into the Ark. My sermons in chapel were said to have taken a queer turn and I had been seen driving around the moors at night with the wolf-child. All this was nonsense of course (though it was true that I'd allowed my sermons to become more ruminative, a little rambling perhaps, on the subject of Saul and Absalom or of Abraham raising the sacrificial sword... painful topics, I admit, but urgent ones). So what if I was seen wiping tears from my eyes when we sang the Nunc Dimittis? *Now lettest thou Thy servant depart in peace, according to Thy word...* it had always moved me. Should I be ashamed to cry? Yet to be honest I too sensed that the old order was falling apart. Examination results had been generally poor, as if my distraction, my abstraction into Egon's world, had sent the entire school into a dream. Parents were complaining, though not to my face—no, it was Alick who had told me this. The captain was missing from the bridge, that was the message as the Governors received it.

Without the reassuring clatter of boys—my crew, mine—even the staircase now seemed to have turned against me. The very walls threatened me with their old photographs and lovingly engraved boards. *Cunliffe T F, Daniel W, Dickson A P J...* what was this but a dreadful mausoleum? The names of the indifferent dead—I'd cherished every one. And now? Was this all I was left with, this shell of piety? Dear God was it possible that Egon, Egon who had filled my life with purpose, would in the end unravel it and leave me emptier than before? I'd never thought of my life as empty; but until now I'd never addressed the reality of a life without the school, only toyed with the idea. Furious, I pitted my shaking legs against the stairs and ran from the building as if it was on fire.

It was in my mind to phone Alick at his fat-faced sister Janet's place in London (she looked uncannily like Alick, indeed she *was* Alick, I sometimes thought, as nature intended Alick to be) and confront him, ask him what he knew—till I remembered that Alick was in the Peloponnese reviewing Grecian bums in the flesh. But wait... Alec Thurgo would know the truth, Alec with his spider's web of gossip, always pestering the Governors. I'd catch him later. No, I'd catch him now, alone, before he left his flat.

'Hello?'

Bewilderingly, it was a woman's voice that answered the phone. I asked to speak to Alec.

'Is that um... one moment—what's his *name*?' she shouted to someone at her end of the line, and after a muffled silence, 'are you Hanbury?'

Ignoring her abrasive tone—who are *you*? I wanted to ask—I repeated, 'Can I speak to Alec, please?'

'Look, if you're the headmaster chap, I've got a message for you. Are you or aren't you?'

'I am, yes.'

'Right. Now, I've been trying to reach you for the past hour or so. Alec said to tell you he might be a little late, and to start without him.'

I groaned. Start without him—and, presumably, the Trimble relatives Alec was bringing? That only left old Trimble, if he deigned to come out of room 26 and join Egon and myself in the library at Webb's. Start *what* without him? 'Where's he gone?'

'It's what he calls his little caucus.' The woman chuckled witheringly. 'You know, backbench plots and such.'

I could picture her now, horsey, a Tory hanger-on. 'Where?

Where do they meet? I've got to get hold of him.'

'Oh, he wouldn't tell *me*, it's all frightfully secret.' Something about her voice nagged at me, familiar. 'Sorry I can't be more help. If he rings, shall I...'

'Tell him to please *not* be late. Tell him to leave a number.'

'Righty-ho,' she brayed, 'I'll do my best.'

Summer sunlight filled the little study with its frayed chintz sofa, the imitation Oriental rug and the pink armchair which would forever conjure Egon perched on the edge of it during our first interviews, a wildcat scrubbed and groomed and tamed into an eager little Prussian officer. Whatever happened I would keep that armchair if I had to steal it with my own hands. I went out to the front door and sifted through the mail still wondering why I'd found the woman's voice familiar on the phone—had I met any of Alec's lady-friends, his totties?—when the unmistakable handwriting stopped me dead.

Even before I opened the letter I knew the day was slipping away from me, swirling beyond my reach. House of Commons notepaper came into view, filched no doubt from Alec's desk...

Dear sir I am somewhat bored here so going to stay with a friend near Wells and if it isn't too much trouble perhaps you could fetch me there. We will make some lunch. An arrow between *make* and *some* led to a hastily inserted *you*. *Make* you *some lunch*. Yes, I was an afterthought. That was it exactly. I sat down, feeling drained.

The rest of the page was taken up with an elaborate tracery of roads and directions straight out of Treasure Island. *Cross stream at foot of hill, climb 200 yards, turn left and follow beech hedge to first track on right...*

This is a map of how to get there. I hope you are having a good holiday, yours sincerely, Egon Lützow.

Wells? My God that was two hours' drive away. I stuffed the remaining letters in my jacket pocket, rose and grabbed the keys from the lobby table and ran to the Wolseley. But only my body was hurrying. My mind was still adrift, serenely enervated, letting mechanical forces take over. When I saw Egon's punctilious hand-writing with its obstinate Gothic traces, the thinking feeling part of me had decided to take the day off. What if the letter hadn't reached me

231

today? I'd be driving slowly to Padstow, to an empty cottage, knocking on the door and peering in at windows, waiting vexed and frantic. But I could feel no alarm at my close shave with this: it made no difference. I knew where my mind was—still staring fascinated at Alick's blackboard, at the words *the indulgent satrap*, and trying to put me off the scent by rendering them into Latin. Instead they came out (with less labour) in French. But this *satrape indulgent* would not be fooled or distracted. The same mechanical forces that were at this moment enabling me to start the car and drive obediently out of the school gates, pausing to check for traffic, were the same forces at work in my life, bellowing what's his *name?* and organizing my journeys, pursuits, appointments, belated invitations—and dismissal, stripped of my honours.

How had it begun? When had I invited them in, these presences, blinding me to... hadn't I treated Penby-Stiers with kindness, yes, with a lenient hand, damn it? Listened, soothed him, sponged his wounds? Oh the stupid voluptuousness of it all—

Yes, blinding me. Even Egon had become Lustio the Wild Boy of Persia while I wasn't looking—or rather while I *was* looking, gazing up at Webb's Hotel from beneath the neon fish; gazing up at Lizzie and missing everything. For this—Trimble's world of icons—was how Egon and Chrissie had met. She was Trimble's latest Madonna. His first Jewish Madonna so far as I was aware, though I hadn't ascertained whether he knew this himself. Chrissie's Aunt Margot had descended to Launceston to take her niece out for the afternoon, had noted nearby Webb's Hotel (*fine granite portico 1837, excellent staircase*) in her guidebook, and brought Chrissie there for tea. Trimble, sitting bleakly unapproachable in his usual corner of the tea-room (brooding, fearing perhaps that after Lizzie there would be no more incarnations) had seen Chrissie enter sallow and erect behind plump rouged Aunt Margot and swooned with certainty. He had never been so close, so physically close: Lizzie Muchmore, like earlier avatars, had been glimpsed from his window as she strolled The Parade. Regularly glimpsed. (In Lizzie's case almost daily, since she revelled in the old painter's gaze.) This one was a visitor and would escape unless he spoke. Happily, widowed Aunt Margot had a weakness for gruff male British courtesy, indeed had buried two elderly

exponents of it, an antique dealer and a moderately eminent architectural historian—in tribute to whom she still sought out fine granite
porticoes, and instructed Chrissie on their virtues in a heavy German
accent. So when 'Mad' Trimble loomed over her at the table, white-
haired and granite-featured (*splendid elderly vicar, 1883-?, good
condition*), Aunt Margot too swooned—or at any rate blushed—with
certainty.

'Mad' was no fool. He was free after all, he was a widower, and
if he had to woo the aunt in order to paint the niece, it was a small
price to pay for resurrecting his vocation.

Would Margot consider letting this exquisite young creature—ah,
her niece? of course, the family resemblance was unmistakable—sit
for him, an amateur dauber but with some small, eccentric reputation, a churchman (sober, reliable) with four daughters himself, now
long since grown-up and their mother gone, alas?

So far, as I understood it from Egon, Trimble had contrived to
ignore Margot's matrimonial hints while encouraging her sufficiently
to guarantee visits along with Chrissie—her excuse, her pretext for
the journey—to Webb's, on as many Sundays as he needed for
artistic purposes. Margot's family were not keen for her to marry
again; in particular Mr Wolfe, as titular head of the clan, found
Margot's continuing flirtatiousness undignified. At seventy enough
was enough. So Chrissie had to be sworn to secrecy. Margot was a
loving and attentive aunt and took her out frequently: that was all
the family needed to know. At fourteen Chrissie Wolfe found herself—much to her amusement, Egon reported—chaperone to two old
trouts. But Margot was not allowed into room 26, while Chrissie sat
for Trimble. Instead she languished in the tea-room, drinking endless
cups of tea until her plump cheeks glowed, and entertaining her
paramour's grandson with tales of Frankfurt in the old days. I
picture them both with one eye on the tea-room door, even as they
laugh. For Egon's mind was of course also in room 26, where like
Margot he longed to be but was barred during painting hours.

Who would not have fallen for Chrissie under such circumstances?
Even to imagine a sitter's face, as the painter scans it in a merciless
agony, is to come under its spell: the more the artist tries to know
the face, to lick its very essence with his eyes, the more the sitter

233

withdraws, leaving only the blank, adorable mask. The Virgin, sublimely ignorant of her magical powers, her fecundity—ah, more than that... what face (and wasn't this why Trimble painted it?), what body can more perfectly represent our ignorance of God than hers? Necessary, inescapable, blameless ignorance, only the more complete the harder we seek to know Him: just as the sitter's essence eludes the painter as soon as he seeks to identify it in her features. And yet—o perfect torment—God *is in* her, in the Madonna's very womb, while she sits patient and thoughtless, reading pious texts (as in Renaissance imagery), or jolts along on the donkey bound for Bethlehem (more like it! to me at least, at this instant, as I wrestle with the gear shift on my doltish, obstinate Wolseley), yes, the godhead is in her and she doesn't even know it! I picture Chrissie returning down the stairs in Webb's, down the excellent, listed staircase with its great wide carpeted treads and lavish mahogany banister. She is behind Trimble, slower than he—Trimble energized, released, still dreamy but as unprotective of his limbs as if he were a young man again, descending a staircase—and life is slowly coming back into her face, the life the painter stole. Or tried to steal. It only withdrew at his glance and now it returns, suffusing her, Chrissie too is dreamy, released from class into a dream-possession of herself. Under Margot and Egon's eyes, they descend the stairs in pensive triumph, like lovers.

'Ach Vilfred!' Aunt Margot breathes (yes, *Wilfred* is Mad's true Christian name, though no-one has uttered it since his wife died), 'When will we *see* it, when will the work be *shown*?' And as Trimble denies her with a modest sigh, 'Just *one* peep for a fond old aunt, won't you permit it?'

'No,' growls old Mad evenly.

Or perhaps she has melted him just a little.

'You know the rules, Margot. More tea?'

As I hear his voice in my head, the penny drops at last—and I hit the brakes, although the lane is long and empty before me and no phone box is in sight.

At the first glimpse of the red sentinel, on the outskirts of a village, I pull up, hurry into the booth and dial Alec's number. My mind is still saying *what difference does it make?* but I ignore it, happy that my body still cares enough to push me on.

The same voice as before barks hello, and I plunge the button home, hearing the coins drop.

'It's me again. Egon's headmaster. Any sign of Alec?'

'None.'

I'm sure now, sure enough to risk a braying laugh if I'm wrong. 'You wouldn't by any chance be one of Egon's aunts?'

'Yes,' she sighs after a brief silence, 'I suppose I am.'

One of old Mad's daughters; that's where I'd heard those tones before. She sounds guarded, and it's my turn to interrogate. 'Which one?'

'Mary.' Her frostiness tells me she knows what's coming.

'Excuse me, but aren't you coming down with Alec? You said *he* might be late... but Alec led me to believe that both you and your sister would—'

'Look. I don't know the boy, I don't know you, and as for our benighted father, he pretends not to have the foggiest idea who we are. Not very promising, is it? Couldn't we sign the letter and be done with it? D'you really need us there?'

'I don't,' I concede, 'if that's how you feel about it. But don't you think it might make a difference to your nephew if he saw that you were sufficiently concerned to make the journey?'

She has the decency to sound abashed: 'Very well, I said I'd come and I will. If and when Alec shows up. Where are *you*?'

'I've no idea,' I answer truthfully, peering vainly through the glass in search of a sign. 'I'll phone again shortly.'

I stepped out of the booth and went in a daze towards the car, trying to attend, trying to *see*. Some part of me was naked to the day, attending, but it wasn't answering my calls; I could feel it, this automaton guiding my legs, focusing my eyes, no doubt it was registering sights and sensations like a photographic plate and with this in mind I tried to get my head under the cloth to see what it was seeing. At my feet a mottled shape seemed to float, to drift on the roadside gravel. Snakeskin. Yes, it moved—and my every muscle told me to jump back. Instead I bent and saw the mass of insects picking at the dead creature, shifting it in their eagerness. Cars roared past us as I studied this microscopic feast until my back ached.

Sitting in the Wolseley I gazed entranced at fields and hedgerows, so determinate. Could a body faint merely by falling behind, losing the tempo linking it—in this instant of concentration—to leaf and stem and berry? I must *not* sleep.

Roused, the car engine seemed dangerously remote. My foot let in the clutch and we were off, swooping through summer valleys bright as stained glass. Nunc Dimittis... here was anguished, demented Denis Towle kneeling like a saint at prayer, chequered green and gold in the sunlit Alfriston vestry; his long thin hands pressed hard together, raised, the fingers tapering, a gothic spire in silhouette; and those hands too had been picked and devoured, long since deli-vered to the microscopic feast. I drove through Devon but memory was more vivid. Tall hedges pillowed my reveries, above them tors peeped from the Somerset Levels like the Islands of the Blest, recalling—unbidden—my father's Sunday expeditions in search of lost Roman remains, and one cherished occasion when he took me with him alone to search wet Berkshire fields for traces of a garrison town whose name...

Whose name I could no longer summon, no matter how hard I tried. I forced myself to stop and phone once more, and this time there was no answer. Snug in the booth I listened to it ring. God willing Alec and the aunts were on their way, through Hammersmith and Chiswick, out past the Gillette building onto the Great West Road... I willed them to go faster in the Alvis, speeding towards Staines... after a time the distant ringing lost its inquisitorial meaning and sank through my ear into my flesh, becoming a part of it like a spoken pulse.

Only now, as I cut the connection at last, does the musty smell of the phone booth rise up to be savoured in its place. Stale booze and fizzy drinks, extinguished cigarettes—like a miniature pub but with some more intimate exhalation, damp clothes and anxiety, *no answer* and *engaged again* encapsulated in one fretful cosy stink, like being trapped with your head inside a sweaty lover's overcoat. The glass is flecking with rain, and for the first time I notice that the sky has clouded over, making the phone box all the cosier... but it's no good, I can't stay here like a bottled exhibit, no matter how pleasant it is.

236

Emerging with regret I see I am not alone in the dusty road lined with grey council housing. Beyond the Wolseley a figure is trudging along towards me in the soft, light rain, slack-faced and open-mouthed—limping indeed, I saw as I watched him—with his eyes fixed on my car as though it were the grail of his entire journey. He is very tall and thin, black drainpipe trousers and a sweat-stained vest, his thin shoulders pulled back by a rucksack. A raised animal quiff of hair—stirring some memory in me—has begun to part beneath the rain, flopping onto his heated forehead to meet his furry insect eyebrows. A red face, mouth twisted in pain. As I start towards the car he accelerates without looking at me, perhaps sensing my presence and, now that I am coming closer to the Wolseley, turning our progress into an absurd race. I'm almost at the car and so is he, his body jerking with the effort, I can see him convulsively licking dry lips... and to my horror I recognize a boy I taught until a few years ago, a local boy, gifted—Dawnay, was it? Dawkins?—and meant, I'd thought, for higher things than this.

'Good heavens!' I cried, 'What are *you* doing here?'

The scarecrow figure reaches the Wolseley and extends both arms to the windows as though about to collapse. As I arrive he looks up at me, panting through a gap-toothed smile.

I stared. He wasn't Dawnay at all, or Dawkins or whatever the boy's name was. Now that my brain had caught up I could see that this wretched creature was older altogether. Who *was* it he reminded me of? Why did my mind keep dropping hints, failing to clear? No matter how briskly I moved I was still a full lap off the pace, befuddled by associations, unable to see or hear directly while my mind hunted through ancient files and dredged up half-witted references. Perhaps I was simply short of sleep, fretting all night and virtually ensuring that I spent the day chasing shadows.

'I am very tired,' he said, speaking my own thoughts, but in a foreign accent I couldn't place, 'from always walking. Why will no British person give me a lift?'

I could have told him why. One look at his fiery face, the lank clothes on the emaciated body, would be enough to guarantee his solitude.

'My friends told me this is a good country for giving lifts. I don't think so.' Was he Greek, Spanish perhaps? There was something Byzantine to his face, the caterpillar eyebrows looped round the drooping lids of a crucified Christ. 'What are you afraid of? I only go to Plymouth, to the train.'

I sigh. 'I'm going the other way, I'm afraid. North. You need to go south.'

'You take me little way south. Please.'

'I'm already late. I couldn't take you far enough to make it worth your while, believe me.'

'Is worth my while. Look at my feet.' If the soles of his shoes were anything like their tattered uppers, I don't want to see his feet. 'You take me little way.'

I shake my head.

To my alarm he turns, releasing his pack to the ground in one violent gesture, and plunges an arm into it, looking up to glare at me as he locates what he's after.

'You take me little way,' he says firmly, confidently now, as his arm comes out of the rucksack.

The hand is balled in a fist, to my relief no threatening blade protrudes from it.

'I pay you, look,' he opens his hand and a five pound note, folded into matchbook size, uncurls on his palm.

It was senseless; a fiver would get him a taxi most of the way to Plymouth or a bus all the way if there was one, but he didn't thank me for pointing this out; instead he began to curse me while I climbed into the car. I offered to take him down the road until we reached a bus station, but by now he was fully occupied releasing all his pent-up rage into invective. To judge by his gestures he cursed in my person the sky, the wet road, and the British nation. Italian curses, I recognized them now. And as I drove off, watching his raging figure recede in the rear-view mirror, I knew who it was he'd reminded me of: Sandro, Sandro Scifo, once the bane of my life.

I didn't want to think about Sandro — indeed perhaps that was why, it occurred to me now, I'd so churlishly refused to give the black-quiffed scarecrow a lift south as he wanted. So what if it made me late for Egon and late returning to Webb's Hotel? I'd done it once without a second thought. For anyone but Sandro, that

238

is, as my vigilant unconscious must have reminded me. Or perhaps this whole Egon business in my life was changing me, contracting me, locating the obstinate purposiveness that I had undone, skein by skein, as I turned my resentment-swollen childhood heart into vacant accomodation, Dr Hanbury's hotel of souls. Of course this rediscovered pith of me was surfacing a little late. But its message was clear: no free-loaders, no lifts. (In my sleep that night this message hammered at me in jumbled, threatening form, distorted like a ball of child's plasticine where the different colours, formerly laid out in distinct, orderly strips, have been coiled into a random rainbow swirl like oil on water; and yet... and yet it's not at all the case that in our dreams we can't *think*, or construct the most elaborate theories of our existence. Acceptable theorems, melodies, even whole poems have been composed in dreams. More commonly awake, of course—but isn't it still the dreaming part that does the work?) Now as I drove on, coming closer at last to Wells—for some reason I kept on thinking I was going to Bath, which fortunately isn't far from Wells—I began to think, or tried to (sometimes it's harder to think when you're awake), about the turbulent two-year progress of Egon through my life: from the infinitesimal German bow of his first appearance in my study, standing to attention beside Alec Thurgo's well-stuffed bulk, to the leather-jacketed delinquent with charcoal streaks on his face, hauled in by the sergeant. Was this my work, this transformation? And what had it wrought in *me*? Instead my mind returned, as to a melody carried by that obstinately dreaming self, to Sandro Scifo.

It was in the winter of 1944, while I was still lamenting my failure to heal Denis Towle's riven spirit, that this strange feline character had arrived at the Ark bearing a battered suitcase full of cloths and rattling ill-assorted cutlery and—so he said, but I never saw it—an honourable discharge from the British Army. In those days vagrants of all kinds had come to hear of the Ark and would show up eagerly at dinnertime or sidle alongside us as we worked in the sloping fields, grabbing a scythe or a spade and setting to work before we could even ask their name. With our limited accommodation (by now the old chapel in the woods housed as many people as cows) we could usually do little more than feed them and send them on their way.

This time there was a room free. Denis's empty attic had been promptly seized by Colin, a deaf-mute who brooked no argument, but no-one had hurried to take Colin's room because it stank, I'm afraid to say, of Colin. The stink mingled incontinence and engine oil, the latter due to Colin's mechanical hobbies. Sandro accepted it without a murmur. He'd known worse, he said; his parents were circus artistes whose life on the road had prepared him for hardship. (As dubious proof of this heritage he juggled apples for us and performed minor conjuring tricks, such as appearing to extract an egg from one of Colin's deaf ears.) They had named him Alessandro after Alexandra Palace, since he was born within sight of this famous venue. We were to call him Ally Pally: it was his professional name. Nonetheless he was at pains to correct our pronunciation of his family name, Scifo ('*Shee*-fo, say with me *Shee*-fo...'), honoured in circus tents but liable to insulting error. Mispronounced *Skee*-fo it meant, as did the Italian *schifo*, loathing or disgust. 'It mean *bleaughhh*!' Sandro explained graphically, pretending to vomit, his hands filling instead with decorously coloured silk scarves.

Eggs and apples we had aplenty, but we were short of entertainment. Sandro played the spoons, threw knives, kept us agog with tales of fat hairy ladies and strong hairy men; made us pasta; even befriended friendless Colin. He was as pally as his nickname. None of this, however, had saved him from being bullied by his fellow squaddies when he was drafted into a Signals unit (I pictured him producing unexpected messages with silk scarves). Scifo—what sort of a name was that? He was on the wrong bloody side, spying for Mussolini. Circus? They'd give him circus. Strapping Sandro to a door they threw knives at him, severing an artery in his leg. Poor Ally Pally: a kindly commanding officer offered him a transfer, suggesting he adopt a British name, at least for the duration of the war. *Skee*-fo could surely be surrendered... '*Shee*-fo! *Shee*-fo!' Sandro had protested to the bitter end, preferring discharge to betrayal of the name emblazoned in red and gold on many a circus caravan.

The Ark applauded this improbable story to the echo. I was less happy with it. More likely he had escaped from an internment camp, and I would be risking my continued tenure at the Ark by harbouring a man on the run. Ally Pally was all hurt puzzlement when I tried to explain this to him. We were already under suspicion, I explained, a despised collection of freaks and traitors. We couldn't afford to shelter criminals. If he was telling the truth, would he show me his papers? But silk scarves and eggs could more easily be summoned from thin air than Sandro's army record from his suitcase. 'Reverend,' he sighed soulfully. 'Is a matter of *trust*. What else you have here? Colin, perhaps he is a killer, a murderer, who knows? You can ask him but he doesn't hear. He cannot speak. You trust him. *He* has no papers. We are here in the lifeboat, on the island like survivors,' (it was true I commonly used these metaphors in my little speeches to the inmates), 'you say it no longer matters what we were, only what we are now. You say this to the others. Why not to Sandro?'

I wanted to say it to Sandro. He cheered us up and I liked him for it. I liked his pasta too. I had to square it with my conscience and as usual my conscience came up with the answer. I took Ally Pally for a walk in the woods. 'You're a Catholic,' I said firmly, hoping to quell any objections from my co-conspirator, 'you understand the privacy of the confessional.' 'No,' said Ally Pally. 'Oh yes you do,' I said and explained my plan. If he told me the truth as his priest (never mind denominations, we were at war and this was no time for ecumenical niceties) I would be vocation-bound not to divulge it. Such would be my defence against any subsequent enquiries; and he could stay at the Ark until these materialized, if they ever did. 'But if you refuse to tell me the truth under these privileged conditions, I cannot permit you to stay without first informing the police. They visit us frequently.' This was no idle threat. We were the first port of call in the hunt for deserters, itinerant thieves and other undesirables. Ally Pally winked at me, untroubled. 'Is why you give me Colin's room, Reverend, with view. I see police car coming, I take back door into the woods. You see? You never have to tell them.' 'Don't you understand, I can *protect* you if you confess to me.' He spread his hands. Mercifully nothing of a humorous nature appeared in them. 'I have no crimes to confess,' he said, 'I swear this.' 'Look,' I said, 'I've known people in the Signals Corps, you know as well as I do that if I started asking you about transmitting messages...' But he shook his head. 'I forget about Signals. I forget many things, is better that way. You are good man, Reverend. Better you sleep well at night, like me.'

I didn't sleep well at all. There was an Italian prisoner-of-war camp nearby, near enough for the vicar of Dobwalls' youngest son, a boy of six, to have equipped himself with sandwiches and set out for it on foot one morning, under the misimpression—it was the vicar's favourite, oft-repeated story—that he was going to visit Italy itself; I made enquiries at the camp, but they knew no Scifo. I might now have slept a little better, if this hadn't been the first insomniac period of my life (the beginning of my Creeper-dom) when even our bees had to suffer midnight inspection, for my peace of mind. Yet what on earth was I on watch against? Perhaps the self that as a morbid, secretive teenager would have doubled up with laughter at the sight of my face above a black robe tied with a thick white ecclesiastical cord at the waist, beating the bounds of my wooded precinct like an anxious St Francis. The wood, the sloping fields, the house and the millrace below it: they were my body. If a bird so much as flew out of my trees and across the valley I regarded it as a deserter, abandoning us. I had some reason, it was true, to feel embattled. We were certainly unpopular, and in Dobwalls we ran the gauntlet of stares and sneers: malingerers safe in our little land flowing with milk and honey, while others fought and died to preserve it. But my 'conchies', my skulking foreigners and nerve-shattered convalescents had fought on the no less honourable battle-field of the spirit, and I was brimming with their wounds.

Individually they had little in common. Captain Powys, who had been with me since the beginning, spent much of the day in prayer but offended the pacifists by wearing uniform and a full complement of medals (I always suspected he was praying for the right to wear these medals proudly, despite the slaughter in which he'd won them and about which he still spoke to me in tears). His hands shook continuously and almost any noise, a car, a slammed door, even a dropped spoon, would make him start as if electrocuted. Major Fellowes, once similarly afflicted by bombardment and invalided out of North Africa with shell-shock, had mastered his fears but now no longer slept at all, night or day, and often accompanied me on my night-time rounds to ease his tedium. Younger soldiers, each carrying his own disabled, haunted look, came and went (Zbiggy, the Pole who had survived German execution, was one of these), but none wanted to tell their stories to the others; only to me; and certainly not to the pacifists who craved them as reassuring evidence of the folly of war.

And they themselves, my 'conchies', had such diverse motives and argued so bitterly that they resembled nothing so much as Balkan conspirators-in-exile, royalist pitted against anarchist in meaningless contention over a long since vanished fiefdom. Charlesworth and Dr Burnham loathed war, Gillies loathed *this* war but approved of other wars, a man called Fraser-Evans (who didn't last long) had a soft spot for Hitler and loathed the English, Durrance believed in war in general, indeed in all wars, but was a self-professed coward and loathed everyone who pretended to be brave, Corporal Harrington (a convert to conscientious objection) loathed officers, and Professor Terry loathed people, especially his fellow-pacifists; but not enough to kill them. Then there were the oddballs: Grissom the cataleptic, whose propensity for dropping off had foiled his call-up board and who hoped to outsleep the war; elderly Miss Platten who came to see, as she put it, how we were all getting on, and never left. She loved only God, and didn't want to hear about the war; why she found the Ark a suitable sanctuary I never understood, since when it came to talk of war our pacifists were a match for Allied High Command. Some of our foreign inmates, Mr and Mrs Mirkovic, Serbians, and Arvo, who I think was Lithuanian, were spared this chatter because they couldn't understand a word of it. And wall-eyed Colin, deaf and dumb, lived in a world of his own.

Ally Pally was his first friend. Colin was a local lad, living with a senile and now neglectful grandmother who had once—so the vicar of Dobwalls told me—been more adept, more patient with the disabled child than his own parents. The boy was out on one of his solitary, shambling walks when he saw me trying to start our decrepit tractor, visibly without success. He walked into the yard, ignoring me but eyeing the tractor like a battered fellow-spirit, and bent over the engine with hands that stroked it into life. Like Miss Platten, Colin stayed for supper and never left. He'd been isolated for so long, perhaps he felt at home for first time in our community of pariahs exiled from each other as well as from the rest of the wartime world.

Though at first we all admired Ally Pally's party tricks, his repertoire was small, and after a while it wasn't only sleep-prone Mr Grissom who fell into a trance when Sandro laboriously attempted to spin his dinner plate on a middle finger (Captain Powys was out of the dining hall like a hunted rabbit) or asked Miss Platten to pick a card. Not so Colin. This was drama without words, 'before your very eyes!' as Ally Pally put it. Did the Italian know, I wondered, that when he drew coloured silks from Colin's gaping lips or the egg from his ear, far from mocking Colin's silent world he was—for Colin—giving it speech? This was a language Colin too could learn, and Ally Pally was a willing teacher. For the first time in the years I'd known him I saw Colin smile as his keen hands quickly outstripped Ally Pally at juggling and legerdemain, and heard for the first time his mirthless croaking laugh, sounding uncannily like our tractor engine on a cold morning, turning over but refusing to catch.

Now it was Ally Pally who watched in rueful wonderment as Colin made Professor Terry's monocle disappear before our very eyes, and reappear dangling among Captain Powys's medals. 'Is my very best pupil!' Ally Pally declared. 'You let me take him to the circus?' It was only when Ally Pally persisted, saying Colin was a natural and could make a career out of sleight of hand—'What else he can do, Reverend? Stay here all his life?'—that I saw he was serious, and began to think the matter over. It would require family consent, which thanks to the vicar of Dobwalls I'd obtained to harbour Colin at the Ark, but it didn't seem altogether a bad idea... assuming that Ally Pally really did have a connection to the circus. And I was beginning to revise my first, sceptical opinion about this, thanks to a series of revelations that brought me closer to Sandro Scifo. I'd liked him well enough as a plausible rogue, but now I was growing more deeply fond of him, seeing his patience and gentleness with Colin, and the absence of envy as the pupil left the teacher fumbling in his wake. Now that it was Colin whose tricks we applauded, Ally Pally had been downgraded from artiste to fairground barker but he showed no resentment. Indeed he revelled in his protégé. 'Colin the Wonder Boy! He hears with his fingers! He speaks with his hands!' he crowed, introducing Colin's latest accomplishments. The slack, withdrawn look had gone from Colin's face. The incontinence too had ceased. Now Colin went everywhere with Ally Pally, always watching him, quick to respond; they had evolved a kind of private sign language. Whatever was to be done with Colin's future, I hoped it would involve Sandro Scifo.

I must admit I'd expected Ally Pally to be gone within a few days, a week or two at most, either under his own wayward steam or by coercion. But the police never called. Then one evening when I was on my rounds I found Ally Pally sobbing on his bed and, without need for the confessional, his story came flooding out.

Still weeping, he showed me a letter, crudely written, unsigned.

If you want your little baby girl you better do something quick. It needs better looking after than she gives it. She don't want it and there's no-one else does, not round here. She can't take care of it properly the way she is now. If you get this don't you say nothing to her about it, just say you come to see her but don't leave it if you're coming come soon.

'Who wrote you this letter?'

Shrugging, he handed me an envelope. Postmarked Truro ten days earlier, it was addressed to Sandro Scifo at a hostel in the Seven Sisters Road in London, and readdressed to The Ark, Dobwalls, Cornwall.

'And is it true, did you get someone pregnant? Is that what you're doing here, Sandro?'

'I hear she is pregnant, I think maybe is not true but I come anyway to look for her, and here in Dobwalls they tell me about this place, the Ark. Is the truth, believe me. I come here but I don't know where she is.' He had begun to snuffle again, 'And now I get this letter and still I don't know.'

'How did they know in London, where you were?'

'I phone them,' again the hands went out, protesting innocence, 'when you let me stay. To give forwarding address.'

'Sandro, it's all lies, isn't it, about your time in the British Army.'

'Reverend, they tell me you have soldiers here, all right? I think, you don't feed me if I am boy from circus.'

'You weren't even born in this country, were you?'

'How you know that?'

I had to smile at his outraged face.

245

'How you know I wasn't born here? My English is very good.'

'Yes, very good. For someone who wasn't born here. Tell me the truth this time, Sandro. Were you in an internment camp?'

'No, no internment.' He grinned. 'I move too fast. But it's true, look, about the circus—look—'

From his case he pulled handbills. *Mottram's Big Top!* they proclaimed in curly Edwardian script, *Manzini The Magnificent! Keller And His Lions! The Death-Defying Scifos!*

'Alice... all I know is Alice.' He was telling me about the girl. 'I met her after the first show in Penzance, then for a week, and then another week in Truro. Maybe she follow us. They come like this, you know, the girls, without names sometimes.' A distressing thought seemed to strike him. 'Maybe is not really Alice.'

'But you would recognize her?'

'Oh yes, certainly I recognize her. She is a very pretty girl.'

'And who told you she was pregnant?'

'This person, I don't know, I thought it was Alice. The same writing. Was a letter asking for money.'

'But you still came to try and find her.'

'Why, you think because I sleep with her, I am bad boy and don't want to look after her? In Penzance I say to her, I want to marry you. She laughed at this. *She* laughed—you understand? But when I hear she is pregnant, I think to myself if I see her, if I find her...'

'But you haven't gone anywhere, these last few weeks.'

He gazed at me sadly. 'I have no money, Reverend.' In true clown fashion he turned his empty pockets inside out and held them away from his body, by the corners. 'You see? No money.'

'I could have taken you to Truro.'

He ignored this. 'And I like it here, I think perhaps Alice will spit in my face if I come with no money... and now...' he waved the letter at me, his face once more streaming with tears.

Where to begin? A pretty girl who might or might not be called Alice, living in or near Truro (or perhaps Penzance), recently delivered of a baby girl... I phoned hospitals, orphanages, church adoption agencies, but located no Alices and no stray baby. We drove to Truro and dallied there and in Penzance, in the forlorn hope of coming across the girl or indeed anyone Ally Pally might remember from the Mottram's Big Top summer tour of Cornwall. Along the way he pointed out several fading posters which had advertised it, along with Manzini the Magnificent and the Death-Defying Scifos—his parents, high wire artistes, Ally Pally explained. On the outskirts of Truro we were made welcome at the imposing granite-fronted hospital that had once been familiar territory to my father, when he was practising medicine in the town; and were sumptuously lunched by the Bishop, a friend of my patron the Dean of Wells. The Bishop was famed for his table, also for a peerless collection of antique silver I had been yearning to see. To tell the truth it was pleasant to get away from the Ark, no matter how futile our journeys were.

All the same I was foolish to ignore the rest of my flock, and when trouble broke out at the Ark it was provoked, I swiftly realized, by my absences. Or rather by Ally Pally's absences. For disconsolate Colin, finding himself abandoned, had developed a new party trick. He made things disappear without bothering to restore them. His victims were not amused. Miss Platten had lost a brooch, Dr Burnham a precious fountain pen, Professor Terry was largely blind without the monocle which now failed to reappear on Captain Powys's chest—where, indeed, one of the medals, the Distinguished Service Order, was also missing. It was pointless to ask Colin to return them. He couldn't hear the request. Sign language had failed, and written notes, passed to Colin, evinced no response either, since Colin had never learned to read. Lifelike sketches (Miss Platten was an artist) of brooch, pen, monocle and medal, had also drawn a blank.

When I visited Colin in the attic I found the missing items neatly arranged on the windowsill, like trophies. He watched me expressionlessly as I gathered them up. I could, I suppose, have wagged a stern finger at him, as at a disobedient pup; but I knew only too well why he'd done it, and it was I who felt ashamed.

Ally Pally had the answer. He would spend some time alone with Colin, to make it up to the boy. Perhaps, Ally Pally suggested shyly, 'you lend me some money, Reverend? I take Colin to London, we stay at the hostel and I bring him back the next day.' Colin had never seen London, had never, so far as I knew, been out of

Cornwall. I was touched, not only at the prospect of this treat for the boy, but at Ally Pally's fatherliness. We had failed to find his baby girl, but he still had Colin in his care.

The trip was such a success that the following week I sponsored a slightly longer one, a weekend including a visit to the seaside at Brighton. Meanwhile I continued to pester hospitals and vicars from coast to Cornish coast (even, in a morbid moment, mortuaries) in search of Ally Pally's child. The Ark was at peace once more, though wary now of conjuring tricks. No more precious articles disappeared. And as the weeks went by, as the war itself drew to an end and I sent Ally Pally and Colin ever further afield, I rejoiced in them as if they were my doves, sent out to find their feet in a world after the flood.

The whole dreadful charade came to an end shortly before Easter with the arrival of the police in an unmarked red Ford Prefect. It had been stolen in London, they informed me, and sold in Liskeard by a young man answering only too exactly to a description of Ally Pally. They also wanted to speak to Colin about a number of shop-lifting offences reported in different parts of the country. And there was more, much more. I listened, sick with grief, remembering a Colin once content to tinker with the farm machinery over which he had such uncanny powers. It had taken Ally Pally to extend Colin's dominion to more roadworthy machines, beyond the confines of the Ark. And legerdemain too had applications more practical than juggling apples or purloining monocles. On each trip they had stolen a car, using Colin's skills, filled it with shoplifted goods to sell, like the car, in London, then stolen another car and driven it back to sell here.

Colin was in the attic. He began to cry, soundlessly, when he saw the policemen enter the room behind me.

Sandro Scifo was long gone, having promptly taken 'back door into the woods' as he'd warned me months before. His room was a treasure trove. Even allowing for whatever he'd managed to take with him as he fled, I could see that few of our journeys to Truro and Penzance had failed to increase his pickings. Empty wallets, purses, pens, a barometer and a brass letter-weight, a silver sugar sifter, notebooks and watches, even handkerchieves, were heaped in cardboard boxes underneath his bed. But the worst was the cutlery, some of which looked too fine to belong to anyone but the Bishop of Truro, who had so kindly indulged my desire to see his collection. I hoped Ally Pally had left these as a sentimental gesture (though in my mind's eye I saw him dashing through the woods burdened by more precious items, silver platters... candelabra...). Yet I shuddered at the prospect of my interview with the Bishop. In all likelihood he had already alerted my superiors.

Ally Pally's abandoned suitcase, mocking me now with its silk scarves and trick devices wrapped up in elastic bands, revealed the full extent of my gullibility. Notes in his own hand matched the anonymous letter he had given me to read: girlfriend and child were of course his invention, and I had not only financed his criminal excursions with Colin but actually taken him foraging myself, as his sponsor and getaway driver.

I weathered the police enquiries with, I think, good grace. At any rate no-one could have found me more ridiculous, more culpable than I already felt myself to be. Some self-forgiving part of me was still intact, too: when no trace of Sandro Scifo could be found, I even felt a spurt of gladness for him. Oh, perversely, if you will. But I couldn't hold my own humiliation against him. I had conspired with it—my first instinct had told me who and what he was, a con-man, a high wire artiste, and from that moment onwards I had stumbled into his trap, but not blindly. In that sense none of us is blind. The darkness in us cleaves to the darkness in others; what would light mean without it? What I could not forgive Ally Pally, or myself, was the destruction of Colin's life. There would be no prosecution, we were told, provided that proper care and supervision could be ensured. This meant in a hospital, as opposed to the loose anchorage provided by the Ark. A place for the boy was found at Truro, at the same old hospital my father had known so well. I tried to persuade myself that this environment could nourish him, they would teach him to read and write, tend him and, God willing, love him. But with the loss of Ally Pally Colin grew increasingly withdrawn, as I feared he would, and though I visited him in Truro for several years he greeted me as though I were only a bitter memory and turned away to the elaborate Meccano engines which sat beside him on his bed.

I had lost Denis Towle, too, to hospital, but Denis seemed happy enough in Horsham—it wasn't until late in '46 that he took his own life there—and at the time this second blow seemed heavier than the first. Once again I had bitten off more than I found I could chew. This time the Ark itself seemed ravaged to me, burglarized. I had beaten the bounds and missed the rot within.

There were saving graces, if you can call them that. Although questions were raised at diocesan meetings, the Ark was allowed to drift quietly aground as war subsided. Had it all happened a year earlier I've no doubt we would have been disbanded, leaving me under a greater cloud, perhaps an indelible one. More mercifully still, none of the silver found in Ally Pally's room had been filched from the Bishop of Truro—my panic-stricken eyes had discerned antiques in hotel and restaurant cutlery. I was too heart-sore to care, remembering how I'd sat opposite Ally Pally in fancy establishments, so proud of my expenditure of time and love and money, as he smiled gratefully and, when my back was turned, slipped the silverware into his clown-sized pockets.

Yes, it was comical, and all too predictable, indeed, that I who was so flattered by my own altruism should make an easy mark. It was a banal incident. But at twenty-seven I had founded my youthful self-esteem not merely on kindness but on filling my spirit with the twisted desires and sufferings of others—to what end, exactly? To show them that nothing in them was alien to me, and so... redeem them from the sense of isolation that (alone, I believed, and decisively) sustained their misery? Ha! In practice these twisted characters I wished to save were so thoroughly alien to me that I couldn't even recognize one while he was pulling me round the county by the nose. I was a joke, certainly, but it was worse than that. My very ambitions for myself were a joke.

While I grieved, the longer-standing inmates of the Ark had formed themselves into a committee, determined to save the Ark from my open-house policy. But the captain, in this instance, was indeed no longer on the bridge. They presented me with draft resolutions—meaningless really, since we could all see that the war would soon be over and the Ark redundant. I was content to be losing control of the place in advance, it was they who were frantic, trying to preserve our absurd community as if it hadn't been fractured and divided from the very start. Peace threatened them with worse. They would have to go home.

So would I. But it was only the contours of the place that I would miss, the woods and sloping fields, the precinct I patrolled each night, glimpsing the sweet small house-front shoehorned into the hill and lit by the glow from ever-wakeful Major Fellowes' window, guiding me home.

I was happy to return to teaching, to contend and rise to be satrap of Egypt, ruling—leniently, yes, but *ruling*, not just serving or seeking to serve. Until Egon came, and I lost my way again.

Don't be a Humphrey all your life, absent attending to others... no wonder I couldn't bring myself to review, as I drove through this treacherous, sunlit countryside, the stages of my Egon-sickness. I would pull him back from the precipice, I who could no longer set Colin free, restore Denis, draw John the First out of the muddy waters. I would be his conduit to himself; he would be mine. Instead it was the police with their seen-it-all faces who arrived once more to set the record straight.

Wells was approaching, it was time to study Egon's map. Would he even be there, if I could find the place? I felt queasy with tension as I glanced at his letter and looked round for landmarks. A pink farmhouse, a hilltop pub, the Coach and Horses, as blandly bogus as its name. And down into the valley full of parched willow-herb, *cross stream at foot of hill, climb 200 yds... turn left*, yes, now I saw it, the private road with its beech hedge on either side, tall as a man, immaculately trimmed and widening as it met the road, then curving outwards to end in small square granite pillars. Deep green the hedge, dark as holly, above expensive golden gravel. *Follow beech hedge to first track on right.* First *track*? I came across nothing that resembled a track, but to the right an opening gave at last onto a vista so gorgeously manicured that I braked merely to gape at it, without turning the wheel. A sloping 'track', if you could call it that, was formed by two narrow tarmac ribbons that glistened in the light, the five foot strip of grass between them shaved as close as the lawn on either side, unspooling past a tennis court, a folly, ornamental ponds, and leading the eye towards the most exquisitely sited house I had ever seen.

There it sat like a sculpted ginger cake, the ochre stone gently pitted and shadowed in tones of marmelade beneath the decorated lintels that curled up at the ends like so many thickly pomaded blond moustaches, cavalry moustaches, many of them askew—the house... but it was impossible to rest on its features while taking in the setting, a great rectangle of raised and golden-walled lawn projecting over the valley beyond and framed by walls of some soft evergreen, feathery apple-green fir, slim walls so tall they made the building seem a cottage, or rather a mansion for dwarves. Beyond the balustraded ha-ha the ground fell away so steeply that nothing could be seen until the valley opposite rose like a far-off map, a few small single trees spaced out across the fields like chess pieces in an abandoned endgame. The house on its high terrace projected alarmingly over this green void—yet sat there in utter repose, in sunlight, supported by the plunging sandstone walls that vanished from sight. A croquet lawn fronted the building, where the level grass ran to the balustrade over the void; and the little white hoops seemed to be dancing on gravity itself, on a flattened mountaintop solid as marble beneath the turf.

What was this place, fit for dukes, for kings—a king's mistress perhaps, a Nell Gwynn hidden from the world—and yet without a soul in sight? Could this be it, my destination? Surely I would have known if any of Egon's schoolfriends owned a house as sumptuously appointed as this. Perhaps a friend of Alec's, landed gentry—but I didn't care if I was at the wrong address, I had to see it closer, and aimed the Wolseley carefully along the ribboned drive. To the left, along the beech hedge, a walled garden came into view, lined with espaliered fruit trees. I slowed and peered in, expecting at any moment to see a gardener, or two indeed, among the vegetables, or Her Ladyship in broad straw hat bending to pick delphiniums. The garden was empty. As I approached the house I rehearsed my excuses, but it was the building, the magnificent facade, and not the act of trespassing that made me breathless and dry-mouthed.

Trails of dismantled ivy seamed the walls, evoking tombstones, and with its pitted blocks like tea-stained shortbread, the house gave off an overpoweringly masculine sense, almost an odour, port and cigar breath exhaled into your face in a panelled room. Making the lintels seem all the more extravagant, the front was gloriously plain, no portico, no mansards above, only the flat, severe, military face, cracked and veined from long exposure, and rising to a roof of mossy tiles that dwindled in size as they receded, the golden moss blending with the orange and khaki-tinted walls beneath it.

Chintzes were visible behind the tall windows. I stepped out of the Wolseley, trembling. I had never coveted a house so much. Beside the tall white-painted door rose sweet sandstone columns, flat-fronted, softly grooved and weathered.

In one of these a bell was inset. A lion-headed knocker stood out from the door. Which to use?

At this moment the door opened, revealing a figure, straight and stern. I stood open-mouthed, afraid that I could no longer control my face and was about to cry.

A young girl stood there in the shadowy doorway, smiling now, a girl with long straight dark hair and a pale thin face and all the responsibilities of adulthood prefigured in her sad, solemn eyes.

'Hello. I'm Chrissie Wolfe. Won't you come in?'

'DO COME IN,' she repeated graciously as I stood there still gathering my thoughts, gaping at her.

She was wearing some kind of summer dress, a print, I couldn't see it clearly yet, sleeves fastened at the wrist, calves bare, short socks and buttoned town shoes. And there were quarry tiles beneath her feet. I was too bewildered, too alarmed by the sense that I'd stepped into the yellowing photograph in my study, to be able to respond. Had I fallen asleep, the car still stationary where the beech hedge parted to reveal the mansion and the grounds?—then it was simple, I was in the dream now, peopling the house with familiar names and images. Chrissie seemed to understand this, she stood there unsurprised by my trance state and waiting calmly till I found my voice.

'Is... is Egon here?'

'Yes, he's here. I've got lunch ready if you'd like to join us.' Somehow this only increased my disbelief. Any moment I would wake in the hot, dusty car. 'That is, join *me*,' she said. 'I'm not sure if Egon's eating or not.'

She pronounced it *Eh*-gon, to my relief, not *Ee*-gon as many others, including Alec, insisted on doing—and at that instant, as I heard her speak it in the German manner, I felt a current run through my back and shoulders, restoring the stiffness of the long drive, and knew I was here, awake and at the right address.

'This way,' she said brightly, and turned to lead me down the corridor, opening a door and vanishing into the light. No more soft tap of heels, but they echoed in my head. As I followed her into the room I braced myself. Despite Chrissie's words—join *me* for lunch—I still expected lordly parents to rise from the chintzes. Only Chrissie awaited me, I saw, as my eyes adjusted to the sunlight reflected off the pale carpets. My head swam again, I almost took a half step back—as much to fend off the aerial view beyond the windows as for the pleasure of taking in the great stone fireplace, the furniture, the paintings. The room was crammed with treasures, exquisite pieces everywhere I looked. Richly inlaid chests and tables, eighteenth century landscapes on the panelled walls, a ceiling adorned with cherubs and nymphs in summery shifts; it was almost too crowded with delights to be authentic. Yes, it was a collector's room, lacking the touch of austerity—the proper British touch, so evident in the architecture. From the mantelpiece a jowly fellow in full wig and regalia, one hand on an obliging spaniel, stared me down.

'Is that a Kneller?'

'Yes.'

Chrissie stood watching me, and when I tore my eyes away from the décor I saw the faintest of smiles on her face.

I couldn't find the words. 'I'm overwhelmed. Heavens above... is this house yours?'

'Well, not really.'

And she blushed. As she stood there tall and slender and composed, her feet together and her hands clasped in front of her, the mistress-of-the-house pose was belied by something in her eyes, a wickedness I hadn't seen till now. Dark eyes, fine dark eyebrows and black hair that crept down at her temples, yes, I could see Trimble's Madonna, straight nose and delicate mouth and the skin

254

swarthy with summer tan, but the sharply pointed chin—it seemed to draw down the flanges of her nose, attractively vixenish—no longer accentuated the solemn sadness of her face at the door. Now it seemed playful, ruthless. The wild thought came into my head that they'd broken in, that she and Egon were making free with this ducal splendour (Archducal perhaps—there *was* something foreign about it) on a teenage lovers' rampage.

'It was my uncle Edward's,' Chrissie said, putting me out of my misery. 'He was a historian. He's dead now.'

'I see. And he left it... to you?'

She laughed. 'Goodness no. Not to me personally, I'm afraid.'

Seeing now that she was enjoying teasing me, I glanced round the sumptuous room again. A large, silver-framed photograph on a commode showed a fox-hunting type with bushy eyebrows, a bow-tie and tweeds, with one arm around a frilly, plumply rouged lady, her faced ringed by a cap of dyed auburn curls. 'You say he was a historian?'

'Well, he was a very rich historian. Chelsom was in his family. Chelsom Place,' she clarified, 'that's its name. And he married my Aunt Margot and now it's hers. It's a wonderful house, isn't it?'

'It's more than that. I can't put it into words—I can't believe I'm standing here—'

'Most people react the same way. Only I don't often get a chance to show them round myself. Would you like to see the rest of it?'

'Yes, yes in a moment. Thank you. I'm still trying to take it all in. This belongs to your aunt, and she... she lets you come and stay here on your own?'

'Oh no. No, I came down with her. She's in Liskeard today.'

'Ah.' It took me a moment to put two and two together. 'You don't mean... seeing old Trimble?'

Chrissie nodded. The wickedness had spread to her entire face. 'No-one in my family's supposed to know. They don't approve. So I'm her alibi.' Smiling, she let her hands slip across each other to hug her arms, watching me. 'And she's mine.'

I was about to ask her what she meant, when I remembered with a start that she was only fourteen and presumably not meant to spend so much time with her boyfriend, unchaperoned; certainly not with a convicted felon and former wolf-child.

'May I ask you something?' she said. 'Do you know Mr Thurgo?'

'Yes.'

'Yes, that's silly of me, I suppose you must do. Then you probably know that he's not all that keen on Egon seeing me.'

'No, I didn't know that. Why not?'

'Because of our ages, I suppose. But—well, Egon says it's because I'm Jewish and Alec... Mr Thurgo,' she corrected herself, 'is terribly anti-Semitic. Is he, d'you think?'

'Not to my knowledge,' I said, withholding my suspicion that Egon had found the mark.

Chrissie studied me; I sensed that my evasive answer was much what she expected. 'Anyway,' she said, 'Aunt Margot lets us meet here. Sort of in exchange for my not telling anyone about her and Wilfred.'

I tried to imagine Chrissie addressing old Mad as Wilfred. Perhaps, the way things were going, as Uncle Wilfred. 'Does she visit him often? I rather thought, at least from what Egon's told me...'

'That she wasn't making any headway? Wait till you meet Aunt Margot.'

'But old... I mean—' I couldn't imagine the brusque old boy in these surroundings, feminine as I saw them now to be, in their clutter; not after years of room 26 at Webb's Hotel.

'What does she see in him? Oh she loves eccentrics, the madder the better. They're her mission in life. Uncle Edward was impossible. I really liked him, though. Just as well, mind you.'

'Oh?' I could see she was longing to expand.

'Sometimes he'd start drinking early in the morning, and then hang out of his dressing room window and use a slingshot on the birds. Or the gardeners, if they got in the way.'

'Yes, I imagined gardeners. It must take quite a team.'

'No, just one. But he's here most of the week, and brings a boy sometimes. And there's someone who comes specially to do the hedges.' She reflected. 'And a tennis court person... you're right, it is a team. I may as well tell you Aunt Margot was stinky rich before she even married Uncle Edward. He was her third. So Wilfred will have to be awfully strong-minded to turn her down, don't you think? Look, are you ready for your tour of inspection? We can't be too long or else the food will spoil.'

She looked so entrancing, so absurdly capable I almost forgot—indeed had quite forgotten till this moment—what I was doing here. 'But where's Egon?'

'Oh, he's fast asleep. In the Yellow Room—we'll peep in and see if he wants anything. The thing is, he walked here from Padstow and he's exhausted.'

'Walked? From Padstow?'

'I know. It took him two days. And we were up all night last night, talking.'

She hesitated; it was our first moment of awkwardness and I wasn't sure—perhaps she wasn't either—which of us had made it so. Why shouldn't they stay up talking?

'We were here on our own, you see. Perhaps I shouldn't be telling you all this.'

'Your aunt went to Liskeard yesterday? And...' I tried to keep the grin off my face but I couldn't, 'stayed at Webb's?'

'I suppose so. But she's not allowed in Wilfred's room,' Chrissie added quickly, 'no-one is, apart from Egon. And me of course.'

'What's it like, his room?' I asked and, seeing her face cloud over, remembered the food she'd said would spoil if we delayed, 'Will you tell me over lunch? I'm afraid I'm almost as curious to know about it as I am to see the rest of this... this glorious place.'

'I'm a bit of a blabbermouth, aren't I,' she said as she walked to the door. 'I'm really not supposed to tell you about Wilfred's room. Will you make do with Chelsom?'

'Oh, reluctantly,' I said, and basked in her smile, in the dimpled cheeks and the chin that almost seemed to fork with amusement.

We climbed the stairs, and I tried to pay attention to Chrissie's charming and well-learnt introductions to the paintings we passed, and to admire the features of the Bishop's room, of Uncle Edward's room, the Turkish room (now Aunt Margot's domain) and the Kandy Suite, forbiddingly wallpapered in shades of indigo, but to tell the truth I was beginning to feel rather faint. I hadn't eaten since my tea and toast at seven a.m., and the aroma of the food Chrissie had promised was now filling the stairwell. At last we reached the Yellow

Room. Without knocking, and with infinite care, Chrissie turned the handle and opened the door a crack, just far enough to peep in, one-eyed. As though in adoration of the door itself, the side of her face that I could see was illuminated by the tenderness on the invisible side, where one eye gazed at Egon. Her mouth was open, slack, like someone listening, all attention, at a door, rather than looking past one. This anxious circumspection breached my heart, I saw myself in it—or rather what I saw was a guilelessness my face could no longer assume, for shame at my susceptibility, at foolish and fatally gullible Hanbury—yes, I saw my own love for Egon stripped of all false dignity, and loved her for it. Envying them both. Then I became aware that Chrissie had been standing there motionless for so long that perhaps, rather then waiting to see if Egon was still asleep... was she rather watching, spying on him, on some activity within? At that instant the thought turned her from the very image of unselfconscious maternal care into a shadowy portrait by Balthus, one of his little wantons, callous and knowing. But now her mouth furled into a smile so generous it mocked me, as she whispered, 'He's awake. Ask him if he wants anything to eat. I'll be in the kitchen—just follow the smells.' And she scuttled quickly back down the stairs, taking them two at a time, loose-limbed, a sure-footed girl in a summer dress.

When I stepped into the room I barely recognized the ragamuffin curled up on the yellow counterpane. The last time I'd seen Egon was outside the court buildings in Bodmin, hair slicked down, face scrubbed, and wearing the best suit Alec could find him, to impress the judge. Now his hair was matted and his face streaked with dirt down one thin cheek. Filthy grey shirt, torn trousers—he looked as if he'd been living rough for weeks, not just for two days tramping the West Country roads. Even my scarecrow hitchhiker had looked more presentable. We'd have to stop at the school, find him some clothes before we went to Webb's to meet the family.

Egon's eyes were closed and he was breathing evenly. My heart ached at the sight of him. I came closer. All the love that Chrissie had rekindled in me as she stood outside the door, unconditional love, flamed in my chest and I wanted to hug him, filthy as he was.

'Egon...'

The sandy eyelashes flickered.

'D'you want some lunch? We'll have to leave in an hour or so.'

His eyes came open and gazed at me, unblinking, with their strange indeterminate grey-green, and the inflexible black mote floating like an eye within an eye. Above the yellow coverlet, beside yellow pillows and wallpaper striped yellow and white, the eyes looked greener, more vivid, refreshed.

'How about some food?' I repeated.

'No thanks, sir.' Like a medium possessed by another voice, the whisper broke into a growl as he spoke again. 'I've got so much to tell you.'

Egon licked his lips as if about to speak. But as he did so his eyelids drooped, the mouth stayed open, he was fast asleep.

THE MEAL, TAKEN in the dining room with the table elaborately laid, was a simple and sensible one, baked potatoes, cold cuts and salad, cole slaw with a mayonnaise made by Chrissie to Aunt Margot's recipe. I enquired about her family and she gave me discreet answers. I think we were both relieved that her 'blabbermouth' fit was over. Our first conversation, with its sly talk of septuagenarian romance, had had the merit of reducing—for a moment almost effacing—the age-gap between us, but it was time to cool things down. I wanted to talk about Egon: was he steady (all appearances to the contrary) in his mind, or unsteady? But this too was an inflammable subject, and I couldn't bring myself to put Chrissie on the spot.

With her composure, her precociously adult ways, she would surely be a calming influence on Egon. Or would she? The vixen chin worked in anticipation as she speared and scoured the baked potato, and again I thought I saw the hellion in her. What did she know of his claustrophobic fits and delusions? Everything or nothing? And how far had they been a pretence to disguise secret meetings with Chrissie? Egon had insisted that there had been no such meetings except at weekends, sanctioned by Aunt Margot's visits to Webb's with Chrissie in tow. Painting sessions had replaced Sunday nature rambles on the moor; when the sitting was over, Trimble and Margot would repair to the tea-room, or stroll the town, while the younger pair hot-footed it to the Ark. To talk, Egon had said.

'Tell me how the fire started,' I said.

Chrissie worked at her ham without looking up. Much as it saddened me to become Dr Hanbury, interrogator, it was no good pretending we were merely newfound pals, linked by our love for Egon. For a moment while we'd lingered at the Yellow Room door, peeping in, it was as if we were his parents. But the truth of our rivalry, like the chasm in age and responsibility to ourselves and to Egon, would out sooner or later. Better sooner.

'I'm afraid I have more than a casual interest in the Ark,' I said. I meant, more than a headmaster's interest in the vandalizing of school property; but now that the tone had altered I knew she would take that as read. 'I lived there for a time during the war. Perhaps Egon told you.'

She nodded. 'He's really proud of what you did, looking after people who didn't want to fight.'

'And people who did fight. As wars go it was worth fighting. Did he say he was proud of me?' I could feel tearfulness suddenly gather in my throat. 'I'm very touched. You know, there were some people... who were caught on the wrong side. Like Egon's father. They were the bravest of all.'

I tried a serious, heartfelt smile and she returned it solemnly, without comment. We ate in silence. The dining room, on the opposite side of the corridor to the drawing room, shared the view over the croquet lawn, the balustrade, and the valley beyond; a dark room with navy walls and an unfortunate ceiling papered in a distracting paisley pattern. I fancied I saw Aunt Margot's hand in this. The backdrop was designed for candlelit intimacy, but in the noonday light, with the French windows open, it was like breakfasting in a bordello.

'It must have been very frightening for you when you realized the Ark was on fire. You were upstairs, Egon said, in the attic.'

She gave a faint nod. There was something wrong, and she wasn't trying very hard to hide it.

'You'd heaped the logs too high in the grate, and one of them rolled out, was that it?'

'I suppose so, yes.'

'You didn't use the fireguard?' Chrissie said nothing. 'Were you somewhere else when Egon made the fire?'

She was elsewhere now, eating mechanically but with sullen misery written all over her face. She was no better at dissembling than Egon was—'Thank God he's half Kraut and doesn't know how to lie,' Alec had said outside the courthouse—unless... unless the other half of him had fooled us all.

'I think you'd better tell me what happened, Chrissie.'

She toyed with her salad for a moment longer. 'Did Egon ever tell you about his place in the woods?'

'I don't think so. What place?'

'It's near the old cowshed, up on the hill.'

'You mean the chapel?'

Her features were flushed and heavy, altered, even her voice was different, slurring resentfully. 'Yes, the chapel. This place, it's a kind of dip, quite deep, it's full of nettles and brambles so no-one goes down there. Egon calls it the bomb-site, but it's probably just a pool that's dried out. He only calls it that to frighten me into thinking there's an unexploded bomb there. Dropped from a Nazi plane, he says. But I don't think there is. It's just his talk.'

'No-one bothered to bomb the Ark, I can promise you that.' I knew the place she was talking about, a little crater full of old badger sets and vicious, forbidding jaws of thorn. 'Have you been down there with him?'

She nodded. 'He's made a sort of cave there. And he wanted me to see it. It was damp and horrible, so we made a fire.' She shrugged, shamefaced. 'It spread up through the brambles, we tried to stop it but we couldn't. Then the wind took it.'

'You mean the fire spread to the house?'

'Yes, everyone thought it started there and burnt its way into the wood. You see, we always lit a fire in the house, first thing.' She glanced at me. 'I'm really sorry. Please understand—he doesn't want anyone to know about the dip. The bomb-site. He says it's because somebody will get themselves blown up but it's really... it's just a secret place. You do understand, don't you?'

'Yes,' I said, disheartened to think that Egon had lied to me, no matter what he was protecting. 'In any case, it was an accident.'

Chrissie nodded. She was studying me, and I felt like the child, a disappointed child, under her gaze.

'Thank you for telling me.' But I wished I hadn't known; a wolf-child of all people, to set a fire in dry summer woods... I saw the canopy of brambles sparking like starfire in the night sky, heard the noise of it, the flames descending like a wild beast on the unguarded Ark.

'The thing is, it doesn't matter now,' Chrissie was saying. 'I wouldn't have told you otherwise. Egon's not going back to school.'

I stared at her. *Not going back?* 'Why not? But Alec—Alec said he wanted to.'

'I'd better let him tell you,' she said, almost stuttering in her haste to get it out, avoiding my eyes. 'Honestly. I shouldn't even have told you about the fire.'

'I won't say anything then. Damn it, the fire doesn't matter.' I felt numb now. Was this her doing? I wanted to shake her. 'Why d'you say he isn't coming back? Whose idea is that?' But Chrissie wouldn't even look at me.

'Perhaps you can talk him out of it,' she said harshly.

The words were blurted out. Was she blaming *me?* Her blazing face began to shed tears onto our plates as she stood and gathered them up, hurrying off towards the kitchen while I sat staring at the paisley ceiling, gulping air, ashamed at my rage but not knowing what to do or how to comfort her. And why on earth was she crying? Surely she wouldn't be seeing less of Egon if he was out of school. More, if anything.

My muddle was compounded by the fact that I was still smarting—oh, it was pitiful, but it was no good pretending otherwise—at the fact that Egon hadn't shown *me* his precious bomb site... as if that mattered now. But I simply couldn't believe he wasn't coming back to the school. It was a mistake, a misunderstanding. When Chrissie didn't return I pushed my chair back and walked towards the light that poured through the French windows as if out of a furnace.

Time to set off—if Egon still wanted to attend the meeting at Webb's. Despite my resolve my mind raced ahead, I saw myself arriving there alone and dully apologetic, braving Alec's wrath with curious indifference. Let them all go hang, the grudging relatives... but wait, wait, *talk him out of it*, she'd said. Where she'd already tried and failed? And talk him out of *what* precisely?

From the valley beyond the balustrade came a horrid mechanical whine, I couldn't see its source, an engine sound too high and light and even to be coming from a chainsaw or a motorbike. Now I remembered that at some point in the last three weeks I'd dreamt that I was sitting behind Egon on his motorbike, riding pillion as we swooped across Bodmin Moor, Egon in a red vest, no helmet, dark sandy hair streaming and flicking at me, and awoken to find the school cat crouching menacingly on my pillow, brushing my face and purring like a two-stroke. I was about to step forwards to try and identify the whining noise from the valley, when to my left I saw Chrissie emerge past the side of the house and walk slowly along the wall of pale green fir, towards the balustrade, her hands twitching and fidgeting at her side. Something about her figure, rendered diminutive by the fifteen-foot-high wave of green hedge, clawed at my guts like vertigo. As if she felt it too, she reached out to the balustrade, and then withdrew her hands as if the sand-blasted surface had burnt her. I watched her run her fingers furiously through her hair until it stood up like a mane by a combination of will and electricity. Was I supposed to be watching these gestures of distress, despair? Were they for me? They seemed rehearsed, like her regal manner when I arrived.

Then it struck me, and the shock of it made my head throb—*was this distress?*... or was it triumph, fluffing up her hair in preening mockery? *Perhaps you can talk him out of it*... what if I'd misread her tone and it hadn't been a plea but a derisive taunt, *he's mine, I've got him... try and talk him out of it, just see how far you get...?* Yes, wasn't that it? *He's not going back to school.* To *you*, to your school. What a patsy I'd been, yet again, feeling sorry for her as I'd felt sorry for Ally Pally while he laughed behind my back, sorry for John the First laughing from beyond the grave... but the dead be damned, for a dizzy moment I was ready to rush forwards, I felt the firm bump of my chest against her body as I took her by her thighs and shoulders and bundled her in one ferocious easy movement up and out into the void, and I wasn't a murderer yet, not yet, only a poor savage beast exulting in a Hanbury I'd never known existed.

But no, no, I was going mad, and when I focused my gaze on Chrissie at the balustrade, glimpses of her face showed her still weeping, wretched. What was happening to me to distort things so? The cataract of hair spilled across her face as I watched her rake through it. Now I wanted to respond to her anguish, to atone; but all the same there was something vile about her actions, something feral, I saw her arming herself with animal weaponry, hiding her pulpy tear-stained face like a squid shrouding itself in ink, a grub bulking up bristles to confuse a predator. It was horrible, I had to retreat at once into the room before she turned and saw me, or else run and stop her before her scalp bled.

At that moment the lazy engine whine from the valley gave a snarl so sharp and close it stopped Chrissie in mid-gesture, and she pulled the hair out of her face to look as the aeroplane soared up in front of us. Then the sound stopped, the red wings blazed gold in the sun as they completed a long slow loop and the tiny distant machine fell nose first in terrifying silence, out of sight.

As the plane hurtled below the parapet, straight down with no room to turn, its disappearance made me flinch. I ran forwards across the lawn, trembling with the sound of the crash about to erupt in my ears. But even before I reached the balustrade I heard the whine resume and stared down in disbelief into serene, uncluttered fields.

Where the hell was the plane? Then I saw it, skimming fast and red across the green like an exotic bird, so small, too small, and my senses swam. It wasn't real, it was a toy plane guided by remote control. Chrissie must have realized it in the same instant, because we turned to each other laughing with the same gasps of relief. A model plane. Like the walls of fir behind the girl, too high for comfortable proportion, the house with its plunging view and valley beyond—near and far at once—seemed to have been laid out with diseased perspectives in mind, a love affair with vertigo.

'D'you know,' I said as I walked unsteadily to her along the balustrade, 'd'you know about Egon and his aeroplane, the one he hijacked?' As I said it I knew this memory had fed my momentary terror.

Chrissie nodded, bat-black hair still mussed and fanning out hugely around her head and neck. As I reached her she took a step forwards and without thinking I reached out and hugged her to me for comfort. It was like holding embers to my chest, and I let my own tears come now that she couldn't see them.

'I gave him some of Uncle Edward's clothes,' came the muffled voice. 'He's getting dressed. I told him he's got to go with you. Talk to him. Please—please tell him not to do it.'

NOT TO LEAVE THE school: that was what I chose to believe Chrissie meant. You're coming back next term, I told Egon briskly as we set off in the Wolseley. And there was no dissent, no argument, no reply at all. He'd chosen the back seat so that he could go on dozing while I drove, and his dazed, newly scrubbed face in the rear-view mirror showed no trace of insubordination. I've got it all fixed, I added for good measure.

Yet I felt strange saying it, as if another Hanbury, the one still hovering at the edge of the terrace and lost in homicidal fantasy, continued to rule my body. I kept recalling it, the violent, imagined sense of assaulting the girl mingling with the feel of her body as I embraced her a few moments later. No doubt it was appalling to have thought such things, even in the grip of deluded rage, but as my mind returned to it, shame kept on yielding to morbid curiosity. What if I'd done it? Absurd, and of course it was easy to pursue such gruesome, childishly vengeful avenues now that I was free and innocent and hadn't actually *done* anything. But wasn't this worse in a way, to dwell on it?... not on the act, I couldn't bear to think of Chrissie's precious body bouncing off terraced walls of rough stone, tumbling like a rag doll into the grass to lie broken and still (but there, of course, I'd thought exactly that); no, what obsessed me, chased me like a fugue down lanes and over hilltops as some automatic part of me drove back through Somerset and Devon and across the Tamar into beloved Cornwall—what obsessed my exhausted mind was how it would feel to have done something so irrevocably dreadful that the mind would have to incorporate it or succumb to madness. And it didn't seem so hard, to go on living normally. As the murderer I would drive Egon back to Liskeard in the Wolseley, at speed. And what did I think I was doing? It was entirely clear: I was reclaiming Egon, and the way to do this was not to talk him out or into anything, it was not to talk at all but to tell him what to do. Precisely as I had done. Before leaving Chelsom I would have discovered a wardrobe full of Uncle Edward's mothballed clothes. They fitted Egon poorly, but happily Edward had been a short, stout historian rather than a tall one, and at least the baggy beige trouser turn-ups didn't billow over Egon's shoes or the sleeves of his hacking jacket, a delicate oatmeal colour, interfere with his hands. (This was the case, though in truth poor Egon had ended up looking rather like an under-age academic, a 1930s *jeune savant*, his jacket and trousers expensively tailored to pre-war fashions.)

My blood-curdling soliloquy continued; I couldn't stop it. Chrissie had mentioned going for a walk, I would have explained to Egon, and since she hadn't returned in time we'd have to leave her a note thanking her for her hospitality. No point in searching the grounds, either she got back in time or she didn't, and perhaps she hadn't wanted to face the goodbyes. Oh, this would have been crazy stuff, of course, and yet not crazy enough to have cleared my head of Chrissie's image crumpled in the field below the house. I was a killer, I had killed. But clearly Egon had seen nothing, and for all anyone could prove, the girl had dallied with the precipice and fallen. Teenage suicide? Such desperate acts were on the increase, everyone knew that. It would be heart-rending for Egon, but in time he would recover... yes, I could almost tell myself that, as the murderer; but even my mind (in his) baulked at so glibly dismissing the grief awaiting Chrissie's family.

This was enough, more than enough, yet the nub of the fascination remained: I had—I would have—done an appalling thing, but did the heavens fall? Did the Lord hurl my car into an avenging tree? Not at all. The Wolseley ran smoothly through brilliant and forgiving landscapes, telling me they'd seen far worse and smiled on it serenely.

I dare say there's nothing too extraordinary about such vengeful daydreams, but dear God this was a child, and one I'd only known for an hour and a half. Then again, I'd given my life to children, so perhaps it was appropriate that I should want to kill one.

That afternoon I nearly did, but Egon would have been the victim, not Chrissie, as I endangered both his life and mine by my negligent driving, my haste to get back to Webb's in time. At the same time my wandering mind showed that a part of me didn't want to get there at all. While waiting for Egon to come down from the Yellow Room I'd stepped into a downstairs cloakroom, charmingly appointed (basin by Superior of Bristol, I noted as I bathed my hands and face in luke-warm water, the ancient porcelain veined with minuscule cracks, the plug itself perished with age, a wide, flat flying-saucer shape with a strong metal hasp at the centre, on a gently sloped boss), offering the visitor good soap, fine prints on the walls and an antique mirror over the basin—but by a truly English oversight, no hand-towel. As I searched through pockets for my handkerchief I came across the letters I'd stuffed into them in my haste to depart that morning. Among these, an envelope bearing the school crest. A letter from the Governors, my dismissal perhaps, I thought as I ripped it open with wet, shaking fingers; but it was a subtler device, a summons to an 'Extraordinary' board meeting to discuss a number of paltry issues including a forthcoming visit by the Inspectorate of Schools. The remaining agenda was 'to be decided'. This paper sword of Damocles lay crumpled in my pocket as I drove back in a trance of elaborate escapes from retribution, a Harry Houdini of the scaffold. I barely recognized myself in this criminal rapture; yet every so often I became aware that in their very perversity my guilty, angry stratagems gave me an opportunity to keep thinking about something other than the school: about Chrissie—yes, even as I pushed her away into the void, annihilated her and walked free.

I was trusting the old Hanbury to drive the car, change gear when necessary, brake at oncoming danger. This was a mistake. Approaching Launceston I began scanning the horizon for Chrissie's school and nearly ran into the back of a truck. Then, emerging from the town and beginning to accelerate again towards high, dreaming ground, a familiar scarecrow figure—the quiff back in place, dry now and perching on his scalp, clothes rippling in the wind, his rucksack at his feet—waved, paused, then danced out into the road to flail at me in recognition. Still trying to get to Plymouth. I sped past without a backward glance. All the same I was eager to rid my rear-view mirror of him, too eager, and hurtled thoughtlessly into the coming bend, a steep right-hander. Too fast, too late to brake. I gripped the wheel as if to lift the car back and away onto the road as the verge reined us in, a whirlpool sucking me into walls of spinning green. When the tyres bit into gravel the steering column seemed to detach into my grasp, becoming part of me, another futile muscle clenched in spasm as we slewed sideways, rattling and bucking on the grass. Any moment now, any instant the waiting hedge would close with us to tear and chew into the metal flank shielding me from its rage. Instead we spiralled out onto a farm track, spinning abruptly and halting just short of the ditch, nose towards the innocent road.

I turned to Egon and saw him still curled in the back seat, asleep without a care. An old horse stood motionless in the field behind us, it too seemed to be asleep. In the stillness I could hear the wind whistling across the moor, and fancied I heard approaching footsteps, running. Before the scarecrow figure could appear—*You crazy man? You crazy? Take me to Plymouth and you go home safe!*—I gunned the engine and swerved back onto the road.

'*JOHN! WHOA THERE!* John!' The voice stopped me as I charged up the hotel stairs.

For a moment I was bewildered to hear myself called by a name no-one had used since my childhood, and turned in alarm, feeling found out. But it was only Dawson, the owner of Webb's, a bluff and guileless countryman forever trying to project himself as a crafty business type, though all his schemes were duds; evidently he had decided that our common status as leading citizens of the town called for the intimacy of my first, given name. 'Message for you,' he said, passing Egon as he climbed the stairs, and gave the boy's outfit a startled glance.

I already knew from Dawson's face what he was going to tell me. As he spoke I could hear Alec's rasping voice: *Sorry, Hanbury. Parliamentary*—he liked to sound all six syllables of this cherished word—*business. Simply couldn't get away. How about next week, eh?*

We stood there for a long moment on the stairs, the three of us like figures representing Bad News from Abroad, the fall of Lucknow or Mafeking; I avoided Dawson's look of you-know-Alec sympathy and gazed, ashamed, at Egon, who was studying the carpet. I'd woken him on the outskirts of Liskeard, and asked him how he felt at the prospect of this first encounter with his aunts—excited, apprehensive?—but he only shook his sleepy head. From where I stood I could smell the mothballs that had embalmed his clothes, and so I'm sure could Dawson, who now took a step or two back down the stairs.

'The old boy's still waiting for you in the library,' he said. 'Says he's meeting you there. I told him Mr Thurgo wasn't coming but he wouldn't budge. You know how he is.'

'You go ahead,' I told Egon, 'see if your grandfather needs anything.' But Egon was already on his way, scuttling up towards the landing. As soon as the boy was out of sight, I turned to Dawson. 'I understand he had a visitor yesterday. Is she still here by any chance?'

Dawson was grinning all over his farmer's face. 'News travels fast, eh? No, Mrs Trevelyan's gone. Left after lunch, looking like the cat that got the cream. And if you want to know where *he* spent the night,' Dawson glanced into the stairwell in mock caution before lowering his voice, 'I can tell you. In her room.' He nodded in gleeful wonderment. 'I told her, if you can prise him out of here, I want one of the paintings, to keep in the window. That's what brings people here, not the old boy himself. D'you know what she said? We'll turn room 26 into a museum, she says, and I'll foot the bill. Yes—and we shook hands on it. Now you go and tell him not to be a silly old bugger and to take his chances while he can. Tell him I'll marry her myself if *he* doesn't.'

I found Egon sitting beside the old man in the gruesome library with its flock wallpaper of faecal brown and founding father Ambrose Truscott, 1827-73, staring from the wall at us with a Regency sneer. Trimble and his grandson, in their neighbouring armchairs, made a matching pair for once—now that Egon was wearing clothes contemporary with Mad's eternal grey suit.

'What time d'ye call this?' Trimble growled.

But there was something less frosty than usual in his demeanour, yes, I don't think I was imagining it, something more Truscott than Trimble, a touch of the Regency buck on the wall. He was almost smiling. The folds around his mouth had long since set like concrete, and I dare say a smile was too much to expect of the chalky lips. But the blue eyes were alive with a wickedness I fancied few had seen since the days of the Know-Thine-Enemy brigade, when the Reverend Mr Trimble had unlocked his pornographic collection to those who could touch pitch and not be defiled.

'I'll fetch you a cup of tea, grandfather.'

Egon patted the powdery old claw on the armchair beside him, and went swiftly out, shutting the door and leaving me with this newly resurrected ancient—priest to priest, I reflected in bemusement, though neither of us was wearing a dog-collar or indeed, since it had taken the memory of Trimble's once scandalous reputation to remind me that he *was* a priest, deserved to be wearing the insignia. My own wild, fantasy-ridden drive was still jangling in my nerves.

'I'm still hoping that Alec Thurgo and your daughters will be able to come down next week,' I began, fully expecting him to ask me *what* daughters? The word appeared to have a different effect on him. His mouth stretched in a grimace—an attempt to remember, even, perhaps, nostalgia?—and he leant his head back on the headrest, closing his eyes. With the best will in the world I couldn't imagine this withered old warhorse spending the night with the frilly, plumply rouged lady I'd seen in the photograph at Chelsom. But he looked happy. 'I could brief you on the situation as I understand it,' I went on, and began to outline the case for Egon's continued attendance at the school. Outside the tall windows Liskeard was bringing its busy day to a close. Departing shoppers honked their horns at speeding tourists on their way to more picturesque locations. Little by little lights came on in the dull, dusty twilight. Now the Empire Fruit Shop's flashing neon sign added a bizarre touch in the growing darkness of the room, bringing a sheen to the outdated, detachable stiff collar that hung so loosely around old Trimble's turkey neck. As we sat there and I rehearsed my party piece amid the bric-à-brac, the antimacassars and the window sashes with their dirty, corded red pom-poms, the cabinet hoards of brown and khaki-backed books featuring illegible titles, untouched for a generation, it

270

was hard to believe we were in the same century as the rest of the town. Trimble himself looked like a corpse stowed in the library at the same time as the books. Was there any point in continuing to harangue him? Probably not, but I kept going. At last Egon arrived with the tea, a full tray for the three of us, and switched on the lights.

Trimble's mouth was open, his nose looked sharper than a pterodactyl's beak, and his eyes seemed to have sunk back into his head, the bruised skin around his eyelids glistening like dark meat. If this was the effect my little speech was going to have on my listeners I'd better reconsider it, I thought, as I watched Egon deposit the tray and take the old man gently by the shoulders.

'Grandfather... grandfather!' Egon shook him patiently for a while, leaning over him. All I could see was the back of the borrowed oatmeal jacket, double vented, bobbing and rustling as Egon tried to rouse the old man. Then the jacket stopped moving, and the pair of them were motionless for several moments, the boy with both hands gripping Trimble's shoulders.

My heart was already pounding when I heard the word 'Sir!' break in a long moan from Egon's lips, and saw him press his head against his grandfather's concave shirt-front to listen for a heartbeat. I ran to them, seeing now the lifeless eagle head lolled back, the features so pared and lean beneath the white hair that they seemed all bone. Try as I might I couldn't feel a pulse. Not a flicker, not a ghost of breath from the old chest, to which his neck seemed to have severed all connection. The face was rigid and the eyes, when I lifted the lids, had rolled up into his head. 'Oh God...' I heard myself mutter, 'what now? What do we do? Come,' I said, taking Egon by the arm, but he only shot me a tearful, angry glance and pulled away. I watched him kneading the old man's hands as though trying to wrench him back to life. Then I ran to the door and down the stairs, trying to keep the panic from my voice as I called for Dawson. Guests everywhere now, the bar was filling up, I saw the glowing red face between the milling heads and gestured frantically.

'I think the old man's dead,' I whispered when he reached me. 'He died while we were sitting there, while I was talking to him.'

Dawson stared, and closed his eyes for a moment—less, I think, in tribute to the dead than to clear his head. He was breathing heavily when he opened them, and I could smell the beer. 'Better call a doctor to confirm it,' he panted. 'You guard the library. Don't let anyone in there.' He rushed off to phone and I clambered back up the stairs, overtaking heavier-footed guests and hoping a little crowd hadn't already gathered on the landing above.

Mercifully no-one frequented the library unless they had to. Opening the door I saw Egon kneeling by the dead man, hugging him, sobbing against his chest. It was more than I could stand to watch his grief—it even shocked me to see him display so much emotion—but when I came and touched his shoulder he shook me off once more and I backed away, feeling like an intruder.

Rather than loiter in the doorway I left Egon with his grandfather, and closed the door on them. I tried not to think of the effect this news would have on Chrissie's Aunt Margot, but failed, unable to resist the gruesome comedy of it. In all truth I felt she was fortunate to be spared closer acquaintance with her paramour—but which of us would have to suffer a sense of having killed him, she or I? Perhaps we would share it. Outside the library door, the landing was immense, spacious enough to have entertained, on occasion, fifty of Liskeard's finest to a buffet meal. Had it once been a reception room, before the floors were sliced up into ever smaller cubicles? Only a huge mahogany table remained, with a billiard table crouching under it on massive legs like a forgotten dinosaur. I slowly circled the table, ready to deflect anyone who looked like heading for the library.

It was only now that the criminal Hanbury, the over-heated fantasist I thought had expired in the shock when I skidded off the road outside Launceston, proved to have been only shamming dead. Down the corridor, as I reached the far end of the monstrous table, I could see '26' glowing in brass on Trimble's chocolate brown door. Was it locked? Or was this my chance, before all hell broke loose, to peep into the sanctuary for a private show of Trimble's Madonnas?—of Chrissie, yes, Chrissie who had not yet replaced Lizzie Muchmore in Trimble's window, who might perhaps never replace her now, unless…

I was filled with a mad desire, not just to see the paintings but to ring the knell of Trimble's death in a way that would at once alert all of Liskeard and celebrate the old boy's life, his triumph, his untiring vision renewed even at the last: I would put Chrissie in the window.

Hopefully it would be the business of a moment. Abandoning my sentry-duty I hurried down the corridor almost laughing at the way the afternoon's fantasies had come to life—I hadn't harmed Chrissie but I'd managed to dispatch Trimble instead, merely by boring him to death... then came a grimmer thought as I hesitated with my hand on the door handle of room 26. I'd invoked death, summoned it like a curse. But hadn't Trimble died happy after a night of bliss? From the look of him perhaps he too was fortunate; it was hard to believe he had many more such nights in him. He had died at the peak. I turned the handle, fully expecting it to be locked. The catch crunched open, the door gave an inch. Then stuck. Was there a chain? None that I could see. All I had to do was push, then.

Once more I hesitated, this time remembering the treehouse door that loomed in Egon's dreams, the undisclosed horror within. Was it my place to enter here? But Egon and Chrissie both, not to mention the hotel cat, had been inside. There were no spooks, no horrors here. The corridor was empty; no-one on the landing beyond. I gave the door a sharp shove and forced my way in.

Darkness. Murky light from the corridor showed only a stretch of bare carpet, and I would have to close the door to prevent discovery. I flicked at the light switch but nothing happened, no light came on. I was ready to back out again, defeated, when I realized that my eyes had adjusted sufficiently to the half-light to make out a table against the wall, littered with dim shapes, mugs, papers, brushes, and something that resembled an old-fashioned taper. Matches beside it. I lit one hastily, and saw that the taper was of the home-made variety, a saucer with a stub of candle in it. But it was enough. I lit the candle and closed the door.

When I turned and raised the taper and saw where I was I stood there trembling, awestruck. Was this how Carter had felt, alone and torch in hand, when he first entered Tutankhamen's tomb? There too he had found a litter of ugly, insignificant grave-goods clustered on the floor—in this case an iron bedstead pulled away from the wall, a paint-spattered chair, a step-ladder, an easel, sheets and rags and more brushes on the floor. But all around and above this debris, every inch of wall and ceiling was alive with frescoes, figures huge and small, crowds, forests, cities, stories. Allowing for the style, which was no less overpowering for being clumsy and childish in outline, I was standing in the midst of the most colossal art work I had ever seen.

Where the ceiling rose had been was now a womb ringed with projecting tongues of fire, stalactites enclosing a Christ-child in the Virgin's lap. But as I held the candle high I saw with a shudder that this was no Madonna but a triple Goddess whose shapes interwove at the fiery rose and fanned out into separate figures, nymph, queen, and aged crone, their arms outstretched in blessing, in gift—ribbons of flowers, grain, animal and human forms spilled from their fingers into every corner of the ceiling—and in terrible possession. *Yn Llys Cerridwen*, ran the ribboned motto on the girdle that wove the three figures into one, *Liskeard, The Court of Cerridwen, The White Lady of Death and Inspiration.*

On the wall facing me, its window hidden by the canvas showing Lizzie's image to the town, Liskeard itself—reproduced in minutest detail—rose to the ceiling to meet the cascade of forms, men and beasts and birds raining into it from the outstretched fingers of nymph-Cerridwen and Queen-Cerridwen. This was Liskeard as it was and as it had been with its castle, garrisons, vanished churches and men and women in costumes ancient and modern, mingling with the Town Hall and the Pipe Well, The Parade and Webb's Hotel itself. Webb's, I saw as I brought the candle closer, with a Madonna peeping from one tiny window. Ah but no Madonna, I understood that now: Trimble's irreverent use of local girls to incarnate a pagan deity, a goddess of death and inspiration, made sense at last. But where were they, all the famous Madonnas, so keenly sought by museums and private collectors? One canvas in the window, one on the easel now—I moved to it and saw, as I raised the candle, Chrissie's portrait smiling back at me with all her devilment, her knowing eyes and narrow pointed chin... and yet I saw it, I confess, with a stab of disappointment, for it was crude work and no match for the original. Or indeed for the frescoes, most of them no doubt painted when Trimble's powers were at their height. These had been failing when he painted Chrissie—or had his thoughts, perhaps, been too much on her aunt? I could see by the candlelight how coarse and thick the paint was... and then I realized where all the old Madonnas were. They were under the new ones. Traces of the earlier paintings showed at the edges of the canvas, where the window-frame would hide them from sight. Yes, the joke was definitely on us: there were only two canvases, now or ever, the one in the window and the one on the easel, each overpainted in turn as icon replaced icon, different and yet the same. Trimble had saved his prodigality for the room itself.

Before me now, as I turned my eyes from Chrissie's image, was a different scene, surrounding the door and spilling along the side walls to meet the city that, on one flank, surrendered to a forest roamed by prehistoric animals and, on the other, opposite the forest, dwindled into moorland, tor and dolmen. Here Trimble's wardrobe intervened, but it had been turned into a gigantic monolith, seeming by a crude *trompe-l'oeil* effect to extend into the scene beyond, where a white-robed, white-haired priest (the artist himself, I took it), his back turned to us, stood half-hidden by the wardrobe-dolmen as he surveyed his moorland kingdom. This was unmistakably Bodmin Moor, with Rough Tor and Brown Willy in the distance. But it was not the deserted, cheerless place I knew. Its circles of wood and stone were crowded with worshippers, dancing among the Hurlers and the Stripple Stones, seemingly unaware of the terrible story unfolding on the adjacent wall, where the doorway cowered. On the ceiling above the worshippers the crone-Cerridwen extended withered arms towards the door, as if to prevent escape. And the figures cascading from her gnarled hands—no, these ones weren't falling, they were being sucked up from the frescoes so liberally peopled by the hands of the nymph and Queen-Cerridwen facing either corner of the window-wall, sucked up as by a tornado into the crone's hands and, beyond them, her slavering jaws. On the doorway wall itself a child fled from her, transforming himself in desperation into other forms, a mouse, a speck of grain, a sail on the sea, only to be devoured at every turn by the avenging goddess, changing shape from owl to sow to all-consuming storm. Again and again the resurrected child sprang up to flee, but the door that beckoned in the wall was denied to every outstretched hand. And now I saw to my horror that the fleeing child's face was Egon's. Egon's too, as I raised the candle to the ceiling rose again, was the face of the child in the fiery womb, the king for a day, the sacrifice.

It was finished, every last corner painted, its bright mediaeval colours rippling with a curiously vegetal effect, thanks to the corrugations of the flock wallpaper beneath the paint. A formidable vision, and I could see a little better now why the collector in Aunt Margot was drawn to Trimble, assuming he'd given her a glimpse of this. A vision completed now. Yes, Trimble had been ready to die; had even, perhaps, in ceremonial fashion—this was a grisly thought but I couldn't keep it out—given himself a night with the all-devouring crone, Lady of Death and Inspiration, to cap his endeavours. I was relieved to note that, on the ceiling above me, aged Cerridwen as the death-goddess did not sport Aunt Margot's rouged and merry face.

Oh but there were still so many details of the frescoes I'd had no time to study. How long had I been here? I couldn't tell if it was five minutes or half an hour, far too long anyway, yet I could hardly bear to leave the room and let the hordes in... did Dawson have the faintest inkling, I wondered, of the pagan chapel under his roof? A primitive Cornish Sistine—yes, Dawson wouldn't need to marry a rich widow now, he was set up for life.

Reluctantly I followed crone-Cerridwen's imperious hands pointing me towards the door, only to remember my mission, the reason I'd entered in the first place. I hurried back to the window, brought the paint-spattered chair, put down the taper (the carpet, I now saw, was the same dull blue that Dawson had installed elsewhere, with whorl designs in paler blue, etched with a darker, petrel shade) and stood on the chair to try and prise out Lizzie. What if she was nailed into place? But no, the window recess narrowed as it approached the windowframe, wedging the canvas, which came out easily. For the first time in many years—years of barely interrupted labour, that much was now clear—light from the town entered room 26. A poor sickly twilight with neon tints, but it made the figures on the wall shrink into mere cartoons, where the candlelight had given them body. No, they should never be seen like this, and never would be, I hoped, as I erased the light with Chrissie's image. I pressed the canvas hard into the window recess. Picking up saucer and candle I saw that the stub was now barely more than a blob of liquid wax, and scrambled towards the door in superstitious haste, banging my knee against Trimble's iron bedstead.

Then as I held out the dwindling flame to light the door I saw what I had missed before, that the door itself stood within the outline of a huge old tree, as if in leaving the room Trimble was immediately entering the forest. And in the branches above the door sat an ugly metal treehouse, its own door opening on darkness.

For a moment I stood mesmerized by this second door, rubbing my blazing knee, and knew that Egon had not only sat for Trimble, but contributed his own story to the legend of the child-hero devoured by the mother goddess. Had Trimble been undoing, week by week, all the work I'd been trying to do, to heal the boy? There was no mercy in this place, it was more Death than Inspiration, and what I wanted now was to get out.

I reached for the handle, turned it and pulled.

But the door, the door in the tree, wouldn't give. By the last guttering flickers of candlelight I felt as much as saw Cerridwen descending on me with her talons, her salivating toothless jaws, her whirlwind.

Any moment now I would be in the dark—I tugged at the door again... what if someone had locked it from the outside while I studied the frescoes in a trance? Could I bring myself to cry 'Help! Let me out!'? How long would it be before anyone heard?

And then the door gave, not by my strength but another's, and I almost fell as it opened towards me.

Dawson stood there in the corridor, one hand on the doorknob, staring at me. I must have looked like a man released from the tomb, but he only shook his head reprovingly.

'I thought as much,' he said. 'You'll get yourself into trouble, John. No-one's supposed to go in there.'

I couldn't find a word to say to him, still dumbstruck and unnerved by the panic of a moment earlier.

Now Dawson began to grin, perhaps seeing how discomfited I was. 'Come on, you're forgiven,' he said, beckoning me out of the room with a gesture of his head. 'Thought you'd steal a march on the rest of us, did you? *I* know what's in there, don't you worry. Or did you reckon I wouldn't take a look round while the old man was out? You'll have to keep mum, though, because he's not ready to hand it over yet.'

'What do you mean, he's not ready?'

'I mean he's not *dead*.'

I gaped at him. 'He's not?'

Dawson shook his head, wryly—even, it struck me, a little ruefully. 'Far from it. Old boy's as right as rain, I reckon he'll bury us all. It shook me though, I don't mind telling you. I mean, we're standing round him waiting for Connock to pronounce him dead, when he opens his eyes, raises his eyebrows and says, "Didn't I ask for a cup of tea?" We all stare at him with our mouths open, not knowing whether to laugh or cry, until finally your kid Egon saves the day and chirps up, "You've got one, Grandfather, but it's probably cold by now, shall I get you another?" He's holding court now, the old bugger, happy as Larry—and I don't think you're quite ready to qualify as a medical doctor, do you? If you don't believe me, come and see for yourself.'

'Wait,' I said as I stumbled after him. 'I've switched the paintings, I've put Chrissie in the window. I'd better switch them back.'

Dawson shrugged, putting one huge arm around my shoulders. 'Time we had a new Madonna. I'll tell him I switched them round when we thought he was dead. How's that?'

When we reached the library Egon gave me a cheerful, sheepish smile. I returned it; after all we'd both jumped to the same conclusions, in sheer panic. Egon was still holding one of Trimble's hands, but the old man seemed oblivious to this, listening with head cocked and alert to stern Dr Connock in the armchair opposite him.

There was a sceptical smile on Trimble's face—young Connock was evidently lecturing him once more on his unhealthy mode of life—and he still looked like a waxwork, though admittedly a perfectly contented one. His head came up as we entered the room, he gazed blearily at me and then at Dawson, seeming at last to recognize him, then sank back onto the head-rest, once more closing his sunken eyes. For a ghastly moment I thought we were about to go through the whole rigmarole again, trapped in some circle of hell devoted to Wilfred Trimble's death and perpetual resurrection, when the chalky mouth opened again, and spoke.

'I know what I wanted to tell you all! Yes... I've got some news for you,' said the cadaver, opening his eyes. 'Dawson, take this filthy tea away. Fetch some champagne. I'm getting married!'

IF IT HAD been a strange day for me, it was a stranger one for Egon. He had lost a grandfather and found him again, grieved as he had never done, perhaps, since his wolf-child days, and been restored. 'You can stay at the school tonight,' I told him as we left the celebrations at Webb's. I wondered how Chrissie and, in due course, her family, would be receiving the glad news. Not with champagne, by all accounts. 'I'll drive you back to Padstow in the morning. Unless you insist on walking.'

'I'm not going back to Padstow, sir.'

I glanced at him. 'Where, then?' He still looked tired, and no doubt he was angry at Alec, with good reason. Suddenly it occurred to me with a lifting heart that I could keep him with me at the school for a few days—maybe for the week, until Alec condescended to come down to Liskeard. Yes, we could patrol the place together, and there were plenty of diversions, the pool, the tennis courts, the cinema in the town. Buoyed by the prospect I left Egon to climb into the car and hurried across the road to the Empire Fruit Shop.

There was enough light from the evening sky to eat our fish and chips by, on the verandah outside my drawing room. The school grounds had never looked more beautiful, I thought, the conifers sharply silhouetted against the darkening blue, the rhododendrons richly coloured, glowing darkly like the friezes around old Trimble's room. My tipsy mind kept returning to his vast and eerie labour of love. What had happened to replace his faith—perhaps never entirely orthodox, but true to time-honoured glimpses of grace and hellfire—with blatant paganism? I was shocked. And surprised at the violence of my reaction: some rump of belief perhaps, some protest stirring within the closet Christian I'd become. *No healing without the Name, without the Holy Spirit to intercede between the healer and the sick...* was it really me, was it Hanbury who'd written those words to Richard Thurgo from the Ark, while poor Denis was still in my care? Nowadays I'd be happy to try and heal an ailing spirit with a hair dryer if I thought it would work.

'I've seen Trimble's room,' I said.

There was a stillness now as the last light dimmed swiftly over lawns and shrubs like the final instants of a play, a stillness before us and behind us as we sat there with our backs to the empty school. *I am sent with broom before, to sweep the dust behind the door...* Egon himself, disguised as Puck, had spoken these words on this very lawn only a month ago, as the serried ranks of the school watched from wooden rostra mounted on the drive. Then too the light had faded as he spoke, narrowing to one faint beam that only just, to straining eyes, picked out his paint-streaked face. Green warpaint. Had it been a mistake to cast him as the wandering spirit of the night, inspiring wanderings of his own? He'd been a rather solemn Puck.

A breeze came, riffling the conifer tips like a deck of cards, sighing in the rooftops above us as if the school itself were exhaling. Such peace, after the frantic alarums of the day. I glanced at Egon but his face was in darkness, I could see no expression. Thinking I must have spoken too softly, I repeated my words about having seen Trimble's room.

'Yes, sir,' he said, 'I'm glad.'

For a moment I wondered foggily where Puck fitted into the pagan scheme of things, but couldn't place him. *Broom before... behind the door.* Behind, before. Time, too, was dissolved by these syllables, and began again, as at the Christ-child's birth. When had Trimble decided to give Egon pride of place, there in the ceiling rose?

'Now that it's no longer a secret, there are things I'd like to know,' I said. 'Had he already begun the frescoes when you first came to visit him from Beale?'

Egon nodded. 'He was working on the ceiling. While his strength lasted, he said.'

'But surely... I don't understand—it was the Virgin he saw in the window, wasn't it? Or did he change his mind about that?'

'He says the Virgin and Cerridwen are the same person. She just changes shape.'

I pondered Egon's neutral tone, forever deferring judgement. 'Do you believe that?'

He gave a faint answering shrug.

'That's up to you, I suppose. But how did you feel about modelling for him? Seeing your face in all those grisly stories?'

'I was there, sir, that's all,' came his voice, amused. 'I don't think he's very good at drawing from imagination.'

'There's more to it than that, Egon. You told him about the treehouse. And he painted you as some kind of prey for this Cerridwen...'

'The hag Cerridwen,' Egon pronounced with relish, 'that's what Grandfather calls her. She's only one face of the Goddess. She's a wolf and a cat and a sow—'

'Yes, I've grasped all that—'

'But I'm not just her prey, sir. When she's a hen she swallows me as a grain of wheat and gets pregnant and gives birth to me in the ceiling rose.'

I hoped he couldn't see the expression on my face.

'Grandfather liked it when I told him about the treehouse. *What is open I shall shut,*' Egon intoned, '*What is shut I shall open.* You see? Because Cerridwen's also the goddess of hinges.'

'I'd no idea hinges had a patron deity,' I said. 'Now I'll know who to pray to when I have trouble with our cupboards.' I could tell he wasn't amused. 'I'm sorry, Egon, I don't mean to be facetious. I'm afraid it's all beyond me.'

'Well, I'll explain to you one day, sir.'

It was dark now, the warmth of the evening and the champagne still lulling me, the lawn, my lawn, dark as calm water before me; in front of it the paler curve of the drive. Yes, Egon would explain to me, in time. And abruptly it was Chrissie's image that passed before my eyes—not the overwrought Chrissie with her hair mussed, on the terrace, nor the sly, composed Chrissie that Trimble had tried to capture and whose image was already slipping from my mind, but the girl with the sad and solemn eyes who'd greeted me in the doorway when I arrived at Chelsom Place.

'I won't be a moment,' I said softly, trying not to break the mood as I slipped out of my chair and passed through the French windows into the darkness of my drawing room. No need for light, I found my way unerringly to the desk. Before switching it on I moved the lamp so it would show what I needed to see.

But when I adjusted my eyes to the glare a stranger gazed back at me from the faded photograph. I barely recognized the thin face with its lank hair and haunted brow—where was the resemblance to Chrissie that had struck me dumb when she opened the door? I'd kept the photograph so long I rarely looked at it closely now, much less with fresh eyes; all I remembered was the mood. Or misremembered it. Chrissie had life, this poor creature was barely worth a second glance. So much for my plan to show Egon their startling similarity; I switched off the light and made my way back, blinded until I reached the verandah again.

Egon sat motionless and erect, gazing out across the grounds. Not quite at ease; preoccupied, yes, but with what? Should I tell him how charming, how remarkable I'd found Chrissie to be? No, any adult compliment would be clumsy and discomfiting to a sixteen-year-old in love. It might even kill the mood stone dead. Yet here was a moment for confidences, in this companionable stillness, with our faces safely hidden by the night. Now, after our safe passage through the shocks of the day.

'I've always hoped that at some stage you'd tell me what you found in the treehouse, when you went back with Ludolf. Was it really so terrible?'

Above Egon the jagged fringe of metal teeth and fleurs de lys that helmeted the edge of the verandah roof, so delicate by day, framed the sky like the fangs of a raised portcullis. I stayed in the doorway, grateful for the darkness, watching Egon's shoulders rise, and fall again as he expelled the breath.

'I had such awful nightmares about it,' he said at last, and shook his head. 'I don't mind telling you. Not now.'

Had he been afraid I'd prescribe treatment, call for a psychiatrist?

'Sometimes there was a body in the treehouse. I couldn't see the face. But I knew it was Herta, because she'd have come back for me, even after what the soldiers did. You see? I saw her lying dead there.'

He glanced round, looking for me.

I said: 'But she didn't die.'

'I know that, sir, she's in Berlin.'

I nodded, unwilling to trust my voice. Was this the time to tell him that Herta was a Hamburg tart? I didn't have to give details of how I'd discovered her trade.

'Uncle Richard wouldn't lie to me about it,' he said, forestalling me. 'And I think I always knew she was alive. But at the time, when the soldiers took her, I must have been afraid of what they'd do to her, and when I came back to the treehouse… in my nightmare there's blood everywhere, in the branches. Everything's slippery. It's all right though,' he said quickly. I could feel his need to reassure me, as he leant forward in the creaking wicker chair, 'Ludolf told me something about the treehouse. Herta kept dead animals in it, mainly rabbits he said, he'd taught her how to stuff and mount them, and she also… she kept some horrible things there. Animal blood in jars. And foetuses and things like that. What it was, I think, the soldiers broke into the treehouse and smashed the jars, and when I came back to the tree and found it all slippery I must have been terrified that it was Herta's blood.' He saw something in my face, or merely in my posture, shuddering at the tale. 'Doesn't that make sense?' he asked.

'Yes, that makes sense. I just… I never pictured the treehouse as quite such a gruesome place.'

'I probably liked it. You know, watching her skinning things.'

'Perhaps. But I'm having trouble imagining you staying there, with all that blood and mess.'

'I was waiting for her to come back. Like an animal would. That was all that mattered, not the blood.' He hesitated. 'I had to wait for her. I've thought about that—waiting and, without realizing, learning how to get by. I think that must have been how it began.'

Something in Egon's voice warned me not to interrupt. I sensed a struggle in him. Whatever it was he had to tell me was too painful to come out easily.

'That's what I've got to talk to you about, sir.'

'I want to hear it all, Egon, you know that.'

'Yes, sir.'

But he sounded inconsolably sad, and a long silence fell as I waited for him to resume.

283

'So... when you went back with Ludolf to the treehouse,' I prompted. 'What did you find?'

'Nothing. I just climbed up and went in. I opened the door and there was nothing there. Only a smell.' He paused. 'I wish I could describe it to you.'

'I'll assume it was unpleasant.'

To my surprise I saw his profiled cheeks widening in a smile. 'D'you remember once, sir, at the end of term, you brought in a little bottle with a sort of orange liquid in it...'

'Yes,' I said, trying to catch up with his sudden change of tone, 'I only do that to classes who've given me a particularly rough ride.'

'You said you did it to everyone,' he protested. 'And you told us it was the worst smell in the world. We had to lie down on the floor before you'd let us take a sniff, in case we fainted. And it *was* horrible, it was so horrible I couldn't smell a thing, it just went straight up into my head and everything went black.'

'I did warn you. You passed out for moment. Everyone does.'

'You said it was crushed bedbugs. But what is it really?'

'Just that. Odour of Crushed Bedbugs, the worst smell in the world.' Now we were laughing, on a balmy evening made for comic reminiscences. As if we hadn't been talking of blood and death and carnage in the woods. 'I've had that bottle since I was eighteen. I got it from a science teacher at my school, and *he* swore it was made from bedbugs. He used it for the same trick—made us lie down and take a sniff. Actually... and I'd rather you kept this to yourself: I stole the bottle.'

'You stole it, sir?'

'Yes, I'm afraid I did. From the science room, on my last day at school. At the time I took it as a sort of dare—that's how I regarded the smell, I mean. It was a challenge, I wanted to master it. And I did, I started by sniffing the open bottle at arm's length, and then a little closer, and gradually I got used to it. Now I can look a bedbug in the face without flinching.'

An owl had begun to hoot in Tupholme Wood; I'd lost Egon again. I came and took the chair beside him.

'I suppose that's how it was for you,' I said, 'with the treehouse. You got used to that too, in time.'

'But I'd forgotten it, you see.' His voice was sombre. 'I could remember how to climb the tree, almost without looking, then I opened the door, and... it was a smell that wasn't a smell at all, it was like going dizzy without knowing why. The same as the bed-bugs—only this was worse, because I couldn't pass out. And it was so familiar. After a bit I realized why it was there inside my head, making me remember something... something that was already there—what I mean is, it wasn't just a memory. It was mine, it was what I'd smelt of, once.' He seemed to rest on the thought, the voice softer. 'It was how I smelt then, my smell. D'you see, sir? It was Egon's smell.'

'I do see, yes. And I can imagine how disturbing that would be. Did it bring back memories?'

He shook his head.

'That's curious, isn't it?' I said. 'Nothing, no memories at all?'

Again he shook his head, as if I'd missed the point.

'You're saying you still remember nothing of the forest years? Perhaps that's not so bad, you know. You may be better off without them.' When Egon said nothing, I blundered on. 'Perhaps there *are* no memories, or nothing we'd call a memory, just instinct—and survival. Days merging into each other, turning into years. What do you think?'

No answer came, and for a time we let the owl speak, throatily at first, rehearsing.

The boy at my side was listening raptly. But to me the sound made the school grounds seem empty. While I wasn't looking they'd turned dark and cheerless. I felt unaccountably depressed. Worse still, I wanted to blame Egon. He was drawing me in, making me feel as fickle and mercurial as he was. Was this what it meant to be sixteen, plunging from one mood to another?

'They don't hoot all year round,' Egon said, 'did you know that, sir? In winter owls don't hoot at all. I read that in a book. But I must have known it once. I knew things like that before I could read.'

'I'm sure you can learn them again,' I began, but as I spoke Egon was saying something too—blurting words I couldn't catch—'I'm sorry?'

'I'm not staying here tonight, sir, I'm going to the Ark.'

I stared at him. 'But... the Ark's not habitable, is it? What's wrong with a room here?'

'I'm not going to sleep in a room. I've made a place in the woods.'

I sighed. 'Chrissie told me about it. The bomb-site. I know the place you mean.' I saw him flush, and decided to press on. 'Yes, she told me about the fire too.'

Anger held him still for a moment, and then he shook his head, relenting.

'She's an honest person, Egon. Which is more than I can say for you, in this instance. Did you have to lie to me about it? Chrissie says you did it to protect your hiding-place. But you could have told me, I wouldn't have minded.'

Egon muttered something under his breath.

'What's that?'

'I said, she's so *stupid*. I had a reason for not telling you where it was.'

'But you told me just now, it's in—'

'I said it was in the woods. I didn't want you to know where, exactly.'

'Why not?'

He was staring at the ground.

'Why not, Egon?'

Now he looked up at me. 'Because I'm going to be there for a long time. And if you come and find me, I'll go somewhere else. I want your word that you won't come and find me.'

I couldn't take it in. 'What are you talking about?'

'I'm going to live there. Please try and understand—I've got to do it. Egon's waiting for me.'

Oh, he said it so simply. *Egon's waiting for me.*

I can still hear him say it, as I write this. There are moments when another person can destroy us with a word; and it's rarely a term of abuse, because abuse arrives too early to destroy us, or of dismissal, which arrives too late. At that instant it was June Caswell's face I saw before me, June turning in the kitchen of her little house in Winchester to tell me that my kind of loving was no love at all... but that had been a modest shock compared to this. Because it wasn't only loss and shame I felt now, the dread of abandonment. It was Egon's sanity, and mine, that I doubted, hearing him speak so calmly of himself in the third person; as another, waiting for him. Whom had I spent the last three years with, then? Whom had I loved? Our lover smiles, disclosing—for the first time—vampire teeth, and everything that is ourself, our certainties, our memories, our very instincts founded on those memories, falls into the abyss.

He was going to live in the dip. Stay there, live there. It was that simple, he insisted.

Simple! For hours I blustered and fought, out on the pitch-dark verandah, protected from the rising wind; I might as well have been talking to it, to the night air. In time I turned on the indoor lights to see him better, to storm and bully and plead some more, but his words had cut the ground from under me. Egon wasn't there with me, he was waiting in the scorched woods above the Ark and I was arguing with a wraith, a figment of my imagination—the moving, speaking simulacrum I had created, who wasn't Egon yet. Not yet: his words. Lord help us, how long did he need, a week, a month? More? Did he have any idea what it would be like to try and spend the winter in a hole in the ground? He only looked at me pityingly. What did *I* know of winters, true Mecklenburg winters? He'd managed once, he could manage again. No, it's too late, I begged him, you can't have them back, the years you've lost—you're not a child any more. D'you really think you can turn yourself into a savage again? You can't do that, nobody can. I tried with all my might to make him see that we were *all* figments, all of us were creatures (prisoners, I almost said) of the lost years, not just of the forgotten years of infancy but of countless moments lost to memory, and surely not even Freud required of us that we recapture every last one. But it wasn't an idea that was driving him. He was deaf to theory. On the long walk from Padstow to Chelsom he had felt possessed, the dark waving night-time trees had taken him to their bosom. They had offered to reclaim him, to school him again and make him whole.

And where did that leave *me*? Alec would have my guts for garters if I authorized this lunatic experiment. No, that would be the least of it—while police scoured the country I'd be sitting blandly on the secret, denying everything, pretending that I didn't know exactly where the wolf-child was, shivering in his hole, frozen to death perhaps...

I felt sick, and had to lean against one of the metal verandah pillars, to steady myself. *I'll go somewhere else*, he'd said. If I didn't agree to the woods above the Ark, he'd simply vanish and find another hiding place. The choice was mine. Would I rather suffer from guilty knowledge, or the lack of it?

Then I began to laugh, and Egon looked up at me in alarm. But I wasn't losing my wits, it was the sight of him that did it, the sight of him sitting there like a pre-war young Tory in his high-buttoned, double-vented Norfolk jacket and Oxford bags—was he really going into the woods dressed like this, a relic of a bygone age? His clothes fitted the period when he'd first entered the German woods, it struck me now, and then the humour of it vanished as I saw a young Peter staring at me, Anglophile Count Peter on his way to Lord's. It was a hideous, mocking image, like pretending you could go back in time merely by dressing for it. Or by hiding in the woods.

'I think I'd better go, sir,' he said, taking pity on me.

'No,' I said. 'You're staying put. Enough of this nonsense.'

For an instant I had a giddy sense that this was all it would take to stop him. Authority, insistence—but the expression on his small, set face wasn't compliance at all, damn the boy, it was compassion.

And what was I going to do? Lock him into a room until he came to his senses? He'd made up his mind—that's what Chrissie had been trying to tell me. Yes, she too had tried to argue him out of it when he arrived at Chelsom and they'd sat up all night, talking. With the thought I felt another surge of anger.

'You seem to think you can do this without so much as a by-your-leave,' I raged at him, 'as though you had no ties, no-one who cared about you. You're leaving Chrissie with your blasted secret—d'you think that's fair? How do you expect *her* to manage? You even made her think you'd be hiding down there with an unexploded bomb... of all the stupid cruel things...'

'It was just a rumour I started,' Egon muttered. 'To keep people away.'

'And is Chrissie supposed to keep away?' I couldn't keep the bitterness out of my voice, 'Or will you have prisoner's visiting days?'

'No!' he shouted, coming out of his trance at last. 'I'm doing it for her, don't you see that?'

'Doing it for her? Marching off and leaving her not knowing whether you're alive or dead?'

He stared at me, panting, rigid, close to tears now but I wanted to press on, to try and push him further if I could. Nothing I might do or say would be as cruel as the weather he would face, the starvation cramps, the misery of boredom, the futility of it... and, in the end, the shame of failure as he hobbled back for food and shelter.

'D'you think she *understands* why you want to do this? Oh, I'm sure you've told her, you've explained it—just as somebody explained it to *you*, when your mother disappeared from one day to the next...' I saw the colour flame into his cheeks, and he stood up trembling, fists balled. 'Now you're doing it to *her*, damn it,' I ranted, 'you're doing it to all of us. But worst of all to Chrissie. And for what? What is it you want, Egon? To go back to the woods and dream that you're still little Count Egon and your mother's coming back to make you king of the castle? Is that what you're really after?' Dear God how easily they came, the taunts, and I could see the shock in his face, shock at my loss of control, 'It's not enough for you to be Egon Lützow here in England with people who love you and a future no-one could have dreamed of for you when that crazy thug Richard hauled you out of the forest screaming and spitting like an animal? Is that it? This isn't good enough for you, is that it? We're none of us good enough for you, is *that* what it is?'

'No!' he howled, and the metal roof of the verandah echoed with it. For a moment I felt dizzy, I was Ludolf in the treehouse cornering the boy to force him to come back and any instant he would jump at me to claw and bite—I saw him take one raging, shaking step towards me, and couldn't move, and in the next instant I felt him pressed sobbing against my chest and hugged him, hugged him as I hadn't dared hug Chrissie, and it's not a wraith I'm holding but the whole firmament, my drowned boy home, my joy, my child.

'I'm doing it for *her*,' he repeated in a whimper, and I wanted to hold him away from me enough to see his face, to try and understand. But he wouldn't let me. 'I do love her, I do. But when I, you know, when I kiss her,' his voice was low, almost inaudible, 'nothing happens—I don't mean... I don't just mean sexually, I mean nothing happens in my head. I don't want anybody else, I never have. But when I touch her I can feel the part that's missing, it's in *here*,' he was breaking free to show me now with a piteous intensity, tapping his temple with one hand to his head, 'it's *here*, I know it is. And if it never comes back, then... you see, I know it might always stay missing. And I know why.' His gaze begged me to understand. 'I'll be all right without it. But I need to know if it's still there.'

Oh, I tried to interrupt, to tell him—what? About the numbing shock of first encounters, adolescent fantasies dissolving into honest panic at the touch of strange, distinct, uncontrollable flesh... but he wouldn't let me speak.

'Don't,' he said, and pulled free. 'I know all about that, sir. You're going to tell me how normal I am. Everyone's been telling me that as long as I can remember.' His voice was charged with bitterness again. 'You're normal, Egon, you're so normal it's amazing, you're an ordinary person like the rest of us. Never mind that you spent nearly five years swinging from the trees, that was just play-time, one long afternoon on the jungle frame. Lucky you—you get all the attention, and it didn't cost a thing.' He turned on me, fierce now. 'Well, it did, it bloody did. It cost me that little connection everybody takes for granted, between *this*,' his hand went back to his head, so hard it rang like a slap, 'and *this*.' Gazing me furiously in the eyes, he gathered the crotch of his billowing, borrowed trousers in one mocking fistful and stood there motionless with one hand at his head and one between his legs, like some dreadful doll with stiffly moving arms that someone had manipulated into an obscene carica-ture, an image of failed, exhausted masturbation.

At last he let his hands fall to his sides. 'I didn't know. I really thought I *was* normal. Just a late starter. But it's not just that I can't do it. I can't even imagine doing it. Please—please don't tell me we're not all sex maniacs. I know that. *You're* not, are you. But you can imagine doing it, can't you.' He steeled himself. 'Look, I'm not the only person who's gone through this. I've read about every wolf-child ever found, and I know how lucky I am compared to most of them. I was three-and-a-half when I started living wild, I could already talk and keep myself clean. The Dodderer told me that if it had happened six months earlier I'd still be an animal. Instead... I'm not. But I've got one thing in common with all the others, the crazy ones and the half-crazy ones who learnt to use a knife and fork and wipe their bottoms, and the ones they dressed up like proper civilized people. Can you guess what it is? Nobody knows why, but not one child recovered from the wild has ever learnt to mate.' He paused at last. 'Did you know that?'

I shook my head.

'I'm going to be the first,' Egon said, and drily now, with a touch of the old defiance, 'if you don't mind, sir.'

He was calm again, his eyes warning me that there would be no more tears, no more outbursts. I was not to comfort him.

'All you have to do is keep the secret.' He gave a tight smile. 'And leave the Ark the way it is, so nobody comes near.'

Spotted snakes... come not near. The echo was there, intended or not. *Not a mouse shall disturb this hallowed house.* This woodland wedding.

'Damn it, this isn't make-believe, Egon, people *die* of exposure—'

But as I said it I remembered that I had been the one on the verge of giving out, in Mecklenburg. Remembered him frolicking, running back and forth in the blizzard.

'Don't worry,' he said, studying me. 'I'll be in my element.'

I gazed at him in silence for a long time, unable to move. Stunned as much by the way he was talking as by what he'd said; by hearing Egon talk about himself as a wolf-child. I never thought he would. So much he'd held back, such distance on himself. So many fears—and plans. It flashed into my mind that he'd deliberately set the Ark on fire, to cauterize his sanctuary. But no, he could have started the fire in the Ark itself, without destroying valuable cover on the hillside above it. And yet... he'd guaranteed himself some precious solitude, if I delayed the long, expensive labour of re-building the place. Cunning ruthless little bastard—he'd engineered a wild-life preserve all to himself, a private Whipsnade.

'And you're just going to walk into the woods, dressed like that?'

'Why not?' he said. 'I like these clothes, they're good and warm. And they remind me of Chrissie.' Now he hesitated. 'I couldn't...

really explain it to her properly. But—either it works, or it doesn't.'

'I see.'

All my arguments had gone, flattened by the books Egon claimed to have read; by the all-powerful curse of the forest. Why—if he was right—why were we neutered by it, why didn't the man-child emerge as sexually rapacious as the beasts, his former fellows? Perhaps he did, perhaps it was the book-learning and the bottom-wiping that undid the 'little connection' as Egon had termed it. Yet book-learning and bottom-wiping didn't do that to the rest of us. Why not? And could the forest itself undo the curse, or only reinforce it? Neither of us knew. Perhaps no wolf-child had ever voluntarily re-submitted himself to the wild—certainly not dressed in a Norfolk jacket and Oxford bags. But what was I to do? Say... come and be a happy eunuch with me, Egon, it isn't so bad?

Instead I heard my own voice, perfectly normal and controlled, saying, 'Well... how do we proceed? D'you want a lift to the Ark? D'you want some supper first?'

'No thank you, sir.'

I shook my head, helpless.

'You know I think this is crazy, don't you—' but his patient nod, even as I added, pleading, '*think* about it—' told me I was once more wasting my breath. He'd thought about it and he was going anyway, no matter what I did or said.

'I didn't want anyone to know,' he said abruptly, as if offering me the best and only present he could find, his last scrap of food, 'but now I'm glad that you and Chrissie know.'

At last I nodded, while he studied me with his pale, small-featured face, hair slicked back, like a subaltern off to war. Going up the line. Should I pack him a suitcase, a warm coat, a change of clothes? A knife?

Then I remembered that old Ludolf had brought the child bread and victuals during Egon's years in the forest, and left them at the foot of the tree, beneath the treehouse.

'Will you let me bring you food now and again?'

For a moment he considered this.

'No need to make the rules harder this time,' I said. 'Some bread, some cheese and fruit? A water bottle?'

He nodded. 'Just leave them in the cowshed.'

'In the cowshed. Very well.'

'If you come looking for me in the dip, even once...' he warned.

'I understand,' I said.

'I won't stay, I'll go somewhere else.'

'Agreed.'

But my heart was rising—it had all become a game, the whole evening a shadow-play, the day itself one long hallucination, and this the final, obligatory charade. All talk, a midsummer hysteria. He wasn't going through with it.

From the Bodmin road a distant police siren rang out, then faded. We both listened to it, smiling.

Abruptly Egon extended a hand towards me. I ignored it, feeling my stomach contract; I wouldn't play, I wasn't ready. But he stood there with arm outstretched, unyielding. Reluctantly I took the boy's hand.

'Goodbye, sir,' he said, holding the handshake. 'Thanks for everything.'

The absurdity of it released me—damn it, he'd rehearsed this. 'Spare me the wartime farewell,' I said. 'You'll be back within a week, you silly bugger.'

'No,' Egon said calmly, 'I won't,' and, letting go of my hand, took a step down from the verandah onto the gravel of the drive. He glanced up at the night sky, and held the pose. 'Look for me there,' he said, 'among the stars.'

THE PARADE IS empty as the Wolseley noses into Liskeard like a beast straying from its habitat, a bear in search of rubbish bins. Empty, cold and dark and tidy, not even a parked, abandoned car.

I'd spent a long time sitting alone at the wheel, in the school drive, unable to start the engine until I knew where I was going.

Before that I'd sat stunned among the slim green pilings of the verandah, a mockery forest with its metal pelmet like a cut-out of leaves fronting a pantomime stage set. Imagining I could still see the pale blot of Egon's jacket vanishing into the rhododendrons. The real, pitiless, stinking shrubbery. The treetops were still now, fixed,

293

no wind. I stared at them until my eyes watered and the silhouettes blurred. Absurd exercise—to try and enter into their trance. He'd know that soon enough. But for a time I felt as if I too had shed myself, all but my eyes, and despite my anxiety I sat there as inert as the landscape I saw.

The day seemed far behind, as if (once I could no longer make out the distant spot where he'd disappeared into the undergrowth) I'd spent the time dreaming here on the verandah, as if I'd imagined it all, the driving and the worrying, hurrying distractedly to fetch the boy and hurry back, scheming and adjusting and forever trying to catch up. And all the while Egon had been calmly planning his departure, running through his lines.

Among the stars... an idiotic piece of vanity, I'd thought when he said it, grandiloquence. But now I understood it differently. I would look up, not for him but for what he saw, wherever he was; yes, for what we shared.

At some point I got up and, for the first time in years, searched for a cigarette. During the term I'd confiscated a packet from Vanstone. Now I couldn't find them. Perhaps Vanstone had stolen them back. My desk drawers were full of surprises, paperwork I hardly recognized; some etchings—I thought I'd lost them—that Egon had done in class, he'd called them abstract (and it was true he couldn't draw for toffee) but to me they always conjured up a mazy web of branches under snow; beneath them I found notices I'd never got round to putting up, unanswered letters, even unopened ones. It came to me at long last that I gave up the school years ago, and that today, like so many seeming turning points, had been no more than the light arriving from that distant place; that place, that point in time when I supposed that I could follow Egon on his journey.

Thomas Merton's Diaries, for so long my comfort, lay before me on the desk. Tom the Trappist in his woodland hut. *My fiftieth year is ending, if I am not ripe for solitude now I never will be.* Could I too become a solitary when the scandal breaks and Alec thunders and the Governors cut me adrift? If my dry throat could laugh I'd laugh along with it. A solitary? Egon's already filled the post.

At length I found a box of cigarettes I dimly recalled as having been abandoned by a parent. God knows how long ago; when I fetched the matches from beside the gas fire and lit one of the cigarettes it tasted so atrocious that I had to down a large whisky to be rid of the stale tobacco-bite.

Then I took the half empty bottle out onto the verandah with me and slowly drained it glass by glass.

I couldn't drive the boy's revelations out of my head. My flesh crawled for him at the thought that his body—that he believed this—was awaiting him in the woods above the Ark. I'd seen those very woods as my own garment, years ago, yes, as a robe, a cloak, a place to hide. As a bestiary too; but a chaste one. No mating at the Ark. Indeed at the beginning of poor Denis Towle's obsession with geminicide, when he was wondering whether he might have garrotted his twin with his umbilical cord as they struggled to emerge from the womb, we sought in vain to confirm or disconfirm the feasibility of this. Not one of us, I found, had witnessed childbirth—unless Colin had, and couldn't tell us. As Richard had put it, we were there at the Ark one by one rather than two by two.

All gone now, one by one, Denis and Richard, Ally Pally and the rest. I'd walked the woods with each of them, singly, all my attention on their words.

Now I pictured myself climbing up to the chapel with fresh food for Egon, only to find the last consignment mouldering there untouched. Do I go and look to see if he's all right, if he's sick? And then at last, perhaps after a few more visits and the food still mouldering, I steel myself to go to the dip and he isn't there, he's gone, I don't know where, and perhaps will never know.

I prayed aloud for strength, but it was something more I wanted, some return, reward: for foolishness, I scolded myself drunkenly, for innocence. But may I not ask to be the hero, after all, of my own life? Why is it that even now they seem so much more substantial to me, the others, even in death, drowned John and poor dead Denis, Egon and Ally Pally too slipping out the back door and away into the forest, gleefully juggling his stolen silver?

After a while I came to, lying fully clothed in a shivering stupor in the bedroom, peering at the little dial on the Teasmade and steeped in the dread of finding that it's almost day, bringing closer—bringing *what* closer? For a moment only the fear. Then, yes: bringing closer the first lies, the first enquiries.

Egon? I'm afraid I've no idea. He simply took off last night.

I couldn't stop him, I'll say, truthfully. Nobody could.

No birdsong, dawn still hours away; only the ticking Teasmade clock and, farther off, with my own heart beating double time to it, the grandfather clock marking time on the landing.

School time. But even if I try to picture the corridors filling up, the term beginning... nothing's changed, my mind is still on Egon underneath the bracken and the gorse.

Lying listening to the Trimble-clock with its heavy, reluctant heartbeat like the patient tock of a judge's gavel. Trying to bring my thoughts to order.

Why didn't you alert the police right away?

Should I say he vanished in the night, while I was sleeping? Can I bring myself to make the first phone calls this morning, contrive bewilderment in the face of the rising alarm, the search, the questions, the recriminations?

Or now—now before it's too late—drive to the Ark and plead with him to take pity on me, make my way by moonlight to the dip, call down into the ferns, *Don't do this to me now, stay with me one more year, wait till you've left school and you're free...*

In the car I sat at the wheel, darkness all around me, the school dark, unable to start the engine until I know where it is I am to go. The interior nauseates me with its residues of the day, the keen scent of my panic as I bounced along the verge on Bodmin Moor. But I can't stay here.

The Parade is empty, empty as the Wolseley noses into Liskeard like a beast straying from its habitat; as I stretch across to peer out from the passenger seat...

Not a light in the windows of Webb's, no candle behind Lizzie's murky canvas form. Old 'Mad' is sleeping the sleep of the betrothed. But wait—o joy, it *isn't* Lizzie, it's my Chrissie in the window, the old boy has left her there.

I park the car in lonely state outside the portico, and climb out for a better look.

For the first time I feel fully awake again as I admire Trimble's handiwork, oddly improved by distance—yes, as though he had learnt over the years how to allow for this, and for the angle of our upward gaze. Now it *was* Chrissie, dark and almond-eyed and pointy-chinned, with the straight nose lending a finicky erotic sensitivity to the fine, supple mouth. Bringing it home to me that I really did go to Chelsom Place today, met this girl and returned to place her image high over Liskeard.

And suddenly the fragments of the day came together in a rush as if I was seeing them, like Trimble's artfully distorted image, at their proper distance at last, as though I'd found the thread connecting them, the thread that was my day, myself, my story. Gazing at the painting—how odd it was, how unashamed! and a far cry from Lizzie Muchmore's round and ruddy cheeks, all rustic innocence, where now stood a knowing, teasing, worldly Madonna, imbued perhaps with some of old Trimble's less devout feelings towards her aunt—I felt quite vividly the part of me that was neither headmaster nor reverend doctor. For so long I had grounded that self in Egon. And still would, surely, while—for as long as he trusted me. But when I sought out Egon in my mind for confirmation I could no longer see my plight in terms of his, or his in mine: police enquiries, blustering relatives, dereliction of duty. No, we were on our own now. But there was more to it than that: even the physical danger, that part of his enterprise to which I was bound while I knew where he was, seemed to recede before a greater danger, one I hadn't yet considered. Never mind whether he was obliged to slink back with his tail between his legs before he froze: what if he stayed, survived, succumbed to a dull mindless rapture from which there was no return at all? His sanity was at stake—that was the gamble. I kept my eyes on Chrissie, drawing strength from her image. Chrissie who shared these fears with me, who was no Madonna or pagan deity but simply a young girl who had found her soul's desire, as I had, in a creature even less accessible than the tongue-tied heroes of school sports: but it wasn't she who gave me strength, it was old Trimble's curious, comical endeavour, so garish among the sullen blocks of granite, the curtains and shutters of the neighbour windows. The terrible power of likeness—its very clumsiness seemed to increase the power—was tearing something out of me, exalting me. Here, close enough to this spot, old Trimble had fainted, looking up at the window of room 26.

And now (by God, if Trimble could give up his sanctuary! I thought, why couldn't I?)—now instead of a revelation I felt called to make a vow—it was a kind of vision too: if Egon could be restored to us intact, if he could heal himself in a manner no textbook ever recommended and no case history had ever told, I'd be his chronicler, yes, neither teach nor preach but be a medium for others' voices; for the living I mean, at last, not the dead; for Egon, and for the tribe who might come, in time, to join him and help us rebuild the Ark.

It was still warm, a night for prowlers and insomniacs. For Creepers, but I was no longer that. I walked through Liskeard in a kind of ecstasy, as though through Trimble's painted town, time cast in stone. The houses were my dead, tenderly loved. Walking slowly down The Parade towards Barras Street, past the doors of the Liskeard Tyre and Battery Company, my footsteps loud in this enchanted cemetery.

If a tree falls in a forest when no-one is there to hear it, is there sound? Absurd question (does God have ears?), I'd always thought: birds, mice, voles, insects... don't *they* hear the vibrations? *He who hath ears to hear, let him hear.* Yes, now I knew why it returned to me, and understood the question. Liskeard was a clock ticking in outer space, a Teasmade town in orbit, suspended and spinning slowly in the dark. Who hears? Its seeming permanence was a Nativity, a Calvary: a piece of time. I was entering it, yielding to it as Egon slipped out of it; surrendering my precious dead, returned to me as I surrender them. Returned as masonry—for at this moment it's the town I love, the sullen unlovely sleeping town. I love its sleep. A time-trance weighing the earth down with its necessary foolish burden of tarmac and stone. Oh, here and there a pleasant building, certainly, but not such as to spoil the ill-assorted, surly line-up, a bunch of raw recruits, some fat and squat, some tall and pimply, all ungainly. All serviceable. A hymn, a monument to ordinariness. I turn at the post office, head down Pond Bridge Hill towards Well Lane and the deserted crutch of the town. Past brand-new walls. Lipton's, formerly Maggs, Son, and Deeble. The human souls asleep around me, Liskeard's mortal portion, its cargo: they're as light as thistledown, shadows left by the bomb-blast. Shuttered buildings, boarded windows, buddleia. Metal advertisements nailed upside down, as if to confess that their products are defunct; making me stop and crane my neck round like a wary bird to read them.

Without doubt
THORLEY'S
CAKE
is the best general
cake in the market

An inverted Liskeard: ton upon ton of foolish stone, cement, roof tiles, chimneys drooping like stalactites into the bowl of night. From silent (as I straighten) streets. Even the seagulls need their sleep. Is Egon sleeping yet, as I patrol the town? Are there owls in the chapel woods? Here there is only sleep. Delapidated Lower Lux Street in a trance of sleep. Most lovable; like a brief, steep portion of a bombed city with its meagre pub, its scrawny, almost extinct shops and the house-sized patches of weedstrewn rubble, enclosed, calling to mind my own roofless abandoned squash courts, between stained and dripping walls. Where (invisible, but I know them) broken cars lurk. As I turn back uphill at Ough the Grocer's with its ochred plaster cracked above the crooked curving shop-front, the slumbering backside of Webb's comes into view, a huge pill-box disguised as a hotel. Inside, the triple goddess sleeps in the darkness of room 26. *Yn llys Cerridwen.* Alive enough to old Trimble; and if to him... yet I know that my own sense of the sacred clings to more prosaic things, simplicities of fascinated sight and sense. A doubter's creed, perhaps. Must I believe in what I cannot see? Seeing is strange enough for me. The wondrous strangeness of these familiar streets and doorways, windows, walls. *How easy is a bush supposed a bear...* but no, there's nothing ominous to it tonight, only a gift I can't think how to use, blind sight. *What is open I shall shut; what is shut I shall open.* Impossible not to wonder (the sleeping stone, if nothing else, seems to demand it) whether there might be some enduring magic here, where there was once a well and sacred water, prayers, incense, ceremony, blessing begged of earth's magnetic will, here beneath the drab stone face of this drab town that happens, Providence alone knows why, to be my destiny. Picture the empty centre of a market town at night, soiled dark stone and glaucous shop fronts: picture it now, at this hour of the night, eerily solid, every detail inordinately clamorous (as touch sometimes distorts, finger-ends turning ticklish-numb as blubbery balloons, mistaking small for huge): the courts of the goddess in her multiplicity, a sow, a swan, a mare, a ship, a grain of wheat. An advertisement, *Take a long look at a Carlton Long Size.* A shuttered cinema. The goose-turd butt, dark and soggy, in the gutter—this too? *And Chips* flashing on and off in the belly of a neon fish? Lighting a painting in a hotel window.

Strolling these streets in latter years I've searched for the same blissful fancy, thinking back to that day when I surrendered Egon and fell murderously in love, thinking of the night that followed and the visions that illuminated it, the dream that greeted me when I went home and fell exhausted into bed—the snow, Mecklenburg snow shrouding the town and the moor, and the boy with his poor drowned lungs convulsing, and Danny, Ally Pally come back from the woods above the Ark to haunt me on a nightmare drive to Liskeard. And then: a death and no death... feverishly I push back the covers and hurry to my desk to scribble down the dream as though...

And have to shake the pen out of my cramped hand when I finish at last. *I was born here*, in a spastic scrawl across the page.

My pyjamas are drenched with sweat and I am wide awake, in the middle of the night.

...WE ARE IN *the car together, driving across the broad plain that leads to the house, and there are memories calling us from either side of the road, too many to keep up with and now we're so close to the house, all that's left is in our eyes, watching for the moment when the house comes into view.*

And there it is, distance pressing it flat against the hill. There it is, so deeply set into the steep hillside that it looks shoehorned into it, as if peeping from a giant foxhole guarded by bushes, the stone facing beneath the roof streaked dark today with melting snow and gleaming like a miniature mansion with its two windows above and two below. The road up to it hidden by the frozen hedge.

Now we're in the lane, invisible, approaching. Traversing the hill. The house slides up beside us like a ship into dock.

And all the changed and unchanged things are one, I can't tell which is stranger, the new door with its unfamiliar contours or the old path up to it. New flowers, trees gone, but nothing that matters has changed; or can.

Alec is standing by the low wooden gate-post with its little wrought-iron gate, still there, his hand on the gate-post's rounded head: I can feel its soft, eroded wood under my palm—bringing a sudden dizziness as the post moves in its socket, as infallibly, as far and no farther, as ever.

I so wish Danny were here, but I know he has fled for good reasons. He warned me; but now I know too, I've guessed it, what he is: yes, an army deserter. The sense of scandal that surrounds his disappearance creates a dark patch in my mind. Yet I'm quite sure I shall see him again.

I know he is tracking us, ahead of us even, watching us approach, watching us now from the edge of the woods where the breeze comes, and the boughs lift, leaves rising like a swarm of starlings.

Eamonn is waving triumphantly from the hedge, a ball in one hand, and I can tell from here where Alec is standing that unless it's shrunk over the years it's not the one we lost, it looks like a squash ball but I wave an Alec-arm joyously back at him anyway. A woman is approaching me along the red-tiled path, walking as carefully as if the grass on either side were ocean, a thin-faced woman, a preoccupied face, she's trying to smile but it looks as though the mere presence of strangers troubles her like a long-anticipated hour of dread.

'Yes?' she ventures.

I've never seen her before but she is suddenly so dear to me, made so absurdly dear merely by walking from the door I set out from to go to Italy with three slices of bread in one hand and an apple in the other, the soft bread yielding till my fingers almost met through them, walking down this path, so dear to me that I smile at her with all my love in my eyes; and she stares back with a sweet, willing, deluded smile, broadening in surprise as though she were about to recognize me...

*There are always a few people who are
in the woods at night, in the rain,
(because if there were not the world
would have ended), and I am one of them.*

—Thomas Merton, *Rain and the Rhinoceros*

MY NAME IS ALDEBARAN. MY NAME
is Franzl, my name is...

No; I know what my name is, and where I should be. My room, my bed, my desk... yet in my mind they now belong to someone else. To the pleasure of knowing that people are looking everywhere for me.

The first mushrooms are coming. Beech-mast, nuts to be stored. Apples growing wild in abandoned farmyards on the lower slopes of the moor.

My cave smells sweet. O, sweet. Lit by oyster fungus and the little flame with velvet feet, *flammulina velutipes*. The day passes so fast, busy taming my dreams. Chrissie, Chrissie won't leave. I've imprisoned her in the beech above me (she won't stay but she'll learn). Alec I've put at a distance, in an upright elm. Sir in the holly tree that guards the dip. And the gnarled oak twisted in pain? It must be Grandfather; my owl drops into it in a fussy clatter of feathers; at night, when I...

When Franzl calls me out to play.

The stream at the foot of the hill leads to the moor, my winding secret trail. Was I always a nocturnal? Was I *then*? *Then* is no help to me. But this I know, that the day with its turning leaf-clock was made for dozing, while the sun reviews our night-work, growing steadily hotter under the collar as it searches for the culprit. Can't find me. Waning at last, waning like a siren on the Bodmin road, like the dogs that bark and pass on, voices sometimes, all gone on.

Gone to search elsewhere for the teasing moon, the hunter's moon that waits for me alone between the branches of my Chrissie-beech. And out I come. To feed, to slide and tumble down the hill, troubling my fellow-badgers in my sport. To scramble up the stream towards the wind, the soft dark turf of the moor spongy as night beneath my feet, to run, my legs demand it, run and run with no horizon. Utterly alone. Aldebaran above me, flaring orange like God's cigarette end. A goad, an infant blaze, a bullseye in the silverpoint of His horns. What am I doing here? Re-learning, but re-learning what? Re-learning not to learn. Learning my place, picking my way back downstream to the dip, without thinking.

The rocks are sharp (see under Treachery) beside the stream. Was I a clumsy wolf-child, picking at my scabs? Blood tastes steely at night, startling as laughter.

Franzl is an interesting case. An interesting fellow. He eats dog's mercury and it does him no harm. One night, I tell him, I might take him back to see my old school, my old room. Show him Tupholme Wood. I'm always making Franzl promises I can't keep.

Where the bee sucks, there suck I. I am allowed no trophies: that's the hardest thing. Franzl is Richard's son, and has his memories. He is a proper Thurgo. But delicate, too delicate. His face, peering down at me from the rim, slack-jawed, is pale from lack of sunlight. And he drools, a bad sign.

May I count, at least? Sir has no berries, and will have none. Seven, ten, twelve-point leaves. Two with fourteen each; joint champions. Grandfather suffers from boils. He has seventeen oak-galls, one so small I had to climb up to confirm the sighting. Number is my... is there a door, in number? Is it the way up or the way down, or a prison? I know I am trying too hard.

And when will it stop being a game (rabbit-run, zig-zag, practising on the moor, dodge back and forth like a mouse, rooting growling like a badger)? Franzl says it's *all* a game. That we can go back to the castle whenever we like, because the soldiers are gone. But they're not gone, I hear them in the day, in their planes droning overhead. They'll never leave us alone. Easy enough not to get caught, easy to hide, to play in the proud fierce dark. Hunter and hunted; but I am neither, I am my playmates' shadow. I can be still sometimes, still as the shade cast by a tree. When will it stop being a game?

I know when, and I dread it.

How then may I look? Night is so convenient, sight shrinks to a lazy—yes, sometimes a treacherous—accomplice, beside touch and smell, the old reliables. And thank God counting ceases. There are no seven seas at night, only the one; no wonder God created light first. Only then: eyes and a man, to witness His work, poor lonely God. Is it from Him I must withdraw my gaze (His boughs, His galls)? But there are still four winds, even at night, to touch and smell. Salt from the south, clay from the west, sweet moorland dung from the north, and from the east, smoke.

My task: to cherish without knowing it. Likeness, the cunning work of light, betrays me. Winter hops forwards on robin's feet, vanishes again; like Christmas decorations, cobwebs and threads of root dangle above me in my badger-scented cave. Like feelers, in my hair. Like lice.

I bury food, like... After gorging myself, I bury it to forget, like dung. No—no, that's wrong, that isn't so; I leave my dung to the north wind.

I CAN'T DO THIS, I

But of course I can do it. Nothing human is—is... and inhuman? What will remain to call my own? Are there even thoughts?

Winter is here, with gloves, a coat left for me in the cowshed. They aren't enough, and I've already rubbed the fingers bare. The world has turned against me, every touch sears my skin it's so cold. Earth and bark and stone, bloodless and harsh. The dead moor splintering beneath my feet. Tonight I found the far end of my cave had fallen in. I've clawed too deep. Oh Chrissie, Chrissie don't come looking for me now, I can't, I must go on.

Do bears seek out a fresh cave for the winter? The moor has grown so bright, I need to hide my head. It's time. But Franzl is afraid. He won't come, he's afraid to die in the dark. My poor, pale Franzl—but I can feel it, feel the great sleep waiting in my body. Does it know, did it know *then* how to live without replenishment? And what will Franzl do without me, will he pine, will he die? He won't explore the moor with me. The long hole beckons with its dark jaws exhaling warmth. I want to drown in it, in earth.

Only one thing scares me about this palatial hole. Not falling, no—the dirt is too firm, the darkness soothing—but intruding. The woods are so polite. Beneath the trees lurk no primeval rats. Only my flock, and they observe the rules, they keep their distance. Will there be rats down here, in the warmth that rises as I slither into an ever warmer, darker world, all touch, all smell? The warmth seems to increase with the darkness. Starfire behind closed eyes, painting the ceiling. The mine shaft slants. I'm in a narrow corridor. What if a further hole opens abruptly as I crawl along? I'll feel it first. Shall I go deeper? How much deeper? Wet rock, tasting warm and salty as blood. Kissing the rockface to quench my thirst. Follow the distant dripping sounds and yes—fresh, warm pools, sweet water when I need it. And warmth, such warmth. The earth's own heat rises here like human breath, as sweet and faintly scented with decay, a mouth gasping between kisses. I love this place.

Every night I dig up my stores, bring pockets crammed with nuts and roots thawing against my body in the dark, a hoard. Time to begin. Let go of sun and moon and stars, bury my head in dreams.

But no dreams come, only the rage for food, waking me over and over till my hoard's all gone and sore limbs drag me up into a melting world. A warm wind, chalky. How long have I slept? On the lower slopes, in the fields, the root clamps stink to high heaven, beckoning me to the feast.

Something has changed, in the wood. Some outline. Eyes straining, unfamiliar work, until I see it now. Elm-Alec has no leaves. He's caught the beetle-death, poor sentry.

Someone has been into the dip. Some... more than one. Rough breakages too large, too careless to be anything but human. Others' footmarks in the clay. Someone has been here and found me gone. No wolf-child, no-one. Now I am truly alone.

No more supplies. For weeks and months, for years.

Oh, for a long time now. My loins are feeble withered things I dare not touch. My clothes are long since rags, like scabs, like strips of skin slowly unpeeling. I am nothing but eyes on a stick of hunger, foraging from one chew to another. No taste, no savour any more. Chew and swallow or chew and spit. I've fought badgers over food, stolen from squirrels, stoned a fox to free his prey, and vomited the feathers and the flesh.

Nights of peculiar triumph when I want to howl and laugh, and dare not but I can feel my great mouth red and panting wide. I dream of running wild through houses where I lived, of people fleeing in alarm.

Today I found Franzl in the leaves. Lying panting on the forest floor, gazing away from me. Soon I must dig a grave.

Summer passes and I forget. Shorter and shorter. Far too soon it's autumn, when the light finds me out and I must build my stores once more.

Under the winter earth I have begun to dream of home at last. The shallow sandy stream, the frogs, the whirling cone of water-flies. The treehouse rattles in my dreams, I am an airman high above. Between the grey arms of the beech. *Du Schweinchen du!* They come for me with nets, hunt me like quail, like fish. I bite until they let me go. *Untier!* I stalk my dreams over and over till they're mine, I know them off by heart. I am entire, but my coat is silence.

When did I meet the old man on the moor? He gave me a coat, his coat. Now it too is in rags, like a mane trailing in the leaves. He spoke to me of... of what? His voice... oh, the voice troubled me... he asked my name and I couldn't speak. He tried to guess my name, and couldn't. All night I lay awake trying to remember what it was, my name. It's time, it's time, before speech dies. I have secrets to tell, they lie deeper than the forest, deep in the warm earth. I've stolen Pluto's gold and I carry it here, in my head. But I don't want to die with it inside. Someone—someone must come, come soon.

How many winters is it now? The great dull spaces have devoured my memory, I feel myself on the edge of the precipice when I am I again, afraid I shall meet myself coming around a tree, or crouching in a corner of the ruined cowshed. It's this spectre (I see myself dividing from myself, a ghost escaping from the crouching husk) that drives me back into the dark, the blind momentum.

I have my own map of the stars, God's semaphore. Between the heart that thunders in the long hole and the great tattoo above (where I can see my own star, my Aldebaran-self sometimes even by day, as I peer up) bristles the wideness of the world, its stinking skin devised for scavenging alone. Like the heavens I gloat over its death as winter comes again.

I am entire, but separate. You see? I am dumb. Who is it that will free me, shatter the forest with a word?

Come to me now, I beg you, come.

I am just down the road, here in the little wood where bramble and thorn have filled the dry gravelly basin of the dip. I am here in your wood beneath the bramble and the thorn, and I can come out at last, if you call correctly. I'm waiting, I can come if you call. My name is Egon.

Acknowledgements:

The author would like to thank the Arts Council of Great Britain for their generous assistance, Catherine Lowe for her inspiration, Lisa Glass and Felicity Bryan for encouragement, Puni and Vanna for accommodation, Berto and Luisa for companionship, and Claire, Zoë, and Chiara Sylvia for making it all worth the candle.

A Selected List of Fiction Available from Minerva

While every effort is made to keep prices low, it is sometimes necessary to increase prices at short notice. Mandarin Paperbacks reserves the right to show new retail prices on covers which may differ from those previously advertised in the text or elsewhere.

The prices shown below were correct at the time of going to press.

☐	7493 91308	**The War of Don Emmanuel's Nether Parts**	Louis de Bernières	£5.99
☐	7493 99627	**Senor Vivo and the Coca Lord**	Louis de Bernières	£5.99
☐	7493 98574	**The Troublesome Offspring of Cardinal Guzman**		
			Louis de Bernières	£6.99
☐	7493 97209	**Man Kills Woman**	D. L. Flusfeder	£6.99
☐	7493 91243	**Honour Thy Father**	Lesley Glaister	£4.99
☐	7493 99600	**Trick or Treat**	Lesley Glaister	£4.99
☐	7493 9112 X	**Hopeful Monsters**	Nicholas Mosley	£6.99
☐	7493 98191	**Lemprière's Dictionary**	Lawrence Norfolk	£6.99
☐	7493 97047	**Ulverton**	Adam Thorpe	£5.99
☐	7493 97470	**Swing Hammer Swing!**	Jeff Torrington	£5.99
☐	7493 91340	**Rebuilding Coventry**	Sue Townsend	£4.99
☐	7493 91510	**Boating for Beginners**	Jeanette Winterson	£4.99

All these books are available at your bookshop or newsagent, or can be ordered direct from the address below. Just tick the titles you want and fill in the form below.

Cash Sales Department, PO Box 5, Rushden, Northants NN10 6YX.
Fax: 01933 414047 : Phone: 01933 414000.

Please send cheque, payable to 'Reed Book Services Ltd.', or postal order for purchase price quoted and allow the following for postage and packing:

£1.00 for the first book, 50p for the second· **FREE POSTAGE AND PACKING FOR THREE BOOKS OR MORE PER ORDER.**

NAME (Block letters) ....

ADDRESS ....

....

☐ I enclose my remittance for ....

☐ I wish to pay by Access/Visa Card Number

Expiry Date

Signature ....

Please quote our reference: MAND